Rising
SUN

RISING
SUN

VICTORIA WEBER

TATE PUBLISHING & Enterprises

Published by Tate Publishing & Enterprises, LLC
127 E. Trade Center Terrace | Mustang, Oklahoma 73064 USA
1.888.361.9473 | www.tatepublishing.com

Tate Publishing is committed to excellence in the publishing industry. The company reflects the philosophy established by the founders, based on Psalm 68:11,
"The Lord gave the word and great was the company of those who published it."

Book design copyright © 2011 by Tate Publishing, LLC. All rights reserved.
Cover design by Lindsay B. Behrens
Interior design by Blake Brasor

Published in the United States of America

ISBN: 978-1-61663-254-0
1. Fiction, Fantasy, Epic
11.06.19

Acknowledgments

First and foremost, to my friends in Rochester and my family. To Alex: without you, I'd still be stuck around chapter five or so. To Kit: your crazy suggestions made me think of things that would actually work. I'm sorry I stopped in the middle of a sentence and left you hanging. To Lauren: you always had a way of suggesting things and critiquing my work that never, ever made me feel stupid. To Kara: for keeping me sane throughout my freshman year at college. To my mom: for all the books we've shared, all the ones you bought me that are still hidden in my room, and all your suggestions and help with my writing. To Aunt Diane: for those first fantasy books that got me hooked on the genre: I owe my love of reading to you. And to Anna: who wanted, like always, to be mentioned specifically. Anna, sorry I'm not always the best older sister. I love you. You will always be my fashion consultant.

To Christina (August 26, 1991–December 27, 2005) and Diana Wang (January 14, 1994–December 27, 2005): you both were amazing. Your love for each other passed beyond the boundaries and loyalties of sisterhood and into the realm of friends. But more than that, you were kind and loving to everyone you met, both friend and relative and complete stranger. You had such a short time in this world; it hardly seems fair to me. I'll always remember your smiles and the good times together.

To Morgan McGinnis (March 2, 1990–November 24, 2009): you were well loved in life and are sorely missed. A talented musician, artist, fellow fantasy fan, and overall kindred spirit—you left all too soon. I'll see you in heaven. I know you're singing and playing with the angels, and I wish I could hear the music, too.

To Lou-Ann Rogers: for help and guidance and NaNoWriMo and, of course, the countless times you've said, "Vicki, stop reading in my class," without once getting mad at me. Thank you.

To everyone who inspired me and inspired some of my characters (I'm not owning up to anything)—thanks for all of your encouragement and support throughout the whole process.

To my editor, Briana: thank you for all your help and for your patience every time I emailed you, saying, "I'm not going to make that deadline."

And of course, to God, for the ability to write, for the gift of being published, and for every other blessing He's given me.

This book is for all of you, and my love goes out to everyone.

PROLOGUE

The elven woman ran so fast the trees around her were mere blurs. Her blond hair whipped in the wind behind her, her breath coming harsh in her throat. She ran almost as fast as a dragon could fly.

Fear spiked through her again. She risked a glance behind her, only to see nothing. But then, even with her enhanced sight, her pursuer could be only yards behind her and she wouldn't be able to see him, not in the thickness of this forest.

Something awful, something evil was looking for her. It had been looking for her for eight months. And it was gaining; each minute that passed brought its servants closer to her, brought her closer to being recaptured.

But there was something else, something perhaps even her pursuers didn't sense. The greatest evil was coming, slowly rebuilding his power. Power enough to transcend the barriers that kept him locked in his domain. And soon he, too, would be after her.

She glanced down at the bundle she cradled so tenderly to her breast. No, not after her. After her child. Her eyes fell from the baby girl who slept in blissful unawareness to the other item she had brought with her from captivity—the only weapon that could defeat the evil from which she fled. A powerful sword, its thin, honed blade glowing like starlight, was tied around her waist. The little green-eyed, blond-haired newborn girl with the pointed ears of an elf and the wings of a dragon had a spiral design wrapped around her left arm, designating her as the next chosen hero.

Why had her child been chosen? This innocent child, only a handful of hours old, who was already being pursued?

With desperation, she began working a spell, one of the few her weak magic could perform. The sword disappeared from her, hidden where only her infant daughter could get to it, and even then, only under certain circumstances. Clutching the child tightly to her chest, she fled. More than her life was at stake here.

A massive shadow flew over her, and she clutched the baby tighter to her, managing not to cry out. But the low-flying dragon overhead bore the glistening, white scales of a Light Dragon. The dragon landed in front of her and swung around, shape-shifting, as older dragons could, into a human form, a thin female. The elf ran to her.

"Please, I need your help," she pleaded.

"Queen Kali sent me to you," the dragon said.

Tears tracked down the elf's cheeks as she kissed her daughter good-bye. The infant's eye's opened, and she gazed solemnly up at her mother.

"Please," the elf whispered brokenly. "Take her to your queen. I need Kali to protect her for me until she is old enough to go to the Academy. Lord Melchizedek is a good man; he will take her in and teach her to fight."

The dragon nodded, holding out her arms for the child. The elf kissed her daughter one more time. The baby began to cry as she changed hands.

The dragon held the child cradled in her arms and regarded the mother with solemn eyes, reading her intentions in her eyes. "You are not coming with us."

It wasn't a question. "I'll lead him away. He'll follow me. But she needs to be kept safe."

"Does she have a name?"

The elf paused and looked back at her daughter. "Her name is Kirin."

Then she tore her eyes away and ran, swinging to the west, as if she were attempting to return to her home. Her heart broke for the child she had held for such a short time.

Within five miles, she was recaptured.

But Kirin was free, hidden, and safe, and that was all that mattered.

Four years later, the Light Dragon landed on the sprawling grounds of the Academy of the Dragon Knights. Before her, an old man with gray-white hair stood ready to greet her. Ready to take her young charge from her.

The dragon shifted smoothly to her human form, arms holding the young child.

"Lord Melchizedek," she greeted, inclining her head.

The man nodded back. "Lady Dragon. And this is her, is it? Little Kirin?"

"It is."

The four-year-old girl swung her head around at the sound of her name, her brilliant green eyes locking on the headmaster of the Academy.

"She's a halfling," he noted.

"My queen has asked me to be sure that Kirin will be taught to fight."

"As much as she is able, I will teach her."

"She is not to be fostered out."

"No. I have a room ready for her. Nurse Anah will help her as she grows."

The dragon nodded again and set Kirin on the ground. Kirin clung to the dragon's leg, still staring up at Melchizedek.

Then the dragon knelt to face Kirin. "Little one, you are going to live here now," she said in her native tongue. Kirin protested, but the dragon spoke over her. "I am going back to Allerion. You will stay here."

When Kirin's lower lip trembled, the dragon smiled sadly and stroked her hair. "You will like it here."

She rose and untangled herself from the child. She nodded one last time to the headmaster, then turned and ran, shifting back into her natural form and taking to the skies. Kirin raced after her, screaming her name.

"Kirin," Melchizedek called after her. She stopped and turned back to him. "You must come back." Her brow furrowed at his words, words spoken in a language she didn't understand. "You must come back," he repeated in Dragons' Tongue.

Head hung, shoulders stooped, Kirin walked back to him. He offered her his hand, and she took it. Together, they walked into the Academy.

There was an older woman waiting inside with a blanket draped over one arm. Her eyes widened at the sight of the small girl with the wings.

"Kirin, this is Nurse Anah," the headmaster told her. To the nurse, he said, "This is our Kirin. Are the boys all in class?"

Anah nodded. "As of last I checked. The masters have agreed to keep them there until we are ready to have them wandering about the castle again."

Melchizedek looked grim. "Then we had better do this sooner rather than later, though I'm not fond of this task."

"It's for the best," Anah said. She wrapped the blanket around Kirin's shoulders to hide her wings, just in case one of the boys was wandering about. Kirin clung to it with her free hand, staring about her nervously at the gray stone of the Academy, so very different from her last home.

The headmaster and the nurse led Kirin to the farthest bed in the infirmary wing, setting her on the bed and drawing the curtains closed. Anah smiled and stroked Kirin's pale hair.

"She's beautiful," she said fondly. She picked up a comb from a small side table as Melchizedek filled a kettle with water and set it on the fire to boil. In slow, gentle strokes, Anah eased the comb through Kirin's windblown hair. Gradually, the little girl relaxed, her eyes falling half-closed. Anah continued to comb Kirin's hair, even after all the knots were out.

Melchizedek handed the child a mug of tea. "Drink, little one."

Kirin drank. Anah combed her hair. Melchizedek watched with grim eyes as the girl fell into a drug-induced sleep. He could only hope that the drugs would keep the pain away. He turned away as Anah stripped Kirin down to just her shift and tied her hair out of the way.

Then he placed his hands on her and began the binding spell.

When he had finished, gone was the halfling elf with the dragon's wings and the spiral mark on her arm. In her place lay a young human girl, green eyes closed in sleep. Her magic bound by his, her inhuman features hidden, she looked … normal.

If anyone was hunting her, they would not recognize her.

She was hidden. And safe.

THE FOURTH ADKISHA

Acold wind blew, making snow dance though the mid-winter air and adding to the five feet of fresh powder already on the ground. The snow-capped tops of the surrounding mountains disappeared through the gray sky.

Nestled between the towering mountains was a vast stone castle called the Academy of the Dragon Knights. The Academy stood nearly in the middle of a valley, and the fields that surrounded it were not farming fields, but training fields.

Those the Academy trained were the elite force of Kyria, known as the Dragon Knights. They were a strange lot, either orphans or runaways, and all were adolescent, the youngest fostered out to the nearby farms until ready to begin training. The Academy took in the unwanted dregs of society at a young age and trained them, teaching them to be something outstanding and special. Though there were only fifty of them, they had all grown up together. They were the closest thing any of them had to a family.

A dozen and a half of the knights were currently dressed in leather armor, their breath misting in front of their faces as they stood at attention on the archery battlefield, the deep snow cleared off of it for the training exercise.

Kirin stood proud and tall among the ranks of her fellow soldiers, or as tall as she could, given the aggravating fact that the rest of the Dragon Knights were mounted on the backs of their dragons. She stood out from her peers—she was the only female present, and the only student at the Academy who wasn't bonded to a dragon.

Why don't they simply throw me out? Kirin thought bitterly. *Surely there must be something wrong with me, seeing as no dragon has chosen me.*

The boy to her left leaned out of his saddle and called, "Give up and go home, whelp. Oh, yes, I've forgotten—you don't have a home. Nobody wants you!"

He was sixteen, tall, and lean. He had black hair and dark eyes that made for a face many young women found handsome. He was wearing loose, black pants tucked into black leather boots and a red shirt under a loose, black tunic. Chainmail and thick leather armor covered both himself and his dragon's weak points. The hilt of his broadsword poked over his shoulder; he preferred to draw from there, already halfway into a strike. Kirin didn't know where in Kyria he was from, only that he, like all the other knights, was native to the country.

"Just you wait, Ethno! I will beat you in training today! Or are you going to fall off again?" Kirin shot back angrily, her fiery temper flaring. She hated the fact that she had to look up at him while she said this.

His dragon snarled at her, bearing his sharp teeth. She stared back coldly, knowing the dark-red male wouldn't harm her.

"It wasn't my fault. Sonard tripped," Ethno hissed defensively.

"In the air?" Kirin snorted, her expression cynical.

The archery master cleared his throat, saving Ethno from having to answer. "I want you each to fly through the rings suspended over the practice field. Kirin will shoot at you, and you will return fire. *No magic.* Your armor should be sufficient enough to sustain the impact. Kirin," he snapped with his usual briskness, fixing his dark brown eyes solely on her, "hit only the armor. Any blood spilled and yours will equal theirs," he threatened. "The same goes for everyone. Begin."

Seventeen dragons took off into the cold winter air, armor gleaming in the bright winter sun while Kirin ran across the training fields. She let fly arrow after arrow, aiming at whoever was near. For half an hour, she ran, shot, and dodged arrows. Her heart pounded in her chest, and though her breathing had long ago settled into a quick, steady rhythm, her lungs burned. Her entire body ached from the exercise, but she could see the end marker, a massive, shimmering bronze ring suspended over the edge of the field. She willed herself to keep going, to actually finish one of the most difficult courses for her. In her mind's eye, she saw Ethno, laughing at her the last time she had passed out from one of these challenges. Her will overpowered her exhaustion, and she pushed onwards.

Someone dove toward her. Kirin, wincing as her sore arms screamed at her, fitted one of her last arrows to the string and fired on her classmate. There was a dull thud as her arrow struck his helmet. He pulled up to a safer height.

There. The end marker. Only twenty feet away. She could see that most of her comrades were already through, watching the fields from the ground.

Keep going, she told herself. *Keep going. You're almost done.*

A shadow darkened the ground around her as Ethno and Sonard swooped low, missing her head by three feet. Kirin clenched her teeth together as she reached for another arrow and swore when she missed her rival.

He dove again, grinning at her as he flew over her head again. Her face set with determination, she waited for him to fly back into her range as her booted feet pounded into the frozen ground, carrying her to the other men.

But before she had time to draw her last arrow, Ethno dove at her and fired. Kirin screamed as his arrow missed her armor and bit deep into her flesh, her vision blurring as she sprawled to the ground. Crimson stained her upper arm.

Weakly, she raised her head to see him laughing, and her anger burned. Without knowing where it came from, a huge burst of fire exploded from her hands and smashed into him, knocking him out of the saddle. Sonard tucked his wings to his flanks and dove, managing to catch his unconscious rider before he hit the ground.

Paralyzed with fear and overwhelmed with the knifing pain, Kirin welcomed the coming darkness, sinking into black oblivion.

Sonard stood protectively over his rider, fighting to remain conscious. Ethno lay in a crumpled heap on the ground, his clothes smoldering slightly, wounded severely. The other knights, both those who had finished and those who had not, raced toward the fallen rivals. The archery master, a middle-aged man with steel-grey hair called Madai ran toward the group.

Zedek knelt by Kirin's side, rapidly examining the arrow wound.

"*Gu tolen!*" he swore under his breath. Four other students looked over his shoulder with eyes clouded in worry.

"Who did she attack?" one of them asked.

"Ethno. Who else?" replied the first, the leader of the group. "Jonathan! Report on Ethno!" he called, pressing his fingers around the edges of the wound.

The brown-haired boy ground his fist into his palm like a mortar and pestle, reducing a selection of plant leaves to a paste.

"Burnt and unconscious, but not bleeding. He'll be fine, Zedek," Ethno's closest friend called.

Zedek nodded, turning to the medic who had knelt beside him. "Peter, can you stop the bleeding before we try to transport her back to the Academy?"

The chestnut-haired knight nodded thoughtfully. "Cut the arrow out of her arm. Jamir, Jakir," he said, addressing the twins to his left, "have bandages ready." He turned slightly to the redhead on his right before speaking again, his voice ever remaining soft, brusque, and pensive. "Ren, take bandages over to Jonathan in case he needs them."

Ren jerked a nod and sprinted over to help Ethno, his ice-blue dragon keeping pace with ease at his side.

Zedek drew his dagger from his right boot and carefully sliced the skin open on either side of the arrow's shaft. The scaled foreleg of another red dragon reached over his shoulder, masterfully pulling the arrowhead free of Kirin's arm.

Immediately, Peter pulled Kirin onto his lap, smearing the mint green paste into and around the wound. He pinched the edges together and bandaged it, muttering a quick "thank you" to Jakir and then Jamir as he reached for the second bandage.

"Well?" inquired the master, who had joined the main group of students, clustered a few steps back to keep out of the way. Peter and Zedek normally had things under control, and if not, no one wanted to be caught in their way. While the student leader never intimidated him, Madai knew it would be more helpful not to interfere. Medicine was not his specialty.

"We can move her now, sir. Hopefully she'll make it back to the Academy without losing too much more blood, though it will take a while to get her there by foot," Zedek reported. "Jonathan says Ethno should be fine; no loss of blood there."

"Have Ethno carried back to the Academy," the master ordered. Zedek nodded. "And who said anything about taking her back by foot?"

Zedek gasped in shock. Behind Madai, students murmured their surprise.

"But, Master Madai! None of us are courting her—etiquette mandates that we cannot fly her," Zedek countered, daring to argue with the master.

"Who finished first?"

"Seran and Amarsa," he answered reluctantly.

"Sir Seran!" Madai bellowed. "Front and center!"

A fifteen-year-old with wild, bronze hair materialized at Madai's side, his flame-red female dragon directly behind him. Amarsa was slim and on the smaller end for a dragon, her wings on the longer side for her size, her body toned and streamlined. She was built for speed.

"Yes, sir?"

"I want you to carry Kirin back to the castle proper and take her directly to Nurse Anah. Understood?"

Seran could not have looked more shocked. "But, sir! The taboo!" he spluttered.

"I am well aware of the taboo. However, if she is not directly touching Amarsa's back, you will not be breaking it. Now move!" he snapped. "I don't want to risk her life by having her carried by foot."

Seran bowed hastily and scooped Kirin up. He had been expecting her to weigh more than she did, and he nearly lost his balance. Cradling her body like one would hold a small child, he scrambled onto his dragon's back and urged her to take flight. She wasn't the fastest dragon at the Academy without reason.

"At last, you're awake. Can you stand?" the nurse's kind voice filled Kirin's head. She nodded slowly and stood up, glancing around at the familiar room to orient herself.

The walls were gray stone, and the floor beneath her bare feet was smooth, made of the same material. Sunlight filtered through the long, narrow windows set high in the eastern wall. A dozen beds covered in clean, white sheets lined the eastern and western walls. A small nightstand stood by each bed. The one that Kirin was bracing herself against held her boot-knife and her shirt and tunic, folded with a precise neatness Kirin couldn't hope to emulate. Her boots, socks, sword, bow, and quiver lay under the table and cot. Because she was partially undressed, curtains had been pulled around her bed, shielding her from anyone else who came to the infirmary wing on the southern end of the second floor of the Academy. Kirin wasn't bothered by her partial nudity in front of Nurse Anah; the gray-haired, brown-eyed woman had needed to remove pieces of Kirin's clothing to heal her before and doubtless would have to do it again.

"Should I bother to ask who started it this time?" the nurse asked, her voice slightly disapproving. But both women knew the nurse had a soft spot for Kirin; after all, they were the only women in the Academy, and the nurse had no children of her own. She had quickly become Kirin's surrogate mother.

"Ethno shot me."

"Hmm. Watch your back for the next few days, sweetheart. He was rather irate when he left," she advised. Then she sighed. "Is it possible for you to keep yourself out of trouble, Kirin? It seems I have to patch you up every other week. And if it's not you, then it's Ethno." She hooked a finger under her young charge's chin and looked Kirin straight in the eyes. Anah smiled. "I swear, child, every day you grow even more into the beautiful woman you will soon become. And with such unusual eyes," she murmured.

Kirin glanced down, self-conscious about her vivid evergreen eyes. No one else at the Academy, or the nearby town, for that fact, had green eyes. "Yes, I'm strange."

"No." Anah stroked her hair. "You're special, and you're beautiful, along with feisty and stubborn, I might add," she teased.

Kirin shrugged, smiling ruefully. "Glass half-empty, glass half-full. What time is it?"

"Midday, five weeks away from Yule."

"How much damage did I do to my arm?" she asked, twisting to see her shoulder as she redressed. *She bandaged it all the way up to my shoulder? It was just one arrow… wasn't it?* she wondered dubiously.

"Your arm is fine, sweetheart. Merely bandaged up. The headmaster wishes to see you though, so I suggest you run along. Don't keep Lord Melchizedek waiting."

Kirin left the comfort of the infirmary wing behind as she headed toward the headmaster's quarters, her heart sinking and her feet heavy. Whispers followed her along the corridor.

"Kirin's awake!"

"Where is she going?"

"Is she in trouble *again*?"

Yes, again. I'm always in trouble! "Kirin, don't do this. Don't do that. Stop fighting with Ethno." *What did I do this time?*

"Hey, idiot." Ethno sneered, walking up beside her. "You are in more trouble than you could dream. You're not allowed to use fire arrows on the practice fields."

"*Really?* I didn't know that," she replied with bitter sarcasm. Then she noticed the massive bandage that ran from his right eye to his right ear all the way down to his shoulder. She could see the red edges of a burn fanning above and below the white cloth.

"Lovely burn. What did you do, put your head in the fireplace?"

"You did it to me, you little whelp!" he exploded, picking her up off her feet by the front of her shirt and smashing her into the wall. Her head struck the wall, but she kept from wincing. "Now I'm scarred for life. I'm fortunate I can still see out of my eye! And it's your fault! I hope you get expelled from the Academy!"

"That's enough!" the headmaster's voice cut through the air like a sword. The small knot of bystanders—who were hoping for a fight—scattered. "Ethno, put her down. Kirin, come with me."

Ethno unceremoniously dropped Kirin, and she nearly fell over, still a little dizzy from loss of blood. He spun on his heel and stormed off toward the closest stairway, heading back to his quarters.

Kirin obediently followed the headmaster through the halls and up three flights of stairs to his study. As they went, she unraveled the bandages around her arm. She was shocked by what she found underneath. Instead of a small wound, a long, thin, silver marking ran in a spiral design from her shoulder to her wrist, splitting into several lines and weaving into a complex, almost web-like pattern on the back of her left hand. A few of the marking's lines ran to her left palm, cumulating at the center of her palm, forming a single point.

What under the stars happened to me? she thought.

Once inside, the headmaster shut the door. "Have a seat, Kirin."

She sat down, closing her eyes in an effort to stop the walls from spinning, and said, "What am I in trouble for this time, sir?"

"Nothing."

His answer shocked her. Her eyes flew open again, her head pounding. "Pardon?" In her confusion, she had to strain to keep her voice respectful.

"You are not in trouble."

"Then why did you want to see me, sir?"

"I wanted to talk to you about what happened out on the training fields," Lord Melchizedek stated. He watched her in silence for a long moment, his eyes tracing the silver lines on her hand, the spiral pattern that ran up her arm. Those eyes paused on the angry red line that marked where Ethno's arrow had struck her. Kirin fidgeted when he lifted his gaze to peer at her face, blue eyes intent upon her, as if seeking the answer to a difficult question.

"Do you remember anything of your life before the Academy?" he finally asked her.

Her brow furrowed as she cast her mind about, hoping to remember some tidbit to tell him.

"White walls, sir. I think. I can't remember much. I'm sorry."

"There's nothing to apologize for." He leaned back in his chair and regarded her pensively. "You used magic yesterday afternoon when you attacked Ethno."

"I was defending myself, sir," she began hotly.

He held up his hand to cut off her protests. "The niceties of it matter little at the present moment. The fact is you used magic. Where did you learn it?"

She faltered. "I . . . sir, I don't know. I simply . . . did. Used magic, I mean."

"Have you read any books on the subject?"

"Of course, sir. My course books, supplemental books, histories—the libraries are full of books on magic."

"The use of magic specifically. How to channel it, control it."

"No, sir."

"Do so in your spare time. Now that you've used it once, you need to learn control."

"Yes, sir."

"I think there are things about you that no one yet knows, things I do not even know yet." The headmaster smiled gently. "Go. Enjoy the rest of your birthday. As of today, you are fifteen, if memory serves me correctly."

Her eyes flew wide open. "Fifteen today!" she gasped. "I'd forgotten."

His smile grew. "Go," he said kindly, nodding to the door.

Kirin stood up, bowed respectfully, and crossed to leave. As her fingers closed around the doorknob, Lord Melchizedek spoke again. "And Kirin?"

She turned back toward him.

"Keep your left arm covered."

Back in her quarters, Kirin jerked her bloodstained clothes off and held them up for consideration. The shirt and tunic she could still wear if she cut off the sleeves near the shoulders and hemmed them. The pants were splattered in dried blood, too much to wash out or be repaired. She sighed and tossed them aside into a corner. At least she could cut off the cleaner fabric on the lower legs to save for patches or binding.

Kirin's quarters, like all of the living quarters at the Academy of the Dragon Knights, were made completely out of gray stone and were large enough for a dragon and its rider to live side by side. A set of large double doors opened into the main room. Opposite the doors was a large window, big enough for the dragon and its rider to fly through. Floor-to-ceiling bookcases stood against the wall on either side of the huge window, slowly accumulating Kirin's books.

The main room of her quarters was where she spent the majority of her time. A low table against the wall held her weapons, including the ones she was repairing, the shield she was making, and the tools she needed for fletching. Another table stood a few feet down the wall, covered in misshapen piles of leather. A shelf above it held the tools she needed to work the leather into light armor, boots, winter gloves, and anything else she might need.

A table and two chairs stood farther down the wall with a small stack of books about dragons on it. Ten feet down the wall, closer to the main door, was a counter for meal preparation with a stone washbasin at one end and several cupboards underneath that held plenty of food and seasonings she would restock as necessary at the nearby town's market. Another shelf ran over the counter that held clay pots of various herbs.

To the right of the main doors, in the corner by the counter, was a large fireplace and a bread oven with a stone hearth wrapped around it. Sitting on the hearth was a cast iron cauldron for cooking stews and soups and a bigger one for washing clothing. A pile of logs stood heaped in the corner, almost out of sight.

To the left of the main doors were a few wooden pegs nailed into the wall that currently held Kirin's thick woolen robe and cloak.

Farther down, two more large, heavy, wooden doors led to the room that would have held a dragon. It was furnished only with a thick, soft rug that covered most of the floor and a stone fireplace to warm the room in the winter. Another pile of logs was stacked in the corner, even though the room had no occupant.

A wooden desk holding Kirin's course books, along with inkpots and quills and parchment, stood against the wall that divided the main room from the dragon's room, surrounded by two more floor-to-ceiling bookcases. Between the dragon's room and the wall with the massive window lay Kirin's bedroom.

Her room was small but comfortable. A bed sat against the wall to the right of the door and the wall opposite of it. Her pillow and sheets were a gentle cream color, and the warm blanket on top was a dark sapphire blue. Against the same wall was a beautifully carved wooden trunk that held all of her clothes. The trunk was carved out of cherry wood and had silver clasps and was decorated around the edges of the lid with vines and flower buds that were beginning to bloom. It had been a gift from Jakir and Ren three years ago, when they had taken a woodcarving class and had built a chest as their final project. On the opposite wall was a nightstand with her washbasin, soap, and cream-colored towel. Jakir had carved up the legs of the nightstand a few months after the chest had been completed; that was what boredom did to people in the dead of the northern Kyrian winter.

Beside the door was a fireplace with its hearth wrapped around it, a pile of logs, and a wicker basket that held the clothes she needed to wash. The fireplace was actually conjoined with the one in the next room—the room a dragon would occupy.

The wall opposite the door held a small bookcase that held all of her personal belongings. The bookcase also held several books from the Masters' Library, one of the Academy's many libraries. It was also the only one the students weren't allowed in. Kirin had gotten good at sneaking around at night to access these forbidden places in the Academy. The Masters' Library held a vast collection of books—books from other worlds, books from other countries in

Kyria, books written in other languages, books on where to find the different dragon lands (but none on the city of Candescere, the last stronghold of the fabled Light Dragons), and books on how to raise and hatch dragons. The headmaster knew everything that happened at the Academy, but he hadn't once reprimanded her for sneaking into the Masters' Library and taking a few books back to her quarters. No one had. So she kept doing it.

Kirin liked her quarters. Most of the material in her quarters was either a deep, rich green, a shade of blue, or a soft cream, her favorite colors. Most of her clothes were also these hues; the only other colors were a maroon sash she had won in a competition; a black cloak; a black shirt, tunic, and pants; her supple, leather boots; and a pale lavender dress she wore when she went to the nearby town or when guests came to the Academy. Kyrian women were expected to wear skirts or dresses, not pants like men wore.

Kirin opened her trunk and sorted through her clothing, dragging on a clean pair of pants. None of her long-sleeved tunics were clean, so she tugged on a short-sleeved one and wrapped a cloak around her shoulders to keep her warm. A sweater would likely be a good idea, but sweaters were difficult to mend and even more difficult to get blood out of, and she would never have the patience to sit down and knit one, even in the middle of the winter.

She checked the bandage around the arrow wound. Satisfied that it wasn't going to bleed through anytime soon, she tugged on her boots, hopping around first on one foot, then the other, in an effort to avoid having to sit down, then wrapped the long bandage around her arm again to hide the silver mark. Nurse Anah and Lord Melchizedek likely had a reason for wanting it out of sight.

Gathering her laundry basket, she elbowed open the door.

Ren, Peter, and the twins were in her main room. Jakir and Jamir were each other's mirror image as they sat opposite each other at her table. Ren leaned his hip against the table, watching Peter stir something over her fire.

Peter looked up. "Happy birthday. How is your arm?"

"Fairly well," she replied, frowning at them. She dropped the basket by her feet and slid it back into her bedroom, closing the door behind it. "What brought this on?"

"Snowstorm." Jakir grinned, pointing over his shoulder toward the window. Sure enough, the outside was a solid wall of white. "We've been stuck inside all day, and we're bored silly. It's your fifteenth birthday. So we brought you supper."

"Besides"—Ren smirked—"this will keep you and Ethno from going another round. The two of you need to withdraw and lick your wounds for a little while."

She snorted. "I'm going to class."

"Tomorrow," Jamir said firmly.

"Tonight. I have astronomy."

"Which has been cancelled due to the snow. Nothing but snow is visible."

"And fist-fighting."

"Master Khalil personally said you were not allowed in his classroom." She scowled.

Jakir rose and held out the chair for her. She turned her scowl at him, and he hit the backs of her knees with the chair, forcing her to sit. "At least pretend to be happy. You're fifteen today."

Peter left the pot to slip up behind her and cover her eyes. She stilled, waiting, listening as the door to her quarters opened and closed. Someone walked over to her, boots sounding against the floor. A tome was pressed into her hands.

"Happy birthday," Zedek said.

Peter uncovered her eyes.

Kirin's eyes lit up. "It's in Elvish!" She stroked the book's cover reverently.

"It's a history," Ren explained.

"We were in Caima a few weeks ago and saw this. A traveler was selling it. We thought you would like it."

"Thank you very much," she breathed, flicking through the first several pages.

"I don't think he realized exactly what he was selling," Peter commented. Jamir smirked, and his brother nodded in agreement.

"What do you mean?"

"Look at the author's name."

She obeyed. "'Eanneth, son of Iloth.' Those are old elven names. Very old."

Zedek nodded, his eyes flashing. "I looked it up. He would have lived around the time of the last Adkish."

Kirin's eyes widened. *The last Adkish. The legendary hero.*

"Thank you," she said again. She ran to hide the valuable book in her room, reemerging to see Ren hunting through her shelves for bowls.

"Up and over one," she instructed. He obeyed, pulling out six bowls. Peter ladeled out large portions of stew, setting them around the table as Zedek poured wine.

The rest of the knights lounged around near the table with their bowls as Zedek said a blessing for the meal before they ate.

"Peter, this is good," Kirin mumbled into her bowl.

"There's more in the pot."

She refilled her bowl and sat back down.

Zedek didn't look up. "So what happened out on the archery field? Between you and Ethno?"

"I don't know. He shot me. I somehow managed to burn him. I'm not sure how I did it. I'm not sure I could recreate it."

"I could try to teach you," Jamir offered.

"So I could ruin your face, too. Ella would love me for that."

"That might help everyone tell them apart," Ren commented. Jamir glared at him.

Jakir laughed. "Wonderful. Then I can be the handsome one."

There were several snickers around the group.

"You're identical twins," Peter laughed. "You look the same."

Kirin smiled around her at the young men who had invaded her room to bring her dinner, company, and a new book. It was times like these she felt as if she truly belonged here.

Dawn found Kirin sitting on her bed with her arms wrapped around her knees, her woolen cloak tucked around her shoulders. She had been unable to sleep because of pain in her ears, of all places.

I wish I had someone to talk to, she thought, staring into the flame burning in the fireplace. The dancing light made strange patterns over the bare skin of her arms, over the odd silver marking. She shivered and rose to throw another log on the flames.

Returning to her bed, she pulled the blankets up over her legs and pulled her cloak tighter around her shoulders. She placed Eanneth's book on her lap, running her fingertips over the engraved lettering on the leather cover.

Translated, it read, *On the History of the Great Heroes*

In other words, the Adkishes.

Intrigued, she opened it and began to read.

Of the Adkishes, there are four. Born into a different major species of our world every ten thousand years, there have been three to date. From the elves, from the kingdom of Ellasar, Ishmael, firstborn son of King Thilyan, became the first of the great heroes. Ten thousand years to the day after his death in battle following the death of his beloved wife in childbirth, Adkish Rurik of the dragons was born. After Rurik came Adkish Charlemagne of the humans, from the country of Kyria, who died, as humans are wont to do, of old age.

Though Charlemagne died only twenty years ago, there has already been some dissension over which race will claim the fourth and final Adkish. The elves, the dragons, and the humans have long been recognized as the major races of our fair world of Kyria—called so, as it is well know, after the largest nation, the realm of the humans— while the vampires, the werewolves, the naiads and dryads, the nymphs, and the Avians have been recognized as the minor races. The Avians, at the time of this penning, claim the next Adkish will be born to them, as they themselves have claim to a country and a king. But the worlds will see in slightly less than ten thousand years.

The Adkish is easily recognized from the moment of his birth. The hero is born with the silver marking spiraling down his dominant magic-arm, culminating at his hand and palm. Some have used tools to help focus their magic, especially at a younger age. Ishmael used a crystal pendant he oftentimes wore around his neck, while Rurik channeled his power through his blade when in human form. It may be interesting to note that Charlemagne, the human Adkish, was the only one who never used an aid to focus his magic.

Kirin stopped reading, her mind spinning. Her eyes wide, she looked at the mark running down her arm. Almost frantically, she looked for the date of the book's penning, checked again for how long it had been since Charlemagne had died. The math wasn't complicated. Ten thousand and fifteen years.

She had the mark. She had been born at the right time. *Am I the next Adkish?* she wondered uneasily.

It would explain why a human had magic.

But the mark had only just appeared, and the author claimed the Adkish was born with the mark.

What if being the fourth Adkish—Adkisha—means I have to leave? I like it here. I don't want to leave. Kirin looked around her room. *This is my home or the closest thing I have to one. And I have friends here.* She thought of Zedek, Peter, Ren, Jakir, and Jamir, who'd been so kind to celebrate her birthday with her, and each of their dragons respectively: Sammerron, Mist, Snowfire, Poseidon, and Zanthys. All dragon riders, especially the elite Dragon Knights, could talk to their dragons—and each other—mentally, a skill called mindspeaking.

But once again, I'm different, Kirin thought. *They would be so mad if they knew that somehow I could speak to all of the dragons.*

She rose, pulled a short-sleeved green tunic over a cream-colored shirt, tugged on her boots, and belted her short sword over her tunic. She wrapped her cloak around her shoulders again and left her quarters for breakfast.

Going to breakfast in the Great Hall was rare; she generally ate by herself. But today she wanted company. As she walked down the aisle between the two huge tables, people stared and whispered.

Scowling, she stopped beside Zedek, one of the few Dragon Knights who didn't seem to mind her presence this morning.

"Why are they staring at me?" she whispered.

"None of us knew you were an elf. Why didn't you tell us?"

"*Pardon?*" she hissed in shock.

"An elf. Your ears are pointed."

"Impossible!" Her hands flew up to feel her ears.

Suddenly Jonathan jumped up and called, "Halfling!"

Everyone began to laugh. She walked up to him, punched him in the stomach, then spun low, kicking his legs out from under him, and continued walking. She grinned wolfishly as she heard his head hit the floor.

Kirin picked up her breakfast and proceeded to dragon-lore class.

THE PRINCE

The headmaster walked down one of the many large hallways of the first floor, leading a stranger. He stopped and knocked on a large oak door to one of the classrooms.

"Come in!" the hand-to-hand combat master called.

Melchizedek entered, followed by the stranger, a young, fair-haired man who looked to be about sixteen. They had arrived just in time to see Ethno punch Jacob in the face, winning the match.

"Good afternoon, Master Khalil."

"Good afternoon, Headmaster," Khalil returned with a bow. Turning to the newcomer, he said, "Greetings. I am Master Khalil."

"I am Callian, son of King Mendez and prince of Giladeth," he replied formally, giving a slight bow. He had a pleasant voice and a handsome face, Kirin noticed as she hid out of sight, waiting and watching him when she knew he wasn't looking her way.

"Welcome to the Academy. It has been a long time since we've entertained anyone from Giladeth, let alone her prince. We are honored. Please, stay and watch the next round. It will be between the reigning champion and Ethno, who is in the ring now," Master Khalil continued, gesturing at the ring.

"Thank you."

Callian smiled, allowing himself to be a normal young man instead of a prince. A good round of fist fighting would be fun to watch.

He was more than a little surprised when a beautiful young woman stepped into the fighting ring holding a crimson sash above her head. She was the most stunning creature he had ever seen. Her beauty was breathtaking, drawn in fine, straight lines, her features sharp. He had never seen another woman like her, and he had met many. Her body was slim to the extreme and athletic-looking. He stared, shocked. She could have been anyone … a warrior or a princess, some great lady, an angel perhaps, or some other celestial being.

She was barely dressed in cream-colored pants rolled up below her knees, revealing her lean calves, sculpted like a goddess's. She wore a midnight-blue strip of material, about twelve inches wide, wrapped tightly around her upperchest, showing off a thin waist; flat stomach; long, bare arms; and a slender, pale throat. A long strip of white bandage was wrapped around her left arm from shoulder to wrist, a glove covering her fingers and palm. Her long, silver-blond hair, a lighter shade than his, was pulled back into a warrior's knot, tied in place by a ribbon the color of the sea.

Never had he seen any woman dressed as she was—and in front of so many men. She must have no embarrassment, no self-consciousness.

He was mildly surprised at her ears, which came to a point, but he did his best not to stare. Still, what really captured his attention were her eyes. They were a brilliant green—deep and intelligent and fierce and lovely. He could stare at them endlessly, lose himself in their depth for eternity.

The man facing her was several inches taller than her five-foot-eight frame, with black hair and a spectacular burn across one side of his face. It looked as if he had angered one of those massive dragons. He was dressed only in blood-red pants, also rolled up below his knees.

Another dark-haired knight moved to stand beside Callian.

"I am Zedek. You seemed surprised," he observed.

Callian tore his gaze off the young woman in the ring. "I wasn't expecting a woman to be the reigning champion of fist fighting, especially while wounded."

Zedek laughed. "That's Kirin. She's the only woman taught here at the Academy. And even wounded, she'll give Ethno a good fight. If it doesn't offend, how old are you?"

"Sixteen. Why?"

"If you're looking for a woman, you'll be disappointed. As I said, we only have one, and that's her." He jerked his chin at the impossibly beautiful figure, drawing Callian's attention back to her. "And she's hasn't come of age yet..." he trailed off, grinning a friendly grin. Zedek watched the prince's expression. "She's not courting anyone," he added with a mischievous grin. "But she's feisty," he warned.

"I can certainly see that." Callian chuckled, his eyes absorbing the cocky, casual way she held herself. It was a stance that said she knew her opponent and expected to win.

"Do you have anyone like her in Giladeth?"

"I've never seen anyone like her." Callian's voice was both impressed and awed. Zedek smirked, and seeing how Callian couldn't take his eyes off her, repeated that she wasn't with anyone yet.

"Begin!" shouted Master Khalil, and the match began. The two opponents circled around each other slowly, waiting patiently, watching. Suddenly, Ethno leapt into the air, swinging into a low-spinning kick. Kirin leapt straight up, impossibly high, kicking his shoulder and off-balancing him as she passed over him. She landed softly on the balls of her feet and waited for him to get up. They inched closer to each other again, rarely landing a blow on each other, though both moved with astounding speed. Both Kirin and Ethno were fantastically good. Callian watched, noting how Kirin's feet barely touched the ground; she was quick as a striking cobra and light on her feet, a deadly combination in fighting. She kept her body loose, her movements fluid and graceful, fighting with intelligence. Her wounded arm didn't seem to impede her in the slightest. Ethno, however, was strong, and power filled his movements. A good blow from him could prove fatal. He seemed to rely on his strength, constantly forcing her to move and dart and duck his blows, trying to wear her out. His hands were constantly balled into tight fists, whereas Kirin's were relaxed. If he could catch her, the match would be over quickly.

With outstanding agility and acrobatic skill, Kirin suddenly flipped over his head and landed a handful of rapid punches at the base of his neck. Ethno fell, dazed, while Kirin landed soundlessly on her feet. He was helped up and out of the arena, and Kirin grinned triumphantly while Master Khalil gave her back the crimson sash, and the rest of the Dragon Knights applauded.

"Amazing," breathed Callian. The fight had barely lasted three minutes.

"Well done, Kirin. My Lord Callian, would you care to go a round?" Master Khalil asked.

"With whom, Master?"

"Why, Kirin, of course."

"Oh." Surprise colored his tone, and Kirin turned to stare at him, her angelic face troubled. "No, thank you. I'd rather not fight a woman."

"Coward!" Kirin called, insulted. Her enthralling expression changed to chagrin.

"Manners, Kirin," warned the headmaster.

"Stand and fight me!" she challenged angrily, striding to the edge of the arena, now scowling fiercely at him.

"I'm not going to hit a young woman," he stated, afraid of accidentally harming her. He eyed the long bandage. Especially when she was already wounded.

"Then draw your sword," she hinted, raising one eyebrow and tilting her head slightly, her eyes daring him to refuse. His eyes slid to her pointed ears again. There were dragons in this country—were there also elves? If so, she could be one of them. Perhaps it would be prudent not to offend her any further.

Callian sighed. "Very well. But I don't want to hurt you." He pulled his boots off and rolled up his pants.

Kirin nearly danced back to the opposite edge of the square arena and drew her own sword. Callian noticed that although she held it expertly, her sword was crude, not the type of weapon he thought a Dragon Knight—or an elf—would carry. The blade was thick and notched, well worn and unbalanced, as if made by a novice and used by far too many people. It was a short sword in the hands of one who could easily dual-wield.

"Slim chance you'll get near enough," she snorted, trying not to stare as he pulled his tunic and shirt off over his head. She tilted her head at him, curious. "I don't remember any Prince Callian in my lessons. Are you from Kyria?"

"No. I'm not from this country. I'm Giladethian," Callian answered, leaping into the fighting ring, his broadsword in his hands. He sank into a fighting stance. Kirin stood calmly, her sword dangling from loose fingers at her side. She closed her eyes and smiled a bit to herself.

"Begin!"

Kirin immediately tucked her sword to her chest and flipped over his head. But he was ready for that and spun around, blocking her blow. They fairly danced around the fighting ring, trading parry for blow, blow for parry. On and on they fought, spinning and twisting, feeling each other out, testing each other's footwork, trying to find a weakness or vulnerability in the other. Kirin slashed viciously at his head, forcing Callian to duck and roll out of harm's way, only to leap back to his feet and block a diagonal blow.

His assumption was correct: she *was* deadly. A faint sheen of sweat began to form on his brow. Even though she was a woman, she was better than half of the knights he had trained with. *Could* he beat her? he wondered.

And then he saw it: a hole in her defense. He brought the flat of his blade smashing down on her right wrist, not hard enough to break it, causing her to drop her sword. He darted behind her, and pinning her wrists to her collarbone with his left arm, he held her body against his, his sword at her throat. Everything had happened so fast that when his sword touched her throat, Kirin's head was forced back against his shoulder.

Silence descended as the Dragon Knights stared in shock. They had not expected Callian to be that good. Neither had Kirin. Master Khalil started to clap, breaking the silence. Then everyone applauded.

When the clapping died down, Kirin, trying fiercely not to blush, snapped under her breath, "Well, are you going to hold me like this all day, or are you planning on letting me go?"

Callian suddenly realized how little they were both wearing and felt the heat rise to his face at the feel of her bare skin against his, her head on his shoulder. He felt her gaze upon him and met her eyes. Callian immediately released her as the rest of the Dragon Knights began to taunt.

Kirin, her face set in stone, leapt out of the arena and wrenched her shirt and boots back on, draping her green tunic and cloak over her unbound arm. As she turned to leave the room, Melchizedek, who had stayed to watch the two matches, calmly said, "Wait please, Kirin."

She stopped, resting her hand against the doorframe, and without turning around, she asked Callian, "Why are you here?"

"Adonai told me to come here, to Kyria. I'm looking for a great warrior—someone known as the Adkisha. Do you know where I might find him?" he asked from the arena, projecting his voice clearly. He held his sword loosely at his side, the tip resting against the wooden arena floor.

Kirin froze. The Dragon Knights whispered amongst themselves in shock at the prince's words. Kirin glanced at her headmaster. She had yet to bring herself to discuss the matter with him, to ask whether it was possible that she, an orphaned, underage female with elven blood in her veins, could be the final Adkish. The Adkisha.

If you truly believe that you are the Adkisha, then you may reveal yourself as the one Prince Callian is looking for, the headmaster mindspoke to her. She was startled to hear his voice in her head.

"Impossible. The fourth Adkish hasn't returned yet," stated Shaun, a seventeen-year-old.

A murmur of agreement went up from the rest of the knights. Kirin pulled the glove off her hand, trying to be subtle about it as she began to unwind the bandage covering the mark on her arm.

"Adonai said I could find him here, in Caima." He looked around. "I am fairly certain I have the correct town."

Free of the bandage but keeping her arm hidden, Kirin took a deep breath and spun around. "What do you want with me?"

Jonathan began to laugh. "You? Ha! That's better than watching you be bested by someone. You must be jesting. You're a *girl*. You can never be the Adkish!"

Kirin's eyes narrowed; she crushed the long strip of white in her fist. Callian thought for a moment about the assumption he'd made. The gender of the warrior had never been made known to him. Was it possible that he was looking for a woman?

"I'm glad to know that you can listen so well," Callian replied icily, suddenly feeling as if he needed to defend her. "I said *Adkisha*, not *Adkish*. Adonai never said that I was looking for a male. I merely assumed that. Although I am surprised Kirin claims to be the one I'm looking for." He immediately regretted his words.

Kirin lost her temper. "I claim nothing! I know who I am, even if you all are too stupid see it!" she shouted, throwing the ball of material at Jonathan.

The older knight's eyes widened as he caught sight of the long, silvery mark. "Impossible," he whispered.

Glaring at him, Kirin turned on her heel and stormed out down the hall.

Callian waited a few seconds amid the astonished murmurs of the other knights before quietly following Kirin down six different hallways, up three flights of stairs, and down two more hallways. Completely lost, he watched her disappear through a set of heavy oaken doors. He counted off a minute and a half—pulling his boots and shirt back on and lacing up the ties around his neck—before knocking once.

The door swung open silently, revealing the main room of Kirin's quarters. He walked in as quietly as he could and, seeing another door ajar, entered carefully into the room where the dragon would have slept. Kirin was in the center of the room on her knees, her head hung and her back to the door, crying silently. His breath caught in his throat. She had let her hair hang down her back, and he could see how *long* it was. How beautiful, the way it cascaded gently, ending at her waist.

Callian knelt beside her, his heart filled with pity for this strange girl. Kirin didn't even notice he was there until he awkwardly put his arm around her shoulders, trying to comfort her. Surprised, her hand snapped up, hitting him in the face, a knee-jerk reaction.

"Ouch!" He scrambled backward.

Bitterly, without looking at him, she snapped, "What do you want?"

"To help. That was what I was sent to do," he said quickly. "I'm sorry they mocked you. And I apologize for holding on to you for so long. I was shocked I had bested you—and that you were so skilled."

She rocked back and hugged her knees to her chest. His attention snagged on the silvery lines down her arm. "It's not a new thing," she murmured quietly. "They're always teasing me. Because I'm differ-ent." Her voice shifted to miserable. "Because I'm a freak."

"Well, they shouldn't," he murmured, keeping his voice gentle. "I've met plenty of women, and none of them know how to defend themselves. Not like you. You're better than them. If you're the per-son I'm supposed to help, then I'm glad you're different. That you know how to fight. And I'm truly sorry I embarrassed you. Perhaps someday we can be friends?" he asked, sounding hopeful.

"Why? Why would you want to be my friend? You must have realized that I have few friends, no family, and no dragon. What would a prince care for my friendship?"

Now she sounded bitter again. This was going to be hard, this girl with her emotions. Callian wondered for a moment if he was in over his head.

"Sir," Kirin said, standing in the doorway of the headmaster's study. "I wanted to ask you about the line of the Adkish. Zedek and his squadron—with the absence of Ethno and Jonathan—gave me a book."

She paused, hoping that he would speak and affirm her specula-tions. When he didn't, she took a deep breath and forged on.

"I really am the Adkisha, aren't I, sir?"

Lord Melchizedek closed his eyes and nodded slowly.

"Why wasn't I born with the mark?"

Those sharp blue eyes opened again. "You were, Kirin," he murmured. "You were. You came to the Academy with it."

"I've never seen it before, sir. But ... it looks ... right. Sir?"

"Do you know what a binding spell is, Kirin?"

"No, sir."

"It is a complicated spell performed in an effort to hide a being by making them appear to be of a different species. No one looking for an elf would pay much attention to a vampire, for example."

Horror crossed her face. "You performed the spell on me," she whispered.

Again, he nodded slowly. "I performed the spell on you. The moment you were brought to the Academy. You were four, and I drugged you into unconsciousness so that it wouldn't hurt you. As the Adkisha, even at four years of age, you had powerful enemies. The original plan was to keep you human until you came of age. Over the course of this year, I had planned on preparing you for your magic, your destiny. But you matured into your powers too rapidly. And now there's nothing to do but wait for the spell to unravel."

"How long will that take?" she demanded, trying not to sound rude.

He watched her gravely. "Not long. Not long at all. The process has already begun." He gestured to her ears.

She felt their pointed tips again. "I have elven blood in me."

"That is my assumption, yes."

"I'm a halfling, though. Correct?"

"Yes."

She waited.

He smiled softly. "Patience is a virtue, Kirin."

"But, with all respect, not one I'm known to possess, sir."

His smiled grew. "But practice perfection makes. Why don't you go to your classes? Oh, and Kirin? Seeing as Adonai sent Prince Callian to be your aide, I think it best if you take over as his host during his stay at the Academy."

"Sir!" she protested.

"Go, Lady Adkisha."

She went.

At the headmaster's request and to Kirin's dismay, Callian accompanied her to her classes the next morning. He found the dragon-lore class to be rather interesting. Master Kish was lecturing on the physical traits of the different types of dragons: Fire, Water, Light, Dark, Twilight, and Shadow. Surprisingly enough, Dark Dragons were no more evil than the rest of the dragons; they were merely black. Callian found himself intently listening to everything Master Kish said. As Giladeth had no dragons, he found them both amazing and terrifying, and kept well away from the ones at the Academy.

He glanced at the young woman sitting silently next to him. She sat just as he did. Her hands were clenched and placed in her lap, and every muscle was stiff. Slightly amused, he figured if he touched her, she would hit the stone roof of the tower they were in. Literally.

Her gorgeous hair swung into her face, obscuring his view. He felt a strange need to brush it back, or at least touch her perfect face. He went back to clenching his hands and attempting to listen to Master Kish. That would probably be safer, assuming he preferred his head attached to his shoulders.

"Dark Dragons love to stir up chaos between the other dragons, between dragons and elves, and even between dragons and humans," Master Kish continued with his lecture. "They, like all dragons, will bond to only one person—of what race, it matters not. However, a single person may have more than one dragon bonded to him. It is possible, just unlikely.

"Fire Dragons are, obviously, different shades of red. They tend to be rather quick to anger, very stubborn, and quite protective of their rider. Fire Dragons will always have an endless fascination with any type of flame—particularly when they are young and cannot yet breathe fire. They also have a prejudice against the Water Dragons. If you are the rider of a Fire Dragon, such as Ethno or Zedek or Jamir, for example, when it comes time for your dragon to mate, you will notice they will never select a Water Dragon as their mate. Same scenario works the other way around. As they say, 'Fire and Water cannot mix.' Does anyone know the name of their queen? Aaron?"

"Queen Quanta," Aaron answered.

"Dragons have queens?" Callian murmured, his brow furrowed in confusion.

Kirin turned to stare at him. He met her gaze. "You didn't know that?" The prince shook his head.

Kirin looked surprised. "Oh. I thought that it was obvious."

"There are no dragons in Giladeth. At least not to the best of my knowledge."

She continued to stare. "Pity," she finally muttered, turning back to the lecture.

"Correct," Master Kish was saying. "Very good, Aaron. No doubt Cináed told you?"

"Yes, sir." Aaron smiled.

Master Kish nodded and returned to his lecture. "Water Dragons are varying shades of blue and blue-green and have the ability to breathe under water, as well as on dry land. They tend to enjoy the taste of raw fish and love the ocean. Water Dragons are slow to anger, but when they do get mad, you do not want to be in their way!

"That brings us to the fourth type of dragon, the Light Dragon. They will actually shine in the dark. During the day, their scales will absorb light and give it off when there is none. They grow stronger as the moon waxes. It is true that no one has seen the Light Dragons in over two hundred years. There are few of them left.

"There are two other types of dragons, though. While it is true that no one has seen a Twilight Dragon in over four thousand years, it is possible that a small population of them live hidden. Can anyone tell me what a Twilight Dragon looks like?" He paused, waiting. Silence met his inquiry. "Anyone? Jonathan?"

"I don't know, sir," Jonathan replied.

Master Kish frowned. "The scales of Twilight Dragons are mainly black, but they are highlighted with a golden tint. Even along their wings, they retain their strange coloring. Furthermore, their eyes are golden, which has led to what assumption? Someone? Yes, Kittim," he called.

"That they are kin to the werewolves and the Avians?" Kittim tried hesitantly.

"All dragons are kin to the werewolves and the Avians. Anyone else? Peter?"

"That they are the original species of dragons and all others were offspring?"

"Correct. Thank you, Peter. Now, how do we know this assumption is false? Aram?"

"There's no record of it. The other species are recorded in history long before the Twilight Dragons appeared."

"Good, good. Now, can someone else tell me of the final type of dragon? Jakir?"

"Shadow Dragons, sir."

Master Kish nodded gravely. "Shadow Dragons. Corrupted dragons, robbed of their intelligence and their natural ability to shift into a human form. They become mere beasts, slaves to those who rule in the Black Fortress in Amalay Kahelith. Someone please translate that Elvish name."

Kirin spoke up. "'The World of Fear,' sir."

"Correct. One world and one country, ruled by three. Someone name for me Nishron's Three."

There was a slight pause, a hush from the scratch of quills on parchment, as if no one quite wanted to answer Master Kish. Then, finally Jamir spoke.

"Morgan, the sorceress. Molyb, the shifter. And Malakieth, the dragon."

Master Kish nodded once, slowly. "Tell me of their fates."

Jakir nudged his brother to speak once more. "Morgan fell to King Nahor of Ellasar's blade during the Battle of Candescere. Molyb has been missing for some time now. And Malakieth rules in the Black Fortress in Amalay Kahelith."

"Correct." The master's voice darkened, and he leaned forward on the podium in the center of the circular tower-room he taught behind. All around him, students also leaned forward behind the oaken tables that surrounded the podium in a large, two-hundred-and-seventy-degree arc, notes forgotten. An intense silence filled the air as they waited for Master Kish to speak.

"Many of you have heard stories and legends about Malakieth. He was once the prince of the Light Dragons. One day he met a woman in the woods of his country, the sorceress Morgan. The two became fast friends. She had been corrupted by power, and soon her poison-covered words seeped into the young prince's mind, corrupting him as well. About half a year after they met, Morgan used her black magic to open a portal to a lush, green world, and the two of them left. Malakieth apprenticed himself to her; they never bonded as dragon and rider. Many years passed. Finally, one day, Malakieth returned to our world, to land of the Light Dragons, his scales glistening with black magic. He and Morgan led an army of Rashek soldiers—powerful and evil creatures created by Morgan's dark magic—against the Light Dragons at the time of the Dark Moon. Caught off guard by Malakieth's treachery, the Light Dragons tried to fight back but to no avail. In the end, many Light Dragons were killed, their queen was injured, and her consort was missing. Morgan, as Jamir has told us, was also killed. The few remaining Light Dragons fled to Candescere, their citadel and last remaining fortress, and have not been seen since.

"A few years ago, the queen of the elves was captured by Malakieth and taken to the world of Amalay Kahelith. Thankfully, she has escaped his prison—with a little inside help, if the report was correct, and has been able to return to our world. I tell you this because the headmaster has received word that she and her eldest son will be traveling here to the Academy of the Dragon Knights. She should be here within a few days, Adonai willing."

A low murmur spread throughout the classroom.

"Class dismissed," Master Kish called over the hum of twenty students talking simultaneously.

Kirin left quickly, a strange look on her face. Callian caught up with her as she entered one of the courtyards.

"Are you all right?" he asked awkwardly.

"No, she's thinking, and it's rather hard work!" called one of the boys who had been in the class with them.

"Shut up, Nemuel. Leave her alone," Ren spoke up. He had his back to a tree and a book in his lap and was carefully sketching his dozing Water Dragon, who lay in the sun a few feet away.

Callian caught Kirin's arm to turn her toward him and then let go as her eyes narrowed.

"Are you all right?" he repeated. "You have … an odd look about you."

Kirin looked away, and for a moment, he thought that she wasn't going to answer. "The castle is made of white stone. During the night, it shines like the moon." She looked back at him. "Castle Candescere, the last fortress of the Light Dragons. I've never been there … never read about or heard of what it looks like. I simply know." She looked away again, her eyes falling on Ren. "But I don't know how I know."

Kirin shook her unsettlement from her and walked over to the red-haired knight, sitting in the dead grass beside him. It was one of the few spots clean of snow. "Ren, Master Kish says the elven queen and the crown prince are coming here soon."

"Hurrah!" he crowed, looking up from his drawing and grinning. Snowfire shot awake and snorted steam at his rider. Ren ignored him and continued. "I've always wanted to meet an elf. They should be fun to draw."

"All right, I'm lost," Callian admitted, shaking his head.

Kirin tried not to laugh, pressing her lips together and closing her eyes.

She had led Callian from the main courtyard up to her favorite library, the one on the fourth floor. It faced north, and the northern wall was filled with windows, showing off an incredible view of the rugged Eludian Mountains.

"You've chosen one of the best times to come to the Academy. Exams are now, but then we have four weeks off, Yule, and another week before classes start up again." She walked over to a long table and grabbed a stack of books. She read their titles and began to put them away. Callian grabbed another stack and followed her. "Summer's fun. There are less classes, and most of them are hands-on, like botany. That's an entertaining class. I'm fairly certain the goal is to survive with all your fingers intact."

"You're jesting, correct?" Callian asked with a laugh.

"Yes, but someone *did* lose a finger. Once."

They walked back to the table. "This is my favorite library, the North Star Library. We're on the fourth floor now. I have anatomy studying to do, if you want to meet my aide. We've named him Turiksö."

"That's a strange name. Where did the lot of you come up with it?" he questioned, his expression curious.

"It's Dragons' Tongue," she told him with a quiet chuckle. She reached into a closet and pulled out a sackcloth bag. "Can you guess what it means?"

"I have no idea."

She pulled out something white from the bag and tossed it to him. He caught it and cried out in surprise, throwing it back at her. She laughed at him, catching the human skull deftly.

"It means 'bone.' Turiksö is one of our human skeletons. We found him buried in the ice at one of the mountain peaks. So now we learn anatomy from him."

"*Human* skeleton? I hesitate to see what other skeletons the Academy stores in her closets."

Kirin laughed again at his joke. "We do have multiple Rashek skeletons—don't ask how we get those." She poured the rest of the bones out of the bag and began to construct the skeleton. "I have to be able to do this in under ten minutes for class this afternoon. I'll eat lunch afterward, but if you'd like to eat earlier, I'll show you the way," she offered.

He handed her the spine, grimacing at the vertebrae that were wired together.

"I'll wait and see this class, if you don't mind."

Twenty minutes later, Callian stood a step behind Kirin, watching her assemble a human skeleton on the long, low table in front of her. She had her teeth bared and her jaw locked, and her eyes flashed in nervousness and concentration in the dark, hot room.

Master Naphtu, who taught human and human-like anatomy and physiology, paced around behind the ten students, making them all more nervous. He had high expectations of everyone. "One minute left, Lady Kirin," Naphtu purred. Callian jumped, not expecting him to be that close. "I hope Prince Callian hasn't been giving you the answers."

"No, sir. Of course not. I can do this by myself," she muttered, staring helplessly at the two roundish bones. She had the rest of the skeleton assembled, and the two that she held seemed to be extras.

Her gaze turned panicked as Master Naphtu began to count down the last thirty seconds from the center of the large, oval-shaped room.

Callian glanced over her shoulder. He smiled thinly and touched the small of her back with one finger. She started and turned her head to stare at him.

He stared back and then looked away and rubbed his kneecap. Catching her gaze again, he once more rubbed his knee.

"The patella!" she hissed under her breath, placing the two bones in the knee.

"Three. Two. One. Stop, and step away from your tables," Naphtu ordered.

Kirin stepped back, close to Callian, and watched the master with apprehension.

"It looks fine to me," Callian murmured in her ear.

"Well, at least it's correct, Sir Carmi," Naphtu announced loudly. "However, if this was a living being, it would be the most hideously deformed creature I've ever seen. Points off, but you pass."

The fifteen-year-old, brown-haired boy he had been talking to heaved a sigh of relief, wiping his hand across his forehead.

"Well, at least he's being nice," she whispered as he worked his way down toward her table, the last one in the room.

"Lady Kirin!" the master snapped, peering at her work. "Do you not know your right hand from your left?" Kirin jumped and stepped over to her table.

"Yes, sir. I did my model with the palms down, as evidenced by the positioning of the ulna and the radius, sir," she said, keeping her voice emotionless. She pointed at the forearm.

Master Naphtu gazed at it and then jerked a nod. "Very well, but next time, palms up! That goes for all of you! Class dismissed."

Kirin was the first out of the door. Callian hid his exasperation. He would likely get himself lost again trying to find her.

But Kirin was waiting outside the doorway, pressed against the wall and breathing hard, every muscle locked up. Callian touched her shoulder.

"Are you all right?" he asked tenderly, his eyes concerned.

"Yes. Merely the adrenaline kicking in. Heaven and hell, I nearly failed that exam. Thank you so much," she said softly, looking at him gratefully.

"Of course. What class do you have next?"

"None. I'm going to go eat, if you're hungry, and then I can show you around if you like," she offered. "And, best of all, no more anatomy for five weeks! That was my final exam."

"Wonderful."

"Very," she agreed.

Callian glanced at her walking along beside him like a friend. She turned to find him watching her.

"Tell me about Giladeth. What is it like? Obviously, you believe in Adonai. You're a prince there, but you can fight decently with a sword, and you know anatomy, and you can read our writing."

"The written and spoken language is the same in Giladeth, which is helpful. I've fought many battles, which is where my skill with a blade comes from. You're still sore that I beat you, aren't you?" he teased.

"I'm not often bested in the arena," she said stiffly.

"It was pure luck," he told her. She stared at him, surprised that he would admit that. "Even the best swordsman can be defeated by a new trick."

She looked down at the stone steps they were descending. "I have to be the best. I have to prove myself to the others. I'm the odd one out, the only female beside Nurse Anah, and so I am constantly singled out, and…I need to be the best," she confided softly.

"If it means anything to you, you are better with a sword than many of the knights at Giladeth, and their weapons are of a better quality—no offense."

"Truly?" she asked, looking up at him. "You think I'm better than them?"

"Yes. So why is the North Star Library your favorite?"

"It has a lot of books about adventures and romance, battles in far off lands, and heroes who are sent on great quests for their king. Besides, the massive fireplace with the furs around it makes a great place to curl up and read in the middle of the winter, and you saw the view. I love to stare out those windows and pretend that I'm flying."

Kirin sat in the sun on a low stone wall out in one of the courtyards, killing time before she had to go and study for her final exam in astronomy, which would take place at midnight. It was her last exam before break started, and she had several hours to wait. But it was nice to sit outside and watch the sunset, bundled up tightly in thick clothes to keep the cold at bay.

Kirin, the elves approach. I've warned Zedek, of course. They carry swords, but walk peacefully. The villagers are curious, Sammerron said, entering her thoughts. Callian was talking with Ren, looking at some of Ren's pictures, leaving her free to speak with the dragon.

How many elves?

Only the queen and the high prince. The queen looks young—thirty-ish, but I don't know how old she truly is. The prince looks to be in his younger twenties.

Suddenly Zedek's voice cut in.

Sammerron? You seem distracted. Are you all right?

Zedek suddenly felt another presence in his dragon's mind. Immediately, he attacked it—finding an unknown something mentally connected to your dragon's head is never a good thing and is always regarded as an enemy at first.

Kirin fought back, desperately trying to protect her mind until Zedek recognized her. The struggle between them was brief, aggression giving way in part to astonishment as secrets were exposed.

A mage! You're a mage!

Kirin! You git, what the bloody hell were you thinking? You can talk to Sammerron—you should have told me! Why didn't you? His angry voice roared in her head.

Because I need friends, too. And if my only friends are other knights' dragons, then so be it. At least they don't hate me!

She heard him sigh, then reply gently to her anger.

Kirin, I don't hate you. And neither do Ren or Peter or half of the other knights. It's just Ethno and his friends that do or, at least, pretend to. The rest of us merely leave you alone. Think about it. If we stood up for you, Ethno and his friends would never stop saying that we were courting. And I don't think that you would like that, now would you?

No, I wouldn't. She hated when he used logic. *You're right, of course. But don't tell anyone that I can talk to their dragons, please?*

I won't if you don't tell anyone that I'm a mage. Oh, and my father wants to see you and Callian in his quarters. He hesitated before asking, *What do you think of him?*

I think the headmaster is very kind.

Not him.

Who?

Callian.

Why? Kirin asked, suspicion in her sweet voice. Zedek could well imagine her narrowing her vibrant green eyes at him.

Because Sammerron and I both think that you two would make quite a pair.

Sammerron eagerly added his agreement.

Kirin was shocked. Suddenly feeling insecure, confused, and unsure, she responded with her usual anger, burying her other emotions deep inside herself.

You mean a courting pair? That we should court? You're lucky that I can't fly, or I'd knock that grin off your face!

He merely laughed a friendly laugh, though he still thought he was right.

Twenty minutes later, she and Callian walked down the hallway toward the headmaster's study. Kirin kept quiet, mulling over what Zedek had said. Obsessing, actually. *What if?* she asked herself, stealing glances when she thought he wasn't looking.

Callian certainly was attractive. His blond hair had a slight wave to it and hung gently around his vividly blue eyes. At six-foot-four, he could easily look over her head. He was lean and strong, yet he was light on his feet. He glanced over to see her staring at him and grinned, unknowingly making her heart jump. He had an attractive smile. Kirin tried to wrench her gaze away from him, afraid he would accuse her of ogling him, but found, much to her chagrin, that she couldn't keep her eyes off him for more than a few seconds. Callian spun around to face her, walking backward in front of her, a crooked grin spreading over his face. As he walked by a window, the sunlight filtering through it and lighting up the golden waves of his hair, he suddenly looked almost... angelic. Kirin felt her breath catch in her throat.

Not able to see where he was heading, he smacked his head into the headmaster's door. *A bit clumsy for an angel.* Kirin laughed softly, a warm and friendly sound. Part of her was surprised. What had made her laugh? Surely not this strange young man's actions?

Callian rubbed his head, muttering, "Ouch." Kirin laughed harder, still trying to get her face and emotions under control.

"Enter, Lady Kirin and Prince Callian," the headmaster called from within. Kirin bit down more laughter at the idea of Callian knocking with his head, struggling to compose her face.

Nurse Anah opened the door for them, ushering them in. Inside sat Lord Melchizedek, a woman who was obviously the elven queen, and the prince, just as Sammerron had described him. He was handsome, as most elves were, with straight honey-blond hair that hung just past his shoulders. His body build was light but strong, his broad shoulders relaxed under his tunic and his sword unbelted and laying casually across his knees. He had light blue eyes and pointed ears. The queen had the same color eyes, but her hair was lighter, more of a silver-blond, and much longer.

The same shade as mine, Kirin thought.

Both elves looked up as soon as the nurse had shut the door behind the warriors. The queen's gaze landed on Kirin and didn't move, drinking the sight of her in as if she was a long-lost love or a childhood friend thought to be dead. There was heartbreak and sorrow in the queen's eyes, such an ancient sorrow that looked out of place on her young face. The prince's eyes were also riveted upon Kirin, slowly scrutinizing every bit of her. Callian felt his teeth clench and his blood flow red-hot through his veins. His hands, which were safely behind his back, were clenched into tight fists, every tendon standing out.

Kirin's eyes flickered around the room, touching on everything and everyone. She was jumpy, nervous, constantly shifting her weight as if ready to fight or run, whichever became necessary. The only court etiquette she had ever been taught had been from Callian twenty minutes ago, when she had begged him to teach her how to interact with royalty other than himself, as he was intent on having her forget that he was the son of a king.

But the elven prince's eyes…They were eyes that knew something, knew something important, something that he wasn't planning on telling anyone.

The headmaster spoke up. "My lady, my lord, this is Kirin, the fourth Adkisha." He gestured toward Callian. "And this is Crown Prince Callian of Giladeth, son of King Mendez. He was sent here by Adonai Himself to assist Kirin. Kirin, Prince Cal-

"Master Patri! A new star! Master Patri!" she called, fear and uncertainty flavoring her words.

Students gathered around them, pointing and whispering.

"Impossible," breathed Master Patri, lowering his telescope. "That's not possible ... and yet ... there it is ... "

Headmaster Melchizedek appeared from the tight spiral steps that led to the rooftop of the astronomy tower, the highest tower of the Academy. The queen followed him gracefully, her head tipped back as she too stared at the star. She joined the group, standing behind her son. The fifteen students that took astronomy this term parted respectfully to let her through.

Ren spoke up. "Sir?"

Queen Ling answered instead. "That is Ashteroth, the star of the Adkish. Ashteroth only lends its power to the Adkish ... or Adkisha. Now that the ten thousand years between the previous Adkish and Kirin have passed, it has returned to grace the night skies with its beauty and power.

"But look to its opposite," she commanded, pointing out a dim red star. "There is the star of Nishron, the Dark Star. It gives its power to the Three.

"I caution you all to stay away from them, particularly Malakieth. I have had ... dealings with him in the past. He is powerful and strong," she whispered, her voice growing soft.

She broke off as if reliving some horror in her past. Ephraim placed a comforting hand on her shoulder, murmuring something in an undertone to her in Elvish.

Kirin watched their exchange intently. *Dealings with Malakieth? Horrors in her past?* she wondered.

Ephraim said something else to his mother, his face grave. Ling looked down, brows drawn together, and then raised her head to look straight at Kirin.

"Lady Adkisha, I would have a word with you in private, if it could be arranged," she murmured.

Kirin looked from Lord Melchizedek, who nodded slightly, to Prince Ephraim, whose hard face gave nothing away, to the queen, whose blue eyes beseeched her. Apprehension filled her, but she nodded.

"Of course, my lady."

Ling led her down the twisting tower stairs, her son close behind her shoulder, as if he was afraid of her disappearing. It made sense—Queen Ling had only recently escaped from imprisonment. Kirin could sense Callian following her, and she was grateful for his presence, a sensation that surprised her.

They reached the hallway, and from behind Callian, the headmaster spoke. "The chamber on the right is empty, Queen Ling."

"Thank you." She opened the door and led their strange procession inside. Lord Melchizedek closed them inside.

Prince Ephraim stoked the glowing embers in the hearth, coaxing a fire back to life with a new log. Ling turned to face Kirin, met her eyes, and then looked away, rubbing her arms. Her son came back to her and wrapped his cloak around her slender shoulders. He murmured what could only be words of encouragement in her ear in their native tongue, his voice too low for Kirin to catch them.

Unease slid through Kirin.

Finally, Ling spoke. "What do you know of your family, Lady Kirin?"

Her unease grew. "Nothing, my lady, save that I am an orphan and that I came to live at the Academy when I was four rather than being fostered by one of the surrounding farmers or townsmen."

"Your family lives."

Callian watched as Kirin's hands clenched into nervous fists behind her back and then relaxed again. She drew a steadying breath.

"And do you know my family, my lady?"

The elven queen closed her eyes. "Well." Those eyes opened again. "You have Ellasarian blood in you."

Kirin inclined her head. "I had guessed as much." Her green eyes flickered to the headmaster and back. "Lord Melchizedek has placed a binding spell on me for my own protection. It is starting to break. My ears have as of recent been pointed like an Ellasarian's."

Ling nodded slowly. "Lady Kirin, you have the blood of the Ella-sarian royalty in you."

Kirin's eyes widened as her face paled. She shook her head mutely, backing up. Callian pressed his hand against her back to stop her retreat.

Ling took a shaky breath. "You are my daughter, Kirin, and I've missed you so much."

Kirin began to tremble, and Callian found himself moving to protect her. But what could he protect her from? Truth was a foe no man could best.

Her mouth worked, trying to speak. Finally, she managed, "Why did you leave me?" The fear and pain in her voice echoed in Callian's mind, and he longed to take that pain away from her.

Queen Ling's voice was just as tortured as she begged her daughter to understand. "I was forced to. Malakieth had pinpointed my location. I was only trying to protect you. I couldn't give him the Adkisha; moreover, I couldn't give him *my daughter*."

"Where ... To whom ..." Kirin floundered.

"Allerion," Ling whispered. "It was the only option I had. You were raised for four years in the courts of Candescere, and then you were brought to the Academy to be taught to fight."

Kirin ducked her head, silently thanking Adonai for the darkness that hid her tears. But Callian noticed, and he longed to comfort her. Ling came forward with graceful steps, closing the distance between herself and the daughter she hadn't been able to raise. She touched Kirin's shoulder with one hand and then embraced her daughter. Kirin hesitated awkwardly then put her arms around Ling and hid her face against the queen's pale hair.

"Am I ... am I ...?" she struggled to ask.

The queen's arms tightened. "No. You are not my husband's daughter. Your father attacked me." She drew back and cupped Kirin's cheek. "But I do not regret you. I love you."

"I ... I need to think."

Ling smiled sadly and brushed tears away from her face. "Good night, my daughter. May Ashteroth shine brightly on you."

Kirin and Callian bowed and left. He half-expected her to run down the hallway back to her quarters, but she walked beside him with calm, even steps. He heard her choke back a sob, and gently placed his arm around her shoulders, trying to comfort her. She moved closer to him, resting her head on his shoulder, crying silently into his tunic in her pain and confusion. She glanced up at Callian, wondering why he cared about how she felt. He looked at her with such an open expression, but with great frustration, Kirin found she couldn't read it.

He opened the door to her quarters and walked with her to her room.

"Good night, Kirin," he said, his angelic voice soft. "And good luck tomorrow with the dragon."

Kirin smiled through her tears. "Thank you, Callian. Good night."

He caught her gaze and smiled at her. Then, simply to make her laugh—for he liked her laugh—he bowed with a flourish to her as if she were royalty. And she was, Kirin realized. Her mother was a queen, which made her a princess. Kirin did laugh, lightly, at Callian's gesture, surprising herself. The sound was music, and it lifted her spirits in the way that only laughter can. She was glad he was here—he seemed like someone she could trust with her every thought, every feeling, every secret.

For deep down inside her, she realized something that shocked and confused her, overwhelming her very core with emotions she had never felt before. As she walked through the door to her bedroom, she paused. Risking a glance at Callian only proved it.

She was in love.

Kirin, frustrated for lack of sleep, crept out of her quarters. She took the hall to the right of her door, silently walking down it for about ten yards and then turning left. She followed that hallway for a half-dozen yards before turning left again down another stone hallway. Finally she stopped before a pair of large oak doors.

Callian, who had been silently trailing her down the darkened hallways, watched as she opened the right door and disappeared inside. He waited outside, not wanting to scare her, not wanting to raise any alarms. A few minutes later, Kirin leapt out the door, landing silently with her knees bent, her arms clutching several books to her chest. She pushed the door closed while Callian hid in the shadows. Like a shadow come back to life, he followed her back to her quarters.

Once inside, he rekindled the fire, causing her to spin and gasp in surprise.

"So what was that room, the one that you snuck into? And what's with all the books?"

"Why did you follow me?" she breathed, placing her right hand over her speeding heart.

"Curiosity kills."

She smiled at his sincere manner with her, her racing heart slowing to a normal pace.

"You are a strange sort of prince," she mused. "Most aren't as open as you are. You are different, and I like that."

He returned her smile. "Answer my question, please."

"That was the Masters' Library."

He liked the mischievous look on her pretty face, the way her eyes gleamed as she said that.

"Students aren't allowed in there. Here," she said, pressing the tomes into his hands, "these are the books. Please don't tell anyone."

"Our secret," he promised. He was surprised, however, at the slight smile and pinkish tinge that crept into her face. He glanced at the titles of the books she handed him: *Finding and Identifying Dragon Eggs*, *Raising Dragons*, *History of Ellasar*, *Legends of the Light Dragons*, *Rise to Power: a History of Lord Malakieth*, and *The Adkish: a Legend Reborn*.

He picked up *Raising Dragons*.

"May I read this? Or were you planning on reading this one first?"

"No, go ahead. I can't sleep, and I have too many questions. So I picked out a few books instead."

Callian glanced out the large window. "You still have a few hours before the dragon comes."

"Will you be there?"

Callian was surprised by the concern in her voice. But then, she was likely worried that the dragon would choose him rather than her.

"No, I'll be wandering around the grounds. I don't want to be chosen. I don't think I could take care of a dragon. I truly don't know that much about them."

"Oh. Enjoy yourself, then." He was once again concerned by the tone of her sweet voice. Was she disappointed? Or was she grateful and simply hiding it?

"Callian?"

He looked back at her. "Yes?"

"Don't go into the forest on the northeast end alone."

She watched as his divine face took on a look of puzzlement.

"The Forgotten Forests are home to vampires and werewolves," she explained.

"Heaven and hell," he breathed. "Are you serious?"

She smiled. "Of course."

They sat together, silently reading until the sun began to turn the surrounding mountains pink, both secretly grateful for the other's company.

Dawn found Kirin by the flight-training field. Callian bade her good-bye and good luck before striding off. A few minutes passed as she waited with the other, younger boys who also had also come, forcing herself to hold still as her heart raced. Then the dragon appeared, running smoothly across the ground.

She was beautiful. Her scales were a deep shade of red, her eyes dark as the glow of dying embers. Her shoulders would have reached Kirin's, testifying to her young age. She was, at most, half a year old. Old enough to know the basics of flying and mindspeech but definitely not old enough to breath fire, or speak out loud, or fly with a rider on her back. Yet. If she chose an older rider—such as Kirin or the thirteen-year-old boy to her right—she would grow rapidly to catch up with her rider's age.

The young female raced straight at Kirin, whose heart soared. Perhaps she would finally be chosen.

The dragon stopped before her. Kirin reached out her hand, fingers trembling as adrenaline coursed through her.

But the dragon dropped her head out of range and scrambled backward. Kirin let her hand fall back to her side, bitterly disappointed, and reached out for the dragon's mind with her own. The dragon searched the small group of prospective riders with a frenzied urgency.

None of these are the right one! Where is he? she howled.

Calm down. Who are you looking for? Kirin asked, keeping her voice gentle and soothing.

But she didn't answer. Instead, she panicked, rearing up to attack Kirin, wings flaring open to balance herself. Kirin stood calmly, begging the dragon to calm down. She knew she wasn't the right one for this young dragon, but she couldn't let the female hurt anyone.

"Get away from her!" Callian was running toward her, sword drawn, fierce determination etched across his face.

"Callian, stay back! You'll get hurt!" she screamed, instantly worried for him. But he ignored her. Kirin looked into his eyes and was afraid of the fire she saw there. He didn't care for his safety; he would protect her.

But the young female took one look at him and dropped back down to all fours. She looked at him again, considering him.

"Callian, lower your blade. Hold out your hand toward her," Kirin whispered. Callian might not know anything about dragons, but she was well versed in their behavior.

He obeyed. The dragon stepped toward him and slid her beautiful head under his hand. He cried out in surprise and jerked his hand away, watching in amazement as a strange mark appeared on his right palm. The dragon touched his mind.

Callian?

"Hush. I'm all right, Tiamat. Tiamat," he mused. "Is that your name?" he asked, stroking her face like he would his warhorse.

Yes.

"How did I know that?"

You are my rider. It was meant to be.

"Why did you attack her?" he breathed.

I was afraid. I didn't know what to do. They frightened me. I am still a dracling, she said sheepishly.

"Dracling?" He frowned.

A young dragon.

Callian turned to Kirin, eyes wide, shocked at the turn of events. He had not wanted this to happen; he had wanted Tiamat to bond to *Kirin.*

Kirin's expression was like stone. Not one emotion crossed her beautiful face. Even her lovely eyes were barren of emotion.

Tiamat began to tease him, immediately catching his thoughts.

Oh, shut up, he thought, exasperated. Tiamat listened, which made him think that perhaps this method—mentally, rather than physically—was the better way of speaking privately with her.

Kirin looked to the headmaster. He nodded at her before turning back toward the impressive stone castle. Kirin turned and walked swiftly toward Callian.

Perhaps she isn't mad, Callian thought.

When she was four feet way, however, she dropped to one knee, her head bent, and said in an emotionless voice, "Follow me, Prince Callian."

She's mad.

Then she turned abruptly and followed Melchizedek back into the castle. The four walked through seemingly endless stone hallways until they reached the hallway to the headmaster's study.

Kirin, I'm sorry, he tried to talk mentally to her. Tiamat supplied the word for him: mindspeak. Kirin stiffened a bit, which he interpreted as her hearing him. *I never meant it to happen. I don't want to take your place.* She didn't answer him. He tried to catch her emotions, but her mind was blank. She let no thought, feeling, or emotion slip.

Kirin, please, talk to me!

You must talk to the headmaster. I have things to attend to. Good day, Prince Callian. He had a feeling that she would like nothing more at that moment than for him to drop dead.

She bowed again and turned to leave. Callian grabbed her arm. Her eyes met his, and he saw cold fire and fear, but there was something else behind that.

Before he had time to ponder this, Callian found himself pinned against the nearest wall. Zedek stood a few paces away, his face dark, right arm raised. Tiamat growled and dropped into a crouch, prepared to attack this man and his magic. But before she could move, Kirin ran to Zedek. He wrapped his left arm around her waist and stepped back with her, vanishing into thin air. The magic that held Callian released him as soon as the mage was gone. Tiamat was still fussing over him as the headmaster called Callian into the study to talk to him.

I have a feeling that Zedek is fond of her. Why else would he have held her like that? Callian told his young dragon.

Perhaps for the magic?

What do you mean by that?

I don't know. Tell Kirin anyway.

Tell Kirin what?

That you are fond of her, the dragon pointed out, as if it was obvious.

Perhaps sometime. Not now.

Zedek and Kirin reappeared at the door to Kirin's quarters. Sammerron was already there. Zedek immediately released his hold on her and stepped back.

"Thank you," she murmured.

"Are you all right?" Zedek asked. "Sammerron sensed your turmoil."

"I'm not sure." Mentally, to his dragon, she said, *Thank you for coming, Sammerron.*

We are friends, he replied softly. *That is what friends do.*

"Good day, Kirin," Zedek said, watching her expression carefully.

"Good day," she whispered, entering her quarters.

He left, leaving her to her confused thoughts.

A Dragon's Heart

Callian and Tiamat had been out together in the forest for three weeks now. In the dead of night after the day Tiamat had chosen him, they had slipped away from the Academy, seeking to give Kirin the space she obviously wanted while Callian and Tiamat explored all the various nuances of the bond, such as the mindspeaking and the magic Tiamat had given him.

That had been one of the strangest things he had discovered.

He had been walking along between his dragon and a frozen stream when she had jumped at something. He had stumbled and lost his footing, falling onto the ice, which had promptly given way underneath him. The stream was only knee-deep, but it was cold, and day was at its end. Tiamat had pulled him out and collected wood, and he had lit a fire to dry and warm his clothing and boots. His dragon, with her warm scales, had curled up around him, trying to warm him. He had wrung out his pants leg. Then, for a reason he couldn't explain, he drew his hand away from his soaked clothing. The water had followed.

They had both stared, surprised.

That isn't normal, Tiamat had murmured.

Callian had simply stared at his hand.

Dragons give their riders magic, but … yours should be fire magic. Not water. The dragon looked at him. *Where did you get water magic from?*

Water magic? he mused, starting to smile. He tried again, once more drawing the water out of his clothing. His smile widened, lighting up his eyes. *My mother always said that I had an affinity for water*, he told Tiamat. *My closest friend, Trig, and I used to pilot small boats around the harbor outside of Haven, the capitol of Giladeth. I've always been a strong swimmer.* He pulled more water from his woolen cloak. *This feels so natural. Shouldn't magic be more difficult to learn?*

Perhaps you've always had it, Tiamat suggested. *Perhaps someone in your bloodline had magic.*

Callian frowned. *But then shouldn't I have always known about it? There have been times where being able to manipulate water would have been rather helpful.*

Tiamat arched her neck, looking proud of herself. *Perhaps I unlocked it when I offered you the bond.*

He grinned at her and rubbed her neck. *Perhaps.*

She nuzzled his hair. *Or perhaps something in your blood is strange and is twisting my magic.*

He laughed. *In my blood?*

She nodded, suddenly serious. *Blood is the seat of magic, dear prince.*

Callian slept fitfully, plagued with dreams.

He was lost, wandering through a woodland shrouded in mist. He could feel the eyes of countless unseen creatures on him. The constant presence of Tiamat was missing, and it was strange, unnerving even, without her by his side.

"How easily you abandon your duty, Prince Callian." The strong male voice echoed on the wind around him, disapproving.

"Lady Kirin hates me now," he called out in defense. His hand crept to his left hip in search of the hilt of his blade, only to find that it, too, was missing.

"How blind you are," the voice replied.

He swung to find its source, but he was still alone.

"I have been bonded to Tiamat in her place. It is a slight she cannot forgive."

"Cannot, or will not?"

"Will not." His eyes swept the trees, but he could not see the tops.

"Tiamat was never meant for her. You know this. And yet, still you shirk from your task."

Callian opened his mouth to defend himself again, but no words came to mind. Shame welled in him. He bowed his head.

"My dear son," the voice whispered soothingly. Callian could feel it wrapping around him in a current of warm air. "You have not failed yet. Tiamat was given to you to give you the means of protecting the Lady Kirin. Go back to her now, back to the Academy, and stand as her protector."

Prince Callian bowed low. "Yes, Lord Adonai."

His eyes opened. Tiamat stirred around him, raising her head to look at him.

"We need to return to the Academy," he told her out loud. Tiamat nodded.

Kirin woke with a gasp from a dream, a dream of pain and fear and of golden eyes watching her, watching over her. Unnerved in the predawn stillness, she scrambled out of bed and dressed hastily, strapping her sword to her side before hurrying from her chambers, heading for the Great Hall and a mug of hot, strong tea. Though she could easily make tea for herself in her quarters, she was too unsettled to be alone at the moment.

There was a figure in the Great Hall sitting slumped at one of the long benches, a Fire Dragon lying on the floor beside him, her head in his lap. Kirin froze in her tracks.

Prince Callian lifted his head to look at her.

He hadn't changed, she noted abstractly. There was no hardening of his jaw or tightness of his eyes or body to tell that she had driven him away in her foolish jealousy and anger.

On shaky legs, she crossed the room to stand before him. He waved his hand at the bench, and she sat. He pushed a mug she hadn't noticed before in front of her.

Hot tea. She took a long, grateful swallow, not caring as she scalded her throat.

"Thank you," she mumbled when she set it down.

He nodded.

The silence stretched awkwardly between them.

Finally, he spoke, simply to break the quiet. "You're awake early."

She looked away. "I had a dream."

"You seem unsettled by it."

"It's become a bit of a theme as of late," she admitted.

"Being unsettled, or the dreams?"

"The unsettling dreams."

"I'm sorry to hear that." He watched her expression. "Is that what unnerved you?"

Kirin shrugged one shoulder and finished off her tea. "I've been getting such awful headaches recently, enough to drive me insane. I don't know who or *what* I am anymore. I feel like there is something hanging over my head, and I don't know when it's going to fall. And my . . . mother and my half-brother have left to go back to Ellasar— my mother to return home after her imprisonment and my brother to guard her and give me time to come to terms with my newfound family. I've wanted a family, a mother, for as long as I can remember, and now that I finally have one, I've no clue what to do or how to behave." She glanced at him. "It's enough to unsettle anyone."

He nodded. "I lost my mother five years ago to an illness that swept through my country. My father and I have long since fallen apart. Trig, my closest friend and heir after me, has come to live at Castle Haven since his home has become unbearable." He looked at her, catching her eyes. "Whatever is hanging over your head, I will be here to support you or guard your back, whichever is necessary."

She gave him the ghost of a smile. "I'll hold you to that." She dropped her eyes from his. "Thank you for coming back."

Callian lay curled up against Tiamat's warm scales that night, almost asleep in the warmth of the castle when a sharp noise caused him to jolt awake. Kirin had cried out in pain. He heard her scream in both his mind and in his ears. He jumped up.

Something's wrong. Tiamat—

Go to the headmaster. Go to the nurse. They are her guardians, she replied, rising to her feet. She moved to guard the doorway to Kirin's room as Callian ran out of Kirin's quarters, turning left down the hallway that would eventually lead to the headmaster's study. But he needn't have worried about how to find him, for the headmaster met him there in the hallway.

"Come with me, lord prince," he said gravely, placing a hand on Callian's shoulder and leading him down a different hallway.

"Where are we going?" he demanded.

"To get Nurse Anah. She can help Kirin."

"How did you know something was wrong?"

"I had a feeling that this would happen soon."

"That *what* would happen?"

"She will be all right," the headmaster answered. "The binding spell is unraveling."

Twenty minutes later found him pacing the floor of Kirin's main room while the nurse, and now the headmaster, tended to Kirin. Finally, both reappeared, looking exhausted, their faces drawn.

"She will be all right," Lord Melchizedek said to him again. "You may go back to sleep if you wish."

The nurse paused on her way out to touch him briefly on the shoulder. "I've left a small kettle of tea on her hearth. She's to drink it when she awakens in the morning. It has herbs in it to ease her."

Callian nodded. "My thanks."

He waited until even Tiamat could no longer hear their footsteps before crossing to Kirin's room to sit in vigil over her. No one deserved to be alone on a night such as this.

He pulled open the door.

"Kirin!" he breathed, his eyes flaring wide.

She lay helplessly on her side on her bed—so much smaller than his at Giladeth—and was bleeding badly from her back. He stared, horrified. What spell could have hurt her like this?

She glanced up, shaking, and feebly reached out to him, whispering his name. He took her hand and knelt on the floor beside her bed as she lost consciousness.

He carefully pulled off the blood-soaked blanket that covered her back and gasped at what he saw.

Hidden, blood-soaked, underneath the blanket was a pair of wings. Dragon wings, by the looks of them. Trying to work his mind past the strangeness he was seeing, he reached for the towel and the pitcher of water the nurse had left beside her bed.

Kirin came to again. She was weak, not even trying to raise her head from the pillow. Barely conscious, she tried to make sense of what was happening to her. Someone was sitting beside her, mopping her forehead with cold water. She muttered one barely audible word before passing out once more: *Father.*

Callian was taken back by what she said, then shook it off. She was in so much pain that she was hallucinating, which was not unheard of after battles. Every now and then she would regain consciousness just long enough to murmur a word or two. A few times, she spoke his name.

Kirin finally sank in a restful sleep, curled up on her side with one hand tucked under her chin. Callian was grateful as he took his first deep breath since she had cried out. Tiamat edged the door open to peek inside.

Surprise covered the dragon's face. Callian felt it through the bond. *She's one of us!* Tiamat grinned. *She's dragon-folk.*

And elven, Callian pointed out. He reached over Kirin's sleeping form to pull several blankets up over her, adding a bearskin on top to keep her warm. He didn't want her to take ill, especially after the amount of blood she seemed to have lost during the course of the night.

Satisfied that she would remain warm even if he dozed and let the fire burn down, he sank down beside the hearth, leaning against the wall and closing his eyes.

She's beautiful, he thought. *Beautiful and strange.*

You're very sweet, Tiamat teased.

He scowled at her. *Oh, shut up.*

You should tell her that when she wakes; tell her that she's still beautiful. Tiamat's mental voice turned pensive. *She's going to be very insecure about her looks now.*

Callian smiled wearily. *She'll likely attack me for saying it.*

Tiamat cocked her head at him and changed the subject. *You should get some sleep.*

He shook his head. *No. I want to be here in case she needs something.*

As you wish. I'll stay at her door.

Thank you.

But despite his best efforts, he still dozed off.

Movement woke him up several hours later, startling him. Kirin moved again in her sleep, burrowing her face deeper into her pillow. Her silky hair parted around her pointed ears.

Might as well wake her up, he mused. *The sun has already risen.*

I wouldn't touch her, Tiamat advised.

"Kirin," he breathed. "Kirin, wake up. Wake up, and lay still."

Her eyes snapped open as she jolted herself to consciousness with a gasp. Ignoring his words, she flung herself upright, clutching the blankets to her, only to groan and fall back down again. She landed on her new wings, winced, and shoved herself up again.

Settle down before you hurt yourself, Lady Kirin, Tiamat advised. Callian opened his mouth to voice her words.

"I am *fine*," Kirin snarled at Tiamat. "Merely light-headed."

"You lost a fair amount of blood last night," he told her, hiding his surprise.

Kirin glared at him. "Why are you in my room?" She paused as his words sunk in. "Last night?"

His brows furrowed. "Don't you remember it?"

She looked down. "I remember being in pain. And I remember someone staying beside me." She looked up, much calmer now, her expression soft. "It was you?"

He nodded. "Lord Melchizedek's binding spell wore off...or unraveled, or what you will."

She frowned again. "It wore off?" Her eyes flared. "It wore off!" Wrapping the blankets around her, she bolted to her feet.

"Where are you going?" he asked, rising.

"To find a mirror. I want to know what I really look like."

"You don't have a mirror?"

She glanced over her shoulder at him, giving him a look that said she thought he was being stupid. "I'm a warrior, not a lady's maid. I have better things to be doing with my time than gazing into mirrors."

He struggled to hide a smile.

She burst into her main room and froze.

What is it, lady? Tiamat asked.

"I think I was blind before." She stared around her, wide-eyed. "My eyesight has changed."

Your eyes have changed.

"Are they still green?"

Yes.

"Then how have they changed?"

Callian picked up one of her carving knives and handed it to her. "Don't panic," he murmured.

Frowning, she tilted it to catch her reflection. And dropped the blade with a gasp.

"No," she breathed, her face paling.

You have dragon blood in you, Tiamat told her. *Your father was—or is—a dragon.*

Kirin took a shuddering breath, clutching the blankets tighter. *I can handle this,* she thought to herself. "Where was the blood coming from last night?"

"Your back." He ran his hand through his hair. "You should know … your appearance has changed a good deal. But you're still lovely."

She raised one brow. "Oh? I'm lovely?"

He flashed her a crooked smile. "Frighteningly so."

Kirin finally smiled, though it was short-lived. "All right, let's get this over with." She let the blankets slip so that her back was bared to him. The sight was strangely attractive. "What do I look like?"

Callian struggled to form a coherent thought. He reached out to touch her and then drew his hand back. "Wings," he finally murmured. "You have dragon's wings. And they become you very well."

Her fingers trembled as she reached back to touch them. His curiosity burned to touch them as well, to know what her wings felt like.

"The nurse left tea by your fire with some sort of herb in it to take away any pain you might be in. She asked that I give it to you."

"I'm not in pain," she whispered faintly. "I need a moment."

She nearly ran into her room, closing the door firmly behind her. Alone at last, she dropped to her knees beside her bed and let only a few tears escape. Drying off her eyes, she rose and opened her chest, changing her underclothing for clean ones. She pulled on a pair of brown pants and her boots and then reached for a shirt.

All at once, her turbulent emotions came back with a vengeance. None of her shirts or tunics would fit anymore. Not with the wings.

Heaven and hell, she had *wings*.

Closing her eyes, she tried to focus on her muscles, attempting to move her wings. Obediently, they fanned out to a good fifteen-foot wingspan. She opened her eyes to look at them. They were a pale color, a gentle cream, jointed exactly like a dragon's. Swallowing, she reached out to touch them again. It was something that she had always longed to do: touch a dragon's wings. They were warm under her fingertips, warm and leathery.

How was she supposed to go about in society like this? She was already labeled as strange for walking about in men's clothing with a sword belted around her waist. How was she supposed to wear a shirt now?

Scowling, she reached for the brown paper package Ling had left in her room before she and Ephraim departed for Ellasar. If this was how she had looked when she was an infant, then her mother should have known about the wings.

She untied the string and pulled open the paper. Inside was an elven riding robe, slit down the back from the waist to the hem to allow the rider to sit astride the horse's back. The front of it was designed to be snug, lacing up the front, the sleeves tight to allow an archer the freedom to fire. Kirin couldn't help but wonder how her mother had come by such a garment if she hadn't even been back to her husband. Had she asked Ephraim to purchase it in a village as they traveled?

It was a shame that those wings wouldn't allow her to wear it. Then her eyes widened. There were slits cut in the back, neatly hemmed. Kirin finally smiled.

It took a good deal of maneuvering to get her wings through the holes, but eventually she got it on and laced up. She took the crimson sash she had won and wound it around her hips to make sure that her stomach wasn't showing.

She washed her face and hands and combed her hair, plaiting it down her back. Somehow, she managed to pull her wings in close to her body. Satisfied that she looked as presentable as she was ever going to get, she opened the door and rejoined Callian and Tiamat in the main room.

You look lovely, Tiamat told her.

Thank you. To Callian, she said, "Stop staring."

He quickly looked away, pulling her teakettle off the fire and pouring tea. She set a loaf of bread on her table with a knife, a small jar of preserves, and two plates. They ate breakfast in silence.

When she had cleaned her plate and mug, she sat down at her worktable and began to fletch a collection of half-done arrows. Callian busied himself softening a deer's hide. After she had finished a few arrows, she looked over at him.

"What are you making?"

"Some form of a saddle. I've seen the ones that the knights here use. I think I could recreate that."

"I could help you," she offered quietly.

He looked up and smiled gently. "I would appreciate that. Thank you."

So she sat at her small table with him, sketching and measuring and planning and finally cutting the leather. They spent over an hour on the art of stitching the leather together to ensure that it would hold up during ill weather and flight before a knock on the door interrupted them.

Kirin bolted to her feet. "Say that I'm asleep," she hissed, fleeing into her room.

Callian answered the door to find the nurse.

"Is she hiding in her room?"

Callian couldn't hide his smile.

Anah shook her head. "It wouldn't be the first time she's done that. Come out, Kirin. It's only me."

Kirin emerged from her room, her wings fluttering nervously behind her. Callian wondered if she was even aware of their movement. He stepped aside to permit the nurse entrance, closing the door behind her.

"Look at you, Kirin. You look so beautiful," Nurse Anah smiled. "I'd almost forgotten what you looked like with those wonderful wings of yours."

Kirin stared. "You knew? You knew, and you didn't tell me?"

The nurse shook her head regretfully. "It was for your own safety. Of course I wanted to. But you wouldn't have believed me, would you?"

Kirin looked away, her expression rueful.

"That coat fits you very well."

"My mother left it for me."

"Good. But I've come to make sure that you were well and to show you how to alter your clothing."

Kirin blushed faintly. "You don't need to do that."

Anah ignored her words. "Go fetch your dress."

"Can we please start with a tunic?" Kirin tried.

"Your dress, Kirin," the nurse's voice was firm, even as she started to smile.

"A shirt?"

"Kirin. You have a prince staying with you. Go fetch your dress."

Kirin threw her hands up in surrender and went to fetch her dress.

The nurse looked at Callian with a smile. "You'll have your hands full trying to protect her, my lord."

Callian chuckled and shook his head. "With those wings, will she be able to fly?"

"I would ask your dragon to be there to help her when she tries."

Tiamat nudged the prince's back in an affectionate way. *I'll be there to catch her if she falls.*

Thank you.

Kirin came back with a dress made from a pale purple fabric, and Callian couldn't help but wonder what she would look like in it.

playfulness. Her shoulders were narrow, being a female, so riding her wasn't that different than a horse, not that he would ever tell her that. She had a bold personality, always ready to spar with him, or hunt for the both of them, or fill his head with her dragonish music whenever he was trying to concentrate. Her scales were burgundy now, having darkened a bit with age. She had an affinity for anything flaming, even allowing him to roast a doe she had once caught. As Tiamat had told him, she was a dragon and preferred her meat uncooked, but burnt to a crisp wasn't all that bad.

She had even taught him a little bit of magic and dragon-lore. And plenty of music. Once she got it into her head to sing, it was difficult to stop her.

His silent musings were cut short by Kirin storming across the fields. She turned one last time to face the Academy, her expression turning sad for a moment. Callian could empathize—he, too, had been forced to leave his home.

She walked over to him. "Are you flying or walking?" she asked briskly.

"I'll travel with you. I'm supposed to be protecting you, aren't I?"

She considered this. "True." She paused. "Well, I'm walking."

"All right. Where exactly are we going?"

"To the eastern forest, on the other side of the mountains. Ellasar is to the east. If we walk, we might see a ghost or a werewolf," she told him eagerly, her voice playfully dark. "Or a vampire."

"Charming," Callian remarked sarcastically, a little uneasy with that idea.

"Or if we're really lucky," she continued, "we might see an Avian."

"A bird?" he guessed.

"That can change into human form at will."

"Odd," he commented dryly. He tugged his outer cloak closer around him to combat the chill in the air as they began to walk, boots crunching through the snow. He continued, his voice quiet, "I had a hunting bird once. But it was shot by another hunter when I was nine."

"I've always wanted a hunting bird," Kirin replied, her voice turning wistful.

They entered the thick forest, the afternoon's sunlight creating strange patterns on the snowy ground as it filtered through the barren branches of the trees. Yule had passed, blessedly forgetting to bring with it fresh snow.

"Truly? Any special breed?"

"Artic gyrfalcon or a peregrine."

"Now those are beautiful birds. I had a red-tailed hawk."

They walked at a brisk pace all day. Occasionally they talked a bit. Callian was happy to maintain Kirin's quick pace for as long as she could sustain it; the movement kept them both warmer. Blessedly, the faint breeze of the early afternoon had ceased, but gray clouds had rolled in, causing Callian to worry about a fresh snowfall.

When nightfall came, they were well into the woods. They stopped and made camp by a tall oak tree where the vast majority of the snow had drifted away, making it easier to clear a spot. Tiamat disappeared and came back with half of a dead tree she had found on the ground and promptly began to shred it to three-foot-long strips. She piled it in a heap and looked at her rider.

"Yes?" he asked, looking up from where he had been idly playing with his boot-knife.

Light it.

"Aren't dragons supposed to breathe fire?"

The answer came from the halfling, who sat with her back to the tree, sharpening her sword. "Tiamat is too young for that. Over time, she will develop the protective scales in the back of her mouth and throat and will be able to breathe fire." Kirin eyed Tiamat. "Probably about a half-year to a year or so."

She put her sword aside and knelt by the wood, beginning to rearrange it. Callian knelt beside her to help.

"Do you know where we're going?" he asked.

"The elven court at the palace in Taure En Alata, the capitol of Ellasar."

"Wonderful," the prince replied with icy sarcasm.

"You don't like court?"

"No. Too many people with their heads in the clouds."

"Must have awfully long necks," she remarked.

Callian burst out laughing. Kirin smiled at him, pleased to have made him laugh.

"No, merely too many rules. I'm not fond of the Giladethian court. Perhaps the elven court will be better."

"You don't like your own court?" Kirin asked.

"No."

"Any reasons?"

"Yes. My father's there."

"You don't get along with your father," she whispered while attempting to light the fire. "Stupid fire," she mumbled under her breath.

I'm going to go find us a couple deer. You two keep talking. And Callian, be nice. Don't anger her, Tiamat told him, walking off. Callian watched as she took flight, her red scales a stark contrast to the gray surroundings.

He wrapped his arms around Kirin's, covering her hands in his. Gently, he struck the flint against the iron. The sparks danced over the kindling, finally catching fire. He let go of the young woman and blew on the tiny flame.

"I could have done that," she told him, irritable for his aid.

"I don't doubt that. I apologize for intervening," he replied genteelly.

She sighed, looking into the fire. "No…I'm sorry I'm so cross. It's merely…this is all so different for me. Usually I do everything myself. It's…it's rather different to have help." She sounded so unsure of herself that Callian felt sorry for her. She was still young and so wild. In a lot of ways, she resembled a wildcat or a shield-maiden.

She glanced at him. "May I see your sword?"

He handed it to her, biting back a cautionary remark about its sharpness. She knew how to handle swords.

Kirin rose, lifting his blade with both hands, admiring it. It was well wrought. "It's a good deal heavier than mine," she commented.

"I've a bigger build that you," he replied. "Its name is Canath, the same as my grandfather's sword. I only hope that it will see me safely through my battles as its namesake did for my grandfather."

She handed Canath back to him, hilt first. He sheathed it as she sat down. "Why don't you get along with your father?" she asked.

"Please don't ask me that, Kirin. It's a sore subject."

"All right." She went back to staring into the fire.

Tiamat soon returned with two small deer. She dropped one next to Callian to be skinned and gutted and walked off back into the woods to eat the other.

ARAMON THE WANDERER

The dark mist swirled around her legs until she could no longer see the ground she walked on, until she could no longer see even the tops of her boots. Tendrils of the strange fog billowed upwards to curl in air that was neither warm nor cool, obscuring the landscape. Still, she walked onwards, surrounded by disembodied voices that whispered in various tongues but seemed to wish her no ill will. A beast walked before her, and she followed it because she felt compelled to, though she could not tell if it was a living creature or a phantom called forth from the mists.

He paused, and called to her in a voice that at once felt both familiar and foreign, though she found that she could not understand the words, or even discern the syllables. Confusion reined as the voices around her started shrieking, the shrill cries those of birds and infants and frightened girls. She dropped to her knees in the thick mist, pressing her hands over her ears, screaming as the noise wrecked havoc on her sensitive hearing.

She bolted upright, narrowly missing Callian, who knelt over her with concern written on his face. Her ears were still ringing, her throat raw.

Callian pressed one hand against the back of her head, the other covering her mouth. The noise was muffled; she had been screaming. She stopped, gasping for breath.

"It was just a dream," he told her, releasing her and twisting to rekindle the fire.

Tiamat picked a wineskin filled with water out of their packs and handed it to Kirin, who took it gratefully.

He turned back to her again, his blue eyes sympathetic and—to Kirin's relief—devoid of any sort of scorn or derision. "Do you want to talk about it? I've an open ear if you'd like it."

She fiddled with the wineskin's strap, searching for a reply. He helped her to sit up without touching her wings. It was forbidden—Tiamat had taught him that much. He still remembered her words: *No one is to touch a dragon's wings, Callian. Even brushing up against a dragon's wing will cause the dragon distress.*

Is there any exception?

Well, yes, one. One dragon, or in Kirin's place, person, can touch another dragon's wing. Between those two, it will feel absolutely amazing.

But how do you know who that one is?

You will know when the time is right.

Kirin's voice brought his thoughts back to the present. "There were voices shrieking at me. It was ... unsettling."

Across the fire, Tiamat's head snapped up.

Someone's coming towards us, Callian, and travelling fast. I hear hoofbeats approaching.

Callian sprang to his feet, grabbing his sword. Kirin threw another branch on the fire and drew her blade, moving to stand beside him.

He glanced at her. "Tiamat and I can hold off whoever's coming long enough for you to throw a cloak over your wings. They make you too identifiable."

"The curse of halflings," she muttered, but wasted no time in obeying, pulling the cowl up to cover her hair and throw shadows over her eyes.

There was a flash of white in the trees in front of them, and then the horseman was upon them, drawing an unbridled white stallion to an abrupt halt at the edge of the firelight, a beautiful longbow drawn and trained on Tiamat, who snarled at him. He, too, wore a cloak, though his was tossed over one shoulder to free his arm to shoot.

After a second, he lowered the bow so that the arrow was aimed towards the ground, though he did not relax the string. He shook his head to dislodge his hood, revealing fair hair that he wore pulled back in a ponytail, clear blue eyes, and ears that were pointed. The stranger wore dark green and brown, a nomad's attire, colored to blend into the woods, and had a quiver slung across his back, over his cloak.

"I heard a woman scream and came to render assistance," he said, his voice melodic with an Ellasarian accent. "You travel perilously close to a Rashek outpost that is not entirely unoccupied. I had thought that perhaps they had attacked the Adkisha."

Callian lowered his sword. "What makes you think that one of us is the Adkisha?"

"I *know* one of you is the Adkisha, and my guess is that she is the one under the cloak, as Adkish Rurik was a dragon and the Adkish is never born into the same species twice. As for how I know, I am a wanderer by nature and was not too far away when the royal family contacted me, asking me to protect you. I am merely grateful that I did not have to travel all the way to the Academy only to find that you had left, Lady."

Kirin sheathed her sword, Callian following suit. "We are traveling to the Ellasarian court. What is your name, elf?"

He replaced his arrow in his quiver, though he did not loosen his bowstring. "I am Aramon." He frowned at them. "Why do you travel to court?"

"To study magic, preferably under King Nahor." Kirin began to pack up the few things they had left out of their packs overnight. "Will you accompany us to Ellasar, since you said that you were asked to protect me?"

He grimaced. "Yes, I will, though I may leave you at the citadel's outskirts. The king and I had a bit of a falling out several years ago, and I'd just as soon avoid another confrontation. Have you considered asking Prince Ephraim to teach you? He's rather skilled at magic."

Kirin nodded under her hood as Callian banked the fire and saddled Tiamat. He looked up to see Kirin approach the stallion, hands held out and cupped before her. The stallion dipped his head obligingly and nibbled her fingertips.

"He's a beautiful creature," she murmured, stroking his cheek.

The horse was fantastic, Callian had to admit. Even though he wasn't too fond of the elf, the stallion he owned was first rate, tall and muscled, with long, fine legs that attested to the speed at which this animal could run and a flowing mane and tail that gave him a regal appearance. He was so white that he nearly glowed in the darkness. For a wanderer, Aramon certainly took good care of his horse.

Aramon smiled fondly, but whether at Kirin or her comment, Callian couldn't tell. "His name is Elindil. His coloring poses some problems for traveling at night, but I am too attached to him to ever give him up. He's a very loyal horse."

An owl screeched nearby, a sudden, startling sound in the quiet of the night. The elf's head snapped to the noise, his horse tossing his mane beneath him. Callian's hand moved to rest on the hilt of his sword.

"About that outpost you mention … ?" he began.

"We had best be off," Aramon replied. "Lady Kirin, is it? I was told that was your name."

She nodded.

"Care to ride?"

"I'll pass," she said, her voice dry. "I scarcely know you." To Callian, she mindspoke, *You should mount. I'll take to the air if danger approaches.*

I would rather you not. You could always ride with me, if you needed to.

Aramon moved Elindil off at a brisk trot, Tiamat easily keeping pace. Kirin jogged beside the Fire Dragon with a long-legged stride, covering the ground with as little exertion possible.

I am glad that you did not ask that aloud—you would have been demonstrating both your lack of knowledge about bonded dragons, through no fault of your own, and how farrin *you are. There is a taboo against another riding a bonded dragon, with very limited exceptions.*

She glanced up in time to see him level a glare at the pommel of his saddle. Refocusing on the ground in front of her, she pressed herself for more speed, slowly overtaking the others. Aramon nudged his horse into an easy canter; Tiamat lengthened her strides to keep pace with Kirin.

They traveled for nearly an hour, until Kirin was stumbling with exhaustion. The second time she tripped, Tiamat drew up short.

"Enough," Callian called to Aramon. "We've traveled a fair distance from where we met you. And besides," he added, glancing at Kirin, whose shoulders heaved for breath, "I'd rather go into a fight rested than exhausted, if there's to be a fight."

Kirin shot him a grateful look.

Wordlessly, Aramon looped his bow across his chest and dismounted, loosening his girth and checking Elindil's hooves for stones. Finding none, he straightened, patted the horse on his neck, and dropped to sit on the ground, pulling his bow and quiver off and unstringing the bow before laying both beside him. Elindil wandered a few feet off to graze.

Kirin lay down a handful of paces away from Aramon, curling in a ball on her side under her cloak. She didn't bother to remove her sword.

Aramon's expression softened. "How old is she?"

Callian turned to his dragon, pulling her saddle off of her. Tiamat nuzzled his hair, then went and lay down near Kirin.

I'll guard her from the elf, Callian, Tiamat murmured to him. *No worries. Get some sleep.*

He smiled at her, then found a relatively bare spot of ground and lay down, unbuckling Canath and laying it beside him.

Aramon was watching him, waiting for an answer.

"Too young," Callian finally replied.

Kirin snorted. Callian looked over at her, but couldn't see her expression.

"You should be asleep," he told her, his voice gentle.

"But then I would miss the conversation. Wake me when it's my turn to keep watch."

Callian turned to Aramon. "Which of us has first watch?"

"Neither. I'll wake if someone approaches, and I'm willing to bet that I'm not the only one who will. There's only a few hours until morning—might as well get what sleep we can get."

Callian nodded, but waited until the wanderer was asleep before letting himself sleep as well.

The next morning dawned grey, the clouds thick and oppressive beyond the bare branches of the trees. They ate quickly and set out, Tiamat slipping off to hunt for her own breakfast. Their travel was a quiet affair. By noon, it began to snow.

Callian glanced up at the sky in surprise. Aramon pulled his hood up and looked over at him. Kirin was surprised to notice that Aramon, though he was tall, was a bit shorter than the younger human.

"Where are you from, rider?" Aramon finally asked. "Your accent marks you as *farrin*."

"Giladeth, from the capital citadel of Haven," Callian replied. "Where it doesn't snow this time of year."

"Your weapon is too fine for a commoner."

"I am the heir to the throne."

Recognition flashed over the elf's face. "You're Prince Achtin, then. I've heard of you."

Callian eyed him strangely. "King Achtin was my grandfather. I am Callian." He nodded to his dragon. "And this is Tiamat."

Kirin grinned. "Aramon, you said that you haven't been to Ellasar in a while?" she asked.

"Not for the last fifteen years. For the past nine decades, I have rarely been at home, appearing for a week at most before leaving again. I'm a wanderer, Lady Kirin. I travel often."

"I wish I could. Get away from my father, I mean. I've been trying to since my mother died," Callian muttered. "I'm finally out of there. I'd rather be here, trying not to get this wildcat of a girl angry at me for the thousandth time, than be there," he joked, elbowing her in the ribs.

"Do you have any younger brothers?" asked the elf.

"No, I'm an only child."

"How old were you when your mother died? What was her name?" Kirin questioned her friend, shoving him back.

"Queen Susanna. I was eight." He looked and sounded so sad that Kirin felt that she really must do something to comfort him. But what? Then she remembered, after she had found out who her mother was, how turbulent her thoughts and emotions had been. If at any time, that would have been an opportune moment to harm her, when she was distracted. Instead, Callian had put his arm around her, trying to comfort *her*. She slid her hand into his, trying to bring the same comfort that he had given her all those days ago in the middle of the winter.

He jumped slightly and stared at her. He had not expected her to be walking so close to him, nor did he expect her to actually touch him. Kirin faltered, confused by her emotions, but she didn't pull away. Callian understood what the friendly gesture meant. He squeezed her fingers.

"How old are you, Aramon?" she asked.

"Much older than you."

"Yes, but *how* old?"

"Two thousand nine hundred and ninety-nine years old."

"You're joking, right?" Callian asked incredulously.

"Oh, I forgot you didn't know. I'm sorry," she apologized quickly, her expression sheepish. "Elves are immortal. Dragon riders, like you, and Dragon Knights will have a very long life span. Your ears will develop a slight point to them, though not as much as mine," Kirin explained, pushing back her hood to show him her ears.

"Hmm," was his reply as he mulled over this revelation.

"You have elven blood in you," Aramon murmured. "I was wondering if you did."

She nodded to him and pulled her hood back over her head.

Tiamat presented Callian with a question, which he promptly asked Kirin. "Are *you* immortal, or do you have just a longer life span?"

"Ephraim said that I'm immortal. I'll take his word."

"What Prince Ephraim said stands to reason," Aramon replied. "Even half-elves tend to be immortal."

Callian looked at his dragon. *So she'll live forever.*

Our lifespan will cross well over a hundred years, dragon rider. Perhaps even three hundred, Tiamat reminded him gently.

Yes, but will she ever age?

She will age normally until she is sixteen. Then she will age very slowly until she looks to be about thirty. After that, she will not age.

Are all elves like that?

And dragons. Riders will just age slowly, but you will always be agile. Do not despair, little rider.

Why shouldn't I, Tiamat? I've come of age; I'm old enough to marry. My father's court is pushing for me to start courting someone, although they would be much happier if I would let them pick the bride. Meanwhile, my life span is three-fold the length of a normal human's but immensely shorter than an elf's. Where do I win? Are there any female riders?

No. That would take extreme circumstances.

So there's no one out there that would live as long as, or as short as, me. Sorrow was evident in the prince's voice.

I thought that you were already in love with someone? Tiamat teased him, trying to lighten his mood. She nudged his back with her nose between his shoulder blades, a friendly gesture that he had grown accustomed to.

Not that she would love me.

You never know. He changed the subject. *Why didn't you choose an immortal as your rider? Doesn't being bonded to a mortal drastically shorten your own life span? Doesn't it take away your immortality?*

Tiamat's reply was gentle. *I wanted you. Not an immortal. And I chose a rider out of loneliness. My cousin raised me when I hatched—my mother had recently perished of illness, and war had claimed my father not long before her death.*

I'm sorry to hear that.

Even immortals die. We merely don't die of old age. She nuzzled his hair briefly. *I will still be young when we die of your mortality, but I would rather spend a shorter span of years with a close, close friend than live out my immortality alone.*

Don't dragons have relationships?

Mates? Yes. And a mating instinct. She laughed once with a dry humor. *I have been told that you will feel my instinct as well. I have been told that many riders, if they if they are not already wed, will lock themselves away when the instinct comes over their female dragons or when their males are near a female under the instinct.*

Oh wonderful. And how long do I have before this charming instinct takes over?

Tiamat chuckled again. *I don't know exactly, but it can't be too long. A bit over a year, I would guess, and then once every couple of years after that. Sooner if I find my mate.* Her eyes narrowed on Aramon, who was talking with Kirin. *And speaking of mates, stay close to Kirin. I don't trust the wanderer.*

Because he's an elf? That's a bit prejudiced.

Watch it, human! the dragon snarled. *Do not question my judgment.*

And is that ever sane? So why don't you trust Aramon? Because he's nomadic?

Because he's hiding something! And he's far too interested in Kirin.

Are you simply responding to my emotions once more?

No, stupid. Look how close he is to her. He's a complete stranger. He's too friendly with her. You know she's beautiful, and she can be charming whenever she wants. She may want to pull information out of him, but how do we know what he wants? How do we know this Aramon is really who he claims to be? He's almost three thousand years old, Callian. He could be anyone. He could be her uncle for all we know. They do look a lot a like. And for another thing, aren't you supposed to be protecting her? "Keep your friends close and your enemies closer."

You've got a point. Kirin, can you hear me? he asked the halfling.

Yes.

Will you listen?

Yes. He could hear the faint tinge of humor in her mental voice.

I don't trust Aramon. I—

Because you're both men.

What? He frowned. *What is that supposed to mean?*

You're jealous. Callian heard her laugh at him.

And what under the stars would give you that idea?

Your expressions are as easy for me to read as if I were reading a book. Most of the time, at least. At other times, you're very difficult to interpret.

I don't trust Aramon because he is a complete stranger to us, and I am your protector.

Ohh. She laughed at him again. *I shall be wary.*

The way she said that simple sentence made Callian's skin crawl. He had no doubt that if Aramon so much as touched her against her will, she would draw blood. Likely large amounts of it.

He sighed, wanting to divert the elf's attention from Kirin without it being too obvious. An idea occurred to him.

"Aramon, you travel often, do you not?"

The elf looked back at the rider. "Yes, why?"

"Have you been all around these woods before?"

"Of course."

"Are there really werewolves and ghosts and the what-do-you-call-them, the Avians?"

"And vampires!" added Kirin. "Don't forget about them. They'll drink your blood."

"Morbid, aren't you?" Callian commented.

"Werewolves and vampires? Yes. Quite a lot, actually," Aramon stated calmly, as if he could care less whether or not they were surrounded by monsters that would eat them for dinner.

Relax, Callian, Tiamat inserted, nuzzling his hair again. *Vampires only drain their victims' bodies of blood and leave the carcass. Werewolves don't bother with sentient beings. Besides, werewolves are cousins to dragons and Avians. And I can protect you from vampires.*

Callian forced his attention back to the elf.

"Avians? If any are left in existence, they are *extremely* secluded. I don't blame them. And ghosts? There are no such things. There are spirits. There are naiads. There are dryads, and there are the nymphs. No ghosts."

Kirin spoke up. "You said that the royal family sent you. Out of curiosity, how did they send you if you haven't been at court for years?" Although her question was to Aramon, all of Kirin's attention was on Callian. The thought made Callian slightly apprehensive, but fiercely and strangely proud. Tiamat nudged his head once more, playfully this time.

"I assure you that I did not lie to you."

"And yet you knew my name and who I was," Kirin replied icily. "How long have you been watching us to know that? Are you some sort of spy?" Tiamat tensed. Kirin felt Callian's hand tighten around hers, and knew that he was ready to pull her out of the way should the other male turn against them.

He sighed. "I am periodically in contact with the royal family through a combination of dreamwalking and scrying," he said, his voice calm.

"Pardon?" Kirin and Callian asked simultaneously.

"Dreamwalking. The ability to enter and—"

"—Influence another's unconscious mind in such a manner that the recipient will awaken with full knowledge of event," Kirin finished. "That much I learned at the Academy."

Aramon nodded. "And scrying. A method of, well, spying on someone without his or her knowledge. Only problem is that you can't hear anything that is said," he explained.

"Teach me," Kirin demanded.

"You may not be able to scry yet—or at all. It's a water-based magic, and there's a certain art to it that many cannot master. There are an abundance of powerful elves who cannot scry, and most elven magic is water-based. It would be better to let the sages at court figure out what sort of magic you have control over now and wait for the rest to come in time."

"Aramon, I've seen the result of some of her magic. The boy she was mad at now carries an impressive scar across his face," Callian put in. If anyone could scry, it was she.

"Flames from my hands," she murmured, looking at both palms.

"Fire magic," Aramon noted. "As I said, I don't think that you can scry. Although, I'm surprised that you started with fire magic. Most elves and half-elves are drawn to either water or light magic."

"Perhaps she is drawn to fire magic on account of her quick temper," Callian teased. He glanced up and grinned at the sky through the branches overhead. "I would love to fly up there," he remarked, his voice soft and wistful.

Aramon snorted. "You have a dragon," he pointed out.

"No." Callian shook his head. "I mean to have wings. To fly on my own."

"Impossible."

"We are surrounded by magic—you yourself are only thought to be a myth in Giladeth. Is it truly impossible for a person to grow wings and fly?"

"Yes. Unless, of course, you're referring to the Avians," he amended.

So he doesn't know about that, Kirin said, entering Callian's thoughts. *Good. Thank you for getting him to tell us that.*

My pleasure.

She smiled shyly at his words and became interested in her boots.

Callian awoke. They had made camp for the night sheltered in the center of a stand of tall trees. He looked around. The moon was almost full tonight, reflecting off the snow, and the stars were out, providing plenty of light to see by. The celestial lights cast a faint glow on the nearby lake, which, with the reflection of the moon and the stars and the bordering pine trees, made it rather picturesque. He searched the area. Something seemed amiss.

Kirin. Where is Kirin? Where did she—Aramon!

He searched for the mysterious wanderer and found him lying nearby. Lying too still. Callian watched the rise and fall of the elf's chest as he breathed. Steady and even. But Kirin was missing, and Callian still suspected Aramon of having ill intentions toward them.

He crept closer to the still wanderer, tense and ready for battle, a knife in his hand.

He was close enough to touch the elf. His chin-length straight blond hair was pulled back from his face. His bow and quiver lay beside him, but his right hand rested on the handle of a hunting knife. Callian breathed a sigh of relief. The elf was asleep.

Her footprints lead off toward the lake, Tiamat commented.

Callian ran toward the lake. *Go back to sleep, Tiamat. Stay with Aramon. I don't want him to think that we abandoned him.*

Fair enough.

He reached the water's edge and stopped. Kirin's footprints stopped, as if she had taken flight. Her cloak lay abandoned but neatly folded nearby. Using all of his tracking skills and wishing his friend Trig were here to help—Trig had always been the better man for following a trail—he searched for a disturbance that would signify someone was near. None came, save the slight breeze that rustled all of the trees around the lake. A cloud blew across the moon, obscuring its light.

You have magic, Tiamat reminded him. *Use it. Reach out with your mind and feel what creatures are near.*

Callian closed his eyes and mentally explored the surrounding forest and lake. Hundreds of fish, plenty of birds, several snakes— and how they were awake and moving in this temperature, he didn't know—even rabbits and mice and other nocturnal creatures. But there were seven oddities: a male elf, a female dragon, two male dragons, and two women—one close by and the other the farthest of the seven. He turned and opened his eyes, following the tendril of thought that led him to the woman closest to him.

Then he saw her. She was sitting on a branch, perfectly balanced, with one knee drawn up to her chest. Her hair was loose, moving gently as the breeze played with it. She was staring out at the lake, unmoving. She must have been at least fifty feet up.

But was it Kirin? Without the silvery light of the almost-full moon to illuminate her, it struck him that she could be anyone—a dryad, a spirit, even an Avian. Possibly an angel. After all, didn't angels have wings?

He swallowed hard. Surrounded in the snowy scenery, her beauty was breathtaking, whoever she was. He quickly scaled her tree, stopping when he could go no farther, and straddled the thick branch, knowing he could fight better from the position he was in and looked up. The woman sat ten feet almost directly above him. He swallowed again. Callian could feel her gaze on him.

"Crave pardon for intruding, my lady," he said softly, feeling it best to be as proper as he could. "But I was wondering if you have seen a young woman? She is missing from our campsite, and I worry for her safety."

The woman gave no answer out loud; rather, she presented him with a feeling. She wanted a description.

"She is about fifteen, and although she is as fierce as a wildcat and one of the best fighters I've ever seen, she is beautiful. She has stunning green eyes, as green as the tree leaves in the summer, and very fair hair. Have you seen her, my lady? I sense something is amiss tonight, and I fear for her."

The woman above him swung both legs around her branch and nimbly leapt onto his, landing with her knees bent, showering the ground below with snow. She walked gracefully and silently toward him, wings extended slightly for balance, and when she reached him, she sat beside him.

"Have you seen someone, my lord? He is my friend, though we were raised in different lands. He has fair hair and eyes bluer than the sky. He is a valiant knight, a noble prince, and a caring friend," the woman next to him whispered, her eyes flashing with mischief.

"Kirin," he breathed, recognizing her sweet voice. She offered him a crooked smile. "Thank Adonai. You had me nervous." He fervently hoped his heart would stop pounding so hard, and was glad that no else had heard what he had said about her.

Or so he thought. Aramon had been awake when Callian had left to look for Kirin. He had waited for Tiamat to fall asleep and then stole out of camp, following Callian. Hidden in the woods, he

WISDOM GAINED

"Heaven and hell," she breathed, terrified. The snake stared at her. She was vaguely aware of Callian inching closer to her side, his sword drawn and gleaming in the moon's light.

The king cobra began to hiss in strange patterns. Listening hard, Kirin began to discern words, *in Elvish*. "*Malakieth ges taban fysgin zei. Jiu, jiu! Lui!*" the snake hissed. It dropped back down to the ground as Callian came within sword reach and disappeared quickly into the blackness of the forest.

Kirin turned to Callian, who stood protectively by her, Tiamat on his other side. Aramon stood by her left. "Flee," she whispered.

"What?"

"Fly! Run! He's found us; he's coming!"

Tiamat swung her dark red head toward the distressed halfling. *Who, Adkisha?*

"Malakieth," she whispered. Aramon leapt fluidly onto Elindil's saddle, his expression hard.

Then we will fight! Tiamat growled.

No, Tiamat! We would die!

Then we would die honorably and not like cowards, fleeing with our backs turned.

Tiamat, I think that I sensed him, when I was looking for Kirin, Callian interjected. *Perhaps it would be wiser to go now. This is a poor place for a defensive stand. I'd rather seek higher ground. If it comes to it, we can fight there.*

Fine. We will flee, Tiamat answered unhappily.

Callian climbed into the saddle and tightened the ties that held his legs into place. He glanced down to see Kirin standing on the ground. She couldn't yet fly well enough to take to the air in escape.

"Come on! Get up here!"

"But—" she stammered. She wasn't allowed to ride Tiamat. It was a proscription she had never broken.

"There's no time for that. We have to go *now!*" he called in a rush. "Hang the rules and forget the traditions for once in your life."

"You don't understand! I *can't* ride Tiamat. It might hurt her. And I've never ridden before," she cried in confusion. Her head whipped around as if looking for Aramon and his horse.

She's never loved before! Tiamat told him in shock, translating her words.

"Kirin, *please!* I'll hold on to you—"

Poor choice of words—Tiamat interrupted.

"You won't fall off. Hurry!" he begged, ignoring Tiamat, his voice desperate.

Kirin hesitated briefly before leaping up in front of him, wings beating frantically a few times to get her the lift she needed, breaking the tradition she held sacred for the first time. Wrapping his arms around her slim waist, they soared into the star-filled sky, both their hearts pounding.

Aramon had already disappeared into the darkness of the wood.

Tiamat? Why would it hurt you?

She is not my rider, and you are not involved in an intimate relationship with her.

Does it bother you?

No.

That's odd. Is it because she's half dragon?

No.

Why, then?

My secret.

He was going to argue with his dragon when she spun into a battle maneuver, corkscrewing to her left and then flying straight up into the sky. Kirin, who had been riding sidesaddle, gave a startled yelp as she lost her balance. Callian held on to her, one arm around her slender waist and the other around her shoulders, pressing her body into his. She fit comfortably curled against his chest, her head tucked against his collarbone, her arms tight around him.

Tiamat leveled out, and Kirin sighed. "That dragon is trying to kill me," she muttered to him.

Tiamat, what was that about? he asked. He wasn't mad, merely curious and a little annoyed.

For fun.

You scared Kirin. She nearly fell off.

But she didn't. You held her on as you said you would. And she could always have flown long enough for us to catch her again. Besides, you enjoyed it, she replied in an irritatingly singsong voice. Her laughter flowed through the mental connection.

Oh, shut up, he retorted.

Kirin relaxed, leaning into him. He held her closer. Up there in the night sky, holding Kirin and riding Tiamat, it was hard to remember that there was great danger in the form of a twisted dragon back down on the land.

"I won't let you fall," he whispered into the young woman's hair.

"It's beautiful up here," she said simply.

Callian looked around at the night sky and then looked down at her. "Yes, it is."

An immeasurable moment passed before she sighed again. "I truly hate to say it, but there's a cave where we can land and spend the night. Aramon and Elindil will be able to get there from the ground." She paused and then, blushing, said, "I enjoy flying." *With you,* she added silently.

"All right, if we must land," Callian finally responded after another long moment of silence. "It's probably safer to be hidden. It was enjoyable while it lasted. Will you fly with me, with us, again?"

"I don't know, Callian. I love this. But I'm breaking so many big rules. And I'm likely hurting Tiamat," she mumbled, her voice filled with wistful longing.

"Tiamat said that it doesn't hurt her when you ride, though she wouldn't tell me why. But please, fly with me again."

She gave him a crooked grin, her teeth white as pearls in the moonlight, and her eyes glinting with mischief. "Are you asking…?" she began, trailing off suggestively.

He started slightly, sure of what she meant but unsure if he was ready for anything like that.

"Err, n-not yet," he stammered like an idiot. "But I *would* like for you to fly with me again."

"I'd like that," she murmured as Tiamat landed skillfully in the cave. A clatter of horse hooves sounded by the cave entrance, announcing Aramon's arrival. He grinned at them.

"Lovely place. Have fun flying?"

"Yes, it was very pleasant," Kirin answered airily as they dismounted.

"You were never asleep," the Giladethian accused as he leapt down behind her.

"True, but you thought I was," Aramon answered evenly, but his smile was gone.

"You were spying on us," Callian continued, placing a protective arm around Kirin's lean stomach. Her blood began to race, though not at the brewing fight.

"I will not deny it," Aramon admitted, his voice and face aggravatingly emotionless.

Callian drew Kirin back, away from the wanderer. "Did you break that branch when Kirin nearly fell out of the tree?"

"I did," the elf answered slowly. Callian drew his sword with his free hand, holding it at ready. Aramon's hand rested on his long knife.

"You could have killed her!" he snarled.

Suddenly, unexpectedly, Aramon turned to Kirin, ignoring the prince. "I wouldn't have cracked that branch if I had known that you would have jumped so badly, Kirin," he said softly. "I was only trying to protect you." His emotionless face had changed with his voice. In fact, he looked at her with an open expression of fondness.

Kirin drew back, nervous and unsure, closer to Callian, whom she trusted more.

Callian wasn't blind; he, too, noticed Aramon's expression and raised his sword, Canath. "Who are you?" he hissed blackly.

Aramon, still directing his words to Kirin, said, "I am Aramon, son of Lord Nahor. I am your ally, a wanderer, and hopefully at least Kirin's friend."

"I don't trust you," Callian spat.

"And I don't trust you. Thus the reason why I broke that branch."

"So you nearly killed her because you don't trust me. *That* makes sense. Thank you for clearing *that* up," he replied with icy sarcasm.

"No, to keep her away from you. I'm not blind, and I'm not stupid. I was asked to protect her, and I will do just that!" Aramon was visibly mad now, his voice raised.

"*I* was told to protect her. By Adonai. Who exactly asked you?" Callian lowered his voice and his sword, but he still held Kirin protectively close to him.

"You were told *by Adonai* to protect Kirin?" Aramon half-closed his eyes in thought, trying to control his quick temper. "It seems as if we should put aside our differences and work together, Prince Callian. My guess is that Malakieth is tracking her through her magic. We stand a better chance of surviving if we band together." He paused, then added, "Prince Ephraim asked me to protect you, Kirin, as the fourth Adkisha, shortly after he visited the Academy."

"Ephraim!" she exclaimed. "He's my half brother!"

Aramon stared at her, eyes flaring wide in shock before narrowing in annoyance. "*Ehin*. He's my brother. I am Ling's second son. And I might need to beat Ephraim for not telling me."

Kirin sat resting against the cave's wall, her mind wandering as she listened to Aramon cook. Callian had lightened up considerably toward Aramon, and Tiamat was still periodically teasing him about that as he rubbed down Tiamat's scales with a soft cloth. She lay on her side with her head in his lap, allowing his ministrations and humming softly.

She closed her eyes, and felt herself slipping into a sort of waking dream.

She was back walking through the mists, and the dark shape rose up in front of her, closer to her than it had ever been. She stopped and held still, reaching out with her left hand for it. The silvery mark down her arm shone in the strange lighting, and she felt warm scales under her palm. Golden eyes snapped open and looked at her imploringly.

"Kirin!" she heard Aramon snap, and she jolted back to alertness.

"Yes?" she asked.

"You were muttering in Elvish," Callian told her. "I couldn't understand you."

"You were narrating whatever it was that you were seeing," Aramon added. "Is this common for you?"

She shook her head. "I've been dreaming of the same thing for a few days now. I didn't realize that I had fallen asleep."

His eyes were grim. "You didn't. Something must have sensed you and is trying to either communicate with you or get your attention, and is somehow blocked."

From what I could tell when Aramon was translating, that might have been a dragon, Tiamat told her. *Perhaps a dracling?*

What dragon has eyes that color? she replied. Then she frowned. "Aramon, how close are we to that outpost you mentioned?"

"The prison? Not far. We've been skirting around its edge."

She looked at Callian and could tell that he was thinking the same thing. "What if Malakieth has taken a dragon prisoner? What if he is calling for aid?"

"Not to sound heartless, but what if, Adkisha?" the elf replied.

"Then we have a duty to free him."

"It's suicide to try to invade that prison. I know the one the Rashek are occupying, though I've never been inside. Other than the gate, there's only a small opening—no more than a refuse hole— in the outer wall. Callian and I could never fit in, not to mention

Tiamat. I'm sorry, but there's no way a fifteen-year-old warrior can take on a whole barrack of Rashek alone and live, in addition to saving the lives of one or several prisoners. It's simply not possible," Aramon stated.

"Even with magic?" she hedged.

"Even with magic."

She scowled at him from across the fire.

"But there has to be some way," Kirin argued. "We can't just leave him there to die."

"What a place for a family reunion," called a new voice. They spun around.

Ephraim was standing by the entrance, a look of sardonic amusement on his face. He was dressed in dark blue with a long, black cloak fastened by a silver brooch. His boots were black leather, and his blond hair was pulled away from his attractive face like Aramon's was.

He stood like the prince that he was. His arms were crossed over his strong chest as he regarded the four of them. He was well armed. The hilt of his sword hung at his left hip, his knife at his thigh, his quiver across his back, and his long bow in his hand.

Standing there, with the firelight playing on his elven features, he looked so much like Aramon that anyone could tell they were related. Kirin wondered how she hadn't seen it before.

"Ephraim! Heaven and hell, you startled me!" she exclaimed. "Do you know of any way to help that prisoner?"

"Yes, though no one is going to like it," the eldest prince told them, walking over to join them. He clapped his brother on the back and nodded to Callian and Tiamat in greeting.

"Tell me!" She looked at him eagerly.

He sighed, looking resigned. "Kirin goes in, alone."

"Absolutely not!" Callian snapped. Tiamat growled her opinion.

"She's the only one who is small enough to fit it. Not to mention that too many people will draw unwanted attention. Kirin has a massive amount of power, Aramon. Callian and Tiamat hide in the woods to the north of the prison, Aramon to the west, and I to the south."

"So we'll be able to help her," stated Callian.

"We'll be able to cause a distraction to buy her some more time if she needs it to get back out with a wounded or weak dragon."

"To the east are the cliffs that shelter us," mused Aramon, thinking it over. "It could actually work."

"And if it doesn't?" demanded Callian.

"I die with honor," Kirin said stiffly.

"No. Absolutely not." He paused and looked at Tiamat, who was watching him. Turning back to Kirin, he said, "I'll accompany you. Tiamat will wait alone."

"You'll never be able to fit inside—you're as tall as I am, if not taller. And even if you could somehow get inside, you'd only increase her chances of being caught," Ephraim told him.

"Oh? I'm quick on my feet and good in a fight if it comes to that."

"You have magic, being a rider. And they're more likely to notice Kirin the more magic there is near her."

Kirin looked around her. Three princes and a dragon, and they were all worried about her. Tiamat turned her head toward the only other female in the room.

Men.

Kirin laughed softly.

You are set on this? Callian's going to worry himself sick if you do this, Tiamat pointed out.

Kirin gazed at her hands, at the silver Adkisha's mark, feeling guilt begin to twist in her stomach. *I can't bring myself to leave that dragon trapped, knowing that I could do something to help.*

Tiamat nodded. Kirin watched her nuzzle Callian's hair, and knew that she was speaking to him. As if they sensed it, Ephraim and Aramon fell silent, waiting for Callian's decision.

Finally, he turned to shoot her an unhappy look. "You must be the only woman to beg to go into someplace dangerous singlehandedly," he groused. But he handed her his knife. "I'm going with you to the entrance."

She rose, and the others rose with her. "Thank you," she whispered to Callian.

WITHIN THE DUNGEON

66 Hello?" Kirin whispered uncertainly into the darkness of the cell. She didn't want to have to enter that nightmarish blackness, but if the dragon or some other prisoner was in there, it was her duty and honor to rescue them.

Carefully, she crept in. When she thought that she might be in the center of the cell, she called out again.

"Hello? Is anyone there?"

There was no answer.

Her heart pounded rapidly in her breast, adrenaline making her jumpy. She conjured up a ball of fire, cradling it in her palm. The small flame lit the surrounding area.

No one was there.

Kirin turned and left.

It had been more difficult than she had imagined, leaving Callian behind to crawl on her stomach through the small hole, especially when he was clearly sizing up the hole as if in hope of making his broad shoulders fit. She wasn't claustrophobic, but the tunnel had been tight and she had hit her head a few times. Being within the prison, in the dark corridors with the black holes of cells, made her heart race with anxiety.

Cell after cell went by, most of them left open. A few were closed, the locks and hinges rusted shut. Kirin didn't bother trying to open them. The only creature that could survive that long without food was a vampire, and a door such as these would be unlikely to hold a vampire against its will. And even assuming that these cells could contain one, she wasn't stupid enough to release it, especially one that was starving. Though many vampires could be very civil and genteel when well fed, underneath the pretty face and the beguiling eyes lay the instincts of a feral animal coupled with an undeniable bloodlust.

She had seen the result of a vampire attack when she was younger. One had come across a farmer's son out in the fields during the harvest time, and the young man hadn't survived. The bloodless corpse had been found by his father, and the father had brought the body to Lord Melchizedek, who had a standing peace treaty with a coven of vampires that lived near the Academy.

Kirin had been shut up in the infirmary wing when the coven leader had come to the Academy to confer with the headmaster about how best to go about hunting for the rogue vampire. She was still healing from a fight that broken out in one of her classes that had resulted in her losing a fair amount of blood and nursing a broken ankle. Thaddeus, the boy who had started it all, had been made to leave the Academy. Even now, she could clearly remember her ire at not being allowed to at least glimpse the vampire male, though it was tempered somewhat by the knowledge that she was not the only one forbidden. Jamir and Jakir and their dragons were locked up with her, and Jakir and Peter, who had volunteered to stay with her, had worked on healing her leg.

Now, navigating the dark corridors alone, she could clearly remember the look Jakir had given her that told her he, at least, understood her ire. It was a look of camaraderie, and now, with her nerves and her heart rate running high, she deeply wished that she could have that look again. Perhaps not from him necessarily, but from someone. She wouldn't mind having a friend in this darkness with her.

Fifteen minutes later, she came to another cell. She quickly opened the lock with the tip of her dagger, a trick she had learned from sneaking around the Academy at night. Bracing her shoulder against the wood, she shoved the heavy door open, grateful when the hinges stayed silent. This cell was not as deep as the other had been.

When her eyes had adjusted to the gloom, she noticed a dark form lying on the floor, either an animal or a very large rock.

The sound of shouting, of the alarm being raised, sent her skittering into the cell. Her anxiety spiked, and she prayed fervently that Callian and her brothers would all remain unharmed.

And that whatever was in the cell wouldn't attack her.

Please don't be dead. Please don't be dead. Please don't attack me, and please don't be dead, she chanted silently.

"Hello?" she barely whispered.

No response came.

"Hello?" she called a little louder.

The thing said nothing. Nothing stirred, nothing breathed. She waited as silently as she could. A few more minutes passed slowly. And then she heard it, the quiet sound of a large creature taking a breath.

"You *are* alive! Are you the dragon I've been looking for? Will you speak to me?" she asked excitedly. She kept her voice muted, both as to not startle the creature into attacking and to keep from alerting anyone else of her presence.

Still the creature said nothing. Slowly, though, it moved, raising its head and opening its bright golden eyes. The shear size of the creature, coupled with the piercing golden eyes staring straight into hers mere inches from her face, scared her. She forced herself not to flinch or cry out.

What creature has eyes that color? Surely not dragons—I should think I would know that. But then, what else would it be? It's much too big for an Avian or vampire. Can it speak? Will it attack?

"Who are you? Are you the dragon that was taken prisoner? Are you a friend?" she questioned.

Still the creature did not speak. It simply stared at her, its golden eyes bright with intelligence and yet wary.

It doesn't trust me, she realized. *But why should it? Still, I'm fairly certain that it* can *talk; it merely won't.*

Out loud, she said, "I am Kirin, the fourth Adkisha. I travel with Callian, son of King Mendez and Crown Prince of Giladeth, Crown

Prince Ephraim of Ellasar, and Prince Aramon, a wanderer. I have come to rescue the prisoners that are trapped here. If you are a friend, you are free to return to your people. But if you are an enemy, then you shall feel my sword in your breast before you can draw another breath. *Amol kahelith uí zei.*"

I do not fear you.

She spoke the last sentence in the language of the elves, knowing that many inhuman creatures understood it. A few more minutes passed while the golden eyes held her gaze.

I am a dragon who was foolish enough to be captured, the rich, male voice echoed softly in her head.

Excited that at last the creature, the dragon, was beginning to trust her enough to speak to her, she forced herself to remain motionless.

I don't think you're foolish. But are you a friend or an enemy?

If I were your enemy, I would say that I was your friend. If I were your friend, my answer would be the same as the deceiver's. But yes, I am your friend. U amo circe.

On my honor.

Kirin nodded in reply. She edged closer to him, trying to see him better, only to stumble over a thick bolt set into the floor. Crouching, she fumbled for it, finding the attached chain, each link as thick around as her finger. She shuddered to feel the engraved symbols— the chain was reinforced by Nishron's magic. The other end of the chain was attached to a manacle around the dragon's foreleg. She ran her fingers over the lock, then set to work with her dagger.

There is much you do not know, Adkisha Kirin, the dragon continued, shifting his weight off of that foot to make her work easier. She could feel his strange, golden eyes on her. *Your past, your family, your future, your powers. You are still young, a mere dracling.*

Her eyes snapped up to meet his again. *My powers? Are there more? Do you know Ling? Do you know who my father is? Will you tell me? Who are you?*

He chuckled softly at her eager questions, then gave her a sharp-toothed grin when she felt the lock spring in her hands. The dragon stretched luxuriously. *My name is Beau. I do not know your mother directly; although, I have heard her story. I am sorry, but I do not know exactly who your father is, though I do have my guesses. But I will tell you more about that when the time is right and not before. As for your powers, you have more raw power coursing though your veins than anyone I've ever seen or heard of. Be careful, Lady Kirin. Releasing too much of this power at one time, especially when you are unprepared to do so, can, and will, be deadly.* He cocked his head, considering her. *I have been calling for you, and I am glad that you came. Are you bonded to a dragon?*

Not yet, she replied.

Do you accept this boon? Think carefully about this decision.

It took Kirin a few seconds to understand his words. *Me? You want* me *as your rider?*

You do not want a dragon? His words were soft and light-hearted. *You do not want to be a dragon rider?*

I do! I would be honored to be your rider. But ... I am dragon-kin myself. Why would you wish to bond to one of your own kind?

You are also a daughter of the elves. And it would be my joy and honor to lend my magic to the Adkisha and to stand beside her as her bonded dragon as she faces Malakieth and his fiends. And though you have wings befitting a Light Dragon, you may never be able to fly as long or as fast as I.

Kirin bowed, hardly daring to believe her luck, and embraced her dragon. Her mind didn't even register the brief spasm of pain that bonding to a dragon brought. There was a rush as his magic joined hers, though she could feel how weak his power was at the present moment, worn down from his captivity.

Beau snorted, obviously pleased with her decision. *Good. On my back then, my little dracling.*

He rose slowly and shook out his wings, responding to her magic. He was tall—through the bond, she could feel that he was much older than she. His memories stretched back far, though she had no ability to look through them unless he allowed her to.

There was a crashing sound, the sound of a gate slamming shut, and Beau bared his teeth toward the cell door.

The others that I travel with are hopefully rendezvousing, she murmured to him.

It's high time we leave this horrid place, he replied, *though I will need your magic to do it. There are no other prisoners here.*

Kirin's heart soared as her dragon, her Beau, combined his power with hers and smashed a hole in the wall, racing out and taking flight, angling upwards so that they would be harder for archers to spot.

Earth magic, Kirin laughed.

Which way?

East, toward the mountains and the rising sun.

That's a long way for you to have traveled, little dracling. Even if you did fly.

Hugging his strong neck, she whispered into the night sky. "It was worth it."

Callian was livid. Kirin still hadn't reappeared, and he couldn't help but fear that *she* had been captured. Tiamat had him pinned to the ground in an attempt to keep him from returning to storm the prison. All of their nerves were running high. Once he had returned, after losing the two Rashek that had taken off after him, Aramon had settled to pacing back and forth, his horse faithfully following and occasionally nickering or snorting. Ephraim was the worst, in Callian's opinion. He rested against the wall, one foot on the ground, the other on the stone of the cave wall. His arms were folded loosely across his chest, his eyes closed, fingers of one hand drumming a tattoo against the opposite arm. His face was completely at ease. Occasionally he would murmur something in an undertone, and Tiamat and Aramon would look up at him before going back to whatever they had been doing. Once, Tiamat had nodded.

Callian had fruitlessly tried to get past her, seeking to go after Kirin. After three failed attempts, Tiamat had simply pinned him to the ground and held him there.

Suddenly, her head snapped up, and she dodged to one side. Callian rolled out of the way to avoid the claws of another dragon.

The two elves and Callian, who was still on the ground, looked at the new dragon with shock. This dragon was bigger than Tiamat and jet-black. His eyes were an unusual golden color, not ocher, but golden, like butterscotch or perhaps amber. He had what looked like veins of the same golden color that streaked across his body, seemingly highlighting his taunt muscles. His tail was long and muscular; it never touched the ground but waved gently back and forth. His body was lean and streamlined. This dragon was built for speed. His claws were dull from imprisonment, but that could be fixed. He looked tired and underfed, and there was a raw patch around the base of one foreleg.

He looked at them, his eyes curious, his great head cocked to one side.

Then Callian noticed something else.

"Kirin!" he cried out. For there she was, beaming at them from the dragon's—*her* dragon's—back. Her gorgeous hair was wind-blown, and her face was flushed, but she was still as perfect as ever.

He leapt up and ran around the dragon to help her off. Tiamat cautiously approached the larger dragon, who stretched out his neck and touched her nose with his. Ephraim and Aramon visibly relaxed.

Callian was too preoccupied with the young female dismounting from the dragon's back. "Are you all right? When we realized you still weren't back, I wanted to come after you. Ephraim seemed a little worried, and Aramon was anxious, but they had decided that it would be better to let you return here. Tiamat wanted me to stay, but I simply couldn't sit and wait. I kept trying to sneak past her, so she pinned me to the floor. I thought that you were going to get yourself killed. I was so worried. But every time I tried to mindspeak with you, Tiamat would overpower me. I tried magic as well, but she was still stronger than me. I'm so sorry. Please tell me you're all right. I feel so guilty. I should have gone with you. I—"

Kirin cut short his torrent of words by placing her cool fingertips against his lips. He fell silent.

"Hush. I'm fine. I'm all right. I'm fine. This is Beau, my dragon. I'm fine; don't worry about me," she told him softly. He relaxed under her touch. Kirin managed only one step before she collapsed. Moving with astonishing speed for a human—even a rider—the Giladethian prince caught her before she hit the ground. She looked into his eyes and found them to be panic-stricken.

"I'm fine, merely tired. The dungeon was far bigger than I expected, and I needed to offer Beau much of my magic to escape. I simply need sleep," she muttered.

Finally Ephraim spoke. "I can't believe it," he whispered in shock.

"Neither can I," agreed Aramon, shaking his head.

Kirin looked at her brothers. "What's got the two of you so surprised? That I can take care of myself? That I proved you wrong? Or that I finally bonded with a dragon?" she asked scornfully.

"The *dragon*, Kirin. Have you *seen* his coloring, his eyes?" Ephraim's voice was incredulous, wistful even. "He's no ordinary dragon. That's a Twilight Dragon. They're supposed to be extinct. Twilight Dragons haven't been seen *in over four thousand years*. They scarcely teach about them anymore. *I* thought they were mere fantasy. This is incredible." The elf was excited by now. "And the fourth Adkisha bonds to one! The court *has* to know about this."

A Twilight Dragon. Of course. Master Kish lectured about them that first day Callian accompanied me to my classes, before Yule. How could I have forgotten?

"I thought elves didn't like dragons," Callian said.

"Well, yes, there's been some strife, but this might be our chance to get the dragons and the elves to work together again."

"Do you think it will work?" Aramon asked.

"If we bring three dragons into their midst, under the white flag of peace and with a Twilight Dragon, it might."

"Hold up, *three* dragons?" Kirin frowned.

"Three and a half, counting you with your wings," the wanderer answered. Kirin gasped. "Speaking of which, *Ephraim*, you might have told me about the wings—and that she was my sister—before you sent me to protect her. All you said was, 'I need you to go protect this girl. Her name is Kirin, she's the next Adkisha, and she's a half-blood. Make sure no harm comes to her.'" Aramon mimicked his brother's voice well.

"Where is the third dragon?" Kirin would not be diverted.

Ephraim exhaled harshly, looking annoyed. "Keep it a secret, both of you," he ordered sharply. Then called out loudly, "Assumptshun!"

A huge dragon, bigger than Beau, flew into the cave. He was a Dark Dragon, and his eyes were a dark blue, almost black. He blew into Kirin and Callian's faces, as Callian was still helping her stand, before walking over to greet the eldest prince.

"You're a rider!" Callian exclaimed.

"Yes," the elf sighed. "And we'd like it if you didn't tell anyone. Ling and Nahor would be irate if they knew. But perhaps, with the Adkisha and her Twilight Dragon and the heir to Giladeth and his Fire Dragon, we all would have a chance of getting the dragons and the elves to cooperate as they did several thousand years ago. If we're going to win this war, we need all the help we can get."

"Wait a moment. *War*? What war? No one told me anything about a war," Kirin told her brother. Callian felt her tense.

"There's been a war going on since Morgan and Malakieth led the Rashek army against the Light Dragons, and it continues even after Morgan's death. It's been small here on our world, on Kyria. But then you showed up. Now, everything, the fate of *all* the worlds, will depend on *your* decisions."

If Kirin had had trouble standing before, this was nothing to what she felt now. Callian picked her up off her feet and carried her to the fireside. He sat down, placing her next to him and helping her support herself.

"Me?" she whispered in a small and scared voice. "The weight of the world is on *my* shoulders? I haven't even come of age yet. How can one child change anything? How am *I* supposed to be able to do this?"

"The weight of *all* the worlds, Kirin. I'm sorry, but you're the Adkisha. It's your duty. Aramon and I will train you, teach you everything we know. Callian can spar with you. You are one of the Academy's best fighters, Kirin. I have faith in you," Ephraim said gently.

Leaning his head down to her ear, Callian whispered, "I will always be there for you. I'll protect you; don't worry. You have Giladeth's support."

"I think she needs sleep. Preferably before she falls in the fire," Aramon suggested.

Callian nodded. He picked the halfling up again and carried her—protesting all the way—to her bedroll in the corner. He laid her down, whispered, "Good night," and left Beau to guard her while she slept.

After a week of training with her brothers and Callian, Kirin was anxious for a break. She jumped at the chance to accompany Beau on a brief flight to scout the nearby forest. They left in the wee hours of the morning, after alerting Assumptshun of their plans, stealing away in silence so as not to awaken the elves.

Who is it that you are looking for, Beau? Kirin asked. *A sweetheart? Your mate? Family?*

An unborn Light Dragon. I found the egg too late to save the mother— it was the smell of blood that alerted me to their location. I hid the egg when Malakieth's servants were after me in hopes of protecting it. I do not know if the dracling has hatched yet, or even if it still lives.

Beau flew for over an hour. To keep herself awake, Kirin gave him her cloak and flew with her own wings, working on building up her stamina and her strength.

Finally, Beau started angling his flight downward. Kirin alighted on his back, and he dropped into an almost-vertical dive, tucking his wings close to his body, only to flare them back out again to catch the wind. He landed in a clearing, running at full speed for a moment before gradually slowing to a stop.

This is where I was taken from, midsummer last year, he told her.

His head near the ground as he hunted for tracks, he bore her on his back into the trees.

The female, though… The female had been the runt of the litter, and yet, when her three sisters had attacked her, she had fought back and killed them. And she had only been days old.

She was Morgan's accomplishment, her super-creature, neither human, were-beast, nor Shadow Dragon, but a mix of all three. It had taken Morgan decades to get her right, decades spent possessing the Spiriter so she could work.

She was fertile, the female. It was important to Morgan that her prized creature be female, not only because Morgan herself was female but because any male warrior would hesitate before raising a weapon to ward her off—and those few seconds would be the last he lived. Morgan's creature was of an attractive humanoid form, lithe and tall, lightweight, agile, fine-featured, and strong. She had the jet-black hair and dark, almost black, eyes that Morgan had bred her for—not to mention the retractable claws and the fangs. The female was perfectly feral, intelligent enough for an animal, and rather aggressive.

Of course, as the female grew up over the course of five years, Morgan, through the Spiriter's body, had had her conditioned to the point that she cowered in fear every time the Spiriter walked into her pen, to the point where any sudden movement made her flinch away. But if one gave her an opening, she would attack.

"The Adkish won't know what hit him." Morgan sneered, watching her creature prowl around restlessly. The female looked up and saw them, baring her fangs and hissing. Morgan raised his hand in a sardonic wave.

Adkisha, my lady. The hero is… a female. We've only just located her.

Morgan's voice was dangerously low, deceptively calm. "Pardon?"

It's a halfling female. We've finally located her; she's traveling east in the company of three dragons, two elves, and a human, as last we knew. The elves are the princes Ephraim and Aramon.

Morgan bared his teeth. "Nahor's sons. Protecting their precious heroine, no doubt. Oh, how I despise that male." She paused. "A halfling?" She eyed her own halfling down below. "Of what cross?"

Dragon, it would seem. Dragon and quite possibly elf.

"Does Malakieth know of this one yet?" she demanded, gesturing toward her pet.

Not yet, my lady. I've kept your creation secret from him as well. The slave that feeds her is sworn to silence on threat of a rather painful death.

"When will you be ready? I grow tired of waiting."

I wait on Lord Molyb, my lady.

"He'll be dead if he doesn't hurry," she snarled. "I will not wait forever. And if Malakieth hears of this—"

He won't, my lady.

"Take one of my men with you, one of your sorcerers. Kill the Adkisha—and *do not play with her*. Destroy her spirit, and let her die."

Consider it done, my queen.

"Good," Morgan snapped. Softer, she continued. "I have been planning this time for centuries. I will not have it ruined, especially not by some mongrel child-hero." She looked again at the female below. "Though, should things go wrong, I do not want to lose everything I have worked for." Her voice hardened; she turned to a waiting Rashek. "Her bloodlines must be preserved. Release the male into her pen, and let them spawn. I will have a new litter to work with."

The Rashek bowed low to her, moving to obey.

To all apparent eyes—and there were eyes watching her—the slave girl appeared apathetic as she was once more led into the female's pen. Internally, she was still screaming at the horror the poor female had been forced to suffer.

Morgan might believe her halfling creation an animal with an animal's intelligence, but she knew the truth. The female could speak, could reason.

The guards let her into the pen, and she approached the female slowly. The poor creature was curled into herself in a corner, trying to hide her tears. The slave girl sat down beside her, placing the things she had been permitted to bring in with her on the ground.

"Nemah," she whispered. It was the name she had given the female, a dragon's name. In their tongue, it meant 'child of sorrow.' "Nemah, love, it's me."

She reached out and lightly touched Nemah's bare shoulder. Nemah flinched and then relaxed under her touch. Her hand crept up to cover the slave girl's, claws extended in her distress.

"I want to die," she breathed.

"Hush," the *rakasheti* murmured soothingly, cringing at the blood smeared on Nemah's pale skin. The male—Nemah called him Leader—had not been gentle. "I'm going to clean your wounds and bandage them. We've done it before, so it's nothing to be nervous about, all right?"

Nemah nodded, extending one arm. As gently as she could, the slave girl washed the wounds left by Leader's claws clean and bound them. Nemah healed quickly—from physical wounds, at least.

"I'm so filthy," Nemah whispered.

The slave girl eyed the water left in the bowl. "We'll get you clean," she promised.

As she worked, she looked about for the rags that Nemah wore, only to find them shredded beyond repair. When Nemah was clean, the *rakasheti* picked up the threadbare blanket she had charmed the guards into letting her bring.

"Can you claw open a hole there?" she asked, holding up a section in the middle.

Nemah nodded, claws easily parting the fabric. The slave girl tugged it on over Nemah's head. She took the last of the bandages and wound it around the blanket, securing it to the halfling's side.

"Thank you," Nemah murmured, wiping her tears away.

The slave girl looked around. No one was about now. She wrapped her arms around Nemah and held her close. Closing her eyes, she sang softly to the female until Nemah fell asleep.

When she was sure that Nemah wasn't going to wake for a few hours, she extracted herself from the broken hybrid's grasp and made her way out of the pen. Chin held high, she made her way through the Black Fortress to her master's tower chambers, letting herself in.

Since she wore the uniform of a *rakasheti*, every male left her alone. *Rakasheti* were slave women with only one master. As the word was in the all-but-forgotten native tongue of the country, not many knew the rough translation into the Common Tongue. But *rakasheti* were, in a word, concubines. Although she herself wasn't a true *rakasheti*; her master never lay with her. She was merely a cook and a companion. The uniform and the status were for her protection.

Her master wasn't there. She changed from her uniform into a tunic and pants and began to cut up vegetables for a soup. A pity they had no meat, but then, he never complained when he went without.

Her knife stilled.

Heaven and hell. She was stunned to find herself crying silently. She *never* cried. And yet... that poor girl...

The door opened as her master came back, setting something on a nearby table. She wiped furiously at her tears as she felt him pause behind her.

Slowly, his arms wound around her shoulders. He had never hugged her before.

Tonight, she needed the comfort; she twisted in his arms to bury her face into the soft fabric of his black shirt. He stroked her hair.

"Talk to me," he rumbled in his low, melodic voice.

She managed to choke out an explanation of what had been done to Nemah. She froze as she felt his massive body coil in anger around her. He exhaled on a sibilant hiss, pale gray smoke curling in the air above her head. The smoke—and occasional flame—that he spat was one of the perils of living with a dragon, even when he wore his human form.

"How long were you watching?" he growled.

"I... I left when... when it started. I couldn't bare to watch."

"Could you hear what the Spiriter was saying?"

"I was too far away."

"What did you sense?"

Magic. It was one of the biggest reasons why she was so important to him, so useful to him. Her forbidden magic. It had drawn

Beau nodded. *Of a sort. My mother was the Light Dragon, my father the Dark Dragon. They loved each other well, though they weren't mates. But love can turn to hate, little halfling—never forget that. My mother found her mate in a fellow Light Dragon, and my father couldn't live with the loss of her. There were horrible things done, little one. My dracling half sister and I were orphaned, and Beryl was too young and too sickly to survive without a mother. And so I remain, and I have both forms of magic. A balance of the two.*

His sorrow washed through her, and she wrapped her arms around his neck and held him closely, resting her cheek against his scales. After a minute, he pulled away.

Show me that spell again, he told her. And she did, slowly calling the shadows to her, wrapping them around her like a cloak to hide her.

The best dark magic is slow and insidious. It's unnerving, and it unsettles your enemies. But never take pride in that, Kirin. Never allow the magic to take too deep a root in you, or it will claim you. Fire magic may wish to consume everything in its path, but dark magic seeks to control and master it. That's why it's so dangerous.

Kirin nodded, dropping the spell. *I am not fond of this magic.*

It is best to be wary. His voice lightened. *Enough of it for now. Come; I will show you light magic.*

The next morning, a steady, cold rain poured from the heavens, washing away the snow. Spring was well on its way. As the weather was too miserable for travel, the group set up camp in a cave and got a fire burning brightly. Both princes taught them some of the elven dances, which Kirin enjoyed learning immensely. Then later that night when the rain petered out and mists began to rise from the melting snow, Tiamat, Callian, and Ephraim attempted to teach Kirin rudimentary water magic, while Beau and Aramon stayed a safe distance away. They stopped once she had the knack of gathering, controlling, and freezing it, to Kirin's dismay.

Ephraim trained Callian and Kirin how to fight from a dragon's back, which was very different than fighting from a horse's. Callian was surprised that Kirin needed to know these skills, having been raised with the Dragon Knights.

I've told you this before, Callian, Tiamat told him. *She has never loved before, so she has never flown with anyone. She had no dragon of her own to learn on, talk to, scheme with, cherish, laugh, cry, or live with. Though she lived with many, she was alone. At least you had Trig after your mother died. She never knew any family. Now that she does, don't you think that she feels a bit left out? Her mother was attacked and is married to a different man than her father. She has two half-brothers who have known each other for thousands of years. Wouldn't you feel out of place like that?*

She always seems so... I don't know... as if she doesn't mind. I never thought about it like that.

Have you ever spoken to her about such matters?

No, I haven't. Have you, Tiamat?

Yes. And then there is this Twilight Dragon. I—

Don't trust him?

Pity him.

Why is that?

Think about it, Callian. The Twilight Dragons are supposed to be extinct. *How then is he here? Did he witness a massacre of his people? Is he the last of the Twilight Dragons, or are there more of his people? Are they as rare as the Avians? Did he ever know any other Twilight Dragon? All these things I have pondered since meeting him. He doesn't speak of his people, and I haven't had the heart to ask.*

Why not?

Sometimes it is better not to know. Her voice was laced with ancient sorrows.

Oh.

Kirin threw a few darts at them, reminding both dragon and rider that they were flying and they had better stop fooling around and focus. Tiamat banked sharply to avoid the danger. Kirin gave a wild cry as Beau dropped next to Tiamat and then surged before

"A gentle voice on the wind. It's difficult to describe," he answered, watching her beautiful face. "But it's typically in my dreams."

Kirin smiled happily. She was completely enthralled by his ability, that he could actually hear Adonai, who had created all the worlds and all the stars and moons.

The spring day was beautiful, the sun dappled on the ground as it filtered through the canopy of new leaves overhead. They walked along in a peaceful sort of silence, the Ellasarian princes leading the way, Elindil following faithfully beside his master. The dragons had disappeared to hunt over an hour ago. Trig had spoken to Callian for a bit about Giladethians that Kirin had never heard of, and she had listened in on the conversation, asking questions on occasion.

Now, in the early afternoon with the silence stretching between them, Callian caught Kirin's eyes for a moment.

May I ask you a question? he mindspoke.

I may not answer, but you are free to ask.

Is the Common Tongue your first language?

I spoke Dragons' Tongue first. I don't remember it well, though it makes sense, given that I was raised in Allerion. Her laughter was pure silver.

Can you commune with all dragons—with all beasts?

Yes, though, apart from that snake months ago, I've never talked with beasts save dragons. I can't imagine that I would want to—it would make hunting more difficult, having your food talk back to you.

He struggled to keep the grin off of his face. *Tiamat thinks that you have some black magic. She says that she has seen in your eyes once that dangerous look that those with black magic have.*

Yes, she said slowly, uneasily. *Beau has been teaching me, though I don't enjoy using it.*

Please, be careful; I don't want you to be corrupted by it.

Confusion swept from her to him.

How can I protect you from you?

She smiled. *You would think of a way. You're rather clever.*

Callian grinned, and Ephraim noticed.

"What are you grinning about, young prince?"

"It's lovely," he said with a shrug, gesturing vaguely at the scenery.

"It is nice in here," Ephraim agreed, his easy smile flashing across his face. He caught Aramon's eye when Callian wasn't looking.

Kirin glanced at Callian, and once again she was unable to look away. The day was warm, and though it was windy, he had removed his dark cloak from around his shoulders and had tucked it into his saddlebag. The breeze played with his clothes and his hair, which had grown longer since she had first met him. The effect was stunning.

Suddenly, Tiamat, Beau, and Assumptshun dove into the clearing, landing simultaneously with an unconscious grace, and ran for their respective riders.

Magic, Callian! Strange magic! Tiamat called.

Nervous, Kirin clutched the strap of the leather bag she had taken to wearing, Beau crowding close to her back, teeth bared. Trig drew his sword and stepped closer to his friend.

"Aramon, grab Trig. We must leave! Hurry!" Ephraim yelled, springing onto his dragon's back.

Callian reached for Kirin's hand, but she didn't move. She was tense and clearly upset.

"Callian? What's going on?" asked Trig, uneasy.

"There is strange magic from an unknown origin. I'm not sure what in the worlds it is, but it's upsetting Kirin."

"It's pulling at me. I can feel it calling to me, grabbing at me like thousands of little fingers," she whispered in horror. Callian wound his arm around her waist.

The air seemed to be charged. Even Aramon stopped, quieting Elindil, to listen, to feel, to think. Tiamat crouched next to her rider, guarding both of the Giladethian men.

Then in an instant, a huge rift opened up only inches from Kirin and Callian, swallowing them, their dragons, and Trig in seconds. Acting fast, the two elves, with their mounts, leapt through the portal. But they knew it was too late. By now, the others would be in a different part of whatever world they had been thrown into. They were on their own.

THE DAMAGE OF A SPIRITER

Callian was flung through the portal, hitting the ground hard. Lying still, he mentally checked himself, making sure it was safe for him to move. There was no pain other than a few bruises; he was fine. He pushed himself into a sitting position, his hand brushing something soft, and glanced around. They were on a beach made of smooth sand, the surf a gentle refrain only yards away.

Heaven and hell, he swore. Kirin lay unconscious a foot or so away from him. Callian reached for her and pressed his fingers to her throat. Well, at least she had a normal pulse. He shook her thin shoulders, but she didn't wake.

He ran his fingers through his hair and groaned, then stood up, crossing to Trig and kicking the sole of his boot. It was not the nicest method of waking a friend, but it was better than getting himself stabbed. People had a bad habit of never living through a wound inflicted by Trig, even when he didn't coat his knives in poison. It was rumored that he could stab a man dead before he was truly awake. Thankfully, he was a light sleeper, so most people simply shouted at him to wake him.

Trig snapped to consciousness, leaping to his feet in one fluid motion, thrusting with his dagger. His blow landed inches short of Callian.

"You missed me," he commented dryly. He had Trig's reaction calculated down to an exact science. Tiamat watched silently, lying beside Beau, who was slowly blinking in the bright sunlight.

"I usually do," Trig shot back. Seeing Kirin unconscious, he scowled, his way of being upset and worried. "What the hell just happened?"

"We were thrown through a portal. I don't know where we are. Kirin is still unconscious and Beau seems stunned, and I have a feeling that something…ill-fated is about to happen."

"Truly, gentlemen?" a cold voice interrupted.

The two of them spun on their heels, Trig throwing his knife in the process. The intruder ducked the weapon, though only just. The Giladethian cursed as the second figure caught his knife and flung it aside.

Two male creatures stood there, clearly not human, though human in form. The one was close to Kirin's height, with black and red skin, the other taller, with skin a pale blue.

But they only had a fraction of a second to notice this before the taller one's spell hit them and the dragons.

No! Callian howled, fighting against the black magic that was pinning them immobile to the ground.

Callian, be silent and listen, Tiamat snapped, responding to his fury. *Beau knows how to break free. But he'll need a lot of magic.* Callian saw the shorter male sprawled beside Kirin, murmuring to her, stroking her face. His infamous anger blazed as red clouded the edges of his vision. It was a pulsating sensation, the bloodlust and magic pounding through his veins in time with his pounding heart. Callian watched as the fiend allowed his hand to trail down, feeling her body. His rage burned, and Beau, drawing magic from Tiamat and Callian, nearly broke free of the spell. But Kirin awoke. Callian watched as she stood up.

And then the devil-spawn attacked her with black magic. Kirin screamed. She was flung backward, hitting the ground hard and sliding on her side. Callian's fury spiked uncontrollably, and Beau seized on his anger, breaking the spell with a furious bellow and surging upward from the ground, only to fall back. In a flash of silver steel, Trig raced toward the shorter one, the one that had touched Kirin. The one that had hurt her. The stronger one. Out of the corner of his eye, Callian saw the taller one draw back his hand for a strike. More black magic. Callian ran him through before he had time to draw the breath and power to kill Trig.

Trig battled the other as Callian ran to Kirin's side, the steel of his sword flashing in the sunlight as he swung towards his opponent's middle. The clash of metal on metal sounded as the creature parried, and Trig feinted to the left before swinging in an uppercut that the other failed to duck. The blade drove home, biting several inches into the creature's neck until stopped by his spine. Trig jerked his sword free. Another swing, and the shorter man's head rolled free of his shoulders.

"Kirin! Kirin, can you hear me?" Callian called.

"Yes," she mumbled, her vision blurring his features. "Where were you?" She shook her head slowly, frowning again. "I mean, what happened?"

Pain crossed his face. "One of the men held us all under an enchantment. I couldn't move, couldn't warn you," he said hastily, lowering his voice so as to not hurt her ears.

"Easy, Callian." Trig's voice seemed to come from afar. He spoke softly, soothingly.

"Better dead than having him—or both of them—take me. Especially in front of a crowd," she mumbled. Trig nodded in agreement. Raw fear flashed through Callian's eyes.

Kirin moaned softly as more pain spasmed through her. Callian slid one arm under her shoulders.

"Callian, you remember the legends and mythology we studied," Trig said. "How do we fix the damage? What has that monster done to her?"

"He's a Spiriter, by the looks of him, so he likely attacked her spirit. I don't think that it's fixable. Her spirit will slowly die, possibly taking her life with it. If only her spirit dies, that man, Mala-whatsit, will probably have some other spirit control her." He spoke through his teeth as fury and fear clamored to reign supreme in him. He could feel his magic building.

Trig backed up a step, and Kirin could no longer see him. Sea spray hit her cheek as the sound of a large wave pounding the shore reached her ears.

You knew this was coming, Tiamat whispered to him. *In your dream. You were forewarned.*

"We have to do something," Callian snarled through clenched teeth. "Adonai, please, help us!"

The air itself seemed to sing before a voice whispered: *"She must find that which belonged to the first Adkish, a crystal imbued with magic. Only then will the damage of the Spiriter leave her."* Then the air was back to normal, the gentle male voice gone. Adonai had stopped speaking.

"We had better hurry," Callian said. And with that, he picked Kirin up, mindful of her wings. Some small part of his subconscious noted wryly that for once she didn't argue as he carried her.

Callian began to survey their situation. There was no sign of game that he could see and no wood for fire or shelter. Beau was as bad off as Kirin, and Tiamat wasn't strong enough to carry two riders and a wounded dragon, so their travel would be slow at best. Somewhere, they would have to find both shelter and a source of fresh water.

"And so the puzzle begins," Kirin heard Callian mutter. A melody drifted through his mind; Tiamat was singing softly, though whether she was singing to herself or to Beau, he didn't know.

"Water," Kirin whispered. No one heard her. She closed her eyes. Her hand moved to Callian's shoulder. She tightened her grip, desperately trying to get his attention.

"Ouch. What is it?" Her tactic worked.

"Water," she repeated. "You might be able to lead us to it. You have water magic."

"And Tiamat's a Fire Dragon. How can you be sure that the two of you won't lead us to something … burning?" Trig asked.

Kirin had no answer for that. She felt Callian begin to walk, still carrying her. "We have to do something," he muttered. Then he stopped, hesitating. "Do you truly think I could?" he whispered to her. "That I could safely lead you and Trig—and Beau—to water?"

She opened her eyes again to find him staring at her with unfathomable blue eyes. "Yes."

Tiamat called to her rider, and he turned to look at her. She stood with one foreleg on either side of Beau's still neck.

You go. I'm going to try to fly Beau and search from the air. I will alert you should I spot water.

Are you sure that you will be able to keep him aloft for that long?

I will no sooner leave him here than you would leave Kirin. I am strong. I can do this, Callian. I have to.

He nodded once, silently, his lips pressed together. "Right."

Behind them, Tiamat strained to pick up Beau, painfully aware that the male outweighed her by a good amount. Though it wasn't easy, she managed to get them both airborne. Callian watched his beloved dragon fly awkwardly inland. It occurred to him that he might never see her again. He shook the thought from his mind.

"Come on, Trig; let's go."

"Lead the way, oh great rider."

Callian smiled. Typical Trig. Some things would never change.

They set off, Callian reaching out with his magic, desperate for some sort of signal to follow. After about half an hour, Trig spoke again. "Callian, if she's too heavy, I can carry her for a bit."

"Surprisingly, she doesn't weigh much." Still, he touched her mind to see if she wanted someone else to carry her. Though her thoughts were muddled and pain-filled, he understood one thing: she was content as long as it was he who held her.

How strange, he thought. *She must be delirious.*

Trig watched his friend out of the corner of his eye. The tension of the situation was undoubtedly making the prince emotional. That much was evident in the way Callian didn't seem to notice he was playing with the ends of Kirin's hair. Still, since Callian's hands were occupied, Trig pulled his bow from his back and strung it, ready to protect them or procure their dinner, whichever became necessary.

They pressed on, trying to keep to as straight of a path as possible. Their surroundings grew darker as the day wore on, until they were blanketed in the deep, shadowy darkness of dusk. They were wearying, with no sign of fresh water or game or shelter. Kirin had long ago curled up against Callian and had fallen asleep with her head cradled against his chest, one hand clutching a fistful of his tunic. It was a strangely powerful feeling, Callian decided, this sensation of protecting her, of having her fall asleep in his arms.

Finally, when strange stars had lit up the sky and twin moons had risen above the horizon, Kirin awoke. Callian watched as she raised her head to peer about with a confused expression.

"Good morning," he teased gently.

She looked up at him, blinking the sleep out of her eyes, and released her grip on his tunic. "I fell asleep?"

"You needed it."

"I can walk now," she told him.

He stopped, Trig stopping beside him, and set her on her feet. She took a few shaky steps, and Trig flashed her a crooked, tired grin. "Come along, little filly."

She shot him a dark look.

They continued onward, the ground sloping upwards now, until they reached the crest of the hill. Something vast and dark loomed up in the distance.

"I'll go see what it is," Callian said, drawing his sword. Carefully, painstakingly, he slipped away from them, travelling down the steep decline of the hill without knocking the small stones loose.

Kirin and Trig followed after him. She stumbled again over the uneven surface, sliding a few feet, her wings flaring out to keep her balance. Dirt tumbled loose, and she breathed a curse. Trig offered her his arm wordlessly, and after a moment, she swallowed her pride and took it.

"May I ask you something?" he said softly. He didn't look at her as he spoke.

She nodded once, eyes downcast as she picked her way over the treacherous ground, and he seemed to see that.

Callian gripped his friend's shoulder. "Perhaps he was mad and death is a mercy."

"He wasn't mad," Kirin said, looking up at them. "Nor was he human." Her eyes slid to Trig. "Excellent shot."

"He wasn't human?" Callian repeated.

"No." She frowned at the corpse, summoning a palm full of fire. Trig cursed again, though milder this time. "He was a Nephilim, the son of a fallen angel."

Callian crouched beside her. "How can you tell?"

"The black blood tends to make it obvious," she told him wryly, "though they are not the only creatures to possess black blood. But were-beasts and Shadow Dragons are rather noticeable, Rashek are broader and bear a bluish tint to their skin, and demons tend to be completely black. That leaves Nephilim and DarkAngels, and since he's dead and we're not, that makes him a Nephilim."

"DarkAngel?" Trig asked, arching a brow. "As in, a fallen angel?"

"As in the sons of Cathas. But they're rare and tend not to be subtle." She turned back to the dead Nephilim. "This is the first one of his kind I've seen in person." Rising to her feet, she extinguished her flame. "He was unarmed save for that knife and has no supplies. I'm willing to bet that he was staying in one of these caves—he might have food and water we can make use of."

Callian nodded, picking up the knife. He offered it to Trig. "Spoils to the victor."

Trig tucked the blade in his belt.

Callian, Tiamat whispered in his mind. *I must land soon. I'm at the end of my strength. Please say you've found water.*

He hoped that she couldn't feel his despair. *We've found and killed a lone Nephilim. We're searching the caves for his campsite now. Are you near?*

Yes. Her mental voice was faint with exhaustion. *I'm landing near you. I must rest.*

Almost immediately, a dark shape detached itself from the blackness that surrounded them. Tiamat set Beau down as gently as she could—which still made Kirin wince—and landed. The landing was nearly a crash. She struggled to her feet, only to think better of it and lay stretched out on the ground, panting for breath. Kirin hurried to Beau, dropping to cradle his head in her lap as Callian left Trig looking through the nearest caves and went to check on Tiamat.

Movement caught his attention, but it was merely Trig returning from one of the caves.

"Are they alive?" Trig asked uncertainly. Callian nodded grimly. "I've found it," he added. "There's a pool in the back of the cave, thank Adonai."

Callian rekindled the dead Nephilim's fire, building it up as high as he dared. Tiamat lay curled up in front of the entrance to block the light from escaping. Trig had pulled his bow and quiver off; they lay with his vambrace, his sword, and his cloak beside him. He sat now with his boots loosened, his head resting on his knees. He looked relaxed and on the verge of sleep, having drank his fill from the pool and bathed, but Callian could see that his right hand hung only inches from the knife he kept in his boot.

"Callian," he finally said, soft enough that his voice wouldn't carry to the pool where Kirin and Beau were bathing and drinking as much of the cool water as they could stomach. "I've been thinking… What if that Nephilim wasn't as alone as we supposed?"

Callian looked up from where he was sorting through their packs. "That did occur to me. But we desperately need the water and the cave is safe and will shelter us for the night. I moved the body into a different cave while you were bathing as a precaution, but… it seemed a risk we had no choice but to take."

Trig lifted his head long enough to meet Callian's eyes, his gaze solemn. "We'll hold this cave if it comes to it. We've been in worse places for defense."

Callian offered him the ghost of a smile. "I'm glad it's you that's here, Trig, selfish as that is of me."

Trig smiled tiredly and dropped his head back down. "It's not my place to ask, but is she your lover?"

Callian stilled. "No, she isn't my lover."

"Are you courting her, then? You're rather fond of her—that much is evident."

Kirin appeared in the ring of firelight with Beau at her side before he could answer, her clothes soaked. Callian felt his breath catch in his throat. Her hair hung loose and damp down her back, parting over her pointed ears. Crossing to her pack, she knelt to search through it, blushing faintly as she found a comb and went to work on her hair. She moved so elegantly, so gracefully. As he watched her, *really* watched her, he saw that all her movements were like dancing, so fluid. It was beautiful to watch.

Her reptilian green eyes flicked up at him and then back down at her long hair as she went back to working the tangles out of it.

You stare, she accused, her melodic voice soft.

Sorry.

Why *do you stare?*

You're beautiful, he admitted. *It's rather distracting.*

She blushed again and smiled shyly at his compliment. *Thank you.* Out loud, she said, "Go to sleep, both of you. I've slept already; I'll keep the first watch." Callian opened his mouth to argue. "Please," she added hastily, looking at him.

He sighed and Tiamat shifted out of the cave entrance as Kirin banked the fire. Leaning back against Tiamat's shoulder, he told her, "Wake me in a few hours, then. You need the sleep; you're wounded. It's either that," he said, seeing the look on her face as she plaited her hair back, "or I stay up with you for the first watch."

"Wake me after you, Callian," Trig mumbled, already half asleep.

She nodded reluctantly, and he let himself drift off to sleep, though not before seeing Beau rest his head in her lap. One fine hand rose to stroke his brow; Callian felt the bitter sting of jealousy twist through his gut. Chiding himself on the ridiculousness of the emotion, he closed his eyes and let sleep wash over him.

He was awakened by a gentle hand on his shoulder. Opening his eyes, he saw that the sun was rising, which meant that Kirin had been on watch much longer than she should have been. He turned to rebuke her, but she gripped his shoulder hard and pressed a finger to her lips.

We have company, she mindspoke. *Move silently and slowly. They can see us.*

His fingers curled around the hilt of his sword. *Nephilim?*

Most likely. They've found the other body.

Don't touch Trig when you wake him, he replied.

Kirin nodded, eyeing the dark-haired Giladethian. From where he lay on his side, the Nephilim likely couldn't see him. *Trig*, she whispered into his mind. *Trig, wake up and lay perfectly still.*

His eyes flipped opened and one brow arched. It was the only part of him that moved.

Nephilim are moving to block us in. They've seen Callian, Tiamat, and myself, but I don't think they've seen you or Beau yet. You're at a bad angle to be seen from the entrance, and Beau blends into the rock—at least until the sun rises a bit further. Tiamat and I will create a distraction, so that you and Beau can escape and come back for us.

His icy eyes narrowed, mouth moving to form a single word: No.

Callian frowned. Fighting back a sigh, Kirin repeated the plan to him. She expected him to take his friend's side and argue, an expectation that Trig clearly held as well, but he was silent.

It was Tiamat who spoke, sounding uncertain. *Beau would leave?*

I have no choice, Beau replied to her, his voice gentle. *It is the best option for Kirin's survival. That mark on her arm declares her as the Adkisha, and they will take her alive—Malakieth will want to pull her and her magic onto his side. He knows it would be the fastest way to end the war.*

Callian was so still that Kirin was half expecting him to refuse to make a decision and let the Nephilim surround the entrance to the cave. Already, they were drawing closer, blades drawn.

Finally, Callian looked at his friend and nodded once. *Go with Beau. Come back for us. We'll need you.*

Trig mouthed a profanity at him. Kirin watched as Beau met and held Tiamat's eyes and felt the need to avert her own gaze. There was something strangely intimate in the promise those golden eyes held.

Slowly, without lifting himself from the ground, Trig pulled his bow, quiver, and pack on his back, strapped his sword to his hip, and wrapped his cloak over all of it. Drawing one knee to his chest, he took something from around his neck and tucked it into his left boot. He threw the cowl over his head and tossed something thin to Callian, who tucked it against his left hip, under his pants where it wouldn't be noticed. He gave Trig the knife he usually carried in his boot, and Kirin handed him every weapon she carried—this time, she would fight solely with magic. There was no sense in losing all of their weapons at once.

Tiamat lunged to her feet. Outside, the Nephilim paused, then grinned at the challenge. Her face set with resolve, green eyes fierce, Kirin rose to stand at the entrance, Callian at her shoulder with his sword drawn. She closed her eyes, drawing as much magic through the bond as Beau could give her.

She screamed as fire erupted, blasting forward and fanning out in an arc. It was an impressive display of magic, and Callian could hear screams as several of the Nephilim were burned. Beau shoved Trig out of the cave, pausing only to lick Kirin's cheek in affection before running after Trig.

Fleeing while Callian remained behind felt like abandonment, but leaving a woman behind felt like cowardice. Aware that he was disobeying direct orders from his prince, he dropped his pack behind a pile of rocks, hands racing to tuck all of the weapons the others had given him inside. Beau slammed to a halt, then pivoted and returned for him, looking furious. Trig bent his bow and knocked an arrow to the string, taking careful aim. The arrow buried itself into the shoulder of a Nephilim near Callian.

The Nephilim weren't stupid. While the majority of them subdued Kirin, Callian, and Tiamat, a party began searching for him.

"Go!" he hissed at Beau, tucking the bow and quiver back into the pack with his sword. The Twilight Dragon bared his teeth. "*Go!*"

Beau snapped his teeth shut only inches from Trig's face in aggravation, then turned, grabbed Trig's pack, and raced off.

Trig palmed his knife and the blade he had taken off of the dead Nephilim, then rose and charged the Nephilim. He managed to kill two and gravely wound five more before they disarmed him and threw him to the ground. A blow to the head sent pain lancing through his entire body, and he knew no more.

Trig came awake to find himself locked in a small, dim cell, his hands bound with rope behind his back. Through the pain in his head and the dull ache in his shoulders, he found himself smiling. He had been hoping that this was how he would end up.

It took a fair amount of effort to draw his knees to his chest and work his hands around his feet, but he managed to get his arms in front of him. He had given Callian his stiletto, which he could only hope their captors hadn't found on him; Trig's own blades were missing, though he had expected as much. They had also taken the liberty of unlacing his boots, presumably to make sure that he didn't have a blade tucked in one. He pushed his fingers under his sock, his bound hands clumsy, and sighed in relief when he found what he was looking for—his lockpick on its chain.

He pushed himself into a sitting position and laced up his boots, then rose and examined the cell door. There was no lock, but the door was fastened by a bolt.

Whoever had locked him inside had been sloppy about it, and Trig couldn't help but wonder if it was because he was only human— not a rider like Callian or a long-awaited heroine like Kirin. Still, being human had its benefits, such as not being thoroughly searched and detained.

It was tricky with his hands bound, but he managed slip his fingers through the small barred grate in the door and catch the loop of

be trapped with you in this hellhole we're stuck in? They've locked Trig—foolish and loyal man that he is—and Tiamat somewhere else, but I refused to leave you alone. They would do nasty things to you here." She could feel a small shudder run down his spine at the thought. "But I'm glad that you are all right."

"We're alone?"

"Yes. For the moment," he murmured softly, helping her sit up.

She looked around. The light was next to nonexistent; she could see the dim outline of the door and Callian. But that was fine. She didn't need to see anything but him. "Where's here?" she asked, leaning into the strength he offered. He wrapped one arm low around her waist, mindful as always of her wings.

Callian chuckled once, darkly. "Hell."

"Seriously?" she asked, alarmed.

"No. We're trapped in some prison to 'await our fate,'" Callian mimicked spitefully. "The executioner comes tomorrow, and we die at 'high noon,' which, in all truth, seems rather poetic to me. I wasn't sure if I would rather you slept through the whole thing so that it wouldn't hurt, or if you would wake up so that we could make our last stand together." His sigh seemed to come from deep inside of himself, equal parts frustration and temporary defeat. "I'm still not sure. But now it's done. You're awake; we might as well enjoy the last day and a half."

He pulled her absentmindedly onto his lap to hold her better and wrapped his arms around her. Kirin thought her heart would stop.

"Hell," she finally agreed in a whisper, allowing herself to nestle against him. *With a bit of heaven. Enjoy the last day and a half? What does he mean by that?*

"I wish that you didn't have to go through this, but at the same time..."

His arms tightened around her. "I will never leave you," he promised solemnly.

She blushed, but smiled up at him. He gazed back down at her, his eyes and expression soft.

Neither spoke for a few moments. It was Kirin who broke the silence. "Now what, Callian? Do you have a plan?"

"No. We die. Unless you have a better plan." He glanced at her sideways, trying to read her expression.

She thought hard, which wasn't easy at the moment. "No," she finally admitted in a subdued voice. "But before we do," she continued, looking away, her nearly-inaudible voice an octave higher in embarrassment, "I ... I want you to—"

There was a light scraping sound at the door, as if someone's key was slipping in the lock. Kirin broke off, staring at the door, ready for a fight. Around her, she could feel Callian coil, tensed for attack. Then someone opened the cell door. Trig grinned and swung his lockpick around in his fingers. A cloaked figure stepped in around him, took one look at them, and said in a light, feminine voice, "Good for you, human. Are you really the Adkisha?"

"Yes. What of it?" Kirin shot back, angry that she had been interrupted. Trig had the grace to look slightly embarrassed.

The girl dropped her voice to a whisper. "Come with me. I can get you all out of here. My name's Natasha."

Kirin looked at Callian, arching a brow. She wanted his opinion.

"I would rather die fighting," he said. She slid off his lap and stood with him, stretching.

"Thank you," she said to their rescuers. "What of Tiamat?"

"Beau's going for her now."

"He's reached her. They're on their way out," Callian added, smiling in relief.

"Follow me, and keep quiet." Natasha slipped back out, leaving the cell door open. They followed her into the passageway, making no sound as she shut and locked the cell behind them.

"Where are we?" Kirin whispered to her.

"A temporary prison, cell block four."

"How old are you?"

"Sixteen. Hush. It's not safe to talk, my lady." Natasha slid down another passage, the halfling and the Giladethians following close behind.

Kirin suddenly fell to her knees, gasping for breath. Natasha, hurrying ahead of them with Trig following close behind, didn't seem to notice. Callian stooped and lifted her up into his arms, easily carrying her with them.

A sudden cry went up, shouting the alarm. They broke into a run. Callian set Kirin back down and took her hand, racing with her over the rough stone ground of the prison.

They burst out of the main entrance into sunlight, with a dozen or more guards on their tail.

"Good luck!" Natasha cried, darting off.

"Wait!" Trig called back, but the sixteen-year-old female had disappeared.

"Kirin, Trig, we need to split, draw them apart!" Callian said as they fled their pursuers. "Please, please, *please* be safe. Promise me."

He released her hand and ran left as soon as she nodded, Trig leaping nimbly over the rough ground and disappearing quickly. Choking back tears, she leapt into the air, snapping out her wings and soaring right.

BRIGHTEST IN THE DARK

She ran through the dim tunnels of the subterranean dungeon. The little flame in her hand flickered, and pain lanced through her body as she rounded another corner in the twisting labyrinth. Wildly, she ran on, following the thread of mental link that was leading her to Callian. She staggered as another wave of pain washed over her. Kirin was tired—though the sleep and the water had been helpful, she was beginning to acutely feel the effects of the Spiriter's spell. She could feel herself… dying, and it was frightening.

She had found Trig and the dragons nearly as soon as she had lost the guards, hoping to find Callian already there. Instead, she had found Tiamat unconscious, with news from Beau that Callian had been recaptured, rendered unconscious, and thrown in some other hellhole of a prison. Redistributing their supplies had been the work of a moment, and miracle of miracles, Beau had managed to find and reclaim Callian's sword during the escape. They had set off, quickly finding the dungeon and dispatching the guards that were there. It was the combing of the dungeon itself that was the difficult part of the task. There was no cloaked Natasha to guide them, and Callian seemed to be flickering in and out of consciousness, making it difficult for Tiamat to locate him. She called out to him again, trying to mindspeak. She could sense Beau's growing frustration and worry—they had spilt up, and still none of them had found any sign of him. The only way that they knew he was alive was that Tiamat hadn't died.

She had been searching, running, for half an hour. She had long ago used up all the stamina she had learned at the Academy. Desperation twisted in her like poison, drawing up gruesome mental images in the gloom of the corridor, visions of Callian trapped in this oppressive darkness, bleeding and in pain, his body mangled, his spirit broken.

Stop it! she commanded herself. Beau rumbled a soothing sound in the back of her mind, and she was glad for his presence.

The corridor emptied into yet another chamber of cells, perhaps a dozen of them, lined in iron bars sunk deep into the floor and ceiling. She didn't need to open them to know that they were empty.

"Help me, Adonai, please," she panted faintly into the darkness.

Follow your heart. What is brightest in the dark? The gentle voice swirled around her, soothing her, filling her with hope.

She ran on, stumbling into another serpentine tunnel, racing against time and fate. If Callian was hurt—and how could he not be?—then the sooner she found him, the sooner she could attempt to heal him. Her brothers had taught her a bit of healing magic—she only hoped that it would be enough, that they hadn't beaten him bloody.

Why all the riddles? Why not: take the first left you come to, run six minutes before turning left again, make an immediate right, and untie Callian? Turning yet another corner, Kirin found herself in a large cavern. She had lost count of how many tunnels and caverns she had searched through. What had looked like perhaps only twenty cells was actually just the surface. The real dungeon stretched over hundreds of yards in every direction underground. No wonder there had only been a few guards. This whole place was a massive, almost pitch-black labyrinth that was mostly abandoned. *If* a prisoner could escape the cell, he would probably starve to death trying find his way out.

Carefully, she lit a nearby lamp hung on the damp wall to her right, grateful when the oily paper that boxed in the flame didn't ignite. The new light revealed several solid iron cell doors lining the back wall. She staggered over to open the first door. Nothing. She tried four more cell doors. All of them were empty. The sixth door held a skeleton—she thought that it might have once been human.

Stay calm, she ordered herself. *I need to find Callian and free him… and tell him.* The seventh and eighth cells held nothing but rusted chains. But as her fingertips brushed against the ninth door, she heard something stir. Something was alive inside that dark, damp cell, and it need not be anything nice.

Slowly she pushed open the door, cringing as it squealed on its hinges. She peered into the gloom.

"Kirin!" a strained voice gasped.

She ran to fetch the lantern. Bringing it back, she set it on a notch in the crudely cut wall, hoping it wouldn't fall.

"Callian!"

He was chained, spread-eagle, to the wall, about six inches off the floor. His clothes were slightly torn, and his right forearm was covered in blood. Kirin immediately ripped his sleeve open, revealing both his wound and his strong arm, and then tore a strip off the bottom of her tunic and bound the wound.

"Are you well?" he asked. She was surprised by the concern in his voice.

She shook her head. "Wretched Spiriter and his bloody spell." She took Canath from her back and belted it around his waist, glad for the semi-darkness of the cell so that he wouldn't see her blushing at being this close to him, touching him…

His blood raced and his breath came shorter as she stretched up against him, standing on her toes to reach the manacle, trying to pick the lock with a dagger. The fire ignited in him, and his heart clenched as another spasm of pain twisted her beautiful face.

"How much longer do you have?"

"If I last the week, I'll be doing well," Kirin replied, gasping for breath after the lancing pain had passed through her fragile body.

She gave up on the lock, tucking her dagger away. Kneeling at his feet, she reached into the leather satchel that hung on from a strap between her wings, pulling out her wineskin she had filled with water from the pool. Her eyes fell on the egg that lay nestled in

My apologies.

Tiamat carefully stepped over to Kirin, trying to avoid stepping on Callian and Trig, who had stupidly decided to try to wrestle with the male dragon. She gently licked Kirin's pointed ear, a sign of affection.

Of course! A dragon's emotions are intertwined with the rider's. I wonder if that means that Beau is in love with Tiamat?

Yes, dracling, I am, Beau answered. He looked up from where he had Trig pinned to the ground with his left forefoot, Callian with his right. He slowly let them back up and laughed along with the two men. *But I have always been that way.*

I was in love with Callian before I met you, silly.

This is different, small one.

Does she love you back?

Yes. The sun will set soon, little dracling, and I know that you are tired. We must at least travel to relative safety.

Kirin nodded. "Let's go back to the ruins we passed by today. That, at least, will provide a bit of shelter."

Trig nodded. "First watch," he said.

Second, Beau replied.

Kirin couldn't help but laugh.

Callian awoke.

It was just a dream. It couldn't be real. She doesn't love me. I must be crazy... or dead, and my mind is playing tricks on me. It can't be real.

And why not? a soft, musical voice whispered in his mind.

It's too good to be true.

Then open your eyes, my dearest prince.

He obeyed, slowly, afraid of disproving her voice. Seeing Kirin so close to him, her beautiful face only inches from his own, her lovely green eyes peering into his, made his heart accelerate. She kissed him gently, her sensitive fingers caressing his ear and neck.

"And why can't I love you?" she whispered so softly only he could hear.

"I must still be dreaming. This is too good to be true," he insisted.

"Then quit complaining," she teased, kissing him again.

Drawing back, she eased out of his arms and sat up, his cloak falling from her shoulders. She smiled at it, touched. He must have draped it over her before taking his shift on watch.

He looked up at her. "I dreamed last night, early in the night." His blue eyes were serious, dampening her mood. "A wall of fire. We walked into it. Or through it."

"I truly hope it was just a dream," Trig mumbled nearby.

"You and I both," Callian muttered.

After a quick meal that finished off all the food they had been able to find in their packs, they broke camp and continued to walk back the way they had come, away from the shore. They planned on skirting around the prison, hoping that they would run into a town—the prison had to be getting its supplies from somewhere.

They walked for what seemed to be forever, always traveling northwestward. It would have been faster to fly, but as Trig had no way of being airborne and they were in a strange land, they decided against it. This world was a horrible place to live. They had yet to find any form of edible wildlife, though they did come across what might have been a village—at least, there were small hut-like structures and a few skinny sheep in poorly made fences, accompanied by a few weary and nervous-looking shepherds. They kept going until everyone was sore and tired and cross with each other and missed the cool cave with the cold pool in the back. Kirin drew her knife and began to polish and sharpen it as they walked.

The air grew steadily hotter and hotter, though it was a dry heat. They had reached a sort of beaten path bordered by cliff-like walls that they hoped would lead them to water, a town, or hunting grounds. The sweat ran down the men's necks as the ground began to slope upwards again, and Kirin could see Beau panting beside Tiamat. They paused to shift Beau's saddlebag to Tiamat, who didn't feel the heat as badly, to give Beau a reprieve. The Giladethians removed their tunics and boot-knives and packed them in Tiamat's saddlebag.

Then suddenly, brilliantly, they broke free of the ravine. In front of them loomed a wall of fire. It was clear now there could be no way of going over or around it.

Kirin walked up to it and tentatively placed her hand against it. It felt hot, of course, but bearable; her own magic protected her. She pushed, but the fire would not let her pass. Exasperated, she turned back to Beau, her hand still on the wall.

He looked at Tiamat, who said in awe, *These are the Fire Caves. We have legends of this place, but to actually see them...* She walked up beside Kirin and pushed her head against the flames. They were as solid as any stone wall. *It is said that inside lies ancient treasure. Perhaps this crystal we seek is within. Of course, not everyone may enter.*

Evidently, I am not allowed to.

Perhaps not alone, Beau said. He walked up to join them, stretching out one foreleg to the wall. Jolting back, he hissed in pain, and Kirin felt the echo of the burn through the bond. Beau looked at his rider, helpless to do anything but bid her farewell and good luck, which he did, adding, *No matter what happens in there, I will always care for you, little one.* Kirin hugged him fiercely.

Tiamat turned to Callian, who had been voicing the conversation out loud for Trig's sake. He paled, but squared his shoulders and stepped forward.

"You're mental," Trig hissed behind him.

"I was asked to protect her," he replied.

Still, he couldn't make himself touch the fire-wall, couldn't make himself walk within arm's reach. Tiamat suddenly lunged at Callian and crushed him to her neck in a fierce, quick hug. If the wall didn't burn him, he was going to have to walk through it. The realization brought paralyzing fear crashing through him. Kirin stepped toward him, approaching him as if he were a spooked horse about to bolt.

Never had he felt such fear before: not fighting a starving, crazed wild beast in the pit as a punishment; not fighting his own father; not charging into battle; nor facing off an angry dragon. Never. His will broke; he planted both feet firmly on the ground and refused to move. He didn't even care that his hands were trembling against Kirin's.

She didn't pull against him, didn't try to force him. Instead, she turned back to Callian, who backed up a step from the unbearably hot wall. She followed him, their fingers now entwined, and her wings flared out gracefully behind her. She took another step, closing the short distance between them. Kirin pressed herself up against his chest, her forehead pressed against his hot neck, one hand gripping his shoulder. She simply stood there, the coolness that radiated from her soothing him, helping him to think clearly.

What she wants is utter insanity, he thought.

But then she simply whispered, "Please," with longing in her voice, and he wrapped his arm firmly around her thin waist, clutching her to him, shifting her aside so he could walk. Fresh determination flowed through him as he took a step forward, then another and another.

He walked into the fire. And burst into flames.

It was so hot. He was going to die; he knew it. The human body was not meant to withstand this heat. Cool blackness enveloped him, and he welcomed it, a relief from the intense heat of the flames.

There was a sudden drop into more heat, and he knew no more.

THE FIRE CAVES

Something cool touched his face, and, begrudgingly, he opened his eyes. An angelic face hovered above him. *Kirin*. So this was Valour. She must have died as well— so young... only fifteen.

"So you *are* awake! I thought I lost you." She sighed, relief flooding her perfect features.

"I'm dead," he pointed out.

"No, you're not dead." Her thin fingers trailed down the planes of his bare chest, igniting emotions that burned through him like a raging fire. Callian bolted upright. His gaze lingered on her pretty face and the cute little smirk on it before dropping to stare at the ground beside him, trying to think coherently. Scraps of burnt, soaked material lay beside him. He stared at them, trying to figure out what they were.

"Strips off my clothes," she murmured, following his gaze. "There's a small pool over there to the left. The water is cold some-how, but not drinkable. I soaked you down."

Frowning in confusion, he looked down at himself. His pants had been ripped off at his knees, the edges charred, and his boots and socks nowhere in sight. Small burns crossed over his legs and arms, aching with a stinging pain. Canath lay beside him; he was grateful that the belt and scabbard were undamaged.

"You were overheating, and even with my wings around you, try-ing to push air into your face, you still collapsed from heat exhaus-tion," Kirin explained. "You were barely breathing. If I didn't do something, you would have died." Kirin looked as if she might cry, and Callian felt his heart ache for her. "I've never been so scared in my life." She sniffed, blinking rapidly, her wings shuddering behind her. "I don't know if there's any more damage," she whispered, eyeing the burns. "I couldn't bring myself to look. I didn't want you furious at me."

"Thank you," he told her.

She offered him a slight smile while rising to her feet.

"I take it we should go?" he asked as he stood up. He belted Canath around his hips.

"Yes. It would be better than having some monster come looking for us. Tiamat is right—this place is supposedly loaded with treasure, the spoils of some legendary beast from its victims. Personally, I don't care about *that*, but what better place to hide the Sword of the Adkish? Perhaps we'll find that while we look for the crystal," she said. "Though I'm not going to *look* for it, exactly. I would simply like to get out of this place."

"Sword of the Adkish?" Callian asked as they walked toward a lit entrance. His hand moved to his own sword, fingers caressing the hilt. "What's that? And what does it look like?" He realized that she was telling him tidbits of information she had picked up to occupy his mind, and he was thankful for it. He reached out and caught her hand.

"It was Adkish Rurik's blade—he fought with it when in his human form and used it to focus his magic, much like Ishmael used the crystal. No one knows what it looks like, or whether it still exists. It's supposed to be some ridiculously powerful blade. Some accounts say it's made of a metal called iridium, some say palladium, some say it's silver, and others say it's pure elemental energy. One account said it was made of pure diamond. It's said to be a beautiful weapon, the treasure of a kingdom, but sadly, it's been lost to the ages." She drew her crude short sword and stepped through the entrance.

His easy smile turned quickly to horror. "Oh no," Callian whispered.

The next room was a giant, burning maze. Kirin was good at flying, but not when she was carrying someone else, and he could

"There's someone up ahead," Ephraim muttered in Elvish. Aramon glanced up at him from Elindil's back, his expression curious. "*Gallen*," Ephraim replied, pointing in front of them, leaning out of Assumptshun's saddle as the dragon flew low to the ground.

Aramon obeyed, eyes narrowing into the waning sunlight to make out the slender form on the shore. The bodies of a Spiriter and a Rashek lay in front of them. Aramon urged his horse forward as they galloped towards the lone being.

"*Mai!*" Aramon called, recognizing the figure bent over the dead bodies. A huge grin spread across his face.

"*Mai!*" Ephraim echoed. Assumptshun landed to greet Ling, swerving as she knocked an arrow and pulled the bowstring taunt.

"What have you done with her?" she screamed.

"*Mai! Mai!* Don't shoot at him!" Aramon called as he galloped over and dismounted. He embraced his mother, fighting back tears. He had not seen her since the day she was taken into Amalay Kahelith sixteen years ago. It was overwhelming to see her again, to see her alive.

"Oh, my son, it is so good to see you again!" she murmured to him. She let go. "Beware, a dragon."

"Don't shoot your own son, *Mai*," he warned.

Her blue eyes grew big. "Ephraim!" she gasped.

Assumptshun slowed to a stop in front of the queen. Ling tensed, preparing to fight. Aramon wrapped an arm around his mother's shoulders, gently restraining her. Ephraim was as tense as Ling.

"Please don't be mad, Mother. This is Assumptshun, and I've been his rider since the Battle of Fazen Dur."

"Three thousand years you've kept this from your father and myself, Ephraim?" she said faintly. "You should have said something."

"I was afraid you would banish us or attack Assumptshun," he admitted. "Then Malakieth attacked you." Ling winced. "And I didn't think that Father would like having his eldest son bonded to a Dark Dragon. I feared that you would be afraid of us."

"That I would remind you too much of Lord Malakieth," Assumptshun added, speaking in the Common Tongue. Being an older dragon, he could speak aloud. Ling closed her eyes and shuddered, all too clearly remembering what Malakieth had done to her. Ephraim and Aramon exchanged a glance, both thinking the same thing: *How long will she have to suffer this pain?*

"Have you told Father about Kirin?" Aramon asked, releasing his mother.

"No," Ling admitted. She opened her eyes, and they were filled with infinite sadness. "I haven't seen Nahor yet—Ephraim and I were waylaid on our return. But you're right; I need to warn him before she crosses the border. That is one discussion I never wanted to have."

"Mother," Ephraim began hesitantly, "after Kirin's birth, when you were recaptured, how exactly were you treated? Does he know about her? *Is* she really...? Did he hurt you again? I'm sorry, but we need to know."

Ling sighed, rubbing the bridge of her nose with two fingers, an old, familiar habit. "Her heritage is foul, unfortunately for her. However, even he does not know her. Yet. I was treated well the second time, but under lock and key and threat of death. No, he did not lay with me a second time. However, he did destroy the Rashek guards that forced the *matiasma* into me and gave me to him. And the rest of his guards were threatened with the same fate if they harmed me."

"He confuses me, *Mai*. And how do you know so much about him, what he will or will not do in different battle situations?"

"You both know that I was once human and that Nahor changed me into an elf before we were married through the conversion spell. How much do you know of my life as a human?"

"Not much," Ephraim admitted.

"No, not much," Aramon echoed.

"When I was young, I had a friend, the prince of the Light Dragons."

"Kanna?" Aramon guessed.

"Kanna's son, Malakieth."

"Malakieth? You jest. Surely not him. He's a monster."

"But he wasn't always." She sighed, looking wearied. "It's late, the sun is setting. Let us make camp for the night, and I will tell you my story in the Common Tongue. No need to make Assumptshun work harder to translate what I'm saying."

"Thank you, my queen."

Ling nodded, her blue eyes widening a bit at Assumptshun's response.

When they had all sat down a little ways off from the bodies and Assumptshun had started a fire, Ling began.

LING'S STORY

I was ten when I met him. I had often dreamed of meeting a dragon face-to-face and was thrilled to find that he could speak the Common Tongue. We soon became fast friends, so close, in fact, that for my fourteenth birthday he took me to his home, Candescere, the capitol of Allerion.

"Look at it, little Ling," he said proudly. "Isn't it beautiful? Someday I will be its king. It is a big responsibility. I always fear that I will fail my people." He hung his great head, dark-blue eyes troubled.

"You won't fail, Malakieth. You'll be a wonderful king. I just know it. As long as you put your people before yourself," I told him.

"My thanks. I can fly you in if you want."

I hesitated. "I'm not certain that I want to be a dragon rider."

He laughed. "No, you can't be. You're a girl. Girls are never dragon riders. What's more, I'm the prince. We don't bond. Why, just last week you gave me a hug. If you were destined to be a rider, you would have gotten the dragon mark the first time you touched me."

"Oh, in that case…" And I scrambled clumsily onto his back. The thrill of flying was something I knew I would always remember. The sense of his power flowed through me as I clung, half-terrified, half-amazed to his neck, for, of course, he wore no saddle.

We soon landed at the palace, which was even more spectacular up close than it was from a distance. The other dragons stared in shock at the small human clinging to the prince's neck, but Malakieth wasn't bothered.

A quiet chuckle sounded from above me. I started badly, looking around wildly for the culprit.

And that's when I first saw him. A man sat calmly in a nearby tree, the afternoon sun filtering down through the trees making him appear green. Then I realized that his tunic *was* green and his pants and shirt were cream-colored, a quiver and bow strapped to his back. His blond, chin-length hair was pulled back, and he had a wry smile on his lips. His eyes were blue, I thought, but it was hard to see, for he was up so high.

"Hello! Why do you laugh, sir?" I called to him.

With inhuman grace and balance, he jumped from the tree, landing softly on his feet a few yards away. "Don't scream," he warned. Then he cocked his head and grinned mischievously. "You kissed a dragon. That's so … disgusting."

I frowned. "Firstly, he kissed me. Secondly, who are you? And thirdly, what are you?" I asked, chagrin in my voice.

"That's only slightly better. My name is Nahor, and I am the prince of Ellasar," the elf—for he was an elf—answered. I gasped, and his grin widened.

Malakieth had often told about elves, how they were not to be trusted, how they were cruel, how they hunted humans for sport, and such. This man didn't seem like anything my friend had told me. Then again, the dragons and the elves had never really gotten along. Perhaps Malakieth was merely prejudiced.

I curtsied. "It's a pleasure to meet you, Prince Nahor."

"No titles, my lady," he corrected as if second nature.

I nodded and examined him closer. He was tall, a full foot and an inch taller than my five-foot-six frame, though I was still growing. He looked only sixteen, though I had no clue how old he really was. He was a beautiful creature.

He moved a bit closer, stopping a foot away, perfectly at ease. It was now easier for me to see more details, like how incredibly strong he looked. Being an elf, he could have lifted my brother's plow horse and thrown the poor creature several yards if he felt like it.

As I was examining him, so he too examined me.

"Do I scare you?" he asked softly, curiosity burning in his velvet voice.

"No." I knew I should be scared, but I wasn't. Fascinated, but not scared.

"What is your name, then, my lady?" As a prince, he treated me, a human nobody that he had seen a dragon kiss, with great respect.

"Ling."

"How old are you, Ling?"

"I turned fourteen today," I answered.

"Happy birthday, then."

"How old are you, Nahor?" He grinned when I said his name.

"Three hundred and forty-eight."

"You look sixteen," I pointed out and then blushed. "My apologies."

He laughed. "Don't fret." He offered me his arm, and I took it, thrilled. I found that simply being close to him made me feel better about today. We began to walk toward my brother's house, but at an angle so that it would take more time. "So, Ling, who is the dragon?"

"My friend, I believe. Prince Malakieth of Allerion."

"Son of Kanna?"

I nodded.

"He kissed you," he mused. "How do you feel about that? You looked confused." He studied my face. "Or perhaps upset. I'm sorry. I'm merely curious. I mean no offense," he said quickly.

"Both," I answered shyly, not offended in the least. "I think he loves me, but I don't feel the same way. Now what am I to do?" I sighed.

"Tell him," he suggested. "Say that you simply want to be friends, nothing more. If he doesn't go for that, tell him that there's someone else. Then he would have to back down."

"Are princes supposed to scheme?" I asked. He grinned at me again, his blue eyes warm. "Well, you do a good job at it. Thank you very much," I added.

"I can see why he likes you. You're amusing, you speak your mind, and you're rather pretty … for a human," he teased. I rolled my eyes, completely forgetting that he was a prince and I was a commoner. He laughed at me.

Nearly eleven months passed since the day I met Nahor. We had met many times, often in the woods, but he would accompany me to the nearby human town occasionally. I retained my friendship with Malakieth, though every now and then he would forget himself and kiss me, and I tried to remain friends with Nahor. But I found that as the days went by, I would look forward to his visits, and when he was gone, I would constantly think about him. Eventually I realized I was in love with the prince of the immortal elves.

It became harder for me to see him, for as I reached my fifteenth birthday, my brother began to invite the town's young men over to supper in hopes of my falling in love. I still hadn't told him about Nahor and my feelings toward him. None of my brother's guests impressed me; to me, Nahor seemed better than all of them put together.

A week after my birthday, I went out into the woods to meet with Nahor, who had seemed like he was mulling over something complicated the last time we had met, three weeks prior. I had resolved to ask him about it. As I was nearly at the meadow where we always met, one of the townsmen, Juab, stepped out of the shadows. He had tried to kiss me several times before, but having a dragon fall in love with one teaches one how to shove a man away.

Juab. I despised him. He was nineteen, unmarried still, but he already had three different sons from three different women. He was cruel, heartless, and cold. I couldn't fathom what my brother was thinking when he invited him to our house.

Fear swept through me.

"Who told you to come here?" I questioned, keeping my voice cold.

"No one. I followed you." He grinned meanly and advanced. Terrified now, I back into a tree.

Malakieth, Nahor, anyone, please help me, I pleaded silently. Juab had reached me by now, and I closed my eyes, knowing what he would do to me. He fingered the neckline of my dress before covering my mouth with his, kissing me roughly as he began to untie the front of my gown.

Juab suddenly released me, falling to the ground with a choking cry. My eyes were still tightly closed, and I trembled all over, nearly hyperventilating.

There was no noise, but suddenly someone's hand caressed my face. "Don't be afraid. I am here. Nothing will harm you," my savior whispered. I stumbled into his embrace, endeavoring not to cry. I could feel his bow pressed against my back, his heartbeat against my cheek. He suddenly shifted, bent down, picked me up, and began to walk off into the woods. My fears were swept away with his smooth stride. After ten minutes, I felt his muscles tense, and I gripped him tighter, my face still buried against his chest. He tightened his hold on me and leapt straight up. After several times, he stopped.

I felt him lower himself down and lean back. His hand crept to cover my eyes.

"Don't scream," he warned me, the same as he had the first time we met.

"Have I ever?" I returned.

He laughed and let me see. I gasped and lost my balance.

"You're ridiculous. And beautiful; that's what got you into trouble in the first place," he murmured, catching me easily. He carefully repositioned me, cradling me against his chest.

We were sitting in a tree that overlooked a shining lake bordered by pine trees.

"Hmm." He exhaled, the tip of his nose gliding along my cheekbone. His warm breath stirred my hair. "Are you well?"

"Yes," I breathed, entranced.

"Then I have a favor to ask of you, Ling. If it's not too much trouble, could you please retie your dress? You're lovely, and I'd rather not be tempted."

I gasped again and did what he asked, turning crimson in the process. "I'd completely forgotten!"

"Too scared after I killed that bastard?" His tone was light and playful as he fiddled with a lock of my hair.

"Too excited to see you, Nahor," I answered, cringing at his choice of words. Then, realizing what I had said, I exclaimed, "Not fair; no mind games!"

"I don't have to. You always tell me everything I want to know." He sighed, serious again, and tucked the lock behind my ear. "I talked with your brother."

This surprised me. "I thought that you didn't want him to know about you," I reminded him. I was also shocked that my brother had never mentioned this. Or perhaps he had, and I hadn't been paying attention.

"Things change," he shrugged. Then he calmly asked, "May I court you?"

I gasped and whirled around, trying to see his face. Instead, I nearly fell out of the tree again. Nahor caught me and then gently pulled me onto his lap so that I sat sideways.

"Are you jesting? But I'm human!"

"But you don't have to be," he told me quietly. "I can give you immortality as an elf; there's a spell I've learned about. It's said to be difficult, but I am sure that I could perform it."

I pressed my forehead and nose against his, closing my eyes. "I would love that," I breathed. His hand caught mine; he slid a thin silver ring into place on my right hand. His fingers glided against mine. I slowly gave him my ring and then caressed his captured hand for a few seconds. He gradually freed his hand from mine, only to braid both of his into my hair, pulling me close. Eagerly, my lips met his.

When I turned sixteen, Nahor proposed, and three months later we were married. As he said, he had fallen in love with a human and was marrying a "newborn" elf.

"Little had I known that while I was courting your father, Malakieth, heartbroken, had met and befriended Morgan. She corrupted him," Ling said, ending her story.

"Seems as if they fell in love, from what I've heard," Aramon commented.

"Morgan doesn't love; she lusts," Ephraim pointed out.

"Ephraim is right; she does not feel love, but she understands it and uses it against people. Be thankful she is dead," Ling replied, her voice sharp.

"Yes."

"Were you tracking Kirin, *Mai*?" Ephraim asked, changing the subject.

"Yes. But the trail ends and begins here."

Aramon's eyes glowed blue as he expanded his senses, blinding himself to the natural world, the present time. It was his own personal skill: the ability to see the way Spirits and other beings had moved in the past and present. After a few minutes, he said, "The Rashek was killed by Callian, the Spiriter by Lord Trig of Giladeth." He used the full title for his mother's sake.

Ephraim whistled. "The humans are impressive."

"But not before the Spiriter attacked Kirin," Aramon continued, his voice hollow, trance-like. "I see Kirin go down, barely alive. Callian picks her up ... and walks inland with Trig. Tiamat flies off with Beau." His eyes reverted to normal. He swore. "I do not like that she is traveling with two men and is unconscious and injured. If one of them does any harm to her, I will personally turn him inside out," he snarled, reverting to his native tongue.

"The trail is not dead, then, *Mai*. We go to inland, and Aramon looks for the trail. You might wish to ride with him, though," Ephraim suggested, ignoring his younger brother.

Aramon whistled a few notes, and Elindil came trotting over, chewing his last mouthful of the short, tough grass that grew sporadically along the shore. Aramon lifted Ling up onto the saddle before leaping up himself. She entwined her hands in the stallion's long, white mane and leaned forward, silently urging her son's horse faster over the rough ground, terrified as to what her former friend would do to her daughter.

ISHMAEL'S CRYSTAL

Callian yanked Canath back out of the Chimera's heart and chest, looking for Kirin. She lay still, too still, in a pool of blood. A huge gash was rent across her body, the wound pulsing in the same sickly green slime of the Chimera's claws.

Poison.

Kneeling beside her, he reached for his magic. It was not unlike pulling the water from his clothing, but Callian still found himself panicking as he drew the venom from her wound, worried that it had already seeped into her bloodstream, that he was too late. Suddenly, he felt her hand brush against his cheekbone.

"Just heal it. There's no more poison," she whispered weakly.

He ran both hands down the gaping wound, pushing his magic into her. He watched in relief as the wound closed, the rush of Kirin's lifeblood stemmed.

He lifted her to her feet, holding her steady until she found her balance again.

"If I'm remembering correctly," she said softly, "Chimera are hoarding creatures."

"So we should try to find its den? What if it has a mate?"

She shook her head. "They tend to be loners—there wouldn't be a mate in residence."

Slowly, they made their way through the tunnel from where the Chimera had emerged. It was short, and the cavern, once they reached it, was a sight to behold. Gold was piled everywhere, interspersed with the occasional precious gem and pieces made of steel, silver, and bronze, not to mention the myriad of skeletons from all manner of creatures. Kirin stopped and nudged a diadem with her toe, and Callian noticed for the first time that her feet were bare—she must have lost her boots as well.

"That's iridium," she told him, pointing to the diadem.

It was a dull, greyish metal that seemed a poor thing to make a crown out of until she nudged it. Rainbows raced across the surface. "It's lovely," he replied.

"And very difficult to work with, especially with the intricate filigree someone did here. All the same, wealth and beauty is dangerous in Amalay Kahelith. We would do best to leave this where it is."

He nodded. "I don't suppose you would know what this crystal is supposed to look like?"

She shook her head.

"At least the air is fresher in here." He knelt and began to search through one pile, grimacing at the skeleton of a slight human. "Woman or child?" he asked softly.

Kirin looked at it, her expression sad. "Likely a child."

"How did all these creatures even get in here?" he wondered out loud. "Even if they walked through the fire-wall and survived, the exit through the maze is too high to reach, and I can't imagine a child making it that far."

"The Chimera would have been able to withstand the heat and could have brought them in to … eat."

Callian sounded skeptical. "Through the fire-wall?"

Kirin shrugged helplessly.

There was a flash of movement over the treasure. Kirin spun and drew her sword with a speed that Callian wouldn't have thought possible. He rose, drawing his own blade, but nothing moved.

Kirin looked around, her heart pounding. She caught sight of the movement again, a rainbow of colors darting over a copper basin.

She glanced up and let out a laugh that was slightly hysterical from relief. "Callian, look up."

He obeyed and grinned, whistling low. "There's the answer to my questions."

High above them was a hole in the cavern's roof that opened up to give a view of the late-afternoon sky, large enough for the Chimera to drop down from. Caught on a bit of jagged rock, the crystal hung on a length of silver chain, catching the light.

"It can't really be that easy, can it?" he asked.

"As you pointed out before, there's the fire-wall, the maze, and the Chimera to get through. All the same..." She stepped up behind him and wrapped her arms around him, wings beating furiously at the air. He said nothing; there was no other way out of the caverns but through that hole, and there was no way he could get to it without her.

No words were needed. As they neared the hole, he reached out with his sword and passed the tip through the chain. It slipped free from the rock and hung from his blade.

The moment he was free of the hole, Kirin threw him forward. He landed hard and rolled, careful to keep from cutting himself or losing the crystal that could save Kirin.

The halfling felt her knees buckle the moment she tried to stand, and she ended up kneeling in the dirt only a few feet away from the edge of the hole, too weary to move. Callian pulled the crystal from his sword and sheathed the weapon. He felt no relief as he held the crystal in his palm—only a deep-seated anxiety that it wouldn't heal her. Under the soot and dirt on her face, he could see how pale she was. The lines of pain in her face seemed permanent.

Slowly, he closed the distance between them, feeling the aches in his own body. He wrapped his long arms around her waist, pulling her close to him, and tilted her chin up to kiss her. He was surprised to feel her trembling against him. Drawing back, he smoothed his palm against her hair, tangling his fingers in the ends where her plait stopped.

She met his eyes, and he nodded at the unspoken request. He lifted the pendant and dropped the chain around her neck. Her eyes closed as the crystal touched her skin under her shredded tunic.

He watched in wonder as her face relaxed, as a smile started to form over her lips. He breathed a prayer of relief, only to feel her arms tight around his neck, her melodic voice near his ear as she murmured foreign words. It took him a moment to realize that she was praying in Elvish.

Kirin was nearly falling asleep while walking as they made their way back to the ruins. Tiamat was taking the first shift, and Trig curled up with his back to the crumbled remains of a wall, his cloak tucked around himself. Beau lay down near Tiamat, who lay at alert between the Twilight Dragon and a pile of rubble, as if even in sleep he was going to protect his female. Trig couldn't help but smirk when he saw that his friend had the same mindset. Kirin was already asleep curled up against the prince, her head on his arm, his cloak covering them both.

As if sensing that he was being watched, Callian turned his head to face Trig and smiled. Trig felt himself smiling back. It had been so long since Callian had looked that happy.

He fell asleep, overjoyed that his closest friend was in love.

A soft, feminine gasp woke Trig up, and he looked about in the pre-dawn greyness to see what was attacking them. Beau lifted his head, blinking; his movement woke Tiamat up, who rubbed her cheek against Beau's neck before dropping back to rest her head on his outstretched forelegs, eyes starting to close again. Trig frowned, confused, and moved to rise.

Tiamat's eyes snapped open, suddenly alert, and Trig froze.

Someone's approaching, he heard Callian's voice murmur in his head. *Someone small. Of course, for once, Kirin was sleeping deeply and startled when I woke her.*

That explained the gasp.

Trig, leave now, as if you are either going to hunt or are abandoning us, then slip around to the west of the ruins and block our newest friend in.

Trig rose and slipped off, keeping to what shadows there were.

Callian drew his sword and placed his back to a ruined wall, motioning for Kirin to do the same. She obeyed, her green eyes alert, pulling the hood of her cloak up to hide her telltale blond hair. He was relieved to see that her skin had regained its color. Beau crouched by one side of an opening, Tiamat by the other. They waited, hardly daring to breathe.

Finally, the silence paid off. A twig snapped nearby. Then a bird took off. To the inexperienced eye, this was nothing. But to someone who has been raised to track and scout and hunt and fight, this meant that there was someone nearby. A few more minutes passed before a young boy dressed in solid black cautiously stepped forward. The dragons pounced. The boy drew a blade and cut Beau's foreleg before Tiamat pinned him to the ground. Callian leapt up beside Tiamat. Kirin ran to Beau and began to heal his wound—her magic had grown stronger with the healing of her spirit—while Callian began to ask questions.

"Who are you?"

"A human."

"What's your name?"

"I don't have one."

"Don't lie," he snarled, the tip of his sword at the boy's throat. Kirin could all too well imagine the blue fire burning in his eyes as he spoke.

"I'm not. We have no names because most have given up hope. And I tell you this because I know that you're not from around here, are you?"

Kirin turned in time to see the boy's cocky smirk.

"Who are you? Why did you follow us? What do you want?"

"I'm called Captain." The boy spoke with the confidence of someone who was in total control of everything. "I'm one of the Council of Five, the leaders of the Resistance. I know that you travel with the Adkisha. I'm looking for her. We need her help, and we can offer her relative safety and shelter."

"How do I know we can trust you?"

"You don't. You just have to take a chance. And your dragon is making it hard to breathe," he stated, scowling at the she-dragon.

"Let him up, Tiamat."

She growled and snapped her teeth by his ear to make her point, then slowly let him up. Kirin heard his gasp of breath as the pressure on his chest was lifted. Tiamat had been slowly crushing him.

"I am to lead the Adkisha and her friends to Dothan, the headquarters of the Resistance, to meet with the rest of the Council," he said, scrambling to his feet.

He immediately turned around and walked back the way he had come. Callian and Kirin exchanged glances, and then proceeded to follow their strange guide.

"Captain, where exactly is your headquarters located?"

"Dothan."

"Yes, I know, you already said that. But where is Dothan?"

"Where Malakieth can't find it."

"And that would be?"

"Underneath the Citadel. We're right under his nose, and he's been looking for us in Tal. Ha!"

"Yes, they'd love to find you, Captain, wouldn't they?" broke in a new voice.

"Who's that?" Kirin asked, a little nervous.

"Thief. He's a member of my band. You won't see him unless he wants you to. Thief is one of our inside men. He will, from time to time, infiltrate Malakieth's fortress and bring supplies and information back to Dothan. Thief is also another one of the Council of Five," Captain explained.

"Ah." She ceased looking for him as Beau stepped closer to her side. "How old is he?"

"Ten and a half," Thief answered from somewhere on her right. Beau's head whipped to the side, and he bared his teeth in a silent warning to the unseen boy.

"Come, let's go," said Captain.

They kept to the shadows, for they had entered the Citadel, a town close to the Black Fortress. The town, if you could call it that, was a wreck. Nearly all the buildings were falling apart. No one was in sight—no person, no dog, no cat, no bird. The only living things that they saw were herds of scrawny sheep, mainly ewes, but every now and then they would pass a ram.

They arrived in front of a beaten-up wooden door. Gingerly, Captain knocked on it, whispering, "Darkness is falling fast. Kindle your lamp, friend, and let the light fill the room."

This must have been a password, for a young girl opened the door. She had ice-blue eyes, and her flaming-red hair and tattered, dark-red outfit made her look like she was on fire. She bowed her head to Kirin and Callian before turning to glare at Captain.

"You're late, Captain. As are you, Thief. Oracle and Sage have been going *crazy* trying to locate you two. Black Two figured that Malakieth was holding you prisoner and was planning on storming the fortress to find you."

"Did he?"

"No. Red Two and I took him down and told the rest to wait."

"Good. Thank you, Red. Oh, Adkisha, this is Red." He motioned to the girl. Kirin wondered if she looked as ragged as Red did and decided that with the amount of tears in her tunic, Red likely looked better. "She's another one of the Council. And this is Thief."

Thief was a dark-haired boy who had appeared from behind them. He, too, was dressed in complete black. There was a hard look to his young face, but there was a hard look to all the faces of the Resistance fighters she had met so far.

Trig materialized behind Thief. "You're rather hard to follow," he said softly, making the smaller boy spin.

"This is our friend, Trig," Kirin told them. "He's rather handy with locks."

Trig smiled at the praise.

Red motioned them inside and led them to the back wall of the little run-down house where there was a small mat that served as a bed. She pushed it over to reveal the stone floor underneath. Bending over, she pried up one of the large stones to reveal a set of steep steps and a tunnel.

Beau, can you and Tiamat fit down there?

Just barely. I won't like it, though.

Captain led the way, followed by Callian and Tiamat, and then Thief and Trig, then by Kirin and Beau and finally by Red.

After half an hour or more, they finally came to a larger tunnel.

"Mount your dragons. You'll be safer—Malakieth and his Shadow Dragons do not have riders."

They did so, Trig walking between the two dragons, and proceeded down the tunnel again. Another quarter hour passed. Kirin grew annoyed with her hood and pushed it off, suffering the keen gaze of the three child-warriors. Finally they came to a large chamber. The chamber was huge and filled with about two hundred people. Children. Not one looked over eleven years. A young girl dressed in red and a young boy with a staff, dressed in green, stood before them. The girl spoke.

"I am called Oracle, for I have been gifted with the ability to see things in the future. I am one of the Council of Five."

"And I am Sage," said the boy. "For I know many things and legends. Welcome, Adkisha. Welcome, Prince Callian and Lord Trig of Giladeth. And welcome, Tiamat and Beau, to Dothan."

Callian spoke up. "Thank you. We are honored. But where are the adults? Surely there are some among you?"

"There are no adults," Thief said bitterly. Oracle took his hand. "None have found the courage to join us. They're all afraid of Malakieth. They no longer give names to their children, for they have lost all hope. They don't know if their children will live to see the next day, for Malakieth's men are cruel and murder for fun."

"How can we help? What can we do?"

"Fight for our freedom. Fight!"

"When do we attack?" Kirin asked, ever the soldier.

"Soon," Sage said. "But we must prepare first. Come; we have a room where you and your friends can stay. You are safe here; Malakieth can't find us."

"Thank you."

Kirin noticed Oracle looking at her, a sort of piercing stare. Kirin felt as if this ten-year-old girl knew something else, something that she was hiding. And Kirin was determined to figure it out. She also felt as if there was something about her that even Oracle didn't know.

"May I speak with you?" Kirin asked in an undertone, dismounting from Beau.

The girl nodded and withdrew a bit from the main body of people in the great cavern.

"Are you elven?"

"I am. I'm the only one here now," Oracle replied. "There's another elf who lives with us from time to time, but she's gone for the moment. The only other elf that we've seen was a prisoner we freed from the Black Fortress." She shook her head. "When Thief came back with the news that Malakieth had an elven prisoner, we could hardly believe it. We snuck into the prison and managed to free her. Heaven and hell, she was so furious at him. I don't know what he must have said or done to her, but she was livid. She said that the elves would never forgive him and that he hadn't seen the last of her. She said that he would never be rid of consequences of his actions. That it would come back to haunt him. It wasn't like he was there it hear it. Perhaps she merely needed to say it." She stopped, for Kirin had gone pale. "Is something wrong?"

"No."

Oracle cocked her head at her, considering her. "Aren't you part elf, Adishka?"

"Yes," said Kirin. "My mother is Queen Ling of Ellasar."

"You're royalty?"

Kirin nodded.

"Oracle! Oracle! Elves!" a boy's voice shouted.

"Thief! What in the worlds; don't scare me!"

"There are elves! Three of them! Two male, one female. And listen—one of the males is riding a Dark Dragon! The other male is on a white stallion, and the female is walking between them!"

Kirin grinned. "I know them!"

She ran out of Dothan on Thief's heels, Callian, Trig, the dragons, and Oracle following her. Finally, they reached the outside
world, though in a much different part from where they had entered
Dothan.

"Ephraim!" Kirin ran to her older brother and hugged him, her
wings lifting herself far enough off the ground to reach him on
Assumptshun's back. She hugged Aramon. Then she turned to Ling.

"It's so good to see you again! How did you find me?" she asked
as she embraced her mother.

"I've been here before," she said coldly.

But of course. Malakieth held her prisoner.

"Well, well, well. Look who we have here. It seems our stray bird
has wandered back home," said an even icier voice.

Kirin whipped around. A tall, dark-haired man stood before
her surrounded by fifteen, no twenty, no *thirty* strong-looking men.
These men were armed with thick, broad swords, thick and strong
enough to crack a man's skull like an egg. Stranger still was the slight
blue tone to their skin.

Callian, she mindspoke, *those are Rashek. Legends say that they are
ten times stronger than they look.*

"Malakieth!" Oracle hissed.

"That's Malakieth? I thought that Malakieth was a dragon," Callian whispered back.

"Older dragons can shape-shift into a human form."

"Oh." He spared a glance at Tiamat, speculative as to what she
would look like.

The man who had spoken wore loose, black pants and a tight,
black shirt that outlined the strength of his upper body. His dark
hair, blacker than the night, hung in his obsidian eyes. Malakieth
was tall, much taller than she was, taller than Callian even. He was
surprisingly attractive, except for his eyes. They were so cold, as if he
didn't care what happened as long as he got his way. He was standing
at ease, watching Ling with a slightly curious expression.

He noticed her staring at him and turned his gaze from Ling to Kirin. His face immediately hardened. Finally he spoke, directing his words to Ling.

"Who's the whelp?"

"I am Kirin, daughter of Ling," she said angrily. Too many times had she been called whelp.

"Ling's daughter, eh?" he sneered. "Another one of Nahor's brood?"

"She's not Nahor's daughter," Ling said, cold hatred obvious in her voice.

Malakieth grinned a familiar, sly grin. Callian froze, staring at him, at Kirin. It couldn't be…

"Ahh. I see. How awful. The queen of the elves was unfaithful. Thought that nothing would come of it, did you? How naïve." His voice was like poisoned honey.

"It's *you* that's naïve, Malakieth. *You* forced me. *You* thought that nothing would come of it!" she shrieked, starting toward him.

Kirin stared in shock and horror at the two of them. "You're my *father*?" she nearly screamed. Callian's hand crept to her shoulder. She wasn't sure if it was for reassurance or to hold her back from lunging at the dragon.

"*What*?" Malakieth's face mirrored hers.

"I'm afraid so, Kirin," answered Ling.

"So *that's* what you meant when we rescued you a half year ago," Oracle exclaimed.

Malakieth suddenly strode up to Ling, his face dark with anger.

"Why didn't you tell me?" he hissed furiously as he picked her up by the front of her shirt. He easily lifted her with one hand. No small wonder she hadn't been able to fight him off.

"I guess it simply slipped my mind." Sarcasm dripped like poison in her voice.

Assumptshun intervened, rescuing Ling before Malakieth could hurt her. Furious, Malakieth commanded his men to attack, then shifted back into his true form and left in a cloud of dust.

The Rashek were strong and skilled with their *hamakus*, the huge, thick, and slightly curved swords that they carried. As they closed in around the small group, Kirin realized this was going to be a short battle. Still, she tensed, holding her crude sword at bay.

I'm not going down without a fight.

That's the spirit, little dracling.

Beau, do you think we stand any chance of winning?

Anything's possible, Kirin. Never forget that.

I won't.

Look out!

An arrow streaked passed her and sunk deep into one of the blue-skinned men's throats. He made a choking sound and fell like a log. Another arrow hissed through the air, then another and another. Four more Rashek fell to the hidden archer's skill.

The attackers rushed, swords raised. Kirin steadied herself for the onslaught, but the first blow still sent her flying. She hit the ground hard, landing on one of her sensitive wings. She cried out as she felt it break. She gathered her strength and struggled back onto her feet. Her sword too far away for her to get to it, she unleashed her magic.

The Rashek directly in front of her dropped dead.

Brilliant! she thought savagely.

Half savage with fury and pain, she held out her left hand, palm facing away from her. The spiral marking on her arm and hand glowed with the power. She lashed out with her magic again. Another sickening crack sounded, and another Rashek died, his neck broken on a rock.

Trig leapt into the fight, knives flashing. He and Callian dispatched three more, fighting back to back as Tiamat ripped through seven. There was a flash of flame as Beau sent four more of the evil creatures to a dragon's version of hell. Assumptshun was airborne, breathing fire as Ephraim shot two more of the creatures with one arrow. Aramon, Oracle, and their mysterious friend killed the remaining six.

The battle over, Kirin sank to her knees amidst the amplified pain in her wings. More damage had been done than she had originally thought. Her left wing was not only broken but cut up as well.

Her right wing also sported a few cuts—and any injury to a dragon's wings was dangerous.

She saw Trig standing against Tiamat's flank, a wicked-looking cut on his forearm. Thief was trying to make sure Oracle wasn't hurt too badly. Satisfied, they disappeared into the hidden entrance to Dothan.

Oracle looks just like Ling, she thought thickly.

Aramon, Callian, and Ephraim were scouting the area, making sure they were safe. Callian seemed to think something was wrong. He called something, but Kirin's hearing had deserted her.

Callian.

Kirin collapsed on the ground. Dimly, she was aware of Callian and Beau running over to her, of them calling her name, and of Callian's strong arms lifting her up before she passed out.

She awoke in a dimly lit room. Vaguely, she was aware of someone lying next to her.

"What is happening?" she asked groggily, closing her eyes again. Even the dim light was too bright for her.

"She's awake," one voice said.

"Hallelujah!" cried a second, definitely feminine.

"Praise Adonai," said a third.

"You were injured, Adkisha, and you fainted. Callian carried you off the battlefield and took you here. He used all the magic he could to save you," the first voice explained.

"But don't worry; he is well. Merely tired," said the third voice. Aramon's voice.

"Aramon?" she asked.

"I'm here, little sister. And Callian is beside you."

"Where am I?"

"Dothan, *kihara*," Ephraim answered.

"You need sleep, my daughter. Afterwards we will talk." Ling sighed. "We have much to talk about."

"But for now, sleep, little *kihara*," Ephraim said gently, touching her forehead with one finger. She sank happily back into the darkness.

"So this is the Adkisha. She's younger than I thought. I saw her out on that battlefield yesterday, and I thought that she was at least eighteen," a female's voice said quietly.

"So you were the archer!" That was Ephraim. "You have skill. What is your name, lady?"

"Elfan. Don't laugh."

"Daughter of elves," Ephraim translated softly. "It's a very nice name. You are Ellasarian?"

"Yes. What is your name?"

"Ephraim, firstborn son of Lord Nahor, king of the elves. My dragon is Assumptshun."

"You're lucky to have him," Elfan murmured.

"My father doesn't know about him. He's not going to like the fact that his son is a dragon rider." He sighed.

They were silent for a moment before Ephraim spoke again, his voice gentle as he tried not to offend her. "Who are your parents, Lady Elfan?"

"I've never known any. I'm an orphan—I wandered around the countryside of Ellasar. A blizzard came up, and I fell or wandered or stumbled or what you will through a rift to Amalay Kahelith. I ended up in a nasty scrape with a bunch of Rashek and a few Shadow Dragons a couple years ago. The Resistance got me out of it, and I've been helping them ever since."

"Do you miss Ellasar?" They sounded like they were standing rather close to each other.

"It's been over five hundred years since I was last there—so no, I don't miss it because I can't honestly remember it," she answered indifferently.

"You can't be that old, then, if you can't remember the past five hundred years," Ephraim mused. Did Elfan catch the same note of sadness in his voice that Kirin did?

"I don't know. Perhaps six hundred. I haven't honestly bothered to remember that, either." She sighed and then whispered, "How old are you?"

"Three thousand one hundred and eighty-three." They were silent for a few minutes, and Kirin thought that they had left.

"Do you know how old Oracle is? Do you know her real name? There aren't any elves on Amalay Kahelith, so where did she come from?" Ephraim asked presently. All right, so perhaps they were still there.

"She's only ten, perhaps ten and a half. She must have come from the world of Kyria, I guess. But I don't know where in Kyria, and I don't know her real name. I'm sorry."

"That's fine." Ephraim said something else, but Kirin had fallen back asleep.

She awoke again to find someone gently stroking her hair, his fingertips brushing up against her pointed ear. Slowly, she opened her eyes to find Callian lying beside her.

Praise Adonai you're all right, Callian whispered in her mind.

It's good to see you, too. I heard that you saved me again. Thank you, she replied, her eyes intense, burning into his.

You used powerful magic out there on the battlefield. Ephraim said now that you can do it, he needs to teach you to control it and use it for fighting. He said he and Aramon should have taught you how to fight with magic from the beginning instead of just healing small wounds and "other minor things." He said you had better heal all the way so he can beat you up better when he trains you. Aramon said you need a better sword. That one you have now is too crude for your skill. I think you need a really nice Ellasarian sword.

That would be nice. How long have you been awake?

Nearly a quarter-hour. But no one knows that yet, he told her cheerfully.

So when did they say all that?

After you fainted. Before I did. Ephraim was annoyed at Aramon, but he was rather stressed.

Are you all right?

Yes, as long as you are.

She smiled at his words. He leaned in slowly and kissed her.

"So you two are awake."

They jolted apart, causing Thief to laugh.

"Don't worry; I won't tell anyone. Didn't mean to scare you. Oh, and the queen wants to talk with you, Adkisha. And then the elder prince wants to train you to fight with magic." He was sitting on an alcove above their heads.

"May I watch?" Callian asked, trying to keep his voice impartial.

"Sure, if you'd like to see me knocked around." Kirin sighed.

"No objections here." He grinned at her, unknowingly making her heart react violently. Callian climbed off the pallet on the cave floor and helped her up. "Can you stand?"

"Yes, I think so. How long was I asleep?"

"A few days. By the way, your clothes are over there. Queen Ling took them off you to try to heal your wings and back. She bandaged you up before they let any man into the room, so don't worry about that," Thief explained, spinning around to face the wall.

"Oh, thanks," she muttered, embarrassed and turning pink.

She quickly dressed, noticing Callian was still dressed like he had been in the Fire Caves. He was still covered in soot and grime, but at least his burns had been healed.

By Adonai, is he handsome! she thought and then rapidly glanced at his face to make sure she hadn't accidentally mindspoken that to him. It didn't look like she had, but she could never be certain with Callian.

Callian tried not to stare at her. She was beautiful, even covered in bandages. One wing was tied tightly to her body, supporting it as the bones mended.

Ephraim keeps calling you kihara, he said, mindspeaking.

She smiled. *Technically, it's Dragons' Tongue for "dragon," but both Beau and Ephraim are using it as an endearment.*

She left the room swiftly, blushing, leaving Callian to talk with Thief.

"So you're in love with the Adkisha?"

"Yes, and don't jest."

"I won't. How did you do it?"

"Do what?"

"Fall in love. Get her to fall in love with you."

"Oh, that. It just sort of happens. You can't control it. And you can't force someone to fall in love with you. Sometimes it happens; sometimes it doesn't. This is the first time for me." He paused, giving the younger boy a sideways glance. "You're a rather friendly boy, Thief. I have a feeling that whoever it is you like may have feelings for you too."

"Ha! Unlikely," he muttered, glancing away.

"So I thought, but Kirin loves me. Just be yourself. So who is she?" he prodded.

"Promise not to tell anyone?"

"I won't if you don't."

"Oracle."

"I can understand why you like her." He flashed the younger boy a quick smile. "Good luck."

He left the room looking for Aramon and Trig.

"So it's true then? I truly am the daughter of Malakieth?" Kirin asked, heartbroken. She had hoped that her father wasn't quite that objectionable.

"Yes, unfortunately, it is true," Ling murmured, taking her daughter's hand. "Yes, he did attack me. And yes, I did conceive. Thankfully, I escaped your father's prison about the time I realized that I was pregnant. I can't tell you who gave me help on the inside for fear that would put her in terrible danger. For several months, I roamed the countryside of Kyria, on the outskirts of Ellasar, ashamed that I carried Malakieth's child. Far too ashamed to travel back to Ellasar and to my husband. When I gave birth to you, I realized that Malakieth had discovered where I was. I had taken with me the only weapon that could have destroyed him, a powerful sword. I gave you to a Light Dragon, who took you to Candescere. I ran, trying to put as much distance between her and myself. Unfortunately, in the attempt to get you to safety, I had to hide the sword away, and I no longer have access to it."

"Oh." Kirin struggled to break the awkward silence between them. "I...I'm almost completely fluent in both Elvish and Dragons' Tongue. But there are always new words to learn or new meanings of a word," she said, touching on a safer subject.

Ling smiled, giving her hand a squeeze. "It is one the attributes of the dragons, the gift of tongues. I am glad that you have inherited it. It is an advantageous skill to have."

Kirin frowned suddenly, remembering the recent skirmish. "There are times when magic simply...comes to me. Where it's instinctive."

"It is a blessing that comes with the power of the Adkish," Ling explained.

"Oh. That's...strange."

"True enough, but it can happen." She released Kirin's hand. "Now, Ephraim has been beating himself up for not teaching you to fight with magic, so go humor him."

Kirin rose. "Thank you for explaining...my father to me."

Ling nodded.

Kirin leaned over to kiss her mother's cheek, surprising Ling, and then turned and jogged down one of the many tunnels to find her half brother.

"Try again."

"I *am* trying, Ephraim," she said testily. She was tired of his snapping at her. She was tired of this stupid magic that wouldn't work.

She was tired of not understanding. And she was tired of the pain from her broken wing, which had been bound tightly to her back and was throwing her balance off-center.

"Then try harder," he replied tersely.

"I'm doing my best!"

"If you were, then that blade would fly. Try harder!"

Kirin reached for her magic for what seemed to be the hundredth time, and again it slipped through her fingers.

Why won't this bloody work? she snarled to herself.

As her anger burned, she felt the power stir within her. She didn't focus on making her crude sword fly; she was too interested in the magic she now felt.

This, she decided, *is wonderful.*

Time, whispered a new voice, a female voice.

Kirin blinked, surprised but not upset by the invasion of a new voice in her mind. She could feel Beau responding, listening curiously to the faint voice. *Who are you?* Kirin asked her.

Time…

Time for what?

Time… is… soon… coming. The last remnant of the voice drifted through her mind. *Tonight…*

In her confusion, the huge wave of magic that had built up was released. A burst of white flame wrapped itself into the shape of a tall, slender dragon. In her shock, the image burst into a thousand sparks that shot everywhere. Many shot off an invisible shield that Ephraim immediately threw up to protect himself. Callian, who had walked into the training room just in time to see the dragon image, was not as fortunate. The wild magic shot straight for him. He threw his arms up to protect his face and cried out as the power Kirin had accidentally unleashed smashed into him, searing his right arm and throwing him backward.

Kirin rushed over to him, tears steaming down her face. He lay unmoving on the floor.

"Callian! Callian! I'm so sorry. I didn't mean to. I lost control. I'm sorry. I'm so sorry! Are you all right?" she sobbed.

She knelt by him, taking his hand in hers.

"I'm fine; no worries," he grunted, sitting up and shaking his head to clear it. "My arm's merely singed. It will heal."

"This is what I mean, Kirin!" Ephraim roared. "You need to learn self-control! You have more raw power than anyone ought to. You need to control it! You're lucky he's not dead! You could have killed him. You have the potential to do a lot of good but also a lot of harm! Do you understand me, Kirin?"

He grabbed her arm, forcing her to look him in the face. The fire he saw in her slotted eyes disturbed him. Pointing her left palm at him, she thrust outward.

Ephraim was blasted backward and rolled to break the fall. He was surprised at the power of her blow; she had barely been able to lift a sword before. Now she had just thrown him, a highly trained elven rider, across the large room.

Kirin turned back to Callian. He, too, saw the raw, uncontrollable power behind her eyes.

"Please calm down, Kirin," he whispered soothingly.

Tears still streaming down her face, she placed her left hand gingerly on his scorched arm, choking back another sob as he winced.

All my fault...

Her eyes met his, green burning into blue. Almost silently, she whispered to him in Elvish, "*Amo forsu senokani a zei.*" I offer healing to you.

A bright, blue-white glow wrapped itself around her hand and his wound. A strange new sensation spread over both of them as their eyes locked. It was as if time was standing still yet moving far too fast, as if they weren't really anywhere in particular, as if they were *between* worlds... or between times. A strange feeling of bliss, almost as if nothing mattered, yet all was important. A sort of floating feeling. It was indescribable. Then, as abruptly as it had started, it ended. Kirin felt her right hand entwined with his left. Her left hand rested on his arm where the wound had been. The huge scorch mark was gone.

She felt exhausted, but she still slipped an arm around his back and helped him to his feet.

"I'm so sorry," she whispered again. "I didn't mean to."

"I know. Don't worry about it. But Ephraim might be mad."

"Mad?" the elf cut in, both brows rising. "I've been trying for an hour to get her to make a blade levitate. She says she can't, and then she causes a seeing—and that hasn't happened in a long time—and then throws me across the room and heals you. And she's still moving. That's more than basic magic. To overpower an elven rider and then completely heal another rider and still be conscious is outstanding."

"So you're not mad at me?" Kirin ventured. *Why is it that men never make any sense?*

"No, you did what I wanted you to do—certainly not as I had expected, but you still did it." He shook his head, starting to smile. "I wish Ling had been here to see that. Callian, did you see the vision she conjured up?"

"Yes. But what does it mean?"

"In truth, I haven't the faintest idea. This has never happened in my time. Kirin, did you hear something when that happened? A voice, anything?"

"Yes," she admitted warily. *Will he think I am insane?*

"What did it say?" he asked.

"'Time is soon coming.' And then it said, 'Tonight,' and disappeared. That's all."

Ephraim frowned. "That's strange. It has to mean something."

"I think that something big is going to happen tonight. I don't know what, but I think that's what the vision meant," Callian spoke up. His thumb rubbed soothing circles over Kirin's fingers, his free hand rising subconsciously to rest on the hilt of his hunting knife.

"I think you're right," Kirin replied. Her fingers tightened around her love's.

"I'll go talk with Ling, Aramon, and the Council. In the meantime, Kirin, you look exhausted and rightly so. You should get some rest. As should you, Callian. I shall see you anon." With that being said, he walked off, leaving Kirin and Callian to talk and look confused.

Eventually they went back to the room they were sharing with Trig and the dragons—one of the few big enough to hold a few dragons—and Callian fell asleep. Kirin, however, was unable to sleep and passed the time reading one the books she had taken with her from the Masters' Library: *Raising Dragons*.

Three hours later, after she had finished the book, Kirin dozed fitfully, her dreams strange and twisted, centered around the young dragon from her vision.

Kirin jolted awake, disturbed and confused by the strange dream.

Dragon?

And then it hit her. The reason for the vision, the purpose of the dream.

Dragon! Hatchling! The egg!

She snatched up the bag where she had kept the Light Dragon egg Beau had found. Looking inside, she found the egg emitting a faint, barely discernable glow in the darkness of the room. Almost frantically, she struggled to recall everything she had read about hatching a dragon's egg.

Light Dragons hatch on the night of a full moon. But how to hatch it? she wondered nervously.

Carefully, she slipped out of the narrow pallet, careful not to disturb Callian, and danced around the tails and limbs of the two sleeping dragons. Trig slept curled in a corner out of the way, fingers curled loosely around the hilt of a curved knife. She spared a thought to wonder where he had learned the habit and why.

Pausing at the door to the hall, she turned and looked back.

Beau, she called softly.

He woke up immediately, looking up at her.

I think the dracling is ready to hatch.

Without reply, he started to untangle himself from his mate. Tiamat roused, as if she was about to wake, and he froze, glancing between her and his rider.

How do I hatch it, Beau?

It should break free by itself. I—

You wish to remain here? she guessed.

He watched her with his golden eyes. *I will follow you in your mind through our bond. I will come if you need me.*

Thank you.

She crept down the tunnel to the cave the Resistance fighters called Dragon Nest. It was a large, circular room. The ceiling was twice as tall as it was wide. A single shelf hung out about fifty feet up the shear wall. No one could climb to it; you would need wings, which Kirin had. She placed the strap of the bag in her mouth as well as in her hands before removing the bandages that bound her wing and taking flight, wincing as her healing bones bore the strain of her weight. It took her less than a minute to reach the shelf, but it was a minute of a burning agony.

And now we wait.

And now we wait, Beau agreed.

Kirin took the egg gingerly out of the bag and lay down with it. She curled herself around it carefully, laying on her side and wrapping her good wing over herself like a dome. Softly, she sang to the hatchling, sang whatever song or bit of melody came into her mind, humming when she couldn't recall the lyrics. She thought briefly about waking Callian up to come and see the hatching but decided against it. This was a private occasion, something only she and Beau would bear witness to. She loved him and knew he would want to see this, but she also knew he shouldn't be there.

It took perhaps a quarter-hour for her to hear the scratching sounds. She sat up and rolled the egg onto her lap. It was glowing brighter than it had before. Looking carefully over the surface, she finally found the crack, running the length of the two-foot-long egg.

Crack! Another deep crack was rent across the smooth, cool surface of the egg. Another, then another followed this crack, until the baby dragon was able to pierce a hole the size of Kirin's fist. The whole egg shook violently until, finally, it exploded, sending shards flying everywhere. Kirin was too concerned with the newborn's safety to notice the shallow cut that ran along her cheekbone. In her mind, Beau sighed with relief.

She's a beauty, the Twilight Dragon breathed.

The newborn looked at Kirin and crawled into her lap. She set to work cleaning the baby off with the edge of her tunic. With a fierce rush of joy and pride, she realized this dracling had chosen her to not only be her future rider but also her surrogate mother. And Kirin knew she could never let any harm come to this baby.

But will I be able to provide for my dragon? Will the hatchling really be safe in my hands? Obviously, she had a lot of enemies.

And the answer came from the baby. Not in words but in a strong feeling of protection.

Do you have a name, she mindspoke to the hatchling, *or is that my job?*

The baby just looked at her, waiting. Naming the dracling was Kirin's task.

Beau? Any ideas?

I find the one you are thinking of to be an acceptable name for an Allerion.

Kirin smiled, stroking the baby. "Your name will be Xzylya."

Content with her name, Xzylya fell asleep curled up in Kirin's lap to the sound of a half-remembered lullaby. But Kirin stayed awake all night, too happy to sleep, sharing the dracling's first moments of life with Beau.

Kirin gently spiraled down off the shelf, hugging Xzylya tightly to her chest. The newborn clung to her adopted mother, looking down at the ground. Callian and Tiamat would be the first to know of her hatching. Kirin might need Tiamat's help caring for the baby. There was no other way she could think of getting aid if the hatchling needed dragon's milk; although, it wasn't like Tiamat had nested recently.

Kirin ran lightly down the tunnel back to her room, the hatchling bouncing along at her heels like an energetic puppy, tripping occasionally as she tried to figure out how to move her legs. She was about the right size, too—for an adolescent wolf. As Kirin approached the doorway to the shared room, she slowed down, asking Xzylya to do the same. Xzylya obeyed and slunk off to hide in the deeper shadows.

Wait here for me, Xzylya.

She walked through the doorway. Callian was still asleep, though he was frowning as if he slept fitfully. But Tiamat was awake, so was Beau.

Where were you? the female snapped accusingly.

Busy. Let me wake Callian up. Then I have something to show all of you.

She crossed the stone floor silently. Stopping by the prince's pallet, she leaned over and kissed him gently.

"It is a nice way to wake up," he murmured softly.

"Come with me. I want to show you something."

"All right, I'm coming."

He still had no shirt on. Kirin led the three of them to the doorway, trying not to blush. Callian was rather attractive, and it was a sort of handsomeness that made her stomach flip, as if she were plummeting through the air.

"What's happening?" Trig groaned from his corner.

Kirin turned to smile at him. "Get up. I have something to show everyone."

He yawned and stretched and stood up, hunting around for his shirt.

"Wait here." She left the room, returning a few seconds later with Xzylya in her arms.

The looks on their faces were amazing. Tiamat and Callian mirrored each other's shock. Trig arched both of his brows but remained silent.

That's a Light Dragon, Adkisha! How...? By all of Ashteroth's power, I never thought I'd ever see one!

Kirin thought it better to explain out loud. "Beau found her egg before he was captured and imprisoned. When he realized he was being followed, he hid the egg away. We slipped away from the campsite one night to go recover it, but we weren't sure if the dracling was still alive. For pride's sake, we kept it a secret. But obviously, the young is healthy; she hatched last night."

A girl?

"Yes, Tiamat. A girl. Her name is Xzylya."

So that's *what you were doing last night!*

"Yes, that was where I was this past night."

"Does the name mean anything?" Callian mused. Xzylya swung her head to stare at him when he spoke, and he gave her a warm smile, his blue eyes soft.

Kirin glanced at Beau before answering. "As far as I'm aware, there's no exact translation from Dragons' Tongue into the Common Tongue, but it's something like 'blessed light' or 'hopeful light.'"

His smile grew broader. "It's a fair name."

Suddenly, a bell rang, assembling the Resistance fighters. Something was wrong. Running, the five soon arrived at the meeting hall. It was already filled with fighters. Nervous in the crowd, Xzylya bumped into Kirin's legs, nearly tripping her. Kirin stooped and picked the dracling up, humming into her mind as if she were mind-speaking to her. The Resistance stared; those closest reached out with wondering fingers to lightly caress the newborn dragon, who soaked up the attention.

"Her name is Xzylya." Kirin shrugged.

At the sound of a gong being struck, the Resistance fighters turned their attention back to the front of the cave, to where Captain was tossing aside the small log he had used to hit a worn shield propped against the wall. Trig shook his head, but Kirin could see the faint smile lifting his cheek.

Oracle stood up, looking pale. Thief rose to stand behind her, his young face hard, one hand resting on her thin shoulder as if for reassurance. Rushes cast their dancing shadows around the room, making the cave seem eerie.

"I've had a vision," she said softly. Even soft, her voice carried over the graveyard-hush of the small crowd.

Kirin looked around for her family and saw them standing in a knot near the back of the crowd. Ling's face was worried; her sons, flanking her, both looked grim, arms crossed. Elfan stood by Eprhaim's shoulder.

"We need to cave in the northeastern tunnels, the ones that lead to Tre, within five days, or the Rashek will get inside Dothan. We also need to start stockpiling supplies—food, water, wood, and anything else we can get our hands on without being noticed." She turned to a small, skinny girl with tangled, brown hair. "Cook, how much food do we have?"

Cook grimaced. "Not much, Oracle. Barely any. Two, three days worth at most."

Oracle nodded as if she was thinking, planning.

Ephraim watched the elven girl.

You wear that same expression, Mai, *when you are deep in thought,* he mindspoke to Ling. *It's... eerie.*

Ling frowned at Oracle, watching her closely.

Oracle looked at Red. "Will you and Captain lead a small group to go scavenge for supplies?"

Red nodded, Captain striding out of the shadows to stand by her side. Together, in low voices, they gathered five from each of their bands and headed into one of the tunnels.

"Sage, I'd like you to oversee the Tre tunnel deconstruction. Brown One, Yellow One, and Blue One are to help him. All three of your bands are to get started as soon as possible. Runners will be sent to you with supplies. I want a portion of Black and a portion of Red to go and guard them, just in case my timing isn't accurate. The rest will stay here and guard Dothan itself. Thief and I are going to go into the Citadel to seek information. Malakieth is too quiet for my liking, especially after learning that the Adkisha and Queen Ling are in the vicinity." She turned to the group of elves, one brow raised, asking a silent question.

Ephraim spoke up. "Ling will remain here. If anyone is wounded, bring them to her. My brother and I will help with the collapse of the tunnels."

"I'm going above to check my traps and see if I can't catch some game to bring back," Elfan said, slinging her quiver across her back. Oracle nodded, and Elfan was gone in a moment.

"And Callian and I will go and help in the tunnels," Kirin said.

Oracle shook her head. "Adkisha, I would rather you and Xzylya and Beau stay here. You're wounded, and Xzylya is just a baby. I would like Beau to remain here in case something does happen so that you are protected. You carry the hope of too many people for us to risk your safety, especially when you are still recovering."

Kirin's mouth tightened in annoyance, but she nodded.

"Callian, Tiamat, and I will still go," Trig said.

Oracle nodded. "Thank you. And now, we go."

And the group dispersed to their various tasks.

The Resistance was amazing. The more time Kirin spent with them, the more she liked them. She got to know those who had titles. She watched them, trying to think of legitimate names for them. There were definitely cliques; certain people would always be together. Thief and Oracle. Captain and Red. Sage and a girl who called herself Cook, who were more like brother and sister. Sage was always teaching Cook different bits of information.

Certain things became obvious. The Resistance could not exist without Sage or Oracle—the only ones who could read. Thief and his apprentice brought in most of the food. Elfan hunted for them.

The different bands seemed to be separated by personality. The Red Band was fiery; the Black Band was tough, quick, and deadly; the Green Band was intelligent and strategic; Blue was caring but could be fierce; Brown didn't kill unless absolutely necessary; and Yellow was an optimistic bunch. The Black and Red Bands were, as Kirin pointed out, sexist. The Black Band held only males, while the Red Band was the opposite.

Callian was now quite fluent in Dragons' Tongue, enabling the two to speak out loud without fear of being overheard.

Every day, Ling and her sons trained Kirin and Callian in magic. Kirin soon became an unstoppable fighting force, though no one told her that. The thing that truly unnerved everyone was when a lone Rashek actually managed to find a way into Dothan. Kirin simply looked him in the eyes, thought about it, and broke his mind. He killed himself in confusion fifteen minutes later. She withdrew into herself... silent, shocked, unwilling to talk or laugh for the remainder of the day. Her eyes took on a haunted look.

"Kirin?" Callian asked softly, tapping on the door to their shared room. When there was no reply, he slowly pushed the door open. She was half-sitting, half-lying on the floor, leaning up against Beau with Xzylya on her lap. "Kirin, you really should come and enjoy yourself. Did you know Thief can imitate nearly any voice? Tiamat's thrilled, and I really think you should come hear him do it."

She didn't reply, choosing instead to stare blankly at the floor and methodically stroke the baby dragon. Callian sighed and came to sit beside her, careful not to lean against either of the two dragons. He wrapped his arm around her, and she turned to unresponsive stone. He blinked, surprised; she hadn't done that since they had first met.

"Do you want me to leave?" he asked quietly.

She shook her head no but remained stiff beside him. Callian caught a lock of her hair with his free hand, twirling it around his fingers.

"What's wrong, princess?" he murmured.

"I'm too *dangerous*," she groaned; her voice cracked. "Every time I lose control, someone gets hurt. And half the time it's you, Callian. How can I live with myself if I kill you?" She took a deep breath, fighting back tears.

He squeezed her thin shoulders. "To me, you have always seemed like the epitome of light, of purity and love and goodness. And I knew, somehow, from the moment I met you that whoever married you, whether me or Trig, a dragon or a Dragon Knight, or even some stranger, that person would be so blessed..." He trailed off when he realized she was in tears. He pulled her to him, comforting her, and kissed her jawline. "Do not fear yourself," he whispered against her skin before kissing her lips until she was so dizzy the walls spun. The spiral mark on her left arm began to glow faintly.

When he broke away, she smiled at him. "Thank you," she whispered.

TAKEN

Kirin leapt up when Callian, along with Tiamat, Trig, and a large portion of the Resistance, came back to the center of Dothan, running to embrace him. Trig walked by them, clasping Callian on the shoulder. "Aramon looks like he's considering stabbing you. I would suggest that you release his sister before he acts on that impulse."

Callian let her go, shooting Aramon a grimace. The elf purposely touched the hilt of his knife before turning away to greet his mother.

Kirin sighed, looking around at the Resistance. "No child should be forced to live like this. I was sewing for them, but it's only a small help."

"Better than nothing," Callian murmured. Kirin stooped and picked Xzylya up, who nipped at her testily.

Stop that, she scolded. *I know that you are hungry. I'm doing the best that I can.*

Beau rose and licked the dracling's cheek as he and Tiamat headed off to Dragon Nest to rest. Kirin and Callian walked back through a tunnel to their room, hand in hand. Trig was absent, but there were signs he had been in there recently; he was likely washing in the Suk River, which dropped at the town Suk, named after the river, to flow underground. In fact, it was by swimming in that river and by being sucked down in a strong current underground that the Council of Five had discovered Dothan. Kirin could only imagine the fear that Oracle must have felt five years ago when she had been pulled under water.

Trig came back into the room, his hair dripping down his neck, dressed in cleaner clothes than the ones he had been wearing, though they were still black. In this hand were his old clothes, soaking wet from being scrubbed clean. He hung them over a wooden stick to dry. Callian disappeared down the hallway to clean up. He met Ephraim by the entryway to the river's tunnel and lifted one hand in greeting. The elf offered him a faint smile.

"Aramon is already inside. Neither of us will have any qualms about it if you don't."

Callian shook his head. "In times of battle, I've bathed with my troops."

Ephraim's smile grew wry. "The Ellasarian women will sometimes fight as archers. If we're out on a march and we come across water, we'll water the horses first and then withdraw to allow the women to bathe." He bent and pulled off his boots. Callian pulled his belt and hunting knife free and set them aside. "After they're done, we bathe, and then everyone washes the horses."

They waded into the cold water with their clothes on. "You all seem to have a great love for your horses."

Aramon looked over. "You've seen Elindil. Ellasarian horses are far superior to any other horses. Without exception."

"No pride there," he remarked wryly.

Aramon flashed a rakish smile, hanging his cleaned clothes up on a rickety wooden rack that someone in the Resistance had made. He grabbed a small piece of a moss-like plant the elves had brought in with them and began to scrub himself down. "The Ellasarian horses are faster. They are a different breed entirely—nearly a different species. I catch them and tame them and train them—"

"His horses are the most coveted in the land," Ephraim interjected.

"And if they decide to accept someone as their rider permanently, it will last forever."

"Forever?" Callian grinned, stripping off his clothes. The water was waist-high, but even so, none of them were looking at each other, and none of them cared. Getting clean felt too good. "As in immortality? Are your horses immortal?"

"We have something that we can give them that stops them from aging. An elixir. It's expensive, but worth it to keep a warrior from having to train a new horse every ten to twenty years."

Callian focused on the elves, no longer joking. "You can make horses immortal?"

Aramon nodded, slipping under the water to rinse clean. Callian turned to Ephraim.

"Could you make a human immortal?" he asked in a low voice.

Ephraim's face was grim. "There was an elven lord once who fell in love with a human woman. She was from southern Kyria—a beauty with sun-darkened skin. He was mad for her and poor with magic. He sought to make her immortal through the elixir and appealed to the elven sages—elves who walked the worlds since the beginning, since time immemorial. They told him plainly that the elixir wouldn't work on a human, that he would regret it. He ignored their warnings, took the elixir, and gave it to her." He shook his head. "She was dead by morning, the elixir working like poison in her body. It wasn't an easy death."

Aramon resurfaced. "Lord Eximere?"

Ephraim nodded.

"Poor girl," he commented, climbing out of the water. He dried off quickly and left without another word.

Callian and Ephraim followed him out, Ephraim wringing out his blond hair. Callian pulled the water off of himself with his magic—it barely required any thought now—and dressed, drying his first set of clothes in a similar manner. Ephraim watched him.

"Don't mind my brother overmuch."

"He's not fond of me," Callian replied, "which only bothers me because I love his sister."

Ephraim gave him a half-smile. "Try to understand, young prince. Aramon and I have already lost one sister."

Callian frowned at him.

"We had a younger sister, the Princess Terah, my father's only daughter. She would be a little over a hundred years old now. She was out playing; we were all out on a day's ride. She must have stumbled through—or was pulled through—a gateway. My father was the first to realize that anything was wrong, but we were too late to make it through the gateway. We searched for her; the sages searched for her. But it was useless. She was never found." His eyes, suddenly so ancient, met Callian's. "She was four." He looked away again, pulling on a clean shirt. "Now, only months ago, Aramon and I find ourselves with another sister. We don't care that she was bastard-born, that Malakieth is her sire. She is our sister, and we'll protect her zealously." He met Callian's eyes again, features stern. "Be careful with her, Prince Callian. Be very careful, lest you harm her and anger Ellasar's princes."

Callian met his gaze evenly. "I would never dream of it."

They gathered up their belongings in silence, listening to the sound of approaching footsteps, the low murmur of female voices. Kirin, Ling, Red, and Cook entered the river tunnel, Xzylya close behind them. Kirin smiled at them as the two males left to give them privacy.

"Ephraim, may I ask you something personal?"

The elf nodded.

"Have you ever loved?"

The elf flashed him a mischievous smile and walked away.

Trig rolled onto his back when Callian walked through the doorway. Callian folded his cleaned clothes and put them away in his saddlebag.

"Almost makes a man miss Castle Haven," Trig commented.

Callian looked at him. "I like being useful here."

"It's the same for me," he replied. "But I would still love to sit in the Great Hall with the soldiers and eat as much food as I could without it dulling my wits."

Callian nodded, picking up a small piece of wood and fiddling with it. "Can you imagine what these poor children would do at a meal like that?"

"Make themselves sick, most likely."

"True. Still, I would love to be able to build a bonfire down here in Dothan and roast a boar for them."

"They'd all have burnt tongues and burnt fingers."

"And full stomachs. It's a shame there's no natural sunlight here, or I would start a garden for them."

Trig chuckled. "Flowers, Callian? You?"

Callian tossed the wood at his friend. "No, stupid. Corn. Wheat. Carrots. Potatoes. Onions. Something that they could grow to feed themselves. I can't even begin to imagine how many they lose to starvation each winter. It isn't right that this war should fall on the shoulders of children."

Trig fingered a faded scar on his left arm, an old knife wound. "Things happen, Callian. You can't stop them all, even with magic and a dragon."

Callian scowled, lying down on the pallet. "A poor king I'd be if I didn't at least try."

Trig looked over at him. "A poor king you'd be if you didn't realize when certain things were out of your power and let them go."

Callian twisted to face him, eyes narrowed. "So what? I'm supposed to not even attempt to take action?"

Trig met his anger coolly. "You can't protect everyone, my friend. You're just one man."

Callian turned away.

"If you protect her too much, she'll pull away from you. You know that. You know her better than I."

Callian was silent for so long that Trig gave up on a reply. "I can't merely sit idly and watch her continuously put herself in harm's way."

"She's the awaited hero," Trig said gently. "That's her destiny. She's been trained to fight all her life. She's brave."

Callian gave a hollow laugh. "You sound like you're half in love with her."

Trig shook his head. "No. I'm in love with the idea that *you're* in love with her. But she's too ... *headstrong* isn't the right word. Brash, perhaps?"

The prince finally smiled. "I like that about her. I like the fact that I can cross blades with her and not have to worry about harming her."

"I never thought that a man would find that attractive," Kirin commented with a wry smile, walking into the room with her clean clothes in her arms. She wore pants and a tough linen tunic that left her arms bare, her sword belt around her waist. The blade lay in its scabbard near the pallet with her bow and quiver on top of her pack and the satchel that had once held Xzylya's egg, but her knife hung in reach of her left arm.

Callian looked at her, the blood rising to faintly color his face. "How long have you been listening?"

She shook her head. "I was merely walking back. I have good hearing." She turned to Trig, trying to suppress a smile. "Headstrong?"

"Brash."

She couldn't hide her smile. "I've been called worse." She crouched beside her pack, storing her clothes, belt, and knife. Callian slid over on the pallet to make room for her, pulling the thin blanket back. She lay down beside him, and he covered her, tucking her in close beside him and stroking her wings. Her eyes closed in bliss.

"Trig?" she murmured. "How did you get that scar? The one on your arm?"

Trig stared at the ceiling, frowning. His fingers traced the line on his skin again. "Did Callian ever tell you that I have a twin sister?"

"No," she replied, turning to look at Callian. His blue eyes were hard.

"Her name is Teresa. Callian was supposed to marry her, but he left Giladeth to help you."

"It was an arranged marriage," Callian said softly in her ear. "I can't stand her, and was considering leaving even before I was told to come protect you. Not to mention that she's tried to kill Trig."

"More than once," Trig muttered.

"Pardon?" she gasped.

"She tried more than once." Trig's expression became sad for a moment before his nonchalance slid back into place. With a jolt, Kirin finally realized that both Trig and Callian had been taught to completely conceal their emotions, to hide everything with cool indifference. No small wonder Callian's emotions could be so confusing at times. "About nine times, actually." He fingered the scar again, as if he were remembering its creation. "This was the proverbial last straw," he continued dispassionately. "The ninth time she tried, she actually managed to give me a decent wound. My father, of course, turned a blind eye, just as he had done every other time. She was obviously his favorite, and they both knew it, and they both knew that I knew. A pity for both of them that I was born an hour and twenty-seven minutes before her.

"She looks like a colder version of my mother, who died a few years ago due to an illness. The same raven-colored hair, the same dark eyes, and the same body build. There is no doubt in anyone's mind that she is beautiful...just like my mother before her. But my mother was a loving person; she would put everyone else before herself. When the epidemic came around, both my mother and I caught it. She took care of me, hurting her own chances of survival. She died, but she saved me in the process. Even to this day, my father blames me for her death.

"My sister reminds him of her. But as I said, there are...differences. After she gave me this wound," he said, once more touching the scar on his arm, "I left. I left my father's estate and went to my closest friends. I went to Haven. Callian and Gannon—a knight who is Callian's mentor and friend, and at times the closest thing either of us have to a real father—gave me a room, and I lived there, training to be a knight. After two years, I took my place as one of Callian's knights."

"Yes," the prince interrupted quietly. "All four of them."

Trig smiled briefly, but his smile soon faded as he continued. "Teresa is...power-hungry. She wants to rule. At first, she would have settled for my father's estate, but...I am still amongst the living. I have little doubt that once I am dead, my father will soon follow. Then Teresa will have the power she craves.

"But will that be enough for her? After committing two murders—both of them the only family she has—will she settle simply for a large estate? Most likely not. Teresa wants to be...queen.

Therefore, she wants Callian. Callian, Sir Gannon, and I know the reasons behind her apparent desires. She has convinced the court that she is in love with Callian, and my father thinks that she wants him as a husband. And what Teresa wants, Teresa usually gets.

"It is our fear that if she were to marry Callian, he would be found dead not long after. And then what? Giladeth would have an evil and cruel queen. I would leave, go into hiding, if I was still alive by then. I have no doubt that I would be the next to die. But I would always be trying to take Teresa out of power.

"You can understand why we dislike her?" he asked, shooting Kirin a sideways glance, his face emotionless.

"Yes," Kirin agreed. "And so you have worn nothing but black since that day you left your home, and you have been taught not to show emotion, and you simply laugh off anything that might make you upset. Along with anything you find remotely funny," she added, her voice quieting again.

Trig was silent for a few minutes. "You are...observant," he finally said. Kirin took that as a confirmation.

Callian stroked her hair. She rolled over and snuggled in against him. In the silence, they listened as Trig and Xzylya's breathing evened out in sleep. Callian pulled away far enough to see her face, her green eyes as she looked over her shoulder at him.

Kirin eyed him speculatively. *You, also, seem to control your feelings very well,* she noted.

I could say the same about you, he replied, his words whispering through her mind. He gave her a roguish glance, suddenly flipping her over to face him. *I wonder how far that control goes,* he mused, lifting one hand from where it rested on her side to brush her hair away from her face.

Her heart hammered in her throat, her blood pulsing quick and hot.

Then swiftly, but so very gently, his mouth was on hers. Her lips parted, and her breath came in an unsteady gasp. She crushed herself to him, her fingers knotted in his hair. This was better than flying.

Leisurely, he drew back, kissing her once … twice … three times. He smiled, opening his eyes slowly. Kirin grinned breathlessly back, her eyes shining with exhilaration.

Not very far, he teased.

Not when you overwhelm me like that, she answered, looking slightly dazed. Callian pulled her close, crushing her once again to his body, her head tucked against his shoulder as he listened to the sounds in the room. The older dragons were curled tightly together, awake but talking silently amongst themselves. Xzylya and Trig were still asleep.

Am I truly that good at kissing? he asked, his smile turning teasing.

You're good at everything, she accused playfully.

He shrugged around her, tightened his arms, and pressed his face into her hair. *You look like an angel. How am I supposed to behave myself?* He brushed his lips along her jaw from her ear to her chin and back again. His fingers trailed gently up the side of her throat, making her shiver in delight; he tilted her chin up and kissed her lips lightly one more time before drawing back. He groaned softly; his expression tortured. *I've waited too long to ask you—I've wanted to ask you almost since I met you. I love you, Kirin.* Her stomach did little flips; her heart was racing far too fast. He paused slightly before asking, *May I court you?*

Drawing back the blanket so that she could see, he offered her a thin silver ring. She inhaled sharply, her heart singing. There were a thousand different things she wanted to say, but none of them seemed right.

With another dazed smile, she took the ring he proffered her and slipped it onto the fourth finger of her right hand—the right hand for courtship, the left for engagement and marriage. She, in turn, rolled out of his arms to rifle through her satchel for a leather thong with a pouch, palming its contents. Sliding back into his embrace, she handed him a silver ring. All girls carried a silver ring with them if they weren't already with someone, usually on a chain or thong around their neck. She was pleasantly surprised that the tradition was held even in Giladeth, on the other side of the world of Kyria, a country with no connections to hers or to Ellasar. This one was thicker than the one she had been given. It had been made of three silver wires, braided and welded together.

He took it gently from her hand and put it on. She flushed slightly as his fingertips brushed against her palm. He caught her eye and grinned in the darkness, that grin that made her heart accelerate, his eyes shining like sapphires.

Callian bent his head to kiss her one more time.

Elfan slipped through the shadows, silent save for the whispering of her borrowed cloak in the wind. She paused for a moment, her back to the flimsy wall of an outlying farmhouse, and tugged the hood up farther over her head, trying to hide her face. The wind swirled the dust and dead leaves around her fraying boots, tugging on the long hem of the cloak. She frowned at it, at the dirt of the land sullying the beautiful fabric of the prince's cloak. It was a shame to have to bring it back to Prince Ephraim dirty, but he had been adamant that she wear it. And she was grateful to him for it. It was still early spring here, and the temperature would drop quickly once the sun finished setting. The wind itself would have chilled her within a quarter hour as it blew through her threadbare clothing. It was only a matter of time before her hands would be too cold to draw an arrow to the string with any sort of accuracy.

She waited until the clouds blew across the waning moons before slipping from the side of the building into the wasteland. She hadn't been able to find the tracks of an animal—none seemed to be about. Her prospects grim, she set off to check her traps. The first five traps she checked were empty, of course. Another had caught a snake, which seemed to have died of starvation. Under a dead-fall, she caught sight of a smashed ball of mangy brown fur—most likely a mouse. She eased the trap off the flattened creature and reset it. Sentimentality urged her to dig a small hole and bury the poor thing; reason pointed out grimly that bigger animals were more likely to come near the trap if there was a greater prospective of something for them to eat.

The final trap she checked was a pit fall that had taken her months to dig. Even from several yards away in the darkness, she could see the debris that usually covered the pit had been broken through by something large. She hurried to the edge, her spirits lifting.

Furious red eyes glared up at her, the massive creature pacing in the tight space. Horrified, Elfan stared down at the were-beast. She'd never seen one up close before. It was so … huge. Certainly not the size of Prince Ephraim's Dark Dragon, but it was close to Prince Aramon's lovely stallion. It was a bulky creature, covered in mangy gray-brown fur.

What was she to do with it? True, it had enough meat on it to fill the stomachs of the Resistance, but were-beasts, as a species, had been created by Nishron's magic and were trained to kill by means of the same magic. How tainted was its body, its flesh? How ill would it make the poor human children that hid in Dothan?

The creature snarled madly at her as she knocked an arrow to the string. Throwing its head back—giving her a prime target that she failed to notice—it howled a long, blood-curdling cry. Far off, yet not far enough to make her feel safe, the members of its pack howled back.

It took her four arrows fired through the beast's skull before it finally died. She didn't bother to remove it from her pit but turned around and fled.

She ran for a solid half-hour, going in random directions as fast as she could before she heard the drumbeat pounding of large paws striking the ground. The pack was behind her and gaining. She ran on, refusing to let despair take over. The beasts may kill her, but they were going to have to work hard for their meal.

There was a flash of what could only be fire to her left, and she bit back a scream, changing course again. The area was unfamiliar to her in the darkness, and she ran blindly, trying to stay ahead of the pack and now trying to dodge this unseen enemy.

Fire flashed to her right, coming closer to her. She put her head down and pushed herself for more speed. Again, fire flashed to the left and slightly behind her, and she realized belatedly that this enemy was herding her. The pack sounded slightly farther behind her. But what was the creature—or creatures—herding her toward? The Black Fortress?

The answer came when it was too late to do anything, to stop, to slow down. With a silent scream, Elfan hurtled off the sheer face of a cliff.

Kirin strapped her bow and quiver to her back, between her wings. Her sword already hung from her hip, her knife tucked into her belt.

Callian came into the room, Trig by his side. Kirin arched a brow at their hunting gear, at Trig sharpening one of his knives on a whetstone.

"Tiamat would like to join you and Beau," Callian explained.

Tiamat entered the room, shooting Beau a glare. *It didn't cross your mind to tell me you were going hunting?*

Beau sighed. *I was going to bring you something back.*

And yet you bring the dracling with you.

Xzylya needs the moonlight as much as she needs water and food.

These chambers are small, and the tunnels twist. Dothan was not meant for dragons. I need space to run. I'm going hunting with you.

"We should probably go now," Kirin pointed out, "before we lose too much more of the night." She scooped up Xzylya and cradled the dracling in her arms. Xzylya's front claws wrapped around her shoulder, biting into her skin.

Together, the group left Dothan to go hunting.

The moons were slim, almost new. Still, Xzylya's eyes fixed on them as they slipped through the barren landscape, looking for game. This whole world looked destroyed.

They had no luck. With only a few hours before dawn, they turned around and made their way back toward Dothan. Xzylya was the only one who wasn't disheartened by the night's failure; she bounded along beside them, chasing insects and bits of debris the wind blew about. She was too young to talk yet—though she was growing at an alarming rate to catch up with her older rider, much the same way that Tiamat had grown to catch up to Callian—but her happiness flowed through the bond into Kirin, making her smile faintly. Xzylya eventually managed to cheer everyone up with her antics. She dove at Tiamat, only to dodge Tiamat's swipe, and then pounced on Beau's tail. He growled at her in warning.

Suddenly, Xzylya froze in her tracks, head up and nostrils flared to catch the wind. Kirin stopped and strung her bow, knocking an arrow to the string as Beau stepped over the dracling in a protective crouch.

The beasts melted out of the darkness and circled in around them, snarling. They were about shoulder-high with mangy brown and black fur and feral, red eyes. Long, jagged, yellow teeth were bared as they growled.

Were-beasts, Beau supplied. *Some of Morgan's creations. They'll go after Trig and Callian first; they'll like the taste of humans.*

Sure enough, one of the beasts grew tired of waiting and leapt at Callian. She released her arrow. It flew straight, through the left eye and into the brain, killing the beast before it could complete the jump. The rest of the pack attacked. The fight was bloody and loud, the air rent with snarls and animalistic screams. One of the beasts caught her from the side, throwing her to the ground. She flung her hands up, calling on her fire magic and charring its foreleg. It roared in pain and snapped at her face, only to have Beau pull it off her and fling it into a tree.

The biggest of the pack launched itself at Tiamat's shoulder, taking her down to the ground and tearing into her foreleg. She cried out, Callian echoing her pain. Trig flung himself in front of his friend, his knife laying open the throat of another were-beast that had reared up to attack Callian.

Tiamat struggled to rise and couldn't. Callian threw his bow down beside his dragon and drew his sword to defend her.

"I think," Trig panted as he warded one off with his knives, "that I like...the Northerners better. They're still...psychotic...but they...go down easier."

"They were once werewolves," Kirin replied. Another one leapt at her, aiming for her throat. She ducked and thrust her blade skyward, gutting the thing. Black blood splattered her. "Legend says that Morgan—" she ducked again as Beau caught one with his teeth and claws and wrenched the thing in half. Her stomach twisted; she swallowed. "—tortured captured werewolves and mutated them with spells to get the were-beasts."

"Morgan's an evil sorceress," Callian added through his teeth, bracing himself as one of the beasts charged him.

It changed course at last minute, slamming into Trig. Kirin cried out in fear as the human's head smashed into the ground, jerking her hunting knife free and throwing it. Her aim was true; the knife buried itself in the creature's throat, killing it.

Callian screamed her name. She spun, sword already up to defend herself. Something hit her head hard, her vision dissolved into starbursts, and she knew no more.

Something grabbed Elfan out of the air, knocking the breath out of her. She clamped her lips together to keep from screaming; she wouldn't give her captor the pleasure.

Slowly, so the creature wouldn't drop her, she craned her neck to see what held her. It could only be a dragon.

The creature's other foreleg carefully wrapped around her, lifting her to hold her against his breast, against his heavy heartbeat and warm scales.

"Are you all right?" he rumbled quietly.

She looked up to see him peering down at her as he flew.

"Assumptshun?" she guessed. Her voice was small and hoarse, breathy.

"Who else?"

She didn't reply, only wrapped her free arm around his forefoot and buried her face against him.

"You're crying," he noted softly.

"I'm sorry."

"There's no need to apologize, elfling." He banked, and Elfan was suddenly glad she couldn't see the ground spin beneath her. "Hold still. I'm taking you back where you belong."

"Hold your breath," he warned only moments before he covered her completely, and they plunged into water.

When he resurfaced and let her see, they were inside Dothan by the Suk River. The dragon released her, she stumbled, and Ephraim caught her, lifting her up out of the water. The elven prince carried her to a room, and she wept into his shirt.

Kirin woke up to darkness and a horrible headache. Sitting up slowly, she was gripped by vertigo. She cradled her hands together to hold a flame.

None came.

Frowning, she reached out for her magic again. It was like running into a wall. Fear crept down her spine. She had no magic here. How was that even possible?

She forced her nerves to settle. She had lived fifteen years with her magic bound. She could handle this.

She looked around her but was completely blind. Raising her hand in front of her face, she touched her nose and then wiggled her fingers. Nothing.

Nervous again, she reached up to touch the back of her head, wincing at the dried blood and the large lump from where she had been hit. Had it blinded her?

She reached out with both hands. Her right hand hit warm scales. She pulled her legs up close to her body only to feel something warm and solid tumble to the ground. She heard a gasp as one of her companions woke up, felt fear trickle through the bond.

Xzylya?

Recognition joined the fear. Relief flowed through Kirin, warming her. At least she had found her dracling.

Xzylya, smell me out. I'm right next to you.

The dracling hit her foot. Kirin felt the pricks of her claws as the baby climbed up her leg and curled up on her lap. Bending, Kirin kissed the top of her head.

Holding the dracling with her left arm, she patted the dragon lying beside her.

Yes? Beau asked. His mental voice was groggy.

Wake up. Can you see?

She heard him lift his head. *No. Is that your hand I feel?*

Yes.

She both felt and heard him rise and turn around. Another dragon, presumably Tiamat, came awake with a snarl.

It's me, she heard Beau tell her.

I'm blind.

I know. As are Kirin and myself.

It's so bloody dark, Kirin complained. *And where are Callian and Trig? Are you two all right?*

I am fine, Beau said.

My shoulder is wounded, but the bleeding seems to have slowed significantly, Tiamat noted.

Beau lay down beside Kirin, licking Xzylya. Tiamat half-limped, half-drug herself over, lying pressed up against Beau. Kirin placed the dracling in their midst, turning herself on her hands and knees to search for the two humans.

She found one, and—after making sure he was still breathing—grabbed a fistful of his tunic and drug him back to the knot of dragons before running her hands up and down his body.

Callian, she heaved a sigh of relief. *He's uninjured; he was probably hit in the head like I was.*

How can you tell who it is by touch? Beau asked. Tiamat leaned over to sniff her rider.

That's Callian, the Fire Dragon confirmed.

Because he's wearing my ring, Beau.

Kirin touched Callian's shoulder, shaking him. "Callian," she whispered. "Callian, love, wake up."

He moaned softly, eyelids fluttering under her fingertips. She lifted his head into her lap, rubbing his arm. "Wake up," she demanded.

"Go away," he muttered back, rolling over.

"Wake. Up." Her fingers bit into his shoulder, wrenching him awake.

"What?" he snapped. He winced and rubbed his head. "What in the worlds hit me?"

"That's a good question," she whispered, pitching her voice low. "Did you see what hit me?"

He shoved himself upright. "I can't see a thing." Kirin touched his face and felt him turn toward her. "It was some sort of creature—possibly Nephilim. I didn't see it very clearly, but it was male. Tall, broad-shouldered, black hair, pale skin … I doubt it was human. Can you see?"

"None of us can. We're in some sort of cell. It must be enchanted or something because it's blocking my magic. Beau, Tiamat, and Xzylya are here with us. I haven't found Trig."

She felt Callian frown. "With any luck, he'll be all right and free to return to your family and the Resistance. He's rather good at getting himself out of scrapes. Tiamat, do you have any idea of where we are?"

No.

Most likely the Black Fortress, Beau answered.

"Tiamat is the only one injured, other than where you and I were hit," Kirin murmured to Callian. "The dragons would have been much easier to subdue once we were—"

She froze, listening. Outside in the direction she took to be the door, two men were talking, their voices growing stronger as they approached.

"My lord, we tried to keep him ignorant."

"You failed miserably," a harsh voice snapped.

"He was Morgan's apprentice. Her castle is his in her absence," the first man replied. He sounded respectful, submissive, and terrified, a subordinate.

The second man snorted in contempt. "Morgan only wanted him because she found him attractive and because he was a prince and, therefore, in a prime position to overthrow his country. He's too weak to truly lead. And you ... you are a hair's breadth from death. Your incompetence is aggravating."

"I most humbly apologize, Lord Sisera."

"I told you quite plainly to *put the others in a different cell from the wench*. I would have thought that even your simple mind could understand that. Clearly, I overestimated your abilities."

"The princeling had magic, my lord. He is a dragon rider. I feared that if I put him in an unguarded cell that he would break free."

He's right, of course, Callian mindspoke to Kirin. Kirin managed a weak smile.

It makes me nervous that this Sisera would want to single me out in a cell that blocks my magic.

Beau's snarl was deafening as it echoed in her mind.

"Your job isn't to think; it's to obey! Forgetting that will get you killed." He broke off. "Well, well, well ... the dragon comes already. What is it about our newest guests that makes him hurry, I wonder?" He raised his voice. "Lord Malakieth! What brings you here?"

"Tales of you neglecting to alert me of the latest additions to my castle," Malakieth rumbled. Callian covered Kirin's mouth with his hand in an attempt to discourage her from yelling at her sire. "It must have merely slipped your mind in all the excitement," the dragon continued silkily. "Although, frankly, I didn't think that you were capable of the feat. Capturing the Adkisha and her company? How extraordinary."

"As you can see," Sisera bit out, "I have her and her magic well contained. And I bid you remember my bloodlines, *my lord*."

Malakieth sounded bored. "I don't care whether or not the Lord Cathas is your grandfather—and I doubt that he does either." He

"A position of slaves. A high position, as it were. And that, dear prince, is all that you need to know about it and all that I will tell you."

"Will you tell me who your master is, then?"

She offered him a sardonic smile. "You are charming, prince. That's a rare thing around here. As is the love you have for the Adkisha. And I have to say, I'm rather flattered by your charm—many of the males here simply resort to brute force." She reached into her bag for a jar of salve, smearing it over the wound. "Malakieth is my master." She packed up her bag and rose. "Lady dragon, I would advise you to keep off that leg as much as possible until you're healed. The medicine will keep it numb for a few hours. It's the best I can do for the moment." She moved to the door, taking her lantern with her. "Good luck, Prince Callian. And the little dragon is adorable."

She shut the door firmly behind her, leaving them alone in the darkness.

"I have to say," Callian remarked softly to her, "at least the last time we were locked in a cell together, there was a hint of light. I'm not fond of this darkness." He paused as he felt Kirin's hand trace his face. Lifting his hands from Tiamat, he reached for her, cradling her face to kiss her.

Elfan fell asleep in Ephraim's arms, exhausted. She awoke not long after in a room that was not her own, listening to the sound of breathing too slow to be any of the children's. Lifting her head, she peered into the darkness.

A small flame was lit with a soft noise, a candle piercing the darkness. The tiny light danced over a strong jaw; prominent cheekbones; straight, honey-blond hair; and tired blue eyes. Prince Ephraim watched her.

He raised one finger to his lips to keep her quiet and then mindspoke to her. It was strange to hear a man's voice in her mind; mindspeaking was not a trait common amongst the elves, though it was a normal skill for a rider to possess.

Ling and Aramon are asleep.

She nodded and carefully made her way over to sit beside him. He took her hand in his, splaying her fingers and stroking them absently.

"Will you thank Assumptshun for me?" she asked, her voice barely audible so as not to wake his family.

A smile tugged on his mouth. *He's here in my mind. He's listening.*

"Oh." She paused, trying to wrap her mind around the idea of two bodies sharing the same mind, no thoughts secret. She wondered if all riders were joined so deeply with their dragons. "Then... thank you for saving me, Assumptshun."

"You're very welcome," Assumptshun rumbled. Ephraim squeezed her hand in reassurance. "Please understand that the were-beasts were too close to allow me to pick you up the conventional way—running you off the cliff was the only option."

"I... thank you."

Ephraim mindspoke again. *I didn't know where your room was, so I brought you here. You're safe in here. U amo circe.*

"Elvish," she whispered wistfully. "I haven't heard it spoken in so long. I'd almost forgotten..."

He smiled in earnest at her, the corners of his summer-sky eyes crinkling charmingly.

They drifted into silence; she, lulled by the sensation of his hand gliding against hers, massaging it. Ephraim watched her profile in the flame of a single candle, his subtle gift trained on her.

He changed hands to free the one closest to her, wrapping that arm loosely around her thin shoulders. Too thin. He couldn't help but envision her in Taure En Alata, well fed, her eyes dancing and her shoulders relaxed, freed from stress, her body garbed in a beautiful dress as befitting a lady of the aristocracy.

Elfan stiffened at first, surprised at the prince's casual embrace, but she couldn't help but relax into him, into the warmth and solidness of his body. It hadn't occurred to her before now how much she had been yearning for someone she could rely on, someone she could relate to.

Ephraim sighed out loud. *Now would likely be a good time to mention that I am gifted.*

She stiffened again. "In what way?"

Empathy. I sense the emotions of others. Merely sense. I have no control over them.

She flushed and buried her face in her free hand.

There's nothing to be embarrassed by, Elfan. I can't read your thoughts. I can only pick up what you're feeling, and I've not noticed anything worth being embarrassed by. He paused, and she was silent. *Would you like me to change the subject?*

"Please."

All right... He searched for a safe topic. *Do the were-beasts usually come that close to Dothan?*

She froze in horror.

What's wrong? he demanded. Assumptshun immediately reawakened.

She looked at him, eyes wide in panic. "What if Oracle and Thief are still out there? What if the beasts catch their scent and go after them?"

Ephraim jumped to his feet, dragging her up with him. They hurried from the room.

Oracle and Thief were coming down the hall toward them. Thief had her tucked against his side; she was crying.

"Sisera has captured Kirin, Callian, and the dragons, and Trig is unconscious somewhere in the wilderness," she sobbed.

Dread washed through Ephraim at her words. His arm tightened subconsciously around Elfan; he had to force himself to loose his grip.

Without a word, he turned and went to awaken his family.

They ended up spending the remainder of the hour lying side by side in the darkness, curled up in each other's arms. Kirin smiled as Callian actually managed to drift off to sleep. Sleep was good. It meant he was relaxed, rather than worried about his upcoming fight.

She woke him up when she heard footsteps approaching from the corridor. Wordlessly, he rose as Kirin coaxed Xzylya behind Beau.

The cell door was flung open so hard it bounced off the wall, sliding back closed. A man with long, dark hair and cold eyes stopped it with his foot. He smirked at Kirin.

"Kiss your lover good-bye, princess."

She stared at him around Callian, hatred burning in her eyes. Callian turned his head to catch her eye.

"I'll return," he said simply.

Sisera laughed. "So optimistic." He grabbed a fistful of Callian's shirt and yanked him out of the cell, slamming the door behind him. "I hear bonded dragons scream as their riders die," he said loudly as their footsteps faded away. "I can't *wait* to see if that's true."

Kirin took an uneven breath, battling the urge to scream Callian's name. It would only unnerve him.

The sound of movement behind her caught her attention; the dragons had piled together into a large knot, as if for comfort. She could well understand their unease. Crossing the few steps to them, she slipped into their midst, curling up against Beau's chest with her arms wrapped around Xzylya.

Kirin, Tiamat mindspoke to her. *You are welcome to listen in on our thoughts. It might give you some knowledge of how Callian fairs in the fight.*

Thank you.

Kirin buried her face against Xzylya's slender neck and opened up her mind to Tiamat's.

His heart thudded painfully as he was led down one corridor and across another, the Nephilim prodding him in the back with a knife. Sisera shoved him down a narrow staircase, laughing as he almost fell.

"I'm so glad I'm amusing you," Callian snarled.

Sisera laughed again. The evil sound of it made his skin crawl. "What does she *see* in you, human?" He didn't wait for an answer, shoving Callian through a doorway at the bottom of the stairs.

Two Rashek waited inside. They grabbed Callian and wrenched his tunic off, then patted down his legs.

"He has no weapons, General Sisera," one grated in an impossibly deep voice.

"Lead him in. At blade-point, fool," he snapped. "No need to deny Lord Malakieth his entertainment."

Callian was led through a short, dimly lit tunnel and thrown through a doorway into a sand arena. The thick door was slammed shut behind him, a heavy beam dropped over it from the other side, locking him in the pit. He looked around to get his bearings. The walls were too sheer and too smooth to be climbed. High above him, Malakieth stood in his true form, looking over the side with an unreadable expression. Sisera joined him, his servant standing behind him and out of his way. Malakieth's serving woman stood beside the dragon's shoulder; he could feel her eyes on him.

There was a wild, savage growl as the beast was herded out from an opposite door. For a moment, before the creature came into view, his minds' eye flashed an image of a great, tawny beast charging him down, of his horse bolting in fear. He had been seven, a child still, traveling with his mother the queen and her courtiers across the great plains of Giladeth to the southwestern port city of Surda. To this day, he feared lions.

The creature that stalked out of a tunnel was bigger and darker than that lion had been. He took deep breath to steady himself, spreading his feet to balance his center of gravity. The beast circled around him, haunches shifting under its mottled fur.

The beast tensed and sprung, and Callian launched himself sideways, rolling through the fall. The creature was faster, landing, spinning, striking out, forcing him to duck again.

The beast backed away, blessedly giving him time to catch his breath. He glanced around without taking his eyes off the creature, looking in vain for something sharp. There was a significant difference between battling a pack of these things with Kirin, Trig, and the dragons—not to mention a bow and Canath—and fighting one unarmed in an arena when he alone was the sole focus of the creature.

The were-beast leapt at him again, and he threw himself to the side once more. The beast's claws caught his upper chest, twisting him as he fell, leaving four deep streaks across his upper body, a bloody sash from shoulder to opposite hip. He hit the ground hard and rolled onto his knees, one hand clutching at the wounds. Already, the pain was starting to fade, to go numb, heralding the shock that was settling over him. The pit and the small group of beings watching his death swayed disconcertingly. The beast moved into his field of vision as it narrowed, prowling toward him, closing in for the kill.

Kirin screamed, seeing Callian hit the arena floor, feeling, through Tiamat, his agony, his fear, feeling her own helplessness. He was dying, dying, and she was powerless to do anything about it, imprisoned in this accursed cell, and stuck helpless with a hatchling and a dying dragon.

Tiamat wailed a high, keening cry, the sound of a dragon sobbing. Beau, teeth bared and tail whipping in fearful frenzy, clutched her to him, rolling instinctually to shield her with his own body. He arched his neck to press his face against hers. Tiamat's breath came in short, labored gasps.

Kirin rubbed Tiamat's flank, Xzylya pressing against her rider and whimpering. Kirin looped an arm around the baby's neck and clung to her, tears running down her cheeks.

Please, please, please let him be safe, she begged to Adonai.

Through Tiamat's mind, she heard Callian's faint voice call out her name, almost a chant. As if he was saying farewell.

She clutched her beloved dracling to her and screamed in denial. The sound rose up, an inhuman sound, silencing all who heard.

Kirin, Kirin, Callian thought in a daze. What would become of her now?

The beast was close enough now that he could feel its hot, fetid breath. It regarded him as a cat might regard a trapped mouse, batting at him once or twice with its paws. Satisfied that he wasn't going anywhere, the creature drew back slightly—and sunk its teeth into his wounded shoulder.

Callian couldn't help but scream in pain. The creature released him and darted away and then came back in for the killing strike. In an act of desperation, he drew back and punched half-blind at the creature's nose, throwing all that was left of his strength behind the blow. But his aim was off. Rather than hit the beast square in the nose, his fist connected solidly to the creature's throat. There was an audible cracking sound; the beast gave a choking cry and fell over dead, its neck broken.

The darkness descended over Callian, claiming him. He never saw Sisera throw up his hands in disgust and leave, never saw Malakieth toss his servant on his back and drop over the wall into the pit with a satisfied smirk.

Kirin lay in the darkness in a stunned detachment. Her throat ached from screaming, but she barely noticed. Xzylya had busied herself with the task of making her rider cease crying, a task she seemed content to accomplish by licking away every tear that ran down Kirin's cheek.

It is said that a dragon will cry when his mate is mortally wounded. The words chased themselves around and around in Kirin's mind. She couldn't feel the hard stone floor beneath her, couldn't feel her arm beneath her head. She was numb.

A dragon's tears are like diamonds.

Her Beau lay with his mate clasped against his underside, against the warmest part of him, where his dragon-flame burned within him. Tiamat's head rested gingerly on one of his forelegs, her eyes closed, breathing shallowly.

Beau breathed a small jet of flame onto his mate over her heart, trying to keep her warm, keep her alive. On his cheek, a single tear glistened, catching the light from his fire.

The door was opened slowly, as if the newcomer didn't want to frighten any of them. Xzylya scrambled to her feet and hissed, bracing her small body in front of her rider to guard her.

The newcomer entered the cell and nudged Kirin.

"I hate you, whoever you are," she mumbled. "Leave me."

"Prince Callian won the fight. You're to be moved to a new location," Malakieth's serving woman said. "Come with me."

"Callian is dying."

The *rakasheti's* voice dropped to a low murmur. "I'm taking you to him, Lady Adkisha."

Beau's golden eyes flipped open. After a moment of staring at the strange girl, of weighing her words, he unwound himself from his mate long enough to lift his rider to her feet. Xzylya shoved her gangly body against Kirin's hip to steady her; Kirin placed her hand on the dracling's back.

The slave girl proffered a thin bronze chain that held a circular disk of the same material. "It is an amulet; it will force any dragon to assume his or her human shape. Painlessly, of course." She nodded toward Tiamat. "May I?"

Beau nodded. The girl knelt and fastened the chain around Tiamat's neck. It was fascinating watching Tiamat change into a lanky, curvy woman, watching her scales turn to red fabrics and wild, curling hair. Beau picked her limp body up gently in his mouth, and they followed the girl out of the cell.

Malakieth waited for them in the corridor, standing in his human form. His servant fell back to walk behind Beau as he laid a heavy hand on his daughter's shoulder, fingers curling behind her neck as if to dissuade her from attacking. He led them through the fortress through what must have been back passageways.

He let them in through a thick door. Kirin's eyes flashed around the comfortably furnished chambers, fastening on a tall, blond young man lying still as death on a long divan.

"Callian!" she gasped, running for him. She dropped down beside him, feeling for a pulse. She breathed a shaky sigh of relief when she found one. It was faint and unsteady, but he was still alive. Blood-

his back to her, stroking the inky scales with one hand. Finally, she couldn't take it anymore. "What did you want to talk to me about?"

His hand stopped. "I … I've changed my mind, actually," he said in a peculiar voice. "I'm sorry to trouble you."

She opened her mouth to comment, to question, but with a snarl, Assumptshun snapped at his rider, coming short a few inches of the prince's shoulder. A warning.

Ephraim glared at him. "All right, all right," he grumbled at the male. He turned to her, and she was surprised to see that his expression was hesitant, unsure.

"I wanted to ask you …" he trailed off as if unsure how to word what he was trying to say. "I was wondering if you would consider coming with me—with us—to Ellasar."

She was stunned. "Leave Dothan?" she blurted out.

He winced slightly, barely noticeable. But she noticed—she had become attuned to him. "That was the general idea, yes. At least temporarily. No one will force you to stay."

"I-I-I can't … I can't just *leave* them here," she cried, shoving her hands in her hair. "They need me. I'm the best archer, the fastest runner. I can't just abandon them, Ephraim. I just *can't*."

He had been so still; now he startled her by surging forward, toward her. The prince took her face in his hands. She stared up at him, eyes huge and wild.

"If that wasn't a concern," he said softly, "would you come?"

"But it is a concern, so why dwell on alternative notions?"

"Would you come?" he replied insistently.

"I … Yes," she whispered. "I would." Suddenly calm, she pulled back, and he let her. "But I can't. I need to stay with the Resistance."

His blue eyes closed; he nodded his head once to show that he understood. Reaching forward, he recaptured her face and pressed his lips to her forehead.

"Then farewell, and keep safe, Elfan, until we meet again."

Turning away from her, he leapt into the saddle, and Assumptshun walked from the room.

Elfan wrapped her arms around herself and wept.

Oracle found her there a few minutes later. Elfan hurried to dry her eyes.

"Is something wrong?" she asked the younger elf.

Oracle raised one brow. "Why are you still here?"

"Because the Resistance needs me, and I won't abandon the lot of you. Not when you saved my life."

Oracle shook her head slowly. "You're miserable."

"Many here are. It is the state of the land."

"Elfan." She frowned. "You have a chance at happiness, and you're letting it walk away."

Elfan looked away, torn, indecisive.

"Go with him, Elfan. *Elfan*." She turned back to the girl. "*Go*."

"Can I catch him?" she whispered.

Oracle smiled and tossed a small pack to her, along with her quiver half-full of arrows and her bow.

"If you hurry."

Elfan strapped the quiver to her back and shouldered the pack. "Thank you, Oracle."

"Hurry," the girl stressed.

Elfan took off at a run.

When, after ten minutes, she still hadn't caught sight of the three elves, she began to worry. She was frightened that they had already gone through the portal. Frightened that perhaps she had gone the wrong way, distracted as she was. Finally, she caught sight of a long, black tail disappearing around a bend in the tunnel.

"Ephraim!" she called out.

Rounding the bend, she saw that he had stopped and was waiting for her, his handsome face hopeful. The portal stood open and shimmering in front of her, so strange and *farrin*. Aramon, Ling, and his horse were nowhere in sight.

She stopped beside the Dark Dragon, unnerved by how close she had been to being left behind. "May I still come?"

Ephraim's face broke out in a grin as Assumptshun knelt. His rider pulled her up into the saddle, setting her before him. He wrapped his arms around her waist as the dragon rose.

"I would be honored," he whispered in her ear.

Assumptshun plunged through the portal.

Hours passed. Kirin dozed sporadically, always waking in terror, afraid that Callian had died while she slept. He didn't, but he didn't show many signs of healing, either. While the bleeding had blessedly slowed, it had yet to stop completely. His breathing remained shallow and pained, his heartbeat sluggish and struggling. His face had a horrible pallor to it.

Malakieth was conspicuously absent, though his servant girl seemed to think that it was normal. She brought food and water to the dragons and to Kirin and helped to tend to Tiamat's wound. She brought Kirin bandages and water for Callian and kept her company. She was a wonderful companion; she seemed to know when Kirin needed her to fill the silence with idle chatter or with a clever story or when Kirin merely desired to be alone with her thoughts.

The first day went by, and while Callian didn't wake, Kirin was able to drip water down his throat, and it seemed to do some small good. The Gilagaithian slave refused to give Kirin some of the amber liquid she had used on Tiamat, saying that the wound was too close to his vitals and that she didn't trust the liquid not to numb his heart or his lungs. Bruises formed over Callian's chest and over his ribs. Kirin ran her hands down his sides only to discover several broken ribs.

"I can set those for you, my lady," the raven-haired girl answered. She set a tray of freshly baked bread down beside Kirin. Xzylya came loping over from the other side of the room to investigate the new food. The girl nudged the dracling away with her toe, and the Light Dragon bounded off again to lie in a puddle of sunshine.

"I shudder at causing him more pain," Kirin murmured.

"It would be better than having them heal wrong," she pointed out.

Kirin nodded, moving over to make room for the girl at Callian's bedside. "Could you do it, then? I have little skill at setting ribs."

The girl nodded, placing her hands on Callian, one above the break and one below. She wrenched his body in one sharp motion; there was a *pop* as the rib snapped back into place. Callian cried out softly, unconsciously, his eyelids fluttering. The girl repeated the motions with the second and third break. Callian struggled, rising back to consciousness. Kirin caught his face, turning him so that she was in his line of vision.

"Callian, Callian, love," she whispered. "It's all right. You're safe; I'm here. Relax, please."

Gradually, his labored breathing slowed. "Kirin," he breathed, sinking back into unconsciousness.

Kirin pressed a kiss to his forehead.

Drawing back, her eyes fell on his shoulder, the unscathed one. It had swollen. She frowned, probing at it with her fingertips.

"Dislocated?" the girl asked. "It wouldn't surprise me given the way he fell in the arena."

Kirin paused, looking up at her. "You were there?"

"Of course," she replied quietly. "I'm Malakieth's personal slave."

Kirin looked away, twining her arm with Callian's. She twisted his shoulder back into place, and his pained expression eased the tiniest bit.

"Where's Malakieth gotten off to?" she finally asked.

"I wouldn't know," the girl replied. "I didn't ask. He'll come back in his own time."

"Likely the gossip will tell."

"I don't believe the gossip, my lady. I find I do better believing what my eyes tell me."

Kirin looked at her again. "You respect him."

The young woman lifted her chin. "I do. He saved my life when I was younger, and he shelters and educates me now that I'm older. I have warm clothes, a fire to sleep by in the wintertime, and more food than most of the slaves here, even the other *rakasheti*. It's a good life, and I'm happy and grateful for it. And it's thanks to Malakieth that I have this life."

Kirin glanced down. "Will you tell me about him?"

She shook her head. "My lady, I know all of his secrets. And I keep them, as he trusts me to."

Kirin met her eyes, beginning to understand. "You could ruin him...because he's not what he seems."

The girl didn't break her gaze. She didn't speak.

"The people of this world don't name their children because they've given up on hope," Kirin murmured. The girl nodded. "Do you have a name?"

She nodded again.

"Will you tell me?"

She shook her head. "Not yet, my lady."

"Malakieth named you."

"Yes."

"How old are you?"

"Sixteen, nearly seventeen. Around the prince's age, I believe. And you?"

"Halfway to sixteen."

"You're merely courting, correct?"

Kirin nodded, a faint blush creeping into her cheeks.

"He'll pull through, my lady. No worries." She reached out and rubbed Kirin's shoulder. "By tomorrow, you'll see. And I think I have something for you to wear if you would like to get out of that."

Kirin glanced down at her clothing, at her bare stomach and the charred edges of her ripped tunic and pants, the fabric splattered with dried, black blood.

Beau looked up at them and nodded.

"That would be marvelous," Kirin said gratefully.

The Gilagaithian jumped up, heading through one of the doors to a different room. She came back holding a crimson dress that looked like—

"Silk?" Kirin laughed in disbelief, at the absurdity of a silk dress in Amalay Kahelith. "Where did you get silk?"

The girl laughed with her. "Don't ask. Suffice to say Malakieth passed several gowns like this down to me."

"You must tell me," Kirin pleaded. "Why would a male dragon have silk gowns?"

The girl smiled wryly, giving in. "They were once Morgan's. Then Nahor killed her, and Malakieth, as her apprentice, inherited all her things. Most of them he got rid of or gave away, but he kept the dresses. When he brought me here, he gave them to me. Unfortunately, I've grown out of several. This is one of them. You're welcome to it."

Kirin took it slowly. "Are you sure? I'll likely ruin it. You can see what I've done to these."

She snorted. "Take it. It's much too small for me. Morgan was closer to your height."

Kirin undressed, slipping into the silk dress. The material was cool and clingy and rather thin. Malakieth's slave girl laced up the back ties to the base of Kirin's wings and tugged on the straps that reached over Kirin's shoulders to make sure that they fit snugly.

"It's a good fit, and it leaves your wings free. How does it feel?"

Kirin eyed the length of wine-red material that hugged her breasts and flowed down over her hips. "Nonexistent?"

The woman rolled her dark eyes. "Keep it. It looks fantastic."

Kirin blushed. "Thank you."

She sank down beside Callian, taking his hand in hers. The girl withdrew, only to return later with a basin and a pitcher full of water, a towel, a chunk of soap, and a comb. She set the bowl behind Kirin and tilted her head back.

"You don't need to do that," Kirin protested.

"I've never had the chance to look after a female before. I plan on enjoying this to the fullest."

"What about Ling?"

"I was an infant when she was here with Malakieth. General Sisera had her recaptured. I was the one that found her in the dungeons, only months ago. We had no idea that she had been back."

"We?"

"Malakieth and I." She poured water on Kirin's hair and then gently began to massage the soap in. Kirin felt the tension in her body relaxing.

"Do you do this for Malakieth?"

The girl snorted. "Once in a blue moon, my lady. I cook for him, sing and play the fiddle for him, clean, talk with him, learn from him, and run errands for him. There isn't much physical contact."

"Oh."

"You seem surprised."

"I had assumed that he ... "

"Used me for pleasure?"

"It made me uncomfortable," Kirin admitted.

The girl laughed. "No, no, nothing like that. Although we pretend that we do."

Kirin frowned. "What do you mean?"

The girl began to rinse Kirin's hair clean. "The word *rakasheti* is a combination of two Gilagaithian words: *rakai*, meaning 'pleasure,' and *shetius*, meaning 'slave' or 'servant.' So a *rakasheti* is a pleasure slave. We're essentially concubines. We serve one master, and we do whatever they want, including give them sons. It's a safe position, especially if your master is good to you. A *rakasheti* must wear the uniform of her status when she goes out it public—it warns the other males that there will be retribution if she's harmed, which is why Malakieth gave me that status. I'm untouchable to all males but him, and he doesn't touch me." She gave Kirin's hair a final rinse and rubbed a towel over it to dry it. "You don't see many beings with blond hair around here. Morgan's Rashek all have black hair, as do their hybrid offspring, and the natives of Gilagaithia typically are dark-haired." She released Kirin's hair to turn her face, looking at her eyes. Satisfied, she picked up the comb and began to work it through the tangles of Kirin's hair. Kirin's thumb tracked gentle circles over the back of Callian's hand, her mind whirling with everything the slave girl had said.

"Your father," the girl said suddenly, "came back not long ago with the most stricken expression on his face. 'She's my daughter,' he told me. 'The Adkisha is my daughter. I have a *daughter*.' It was like he was in disbelief. Then the next thing out of his mouth was, 'She has my father's eyes.' I thought you might like to know that."

Kirin smiled slightly. "It's so strange," she confided. "I grew up thinking I had no family, and now... I mean, I had always guessed I was illegitimate, but to find out I had a family..." She shook her head, and the girl knocked the comb against her shoulder.

"Sorry," she apologized. The girl shrugged.

"Callian is right; you do seem familiar," Kirin murmured. The girl said nothing.

They sat in silence while the girl finished with Kirin's hair, plaiting it tightly for her.

"Your prince will heal. You'll see," she said, rising with her tray. She turned to the dracling. "Xzylya! Come to another room with me, and I'll teach you a song."

Go, Kirin whispered to the baby.

Xzylya bounded over to her rider, licked Kirin's cheek and received a kiss, and raced off after the young woman with the dark hair.

Kirin woke up in the middle of the night to the sound of weak coughing. Adrenaline spiking through her body, she rose and attempted to roll Callian onto his side. Beau rose from Tiamat's side, reaching over her with one foreleg to help. Still unconscious, Callian coughed out blood before settling, his breath rattling harsh and wet in his throat.

Kirin stared at the blood in frozen horror, Beau standing stiffly beside her. Xzylya came to them and pressed up against Kirin's hip, trying to offer her rider hope. She was too young still to understand what that blood meant.

Internal bleeding.

Callian was dying.

She put her ear to his chest, listening to the rattle of fluid inside his lungs, fluid where there shouldn't *be* fluid. Tears rolled down her cheek.

"My lady?" the slave girl asked, coming with a candle from an adjacent room.

The main door opened, the master of the chambers striding through. Malakieth froze as he looked at them and then snapped into action, breathing flame into the hearth to rekindle the fire.

Kirin snapped into a defensive crouch as he came near where Callian lay. "Stay away from him!" she snarled.

"Is he dying?" Malakieth demanded.

"What does it matter to you? Leave us!"

The *rakasheti* slipped past Beau to look at Callian. "Yes," she said, answering her master's question.

Beau swiped at her—a warning—and the girl darted away. Malakieth barely restrained himself from lunging at the Twilight Dragon.

"Leave!" Kirin demanded again.

"Answer a few questions first," Malakieth replied. "What does a vampire do when his mate is a human?"

Kirin stared at him, confused by his question. What was he getting at? "Bite his mate and make her like him."

"And what would a werewolf do?"

"His mate would lose her mortality with the consummation of their bond."

"And a dragon?"

"The same. As would Avians."

"What about an elf?"

Kirin paused. "There's nothing to be done. One is mortal, the other immortal."

Malakieth shook his head. "Think, daughter, think. Your mother was once human."

Kirin blinked in surprise. Behind her, Callian went into another coughing fit, choking out more blood. She knelt and smoothed his hair away from his face.

"*Think*," Malakieth ordered.

"I don't know *how* Nahor changed her," she replied hotly. "I've never even met the king."

"Think!"

"I don't know—" Kirin broke off, her green eyes widening. "*Animai conveinos*," she breathed in Elvish. "Conversion."

"Yes," her father rumbled. "Elves are stronger and heal faster than humans." He turned to his servant girl. "Come, Natasha. We'll leave them in peace."

Kirin startled to attention. "Natasha? That's your name?"

The *rakasheti* Natasha smiled; she followed Malakieth into a different room. "You look better than the last time I saw you, my lady."

"*Natasha*," Malakieth insisted.

She vanished, closing the door behind her.

Bewildered and surprised and worried all at once, Kirin turned back to Callian. He was deathly pale, his face drawn in pain, and his lips painted red with blood. She tried to remain calm as she cast her mind back to what she had learned at the Academy.

Animai conveinos—meaning "spirits combined"—was a powerful piece of magic that pulled the spirit out of one being—the mortal—and drew it into the other—the immortal—who was working the magic. When the two souls touched, the immortal literally shared enough of their magic to give the mortal an eternal life span. It was said to be painless. The one controlling the magic had to be in contact with the other at all times during the conversion; the other's body could die if the contact was broken, leaving his or her spirit trapped with the first's body. And the spell didn't work on just anyone. The two had to be in love, deeply in love. Soul mates. It was where the term had originated.

Kirin hardly dared to breathe as she pulled the crystal pendant out of the small pouch on the thong that had once held the ring she had given Callian and dropped it over her head once more. Climbing onto the divan, she straddled Callian's legs, locking her ankles together behind his knees. She would not risk his life; she refused to let the contact between them break during the spell. She wound her right hand in his hair, placing her left palm over his heart and feeling the erratic beat. Nervous, she swallowed hard and closed her eyes, aware of little Xzylya standing like a silent sentinel beside them, aware of Beau stretching out beside his mate.

She forced herself to focus on her magic, reaching for it. It rushed to her command, making her palm tingle and setting Ishmael's crystal and the Adkisha's marking on her arm aglow.

She sent the magic spiraling into Callian, searching, aiming to change rather than heal. He arched under her hands, eyes flying open as he was pulled back to consciousness.

Kirin opened her eyes to see Callian staring at her. "I'm going to save you," she whispered.

Her magic found his spirit, and she drew back, tugging at it, at him. His eyes were trusting as he surrendered to her magic.

Kirin gasped as his spirit rose out of his body and entered hers.

Beneath her, Callian's eyes closed.

ELF

Sisera walked out into the pit. It wasn't the ideal place to perform the ceremony, but it would have to do. It was large and easily concealed from that bloody dragon, since the fool rarely came down to watch the executions that took place in the pit.

All of the sand and dirt had been cleaned and raked until it was even. The slaves had trampled it down until it was hard-packed.

Even more care had been put into readying the pentagram that now lay in the center, red-brown in color, the color of dried blood. And that was what it had been made from. Sheep's blood, used as paint to dye the floor of the pit. Symbols written in Nishron's Tongue ringed the inside of it, made from the blood of chickens.

Those who had been taught to work the looms had been kept busy making white cloth while others had been sewing that cloth into shifts. Slave labor was a beautiful thing. Either they worked, or they died.

His Nephilim had been out across the countryside, gathering the necessary humans. He looked at them now, eyes burning with hatred. He hated humans, especially these humans. They were untouchable. The ritual demanded fifty virgins, and no one dared to ruin this ritual. The consequences for failure were unspeakable.

His half-brother, Jurrinius, approached hesitantly and bowed. "My lord, we are nearly ready."

Sisera rolled his eyes at the useless piece of scum. How could his father have allowed such a failure of a Nephilim to live?

to protect Kirin while she's working this spell. If she breaks contact with the prince, he'll die."

"May I use magic?"

Malakieth met her eyes solemnly. Her use of magic was one of the few restrictions he had given her, and, like the rest of the restrictions, it was to keep her safe, keep her hidden away. "If it comes to that, yes. But Natasha? If it comes to needing magic, fight to kill, not to ward off."

Natasha nodded once. Malakieth slipped out of the room, past his daughter, and out of his chambers, following the pull of the magic.

He froze outside of the pit, his blood flowing cold through his veins. That wild laugh echoed around him.

No. It can't be…

He knew that laugh. It was so horribly familiar.

Making his way to the edge of the pit, he saw the horrible view below him, saw the pentagram, the slaughtered sacrifice—*human* sacrifice—saw the crowd of Nephilim, Sisera, and Molyb. And at the center of it all, Morgan stood, face pointed skyward.

Numb with shock, he turned and fled before she could see him, racing through deserted hallways back to his own chamber. He had to protect Natasha and his daughter.

Ephraim regretted setting Elfan in front of him rather than behind the moment they were through the portal. He barely had time to throw up a shield to deflect the arrows fired at his dragon, pushing her down against Assumptshun's neck. One of them shattered through the shield—a light arrow—and burned the dragon's foreleg. He felt the echoing pain in his own arm. Assumptshun took the hit mutely, restraining himself as Aramon galloped in front of them and bellowed the order to cease-fire.

"Stay very still," he grated in Elfan's ear as he leapt down. A familiar-looking male on a gray charger stepped forward, eyes widening in surprise.

Aramon backed his horse out of the way, shielding his mother with his body. So far, the band of elven archers hadn't noticed her, preoccupied with the Dark Dragon that had come through a portal into their land during the new moon.

"Captain Raynis, do not, in any circumstance, open fire on my dragon again," Ephraim snapped.

Raynis was, for once, speechless; he stammered an apology, bowing and staring up at the dragon wide-eyed. Ephraim cut off his words. "This is Assumptshun, my bonded dragon."

He bent over to check out the wound. Light arrows took a skill at magic that he himself didn't possess, though his father did. Raynis, thankfully, had only grazed the side of the dragon's leg.

I'll be fine. It stings a bit; that's all, the dragon said gruffly. *Go introduce your female.*

Heaven and hell, we're not courting.

Assumptshun just growled at him, making Raynis step back. His fingers itched for his bow, but he heeded Ephraim's command.

The prince reached up for Elfan. "Come down, and meet more of your kind," he murmured.

She swallowed and allowed him to help her down, fidgeting with her threadbare clothing, one knee of her too-short pants torn, the hem of her tunic fraying. Raynis's entire company stared at her; she blushed and looked away.

Ephraim placed a hand on her shoulder and gave them a hard, warning look. "This is Lady Elfan. She is my guest and has been living for some time on Amalay Kahelith with a band of brave fighters who seek to liberate their world. She has an admirable skill with a bow."

Look up, Elfan, he coaxed. *See how they smile at you? Here, a woman with a skill at archery is praised, for she can defend herself in her husband or kinsman's absence.*

Elfan smiled hesitantly at the elven company. One of the women smiled back.

"Permission to approach?" she called.

Ephraim nodded. She trotted her horse up to them, dismounting near Elfan. She pulled something from her saddlebag and offered it to the taller woman.

Take it with no arguments, Ephraim mindspoke to her hurriedly. *Don't offend her.*

Elfan took the material, unfolding it to see a midnight-blue cloak, a silver tree embroidered on the back. She stared at it in wonder, running her fingers over the material.

"It's beautiful," she breathed.

The woman beamed. "It was my daughter's. She died of an illness no healer could cure a few years before."

"You're giving this to me?" she asked incredulous, stroking the fabric again.

The woman smiled gently. "You would honor me by wearing it."

Elfan met the female archer's eyes. "Thank you very much," she said earnestly. The woman beamed, curtsied, and remounted, resuming her place in the company. Ephraim wrapped the cloak around Elfan's shoulders.

Aramon stayed silent and still, letting his brother do the talking, draw the attention. He was very aware of his mother sitting stiffly behind him, not actually touching him, his cloak around her shoulders and closed in front of her, the hood drawn up to hide her face. If anyone noticed her and inquired, he had only to say she was his childhood friend, Niamh, and no one would breathe a word or think anything odd about it. It was commonplace for him to steal her away, to come riding into Taure En Alata with her on the back of his saddle or on his pommel. No one would expect that it was the missing queen.

Ling had been like that for the whole short ride through Dothan, not touching him, declining his help while mounting. She wasn't a tall creature, and it had taken some effort for her to get in the saddle. She hadn't touched him since they had first met, when she had embraced him. Now it seemed as if she couldn't bear male contact—the young boys of Dothan the exception. It stung, but he could understand, given what she had been through. Once, she had been a smiling, laughing woman who, when she was with her husband, always stood close beside him, holding his hand, touching him, and smiling at some private comment or joke. Now she was riding into her citadel in obscurity.

And that was the way all of them wanted it, especially Ling. After being gone for sixteen years, having been raped, and having a daughter out of wedlock, even she was unsure of the reception she would receive from her husband.

When Ling had quietly voiced her concern in the tunnels of Dothan, Ephraim had caught his eye, and Aramon could tell his brother had been thinking the same thing: if Nahor blamed Ling for what had happened to her, they would personally beat the male, even though he was the king and their father and they respected him as both a warrior and a man.

Finished talking with Captain Raynis, Ephraim turned and half-lifted, half-tossed Elfan into the saddle. The gesture, while it went over Elfan's head, was not lost on Raynis's archers. It was a gesture that clearly stated this was the woman Ephraim wanted, which was the real reason the woman had given Elfan the cloak—a gift for one who might very well be the future queen.

Ephraim leapt up behind Elfan, resting his palms loosely on her hips. Raynis's company fanned out in front of them as an honor guard as the dragon started off toward the citadel, Aramon quietly falling into step behind Assumptshun.

Within moments, Taure En Alata came into view. Aramon heard Ling sigh behind him; with what, he wasn't sure.

Of course, there was much chaos when they rode into the capitol, both from the princes' return and the dragon that bore the heir home. Ephraim lifted one hand to wave good-naturedly to the crowd, Elfan smiling shyly in front of him, tucked inside the cloak. Aramon kept his head down and ignored the people, Ling doing the same behind him, keeping the attention on the trio in front of them and fading into the background.

As soon as he could, he broke off from the group and rode his horse directly into the stables, stopping only when Elindil was inside his stall. Ling slid off awkwardly, staggering back a step before she regained her balance. He could understand. She hadn't ridden a horse in sixteen years. It was long enough to make even an immortal ungraceful.

He swung his leg over the saddle and dropped down into the thick straw, quickly pulling his saddle off, saddlebags still attached. He tossed them over his shoulder, grabbed a brush from inside one bag and a hoofpick from another, and groomed his horse down, pulling the deep-green blanket with the silver embroidery off the rack outside the stall and draping it over his horse, buckling it at the chest. Ling followed him from the stall, silent as a shadow, latching the door behind her. Aramon put his tack away and led the way into the castle proper.

He was careful to keep his mind clear of all thoughts of Ling, in case his father—with his mind-hearing gift—was near and alert. Hopefully, though, Nahor was watching his eldest son come into the citadel on the back of a Dark Dragon with an unknown woman riding in front of him.

They encountered no resistance or questions as they made their way to Nahor and Ling's chambers—likely everyone who would question them was busy with the distraction Ephraim and Assumpt-shun had created.

At the doorway into the rooms, Ling turned to face her son, lifting her chin up to look at his face. "Thank you," she whispered in his native tongue. She lifted her hand as if to touch his cheek; instead, her fingers closed on a lock of his hair. "My beloved son."

He captured her hand and kissed her knuckles before she had a chance to pull away. "Mai," he replied.

She smiled at him, turning and entering the room. He spun on his heel to go watch his father interrogate his brother.

Nahor stood on the balcony, hands resting on the ornate railing, and looked down upon the scene that greeted him. His face was calm, a careful mask.

His thoughts, however, were as turbulent as the sea during a storm. His eldest son, his heir, was a dragon rider.

He focused on Ephraim's thoughts, thoughts that he could hear so clearly. Such was the nature of his gift.

How long have you been bonded to a Dark Dragon? he mindspoke to his son, careful to keep his mental voice calm and even. Controlled. Not for the first time, he was grateful that his gift gave him the ability to mindspeak.

Ephraim's eyes flicked up to his and back to the crowd.

Since the Battle of Fazen Dur. Ephraim didn't bother to project his thoughts, didn't bother mindspeaking. He knew his father would hear. *We bonded on the battlefield, both cut off from our armies, after we had spent several hours fighting side by side until my quiver was empty. The power that came from bonding with him saved my life... saved both of our lives.*

I am glad of that, at least. Though you should have told me.

Those blue eyes flickered up to his again briefly, his son flashing him a quick, rueful half-smile. *I'm no fool, Abbo. I know well how much you detest dragons.*

Primarily Malakieth. And Shadow Dragons. And any of his species that side with him.

Thankfully, then, the dragon cut in wryly, *I do not side with Malakieth.*

Your name, dragon, bonded to my son?

Assumptshun, descended of Zeripath.

Well met. Welcome to Ellasar.

Both his son and the dragon seemed surprised. Nahor had to work to keep the amused smile off his face. His son had successfully hidden all thoughts of the dragon—Assumptshun—for three thousand years from a skilled mind-reader. Yes, Ephraim would make a good king.

Nahor looked more closely at the wide-eyed girl. Though she had a well-made cloak about her shoulders, it was not one of Ephraim's; someone in Raynis's company must have given it to her. The clothing underneath was dirty and in disrepair, and the quiver and bow on her back were not of a good quality but had a well-used air about them. Whoever she was, two things were clear: Ephraim was fond of her, and she was young and malnourished.

Where *had* Ephraim found her?

And now, my dear son, who have you brought with you?

Elfan.

Daughter of?

She does not know who her parents are. She's been stranded on Amalay Kahelith for years. There's an underground resistance there that she's fallen in with; she's a good shot with a bow.

She could use a better one. As well as better clothes.

I plan to take care of that.

As well as decent food. She's nearly emaciated.

Again, I plan on remedying that. The Resistance is made up of mainly children. She gives most of the food she either hunts or scavenges to them.

So she has a good heart.

Thus why she's riding on my dragon.

"My lord king?"

Nahor turned at his steward's voice. Dolon was older than he, had at one point been Nahor's tutor, and had had to put up with Nahor pulling all the stunts Aramon often pulled.

"What is it, Dolon?" he asked.

Dolon frowned, coming forward. "I came to ask if you'd seen Prince Aramon. Captain Raynis said that he had also returned to the castle but, as usual, had disappeared in the chaos."

Nahor gave the man a small smile. "And you're worried that he'll disappear completely again before anyone gets a chance to speak to him?"

Dolon didn't smile, per se, but his eyes, those ancient eyes set in such a young face, were warm. "Like father like son, dear king."

Nahor walked away from the balcony. He had seen all that he had needed to see, and Ephraim could easily handle the crowds.

"Walk with me, Dolon. With any luck, Aramon is somewhere within the castle. If he's just come from Amalay Kahelith, I'd start with the kitchens. Likely he's somewhere in there charming a maid or two into an early meal."

Dolon finally smiled. "Verily, no doubt. If I may ask, dear king, what do you make of the dragon Prince Ephraim seems to be acquainted with?"

They were passing by a corridor that would lead past Nahor's own rooms, talking about the dragon and the girl Ephraim had brought home with him, when Nahor sensed it. He froze in his tracks, his steward stopping instantly beside him.

Both men stood still and quiet a moment as Nahor listened with his gift, straining to catch what he had thought he had heard.

"My lord?" Dolon finally ventured to ask.

"Hush. I thought I heard…" He closed his eyes to blind himself to the world, shutting out distractions as he reached out with his gift, something he very seldom did for the sheer agony of the onslaught of noise that would invade his mind.

There. He swung to face the sound, the sensation of the mind he knew as well as his own, better than Dolon's even. His eyes opened to show him the corner of the corridor they had just passed.

"Dolon, there is something I must attend to. We will further this discussion another time. Meanwhile, allow no one near my chambers, especially those with sensory gifts, including both of my sons, and if you do find Aramon, ask if he would be so kind as to allow me to speak with him before he wanders off again."

He took off running after the mind before Dolon had even finished acknowledging his instructions.

It was addicting, this sensation. Hosting Callian's spirit was … addicting. She could soar, lose herself in forever, and he would always be there beside her. He would always be hers and she his.

She could feel his spirit resting beside hers, not quite touching. That wasn't close enough, not for her. He caught hold of her ideas, her fiery passions, and eagerly threw himself into her.

Kirin couldn't breathe. It felt better than anything she had ever felt before. Nothing in her memory could compare to this.

And suddenly, he was holding her, cradled in his strong arms like a little child, and they turned to watch as a vision of a possible future came to them.

They were looking at themselves in front of a huge, glittering white castle. They were older, looking about thirty, and he held her close, forearms clasped over her lower stomach, pulling her body back against his. A young, blond-haired, green-eyed girl with walnut-colored wings came running over, her hair slightly curly and parting over her pointed ears. She was laughing as she took Kirin's hand. The scene shifted, and the girl was a few years older. She held the hand of another girl—a toddler, darker blond, but with the same brilliant green eyes, leaf-shaped ears, and the slightly wavy hair that Callian had. Her pupils were shaped like Kirin's. The vision shifted once more, and Kirin and Callian saw a third child enter the picture: a young boy, his hair darker than either of the two girls', almost walnut. He, too, had evergreen eyes and pointed ears.

The vision faded, and Kirin opened her eyes to stare down at Callian's body, at his regular breathing, at the normal flush returning to his skin. She watched as his ears grew more pointed, until they looked like an elf's ears might. His facial features didn't change much; he already closely resembled the Ellasarians. She stared down at his healing shoulder and chest—the wounds left by his fight with the were-beast no longer releasing his lifeblood—and at the perfect musculature of his upper body, unhidden by clothing. She traced her fingers down the smooth planes of his strong chest, careful to avoid the wounds.

His beauty was surreal.

She bent her head to him, listening to his steady heart rate, to the sound of his breathing. Gone was the wet, strained sound. She wanted to laugh with joy.

The transformation was complete, and Kirin felt Callian's spirit slowly leaving her body, drawn back into his own.

His blue eyes opened. Kirin was tired, so very tired from the amount of magic she had used, but she felt *physical* again. She felt bound to this solid world.

She smiled down at him. He reached up slowly with one hand and brushed his thumb against her cheek.

"You're crying," he whispered.

"I'm happy," she explained.

His eyes shifted briefly to Tiamat. Kirin glanced at Beau, feeling his relief and joy.

You did it, little kihara, he told her.

A slow grin spread across her face. Xzylya bounded around the room, overjoyed, and came running for the divan where Kirin and Callian were. She nuzzled in close to them, and Callian smiled and rubbed her head. She bounded away to jump on Beau and Tiamat, who laughed.

Callian looked at her. "You're all right?"

Kirin nodded, fresh tears running down her face. "And you will be, too." She leaned down to kiss his throat. "You nearly died. It was...so horrible. I don't ever want to have to go through that again."

He managed a weak smile, sinking his hand into her hair. "No worries. I don't plan on fighting another were-beast unarmed again."

Kirin drew back and dried her eyes, smiling at him as she slipped off him to kneel beside the divan. He took her hand in his, kissing her fingers as he looked at his surroundings.

"Where are we?"

"Malakieth's chambers. He brought the dragons and I here after you killed the were-beast. His servant and I have been tending to you. His servant Natasha."

It took a few minutes for the name to sink in. "That Natasha? The one who helped us escape from that prison?"

Kirin nodded, gently pushing him back down when he tried to sit up. "She made some comment in front of him about having seen us before, and he didn't react."

"Has he been treating you well?"

"He's been absent most of the time, but Callian..."

He looked at her and caught her gaze with his. "Yes, I have the ability and the knowledge to perform one. But I would never do it."

"Even if it was your mate who had died?"

His eyes were hard. "Even then."

Natasha's face paled. "So it involves a sacrifice," she breathed. "A ... human sacrifice."

Malakieth nodded at her.

"It's good to know that you have some morals," Kirin said acidly.

He glared at her. "I am in no mood to be nettled, daughter, not when I have to deal with that vicious, black-hearted daughter of a dog," he growled, stalking away into a different room.

Kirin turned to looked at Natasha, one brow rising. "Bitter, isn't he?"

"She ruined his life," Natasha explained. "You would be bitter as well."

"I always thought that he had fallen in love with her, or at least was attracted to her after Ling married Nahor."

Natasha shook her head. "Is that what they tell you on your world, Adkisha? Malakieth can't stand Morgan. I asked him once if he had ever loved her. He told me that the only time he didn't hate her was in the beginning when her lies comforted him." She looked at the door Malakieth had gone through. "I'm going to leave the lot of you alone now and go ease him. But, Lady Adkisha, try to see him with an open mind. Judge him on what he *does*, not on what the stories *say* he does."

Kirin nodded grimly, striding back to Callian. Tiamat rose up and limped over to where her rider lay, nuzzling his hair affectionately. Beau was entertaining Xzylya, knocking her back as she leapt for his horns. Kirin's shoulder panged when the Light Dragon landed particularly hard, but Xzylya bounded up undeterred.

Callian smiled, watching them play.

Nothing dampens that one's joy, he commented to his dragon.

She's young, and she doesn't seem to let the evil in the worlds drag her down. She's a very loving little creature, and I'm glad Beau and Kirin found her.

The silence stretched between them as they watched Xzylya leap into the air again, managing to finally get past Beau and clamp onto one of his horns. Beau lay down slowly and rolled over. Xzylya pounced on him, getting a better grip, and growled. Beau tugged on her tail, and she squealed and released his horn, diving for the offending foreleg.

He'll make a good father, Tiamat commented.

Kirin came over and sat down beside them, watching her dragons.

"Go play with them," Callian murmured.

She shook her head. "I'm too..."

"Nervous?"

"And apprehensive. Unsure. Rather confused," she admitted.

"About Malakieth?"

"About everything. Malakieth. And now Morgan and Molyb."

"Not that I'm the expert on anything here, but on a whim, I'd say that Morgan must be the worst of the evil if the other evils resurrected her. They've got to have some good reason to bring her back if they're all as heartless as everyone else makes them out to be."

"So Morgan is the worst of the worst," she said glumly.

"Currently. At least, that's my impression."

She slipped her hand into his; he squeezed her fingers tightly. Kirin winced. "Ouch, love, careful. You've gotten stronger, you know."

He frowned. "Have I? Strange for a man that's nearly died."

She looked at him, suddenly unsure. He gripped her fingers again, though not as hard as before, nervous without truly understanding why he was nervous. A small portion of his mind noted that the dragons had ceased playing, that Xzylya was slinking over to her rider—to protect her or comfort her, he wasn't sure.

"What's happened?" he whispered to Kirin. "What's wrong?"

She ducked her head, slumping down and resting her forehead against their joined hands. Slowly, she raised her free hand and ran her fingertips along his ear. He frowned as he reached up to feel what she was feeling, freezing when he felt the way the top came to a point.

Like an elf's, he realized.

"*Animai conveinos*," she mumbled into the divan. Even though he should have had problems hearing her, her words were easily understood. "It's Elvish, roughly translated into 'spirits combined.' More commonly called the elven conversion, or simply conversion."

His mind was numb; he couldn't think straight, couldn't get his thoughts in order. "Are you saying that ... ?" He trailed off, unsure of what he was even trying to say.

Kirin gripped his hand harder. "It was what I had to do to save you—turn you into an elf, make you immortal. I'm sorry, Callian. I ... I couldn't bear merely letting you die," she whispered faintly.

"Your healing magic," he managed.

"It wasn't enough. You ... you were dying on me. I couldn't just ... let go. I'm so sorry." Dimly, something in his head recognized that the hand she was bowed over was growing wet, that Kirin's sides were moving with rough breath, that her wings were trembling. One thing connected with another, and he realized that she was *crying*.

He reached out to comfort her automatically, his palm landing softly on her shoulder. His fingers felt warm skin and cool silk, and his mind suddenly seized on the most important thing she had said.

"I'm immortal?"

She finally raised her head to look up at him, and his heart nearly broke to see the tears running silently down her cheeks. His hand moved from her shoulder to her cheek, his thumb brushing away the wetness. She closed her eyes and leaned into his palm as if she were starved for comfort, nodding in answer to his question.

He was ... immortal.

"I won't age, won't grow old and die? You won't outlive me?" he asked quickly.

"You will never die of old age," she whispered to him.

Abruptly, he felt like laughing in triumph. Kirin wouldn't outlive him. Tiamat wouldn't have to die a premature death. And hadn't that been two of his biggest concerns all along? The early death of his dragon and the vast difference in life span between himself and the young woman he loved?

His dragon realized at the same moment he did. Giddy, she nipped at her mate, who heaved a great sigh of relief and sprawled out next to her, head resting on her forelegs.

He, an elf. He would be stronger now, strong enough to protect her better. A harder, faster opponent to overcome in battle.

Leaning over, he freed his hands long enough to grasp her upper arms—gently, now, lest he hurt her—and helped her up far enough that she could sit on the edge of the divan. She looked down at him, her expression pained and unsure and so horribly insecure. Callian edged over to make room and tugged her down to lie beside him. She obeyed, but her expression never eased.

"Callian, I'm so sor—"

He placed his fingertips over her lips to keep her from apologizing again. "Hush, Kirin. No more apologies."

"Aren't you mad?" she breathed against his fingers. He was distracted briefly by the perfume of her skin, her breath, something he had never truly realized was this alluring.

"Mad? No. I think you're bloody brilliant. How in the worlds did you do it?"

Her expression finally changed to surprise; hope shone in her eyes. "You're not angry with me?"

"For saving my life?" he asked incredulously. "For doing what I've been trying to figure out how to do? I talked to Ephraim not long ago, trying to figure out some way to extend my life, Tiamat's life. I couldn't stand the thought that your life would just be starting when mine was ending. It was one of the few reasons why I waited so long to court you. I'll admit, another was fear of your refusal, as cowardly as it sounds for me." She smiled slightly, and he returned the smile, glad that he could cheer her up a bit. Then he became more serious, reaching out to stroke her hair. "Oh, Kirin ... How could I ever be angry with you? Frustrated, yes; occasionally I can manage that, especially when you're being stubborn or are trying to pick a fight. But never angry."

He cupped the back of her neck and leaned over to kiss her. She sighed, relieved, the tension melting out of her. Her hand moved to cradle his jaw, one wing flaring out and over them.

When they broke apart—after hearing Xzylya leave to curl at the head of the divan, satisfied that her rider was all right—Callian grinned.

"That was better than I remember, although, after that fight and the shock of finding out that I'm now immortal, it wouldn't surprise me very much if my memory's been affected," he remarked.

Kirin smiled slyly, taking his breath away. "You're an elf now; your senses are sharper."

The grin he gave her was nothing but wickedness. He kissed her again, and she gasped, her hands reaching up to grip the back of his neck, tangle in his hair.

They drew back, and he ran his hand down her side. He drew back, fingering the material over her hip where the skirt's gentle flare began.

"Where did you get this?" he asked.

"Malakieth gave it to Natasha and she to me. She said that she's outgrown it, and, wearing it, I can see why. She has several inches on me. Though the back of the gown is nice—my wings fit through without alteration." His hand slid up her spine to the warm place where her wings flowed into her back. "I'm hoping not to ruin this dress."

"It's a fine quality," he remarked. "And it looks fantastic on you with your green eyes and lovely blond hair. I'll have to thank Natasha for giving it to you."

Callian pressed his lips against hers briefly before turning serious once more. "How are we going to get out of here, especially now that Morgan is here?"

She buried her face against his chest, eased by his steady heartbeat, so different than it had been mere hours ago, and spoke into his skin. "I don't know. I don't even want to think about it tonight. It's been stressful enough."

"Fair enough," he whispered to her hair.

Within moments, she was asleep.

LING'S RETURN

Nahor opened the door to his room, hardly daring to hope.

The figure by the window stood as if spellbound by the beautiful view. She still wore the hood of her too-long cloak over her head, the material draped over thin shoulders, thinner than he had remembered. Those shoulders curved as if they bore the weight of the worlds, and the sight made him ache.

He shut the door softly behind him, and she stiffened, proving that she was aware of his presence.

"Ling?" he dared to whisper.

She didn't speak, but her voice filled his head as she thought words for him.

Hello, Nahor.

He couldn't even begin to decipher the myriad of emotions in those two words. He would have needed Ephraim to be nearby.

He strode forward in a sudden movement and then stopped just as abruptly, unsure, awkward around the woman he had known for most of his very long life. He had dreamed of this moment for years, but now that it had come, he had no idea what to do.

"Ling," he murmured, almost a plea, praying for her to turn so he could see her face.

She seemed to understand. Turning, her hands lifted to lower the hood, and he nearly cried out in dismay. She had always been on the thinner side, but now she was emaciated, as if she had been starved, her skin paler than usual, as if she had gone far too long without seeing sunlight. Her clothing was dirty and torn, ill-fitting, bare feet peeking out under the hem of the borrowed cloak.

"*Ehin*," he swore suddenly. She was crying. *Crying.*

He closed the distance between them, cupping her face, searching her eyes as well as her mind in an effort to understand what was wrong without having to make her say it.

"What is it, Ling? What is wrong?" he whispered to her.

She backed out of his touch, eyes fearful. "I'm so sorry," she murmured.

He reached for her again. "Ling, please, what can I do for you?"

She flinched away, and he dropped his hand, dread curling through him. Her words confirmed his fears.

"Don't touch me. I'll get you filthy."

Fresh tears ran down her cheeks when she saw that he understood what she either couldn't or wouldn't say.

Ling had been raped.

His mind worked furiously, trying to fathom who could be cruel enough to harm her. Who in his right mind could do that to her?

She turned away, wrapping her arms around herself, displaying more prominently how wasted away she was. How long had she been on Amalay Kahelith? Where on that cursed land had she been?

He pushed the questions away. He would ask her for details later, perhaps much later when the wounds weren't as fresh, and simply let her offer up anything she wished to tell him. The first thing to do, even before letting her soak in warm water, was to get some food in her.

He stepped up to her carefully, moving slowly on silent feet, cautious not to make her feel trapped. Laying his hand on her arm lightly, he led her to the divan near the hearth, seating her. There was a blanket nearby, folded on the end of the low bed; he offered it to her. She took it without looking at him and slid off the borrowed cloak, wrapping the blanket around her. He hung the cloak by the door and coaxed a fire to life, setting a teakettle to boil. There was food set out on the low table against the wall; he took two plates and a knife, along with a shallow bowl of olive oil, a bowl of fruit, and a loaf of bread, and brought them to her.

She stared longingly at the bread, and he ripped a large piece off the loaf and handed it to her, not bothering with the knife.

"Eat, my love," he said gently. "You look famished."

She dried her eyes on a corner of the blanket and took what he offered, eating it in small pieces. His gift told him that she was trying to pace herself.

"Thank you."

"Any time," he whispered back, sitting on the floor in front of her, the fruit between them and the oil balanced on the divan beside her.

He watched her fingers tear another piece free and dip it in the oil. She still wore the rings he had given her so very long ago. The sight warmed him.

How do you not hate me now that you know? The thought flowed unbidden from her. She looked away, ashamed.

Nahor moved so that he was in her line of vision, forcing her to see his face. "How could I?"

Thank you, she thought again.

"You don't need to thank me for that."

She glanced up at the door.

"No one's outside, love. No worries. I asked Dolon to keep everyone away from me for a little while."

Relief crossed her face for the briefest of moments. And then she whispered, "Aren't you going to ask me who ... who it was?"

He turned slightly to lean his shoulder against the couch, nudging the bowl of fruit out of his way to stretch his legs out, crossing them at the ankle.

"I figured you didn't need that sort of torment right now," he finally answered. He picked up a piece of fruit—*pulmena*, one of her favorites—and began carefully removing the tough outer skin with his knife. The sweet flesh inside was a vivid blue color.

She looked down and then back at him. He watched her, meeting her eyes when she looked at him. Still holding her gaze, listening to her thoughts churn, he offered her a slice on the tip of his knife. She took it and simply held it in her mouth, eyes closed as she finally smiled.

I've missed these. I'd forgotten what they tasted like.

This is the time of year when they're the ripest, he reminded her. He cut himself a small piece, slicing off a bigger one for her, knowing her well enough to know that she would feel uncomfortable eating alone. *It has been a good spring for their trees—there are an abundance of the fruits for you to eat.*

She placed her fingers on his hand, and he transferred the knife to the opposite one to set it down, turning his captured hand over so that her fingers touched his palm. After a moment, she flattened her hand, pressing her palm against his, and he wrapped his fingers around hers. Her smile faded.

I thought about you, she murmured.

And I you, he returned.

It kept me going. I kept thinking that I had lost the will to live, that I was ready to die, and yet, every time I was given food, I ate. It took a while, longer than it should have, but I realized that I was holding on for you. I didn't want to lose you. I spent nearly fifteen years in that jail cell in the darkness. I couldn't seem to manage any magic even though the cell was unguarded by runes or demonmarks.

She fell silent, and through his gift he saw pieces of her memory of the place: a cold, dank stone hollow with iron bars bigger than her wrists marking the doorway. The Dark Fortress. Fear, loneliness, horror, grief, hunger, self-hatred, and longing tinged the memory.

The Resistance freed me with a little inside help, she continued.

He couldn't help but ask. *There is insurrection within the Dark Fortress?*

Not that I know of. The Resistance calls her the Traveler. She garbs herself completely in cloaks and veils her face; it is only possible to tell her gender when she speaks. But she came in one day—or night, I wouldn't know—and saw me, and the next day some of the Resistance was there and she with them. She was able to open the cell—I'm not sure how, though my guess would be that she had a lockpick or a skeleton key of some sort.

Again, her mental voice fell silent, her thoughts quieting. He held her hand and cut her another piece of *pulmena* with his left hand.

I want you to promise me not to go after him. I don't want you hunting him down.

His eyes hardened. *I can't promise that, Ling. Not even to you. You know that I plan on killing whoever hurt you. As I did when you were fourteen, just before we started courting.*

She reached over and touched a lock of his hair with her free hand. "Nahor, please," she said aloud. "I don't want you risking yourself. It's not that I'm trying to protect him. I'm trying to protect you. I ... I couldn't stand it if he took you from me, if he killed you. I—"

He caught the hand that touched his hair and pressed it to his lips to quiet her. Releasing her, he looked her in the eye; his voice solemn, he said, "I vow to you that I will not actively hunt him down, but should our paths ever cross, if by chance or in battle, I will kill him." He drew a blade from a hidden sheath on his leg, showing it to her. It was an assassin's blade, the edge slightly curved and wickedly serrated, the handle slim and fine. "This blade will rest in his heart."

He held her eyes as she thought over his words, sheathing his knife. She must have decided that it was the best he could give.

She dropped his gaze, gripping his hand tighter. *Malakieth. It was Malakieth.*

He made some sort of strangled noise in the back of his throat before he could stop himself, dropping his head to rest on the divan near their hands. She continued.

It was only once, when I first arrived. Some of the Rashek drugged me so much that I couldn't move. I tried to fight him off. I truly did. He was too strong. Please, believe—

I do, love. I do. But tell me this if you can. Was he in his true form or his human one?

Human. And it was only once, but still, Nahor—

Relax, my love. You don't need to tell me if you don't want to.

She shook her head. "No," she whispered. "This you need to know."

He looked up at her, dreading what he was about to hear.

One lone tear ran down Ling's cheek; he reached out to catch it, surprised when she let him touch her.

"Her name is Kirin. She's fifteen. I had to give her to the captain of Kali's personal guard to keep her from falling into her father's hands only hours after she was born."

His mind was numb in shock. He said the first thing that came to his mind. "He doesn't know about her?"

"He just found out."

"Because pregnancy is such a subtle thing," he snorted without thinking.

Ling ducked her head, shame washing through her. Guilt slammed into him, clearing his mind, making him feel wretched.

I do not hold you responsible or in any way blame you for the hell you were put through, beloved, he murmured into her mind.

A silent sob shook her shoulders. *But this was my fault. No, listen,* she said when he tried to interrupt, to calm her. *I was such a fool. I could have come home. A month and a half after it happened, I realized that I was pregnant, and the only thing I could think of was that I had to leave or else die trying. I slipped out in the dead of night under the light of the full moon and eventually stumbled across a portal back to this world, to the country of Kyria. I traveled near Ellasar but never entered. All because I couldn't bear the thought of returning home pregnant with another's child.* Ling tried to stop, but the words flowed from her, uncontrollable. *And so I gave birth alone and had only a few hours to recover before I realized that there were Shadow Dragons closing in on me. I fled with Kirin, fled without thinking of which way to go, when Kali's captain found me and agreed to take Kirin into Allerion to Candescere. She couldn't protect the both of us. I turned and ran for Ellasar. It didn't take long for them to catch me and bring me back to the Dark Fortress. I thought that Malakieth had guessed about Kirin, but I was wrong. It was a Nephilim general called Sisera who had captured me. That's how I ended up in that horrid cell. Because I was too stupid and too cowardly to come immediately home while I had the chance.*

Nahor set the food on the floor and eased himself up onto the divan to sit beside her. She dropped her head to rest on his shoulder, seeking comfort, and he rubbed her back while she cried.

Does Kirin still live with her grandmother? Allerion isn't too far from here; we could send for her, he offered.

Ling shook her head. *I asked that Kali have her taken to the Academy of the Dragon Knights near Caima, Kyria.*

That's a good deal farther but still doable, if you would like.

She left in the early spring, traveling here—

Perfect. We could send Ephraim and his dragon. I'd suggest Aramon, but he has an aggravating habit of not returning.

Ling finally smiled, though it was brief. *Kirin ended up in Amalay Kahelith, where we met again. But then she was captured by were-beasts and is in her father's castle with three dragons and a human prince, all of whom guard her passionately.*

Nahor managed a smile, more for Ling's sake than any humor. "Is she so beautiful that she attracts the guardianship of so many suitors? If so, I fear that the human prince will have the hardest time, given that he has the shortest life span."

He could see her tension ease at his gentle teasing. "No, he's the one she loves. Prince Callian of Giladeth. Of the dragons, one, a female, has bonded to Callian, with the male and the dracling female bonded to Kirin."

"Ahh. What sort of dragons are they?"

"Callian's is a Fire Dragon; Kirin's female is a Light Dragon, the male a Twilight."

Nahor made an impressed noise. "I hadn't realized that there were any left."

They were silent for a long moment. Ling had almost drifted off to sleep when she murmured, "Nahor, she's the Adkisha. Kirin is the fourth and final Adkisha."

FAMILY MATTERS

Kirin woke up alone on the divan. Groggy, confused, she sat up, looking around the main room. Beau looked back at her, lying perfectly still to keep from waking Xzylya.

She's been so tired, he whispered to his rider. *So young, and yet she kept herself going to support you and I while Tiamat and Callian lay dying.*

Kirin stood up and crossed over to the pair. Tiamat was nowhere in sight; likely she was with Callian, wherever he was.

Sitting on the cold floor, she leaned against Beau's warm shoulder, feeling the taunt muscles under the dark scales. Xzylya lifted her small head and yawned at her rider, and Kirin drew her close.

Come, darling, and rest with me. You have done so well recently.

The dracling made a contented sound in the back of her throat and rested her head on Kirin's lap, forelegs curled up against her breast, her tail wrapping around Kirin's calf, and her wings spread haphazardly on the ground. Kirin smiled and stroked the hatchling's neck, humming bits of mostly forgotten lullabies.

Beau rumbled happily and laid his head down again, neck curling so that his cheek touched her other leg. With her free hand, she traced the planes of his face.

Dragons are such beautiful creatures, she marveled.

Very powerful, Beau reminded her.

And yet so very gentle. There are times that I can't help but notice how human you all seem. But then I find myself wondering: are you like the humans, or are the humans like you?

His golden eyes opened and focused on her. *You are not the first to wonder that, little one. To my knowledge, though, none have ever come up with that answer.* His voice turned to musing. *If I should die, I should like to remember to ask Adonai that question. I should like to learn the answer.*

Kirin looked away. *I am afraid of death, of dying.*

He frowned, his dark brow pulling down over his eyes. It was a strangely humanoid gesture. *What is there to be afraid of?*

She hung her head, slightly embarrassed. *Of pain. Of failure. Of… not being able to be with the ones I love. Of course, my death would now mean yours and Xzylya's, the poor babe, but for years I had no ancestors to look forward to meeting should I die.* She tossed her braid over her shoulder as if shrugging off her fears. *But now, why worry?* she said flippantly. *Now when I know that I am immortal, I merely have to avoid dying by the blade in battle.*

Beau said nothing in reply, but he didn't have to. Kirin was well aware that, as the Adkisha, she was a prime target for enemies in battle.

They lay in silence, feeling the rising sun warm their backs through the gap in the curtained windows. It was very relaxing, and she felt her eyelids drooping.

A disconcerting thought drifted through her mind, and she shifted uncomfortably. Xzylya grumbled softly as she woke up.

Beau? she asked hesitantly.

One eye reopened to focus on her. *What is it, lady?*

She actually blushed at the title. *There was something I read before leaving the Academy that worries me. About the line of the Adkish.*

Don't believe everything you read, he snorted.

It was written by an elf who would have been alive during the time of Adkish Charlemagne.

He grew serious. *What about his writings unnerves you?*

There are only ever four Adkishes mentioned—expected. And I am that fourth one. I can't seem to help but wonder if that means that I will never die, or else be destroyed in some brutally horrendous way that the powers of the Adkish cannot pass on to someone else.

Beau lifted his chin to lick his rider's cheek, his long tongue flicking at her ears and making her giggle. *Know this well, Kirin. There is nothing that Adonai cannot do. Yes, there were only four Adkishes prophesied in the early ages of the worlds, and yes, you are the fourth and final Adkisha. But prophecies are rarely straightforward and seldom work out the way one might think that they would, and so it is often just as good, if not better, to live as if you've never heard of the prophecy.*

Do you think that we will live forever?

Beau's eyes closed once more, and he nestled his head back against her. *I do not know,* kihara. *I only know that I will make the best of as many days as I have been given, living to the fullest and the greatest as I can, whether it is ten days or ten thousand years.*

There was a certain wisdom in his words that Kirin admired, and it calmed her.

Her eyelids grew heavy with the warm sun on her back. She fought to stay awake.

Sleep, Beau murmured. *You're safe.*

How can I be safe in the Black Fortress?

Because you are in your father's castle, and his previous actions prove that he has no ill will toward you. You are his daughter, and in his own way, he cares for you.

Kirin let her eyes close and was fast asleep.

Callian lifted his arm just in time to block the blow. She lashed out with her left hand and caught him in the hip.

"Focus," she demanded. "Or do your injuries handicap you overmuch?"

He grit his teeth and lashed out in series of too-fast blows. He wasn't used to this speed.

She, however, seemed fine with it, blocking him easily. "Stop pulling your punches."

"I can't help that I was trained not to hit a woman."

She kicked her leg up in a fluid arch that made him duck. He swung low, taking out her ankle, but she rolled with the fall and sprang back to her feet undeterred. "Likely you spar with Kirin. Think of me as you would her." She snapped out and caught his shoulder, causing him to stagger backward. "At least in terms of an opponent."

"No good." He grit his teeth to ward off the pain in his body. "I plan on pulling my punches with her now as well."

She caught his fist in her open palm, and the sparring turned into a grappling match.

"Prince Callian, be serious and put your weight behind it," she snapped through bared teeth. "You have the advantage, so use it."

He forced her back a few steps. "You've been kind to us, Natasha. I don't want to hurt you."

"I spar with Malakieth all the time. I'm tough. Not to mention that I'm not fully human."

He paused in surprise, and she shoved him back. He threw his weight forward into her and twisted his arms, flipping her off her feet. She landed hard on her side and took a moment to get back to her feet, wincing as she did.

"Are you all right?"

"Yes, fine. A good fall with an ungraceful landing. It was well done, though." She shook herself and walked to the wall, bracing her left arm against it.

"This is why I wasn't throwing my weight around like I would against a male. I don't know my own strength anymore."

"It's fine, it's fine." She wrenched her shoulder back into place without crying out. "There's really only one way to learn. Give me a moment to catch my breath, though."

He nodded and sat down. She slid down the wall, resting her elbows on her knees. "You're a halfling?" he asked.

She nodded. "My mother was human."

"And your father?"

"A Rashek warrior. Imagine how I was conceived." Her voice dripped with sarcasm.

"I am sorry for your mother, and for you, for having such a sire."

"I never knew either. The women here give up their halfling children at birth. She was a slave, I would guess. I am one."

"Do you mind it? Slavery?"

She shook her head. "It is all I have ever known. From an early age, you were taught to think independently and to lead others. From infancy, I was taught that disobedience meant death. Belonging to Malakieth has its advantages—more freedoms, more liberties, more food, more clothing." She flashed an impish grin and raised her voice a bit. "Not to mention that he's *such* a handsome male."

"You're very amusing, Natasha," Malakieth returned, walking by the doorway in his true form.

Her grin grew. "I strive to be a source of constant amusement for you."

He rumbled a laugh.

She seemed pleased with her efforts. Callian watched the doorway that the dragon had walked by.

"When we met you before, in the prison ..." he trailed off.

She nodded. "Malakieth was the one to have found you and your lady. He sent me to free you."

"You said that you were betraying your people."

"I am half Rashek. In one sense, I was. And still am."

"Why did he do it? Why bother to free us at all? He must know—you must know that sooner or later, Kirin will have to challenge him in battle."

Her face grew troubled. "Prince Callian, I like you. I truly do. You are good and honorable and charming, and around here, you're very innocent as well. And I admire that—please don't take insult. But know that if and when that time comes, I will be at Malakieth's side, and I will not hesitate to harm you if it means protecting him."

"I hope that you would not be in that battle, Natasha. Harming you would be a poor way of repaying you for everything you've done for us. And it will be a cruel, horrid day when a daughter must fight her father."

She looked at the ground. "I wish that there were some way to prevent that day from occurring," she whispered. "If Malakieth defeats her, he will despise himself forever. But if he loses ... He's all I really have, Prince Callian. I do not know what I would do without him." She was silent for a moment. Then her shoulders squared and she stood up. "Enough with depressing subjects. Care for another round?"

Kirin woke up when her father entered the room.

Malakieth caught her eye. "Come. You and yours need to move into a more discreet room. And please, refrain from using magic. It is possible for Morgan to sense it, and having her come up here could place Natasha in jeopardy as well."

Xzylya stuck close to her side as Kirin moved toward her father. Beau moved in front of her, reaching the taller male first.

Can we trust you? he challenged.

Malakieth's eyes narrowed. *That is a question you must decide for yourself. I have no honor to swear on, but I will do what I feel is best for my daughter.*

Beau watched the male as he passed him, heading for the room Malakieth gestured to.

Come, little one, he called to Xzylya. She came bounding after him, giving Malakieth a wide birth.

Malakieth reached out and placed his hand on Kirin's shoulder to stop her.

"I was wondering if we could have a chance to talk privately," he murmured.

She didn't look at him. "There is nothing I have to say to you that isn't inappropriate."

"Everyone decent has nothing but inappropriate things to say to me."

"You brought that upon yourself."

"I am well aware of that."

"Then you are also aware I will eventually escape from here."

"I trust that you do not find yourself a prisoner. Staying in here is much safer than the rest of the fortress."

he would be forced to battle. Of course she would be his biggest mistake. It was only reasonable.

A pity that the knowledge still hurt—a pity that anything he said could hurt her so quickly and so sharply. Heaven and hell. He had betrayed his own people, started a war that had been raging for nearly four thousand years—by far the longest war in the history of all the worlds, to the best of her knowledge—and ruled over an entire world with a harsh, bloodthirsty army that made a habit of pillaging, raping, torturing, and murdering.

And yet, no matter how hard she searched for the anger, the righteous fury at this creature and his actions, she couldn't seem to find it. The knowledge, that lack of anger, scared her. How could she face him in battle without it?

Malakieth looked over at her, looking first confused and then shocked. She must have made some sort of noise.

"You're crying. *Gu tolen*. Why are you crying?" he asked, coming over to her. Shifting to his human form, he knelt in front of her, capturing her face when she tried to turn away from him. She wiped furiously at the tears, traitorous little things that they were. Why couldn't she have been born like he had been and shed crystals for tears? Dragons rarely ever cried; they just didn't seem to be able to unless someone they loved had died.

"Kirin?"

She swallowed, forcing her voice to sound normal. Her words still sounded choked, despite her best effort. "I'm your worst mistake. It...it shouldn't bother me. I don't know why it does." *Shut up, Kirin*, she commanded herself.

He flinched slightly; if he hadn't been touching her, she doubted that she would have felt it. Gently, he dried her cheeks with the edge of his sleeve. "You are not a mistake. What I did to Ling was wrong. It can never be undone. It may not ever be able to heal. But you— you are a wonderful being. You're a spitfire—Adonai only knows where that came from—and you have your grandfather's eyes." He touched her hair. "This is your mother's hair and her ears," he murmured. "But I've seen the fire that flashes in your eyes when you move to defend those you love. That comes from my people. And your wings—their color is only yours to claim." She smiled briefly. "You're a fantastic creature. How have I never heard of you before?"

"I grew up hidden within the Academy of the Dragon Knights of Kyria."

"And thus your ability to fight. Still, word would have leaked of a young halfling female learning sword play, especially given that you must be rather good at it."

She actually blushed at his praise. She was such a fool. "Lord Melchizedek had placed a binding spell on me. I was unaware of it until it started to unravel when I grew into my powers as the Adkisha."

"Brilliant of him."

"Growing wings is a painful process."

"And one that I apologize for."

She snorted. "As if you made me do it."

Both brows rose incredulously. "Unless Ling is hiding something important, I am fairly certain that your wings came from my genetics. They tend to run in my family."

She flashed him a grin.

He cocked his head at her, considering her. "So you grew up in the Academy."

"From four to fifteen, when I left to travel to Ellasar in hopes of being taught by Nahor."

His face twisted in a grimace. "Nahor." Then he frowned. "Where were you until you were four?"

"Castle Candescere."

His eyes widened; he leaned forward. "Under whose care?"

"I was never told."

He leaned back, and she couldn't tell if he was disappointed with her lack of knowledge or not.

"Have you always known who your parents were?"

She crossed her arms. "I thought you wanted to apologize, not interrogate me."

"I do, and I will. Soon. But I find myself, for the first time, getting to know the daughter I never knew I had. I want to know you, Kirin, your past, your travels, how much you were taught at the Academy. I want to know how you came to meet Beau and Xzylya and Prince Callian and Tiamat. I want to know everything—everything you'll tell me—and I'm hoping you'll humor me."

He waited for her reply. Her arms loosened. "Then you'll have to answer my questions. Truthfully."

He bowed his head to her. "Of course. Now, back to my previous question. How long have you known?"

"Not long," she admitted. "Not long after I found out that I was the Adkisha—Lord Melchizedek's spell hid the mark, as well as suppressing my magic—I met Callian. Only days after that, I met Ling and discovered she was my mother and Ephraim was my brother. I met Aramon while traveling, and it wasn't until Ephraim rejoined us that I found out he was my brother as well. I haven't met Nahor yet. And I first found out about you when we met that first time, although I should have suspected it."

He didn't bother to hide his regret. "I wish I had known about you from the beginning."

She cocked one brow at him. "So you could have raised me to be evil? Raised me here in the Black Fortress?"

"The latter. I would have liked to have raised you. I would have protected you, kept you happy. Natasha could have been your playmate."

"Have you raised her from infancy?"

"From age eleven."

Kirin shook her head. "I need freedom and the chance to prove myself and make my own mistakes. I couldn't have gotten that here."

"You're likely right." He sounded rueful. Quickly, he changed the subject. "Were you content at the Academy?"

Kirin thought about that. "I was," she finally replied. "I had several friends there, friends who would invade my quarters on my birthday to bring me dinner and a new book and who would claim they were only doing it because they were bored silly by the blizzard outside." She smiled with the memory, knowing she was blind for not having seen the depth of the friendship she had with Zedek and the majority of his squadron earlier.

Malakieth smiled with her. "Your birthday," he repeated. "How old are you?"

"Going on sixteen."

"How soon?"

She shrugged. "A few months."

"You don't know your date of birth?"

"I grew up an orphan," she reminded him coolly.

"Ah, yes. Did you court any of the Dragon Knights?"

She shook her head. "No. Although it was always assumed by everyone who knew us that when it came time to settle down and start rearing a family, I would wed Sir Jakir. He was one of the few that I didn't get into fights with, and he could have handled having a warrior for a wife." She smiled. "But then I met Callian."

"Would this Sir Jakir be jealous?"

Her grin grew. "Perhaps relieved. I'm not a normal Kyrian woman, a fact that I am well aware of. But yes, if I hadn't met Callian, we would have likely wed within a few years. He would have wanted to stay near his brother, who is courting a girl from Caima, and I wouldn't have wanted to leave the Academy. It would have been a practical arrangement—until I found out that I wasn't human." She shrugged one shoulder. "Callian is better for me, even though we did fight in the beginning."

"As a prince—Giladethian, correct?—he'll need to live in his own country. You would likely need to leave the Academy."

She looked at him. "I've already left," she murmured.

"Tell me about your travels, then. You said you were going to Ellasar? Amalay Kahelith is a far cry from there."

So she launched into the tale, telling him of all that had happened until she had met Beau.

"Why did you imprison him?"

"I didn't. A lot of things—wicked things—are done in my name, oftentimes without my knowledge. I had heard there was a Twilight

Dragon that had been imprisoned by Nephilim, but I didn't truly believe it until I went to see for myself. I saw your Beau and had no idea what to do with him. The next night, he was gone, leaving only a hole in the wall."

"We broke out," she explained. "He bonded to me and used my magic to escape."

His mouth twisted in a wry smile. "Hindsight had revealed as much. Go on."

She continued with her story until she reached the Spiriter. His eyes narrowed in anger.

"Is he dead?"

She nodded. "Trig killed him."

"Good for the human."

She frowned. "Wasn't he your man?"

Malakieth shook his head. "Morgan's. He's always been Morgan's. It bothers me that she knows about you."

"Perhaps she thinks I am dead."

"Unlikely. Continue, please."

Kirin told him of the imprisonment, and blushing, she told him of her trip into the underground dungeon to reclaim Callian, but left out the kiss they had shared. If Malakieth could tell she was omitting things, he said nothing. She told him of the long trek to the Fire Caves; his eyes widened as she told him of walking through the fire, of the burning maze, of flying with Callian, of the battle with the Chimera, and of being poisoned.

"You're lucky he was able to save you, especially given that he is new to magic," Malakieth murmured.

She nodded. "It was a near miss."

"You seem to have an abundance of those, daughter. How many times have you nearly died?"

She shrugged one shoulder. "I haven't kept count. I know that each time I near death, I am grateful to be alive."

He nodded, motioning to her to continue. She told him of finding the crystal and the healing that it had brought. "The curious thing," she said, looking at him pointedly, "is that during the imprisonment, your Natasha helped to free us."

Malakieth looked down at his hands, folded in his lap. "I had heard the Adkisha had been captured and was awaiting execution. By that point, the reports were saying the great hero was actually a young woman not yet of age. I don't know what made me do it—send Natasha to free you. I only know that it seemed a cruel twist of destiny that this hero was so young, and at the time, I assumed you had never been taught to fight. Adonai's choice didn't make any sense. And I couldn't simply leave you there to be executed. I'd have rather vanquished this child-hero in an honorable fight. At least you would have had a chance of defending yourself. Now though … things are different. So very different. But continue. Natasha came and freed you, you reclaimed Callian from the labyrinth, and you found Ishmael's crystal."

"We traveled back to the ruins to spend the night—likely our first night where something horrible wasn't happening, I might add … " She told him about meeting the child with no given name. She was intentionally vague about the Resistance, but he showed scant interest in them or in Dothan itself.

"And then we met and found out we were related to one another, and you picked Ling up and snarled at her." She stopped and waited for him to speak.

He looked down at his hands again. "And now it is my turn to apologize," he murmured. "And to explain."

He was silent for several long minutes, as if he were trying to organize his thoughts. "When we met, it stunned me to learn that I had a daughter. I had never even guessed I had gotten Ling pregnant. She fled the fortress in the middle of the night about a month after … after it happened. I assumed she was heading for the Resistance or even that she had found a portal back to Ellasar. I watched as she ran and let her go. I had already proven how bad I was for her. But seeing you … it was the first time I'd ever seen you. And there was no way to deny we were related. I didn't think, merely reacted, and I am sorry that I reacted in the manner I did. But I had to get out of there. My daughter was the Adkisha, the warrior I would one day have to battle. It was only later, once I was back in my tower where I could completely lose my mind and only Natasha would be the wiser, that I realized you might have been killed. I spent the next few days anxiously listening for the rumors, for the news that you were alive."

"I was thrown around a bit. I don't weigh much, and Rashek are rather powerful creatures. Both of my wings were wounded, and I broke one."

The look of horror on his face was almost comical. "How did you heal so quickly?" he whispered.

"Ling. And Callian. He also has healing magic."

He relaxed, looking relieved. "A boon. Even as a Light Dragon, I had no skill at healing."

"Does Natasha?"

He snorted, lowering his voice to make sure that it didn't carry. "No more than a skilled human might."

When he said nothing for a moment, she spoke, her voice firm. "It is now my turn to ask questions."

She watched his chest expand with a deep breath. Reluctantly, as if he were dreading what he knew she was going to ask, he nodded once.

"If you loved Ling . . . if you loved her, how could you do that to her?"

"Are you aware that she was drugged?" he mumbled.

That made her pause. "No matter. That's no excuse."

"It's the only one I've got," he said defensively. He paused and took another deep breath. "She must have wandered too close to a portal or even through one. But a group of Rashek soldiers captured her and brought her to the fortress. I'm still not sure if they thought that they were doing me a favor, or if they were trying to endear themselves to me, or if it was their idea of a good joke—though they did know that I loved her. Before they brought her to me, though, they drugged her with *matiasma*—the one substance that can make me lose control. It used to work on Morgan, by the way, but it doesn't anymore. Molyb found a way to block that effect for her, and since he tested it on himself, he is also immune. He offered to do the same to me, but the side effect is not something I would want. If you inject it into someone with any other kind of magic, such as light magic, Ashteroth's power, like yourself, or water magic, like your mother, it will temporarily knock out your power and, after that, your ability to move. To someone like me, it will make me crazy—I draw most of my power from Nishron now. But the Rashek that had found her, they gave her so much of that sludge she could barely move. And flying in through the window to find Ling in here…" He trailed off, his eyes trained on his hands in his lap, on the floor that he sat cross-legged on, anywhere but on her. "Seeing her again after so many years was like seeing Valour. Of course, simply being near the *matiasma* made me insane, and I was already emotionally excited to see her again. I just…lost control. And it didn't seem like she was resisting me. I…wasn't myself. I can't even remember it clearly, but I wouldn't have done anything at all to her if she hadn't been drugged with the one substance that usurps my control." He looked up to meet her eyes. "To this day, I still can't believe I did that to her. And I wish I could explain that to her."

"Why didn't you, then? When you recaptured her and deprived me of a mother? Why didn't you explain yourself then?"

His countenance was open, allowing her to read his emotions. "I didn't know she was here. My guess is that her recapture was Sisera's doing, or perhaps one of the other Nephilim leaders. I don't think she was harmed a second time, blessedly. But not long ago, Natasha was running an errand for me down by the dungeons and stumbled across her. She ran to tell me of her discovery, and I sent her—in disguise, of course—to the Resistance. She led them into the dungeon and helped them escape with Ling."

His words stunned her. "You have a way to contact the Resistance? Aren't they supposed to be your enemies?"

He gave her a sly, secretive smile. "Dearest daughter, I am *infamous* for being a traitor. You've seen Natasha under her cloaks. If she didn't speak or didn't give out her name, you would be hard pressed to guess what was hidden underneath. Is it a male? A female? Human? Nephilim? Elf? That is the point of the robes. Obscurity.

The Resistance calls her the Traveler. I know many of the openings to Dothan, if not all of them. Natasha brings them supplies when they need them desperately." His grin grew. "There's no need to look so surprised, Kirin. My fight isn't with children."

"Then who is it with?" she challenged.

He was silent, not looking away from her eyes. "I will let you know when I figure that out."

They were quiet for several minutes. Malakieth eventually shoved himself back, away from her, and resumed his true form, lying curled on the floor. Hesitantly, as if unsure of where they stood with each other, he inched closer until his head was in arm's reach of his daughter, then closed his eyes.

"Do you regret knowing about me?" she finally whispered.

One eye opened to look up at her. "No. Of course not."

"Even though it makes things harder, more complicated?"

"I am glad to call you mine." Cautiously, he rested his head on her knees. After a hesitant moment, she placed her hand on his black scales, feeling the power he contained. Her fingers traced around the edges of his horns.

"Why did you help me save Callian? I'm glad that you did," she said quickly, "but I don't understand your reasoning."

He snorted pale-gray smoke. "Kirin, I have fallen in love and had it ripped from me. Do you possibly think that I would wish the same fate upon my daughter? Especially if it is in my power to stop it?"

She didn't reply. After a moment, he spoke again, his voice filled with mischievousness. "And I approve of Callian."

"I'm so glad that you give your consent," she returned, smiling at his misplaced humor.

"A father's consent is very important," he teased.

It was becoming easier with each passing moment, talking with Malakieth. Here she sat in the Black Fortress with Malakieth resting his head on her lap. Here was the great betrayer, the destroyer of worlds, Morgan's apprentice ... and they were making jokes and laughing. Like any father and daughter from any country might.

Her smile faded.

"I don't want to fight you," she breathed.

"There has to be a way out of this fate," he replied. "I deserve punishment, but surely Adonai won't punish you as well. No child should be held accountable for the sins of their parents—or parent, in this case."

"I need to leave here. You know that."

His eyes opened to look at her solemnly. His words were a vow. "I'll think of a way."

REVELATIONS

Nahor stepped into the small, semi-private room where he and his family often broke their fast, his thoughts too distracted and preoccupied to notice at first there was a stranger in the room.

He paused, a mug of hot tea raised in one hand, and regarded her over it. "Elfan?" he guessed.

She nodded, nervous to meet him.

"Welcome to Taure En Alata." He took a sip of the tea. "And good morning. I hope you'll forgive me my rudeness. I find I have overmuch on my mind."

"Of course, my lord. And thank you for your hospitality."

He glanced around for his eldest son and didn't see him. Perfect. "Believe me, any woman to catch Ephraim's attention is more than welcome here. I've been trying to marry that man off for decades."

She blushed vividly.

One brow rose. "Or have I been reading this incorrectly?"

She blushed harder and seemed to search for a reply. Ephraim walked into the room then, Dolon at his side, both males bearing plates of food.

"It eternally sends them into a tizzy when I seek to bring the food to the dining rooms," his son stated. Across the room, Aramon flashed him a smile. Ephraim's eyes sought out Elfan, and he frowned, looking between her and his father. "What have you been saying to her to make her blush like that, *Abbo*?"

"Nothing at all."

"Other than that he has not been able to marry you off yet," Aramon added from the corner.

Ephraim shot his father a dark look. Nahor offered him a slight smile, drinking more of his tea.

"Although the same could be said of you as well, Aramon," he returned.

"*Abbo*, you know why—"

Nahor continued as if he hadn't heard him. "Though in your case it is not the lack of someone who interests you but sheer stubbornness."

"I'd make a horrid husband, always wandering off—"

"So hash it out with Niamh. Ask for her opinion on the matter."

"She says that it doesn't matter—"

"Then where is the problem?"

Aramon simply scowled at him.

"See, Dolon? Sheer stubbornness."

Dolon smiled. "I dare say that he takes after his father quite well."

Aramon grinned victoriously. "Thank you, Dolon, for pointing that out." He snatched a pastry off one of the dishes.

Ephraim was explaining the different foods in an undertone to Elfan. Aramon dropped into a chair. Dolon crossed his legs and leaned his shoulders back against the corner closest to the door, ready to be both a companion, a steward, and a guard at a moment's notice.

With the bantering gone, Nahor had plenty of time to be overwhelmed by his thoughts again.

Someone rapped on the table near him, making him flinch in surprise. Dolon frowned at the king. Ephraim withdrew his hand, eyes narrowing at his father.

"You are extremely distracted this morning."

It wasn't a question, and something in his tone made Nahor's temper flare, his eyes narrowing.

Ephraim's gift picked up on that, making him want to lash out defensively. Instead, he crossed his arms and forced his body back into his chair. Aramon looked between the two, eyes starting to glow bright blue as he called on his gift. Dolon and Elfan looked confused.

Nahor reined in his temper before he did something rash. His sons relaxed. Leaning back in his chair, mimicking Ephraim's posture, he regarded them.

"Dolon, close the door, please."

When the door was shut, he met both of his sons' eyes, first Ephraim, the eldest and the best with magic, and then Aramon, the rasher, more unpredictable of the two.

"You are both ready to attack me," he stated, his voice dangerously quiet. "Why." It wasn't a question.

Blatant disbelief crossed both of their faces.

Don't even tell me she slipped off before he could see her. The thought went spinning through Aramon's mind.

Does he know that I am still here? That was Elfan.

Ehin. Didn't he talk to her? Or did she refuse to say anything? Ephraim.

King Nahor, Dolon thought to him. *Would you prefer it if I left?*

Nahor held up his hand, but there was no way to completely silence the thoughts of others that spun inside his mind.

"No, Dolon, you may stay. Likely everyone else in the room already knows—knew before me." He leveled a hard glare on his sons. "And you're nearly family. Yes, Lady Elfan, I am still aware that you are here. Aramon and Ephraim—yes, she is still here, and yes, I did talk to her. Why else would I be so distracted?" He turned to Elfan. "How much, exactly, do you know of this?"

She slid closer to Ephraim. "All of it, lord king."

His gaze returned to his sons. "And how long did the two of you know?"

They looked at each other.

"I found out around Yule," Ephraim admitted.

"I learned several months after him," his brother added.

"Half a year. Half a year, and neither of you thought to tell me?" he demanded, incredulous.

"That's not the sort of thing you'd want to find out in a letter," Aramon snapped defensively.

"You can *dreamwalk*. You could have at least mentioned something months ago."

"Dreamwalking is a difficult process—"

"And one that you've perfected. I'm well aware that you communicate with Niamh that way all the time."

"And what am I supposed to say? Come visit you in a dream some random night and say, 'Oh, by the way?' You would have been after me with questions, wanting to speak to her, and I was out there trying to protect the Adkisha."

Nahor took a deep breath to calm himself.

"You've found the Adkisha, then?" Dolon asked mildly.

"Yes, and she happens to be my daughter."

Dolon choked on the tea he had just taken a drink of. "Princess Terah?"

"No."

Dolon paled. "Heaven and hell," he breathed. "How did you manage to keep it secretive? Surely there would have been at least one rumor."

"She's not actually my blooded daughter," Nahor stated quietly. Turning to look his sons in the eye, he added, "Though I'm willing to claim her as such, if she'll have me."

He could see Elfan starting to smile. Both of the princes relaxed completely, looking relieved.

"We were afraid that you were going to be unreasonable," Ephraim admitted, smiling.

Dolon was staring at him. "You've found the queen," he whispered, as if by talking too loud she might disappear again. "Ling is home."

Nahor nodded. "She's asleep in our room. Which, until further notice, is inaccessible by any and all males, regardless of who they might be."

Dolon started to smile. He had always had a fondness for Ling, for the kind-hearted human girl who had stolen Nahor's heart when he was young, for the beautiful, loving elven queen she had grow up to be. "I'll simply have to wait until you see fit to bring her out into the rest of the castle to greet her, then."

Nahor didn't smile. "I'm afraid that I have to ask you not to touch her."

"Truly, my lord. She won't disappear again."

The king could see the moment his steward understood. The blood drained from the elder elf's face. "The queen had a daughter. A daughter who is not yours." He shook his head. "Impossible. Ling would never do that to you."

"She wasn't given a choice," Nahor replied softly.

Dolon swore in an undertone in their native tongue. "Who would do such a thing?"

Nahor's eyes were hard. "Malakieth." Abruptly, he began to gather together a plate of food to take to his wife. "The girl's name is Kirin. She's nearly sixteen. And she is currently with her father in the Black Fortress. When that situation is rectified, she will be invited here. And in the meantime, I will tend to my wife." He stood to go, pausing to turn to Elfan. "I am glad to have met you, however strange this brief meeting may have been, and I hope you will honor my family with your presence for as long as you see fit. It's not always as … dramatic around here was it was this morning, and for that, I apologize."

And then he was gone, heading toward his chambers and his beloved wife in hopes of starting the long healing process that loomed on the horizon.

Malakieth showed Kirin to the small room where she, Callian, and the dragons would be staying. Callian was already inside, sitting on the ground with his back against Tiamat's shoulder, cleaning his sword. He looked up and smiled at her in welcome. She could see the tiredness etched in his face, but his pleasure showed through.

"Natasha has been sparring with him for the past several hours; he'll need practice relearning his own speed and strength now that you've changed him," Malakieth murmured to her. Raising his voice, he spoke to them both. "A word of caution, daughter, Prince Callian—stay within these rooms, be prepared to be absolutely silent at a moment's notice, and use no magic. Morgan once had a habit of coming up here unannounced, and I doubt that has changed much, no matter how many years have gone by. Immortals tend to be horribly tenacious."

He turned to his daughter but was distracted by someone bumping his hip. Looking down, he saw the hatchling, Xzylya, looking up at him.

He knelt so that he was her level. *Greetings, little Xzylya,* he mindspoke to her, *dracling of my own race, bonded to my daughter.*

She arched her neck, pleased by his formal greeting. She turned to her rider, and Kirin heard her voice for the first time, speaking in Dragons' Tongue. *Koyoi, dasha.* Hello, rider.

Kirin grinned, throwing her arms around the young dragon's neck. Koyoi, *Xzylya, little love,* she replied. *Greet my father.*

Xzylya turned to look at Malakieth. "*Koyoi,*" he murmured to her. He straightened, turning back to Kirin. "I will leave you now. I thank you for talking with me."

Kirin bowed her head. "Thank you."

Malakieth returned the bow and left, closing the door most of the way behind him. Kirin smiled and sat down beside Callian, Xzylya standing over them.

"She's learning to speak."

Callian reached out to rub Xzylya's scales. "So Beau told Tiamat, who in turn told me." He stroked Kirin's hair, feeling the way the silken strands twisted in her braid. "How have you been?"

"I'm..." She sighed. "I am good. I am confused. I am...unsure. A little afraid," she admitted sheepishly.

He pulled her against his side. She sighed again and buried her face against his shoulder. He smelled of male and dragon and of the polish he had found to clean the steel of his sword.

"You are a young woman in the middle of a destiny she didn't want and didn't ask for, trapped in a place with a horrible reputation. Anyone with any sense would be frightened," he whispered into her hair.

wouldn't have to bend. His hands cupped her hips, holding her close, sliding to her back, her wings. She locked her hands against the back of his neck, her fingers knotting in his hair.

Kirin, Beau warned, his voice low.

Dasha?

Kirin ignored them, too swept up in the moment to care.

And then Callian pulled back, breaking the kiss slowly.

Common sense returned to her. She leaned back, but not before she nuzzled into him and placed a quick kiss under his jaw.

"Yes, I'd say that counted," Callian replied, eyes dancing.

It took Kirin a moment to remember what they had been talking about. She blushed and picked up her sword again, giving the blade one last wipe and sheathing it. Reaching for her knife, she set to work again.

They spent the better part of three hours like that, tending to their weapons and their leather and kissing. Each kiss served to inflame Kirin more, building up the flames by adding dry kindling until she thought she would erupt. She was surprised that she had not yet lit anything on fire.

Callian leaned forward and grabbed Beau's saddle and the harness that kept it in place. Kirin admired the way his shoulders and arms moved under his shirt as he lifted it up, muscles flexing as he twisted, watching the way the setting sun slanted across his cheekbones through the slight part in the drapes, the way it touched his eyes, the way his blond hair fell haphazardly over his brow. *It needs to be cut,* she noted abstractly.

She wondered if he was the sort to allow his skin to grow dark during the summer when he was in his homeland. In Kyria, no noble would be caught with sun-darkened skin.

"What are you thinking about?" Callian asked, breaking into her thoughts.

She felt herself start to blush. "Vanity and skin tone."

He blinked in surprise. "What about it?"

"Does your skin darken in the summertime?"

"It's a natural process, so, yes."

"Giladeth's nobles promote that? Letting one's skin darken?"

He frowned. "Giladeth's nobility does not promote it in other nobles. It's a mark of physical labor. The knights and the army often grow dark, though, and I with them. While the nobles don't enjoy it, the common folk do. They like *me* because I attend the nearby festivals and help with the planting and the harvest and walk through the towns and villages. And that's the sort of approval I want when I am king. The commoners'. After all, they are the backbone of any country."

He is wise beyond his years, Beau murmured.

Someone rapped on the door before pushing it open. Natasha came inside with a tray laden with bowls of stew, warm brown bread, and a small square of cheese. Tea steamed in ceramic cups.

"Natasha, I could have helped with that," Kirin protested, rising.

"Sit down, sit down," Natasha returned. "This is what I'm here for. Making meals from scanty food."

Seeing as your master is the leader here, wouldn't there be more food? Tiamat wondered. Callian relayed her words.

Natasha looked at the Fire Dragon, her head tilted sideways. "The army eats a great deal. The people of the land have almost nothing to survive on. Malakieth hunts what he can in the places the people cannot reach, and tries to be as frugal as possible."

Tiamat dipped her head to show she understood. Natasha handed the tray to Kirin and left them alone for the night.

They sat down to eat, Beau nipping at Xzylya's tail when the dracling tried to butt in. Xzylya spun to snarl at him and was met by bared teeth. She dipped her head in submission and slipped away to curl docilely on the far side of Kirin.

Callian cut the bread and the cheese in quarters, giving each dragon a share. The remaining quarter he divided between Kirin and himself, making sure that her pieces were slightly bigger. The bread, though made from coarse grain, was filling and homey. The stew was delicious, filled with potatoes and carrots and wild rice and flavored with onions. There was some type of meat in the stew, but she couldn't identify it, nor could she taste it—the onions hid it too well.

Callian looked up. *Any idea what this is that we're eating?* he mindspoke to her.

No. Sometimes it is best not to ask. It tastes fine to me.

Kyrian food tastes fine to me, though Giladethians don't seem to eat onions.

A pity.

He watched her, his eyes suddenly strange.

What is it, love? she asked.

I should like to take you to Giladeth and show you around Haven and the castle.

Kirin looked down. *Your court would not approve of me. I am too farrin for a land unaccustomed to dragons.*

They will learn in time. But I would take you dancing at the castle and take you hunting with falcons and hounds and to Haven on market day. It's easier for me to imagine than I thought it would be, and even in my mind, seeing you in Castle Haven . . . it's a lovely sight. You would bring so much beauty to the castle. He paused. *In all honesty,* would *you like to go to Giladeth someday?*

Kirin was silent for a long time before replying. *I am always ready for a new adventure. But I would miss Kyria and her wild winters and the deep forests around the Academy. I don't know Ellasar or Allerion well enough to miss them.*

We would return before long. When my time as king is over, where else are we to go? I am now immortal and in line by blood for the throne of a country of mortals. I cannot rule Giladeth forever. I'll marry, settle down, raise a family, and let one succeed me to the throne in the same time span that I would if I were mortal.

Kirin looked at him, gauging his reaction. *There are two flaws to your plan, Callian. The first and most obvious is that you are planning to leave Giladeth after your time on the throne, but you plan to have your son succeed you to the throne. Are you planning on living on one side of the world while your son and daughter-in-law rule on the other? And the second is something that is a side effect of immortality.* She took a deep breath, steeling herself against any reaction that he might have. *Immortals are not very fertile. As a turned mortal, you may be more so than most, but if you wanted a chance at having a son within the next five or ten years, it would not be with me. I will not be fertile for many more years.* That's *why the immortal populations are a normal size.*

Callian's expression was carefully arranged so as not to hurt her. She had had no choice in the matter over changing him; he had been dying—it wasn't as if she could have explained everything in advanced and then asked if he still wanted immortality. He should have expected that there would be some down side, some negative to being immortal. Kirin hadn't said that he *couldn't* have children, only that it would be *harder* to. And if he wanted to sire her children, he would have to wait and be patient.

Most immortals start to be fertile around one thousand nine hundred years of age, Kirin added softly. *Roughly.*

You have a while to wait, then. I have a while to wait.

Sorry.

I don't blame you. Quite honestly, if our places had been reversed, and I had been given your powers and you had lain dying in front of me, I would have done the same.

Kirin smiled at him, her eyes tender.

He smiled back, setting his empty bowl back on the tray and grabbing his pack. He shoved it against the wall and lay down, resting his head on it.

"May I ask you something personal?" he murmured.

She set her own bowl beside his and drew her knees up to her chest, wrapping her arms around her legs. Her wings flared out to keep her balanced. "Of course."

"Do you want children? Someday?"

Kirin nodded. "At least one. Hopefully more. Do you? Or rather, would you if your court didn't demand it of you?"

"I've never really thought of it that way, to be truthful. My whole life has been in preparation for ruling the country. A wife and an heir were always assumed."

"Would you have had a choice in a wife?"

He snorted. "If you'll remember, I ran off to Kyria before they could make me marry Teresa."

She grimaced. "Ah. Yes. Her."

He gave her a half-smile. "I prefer blond-haired women," he teased.

"Rogue," she shot back.

He grinned at her, and she smiled back, and for the moment, everything was right in the world.

PRINCESS

Ephraim knocked on the door to his father's rooms, still hesitant even though his gift let him know there was no passion in the room, nothing that he was intruding upon.

"Come in, Ephraim," his mother called from inside.

It was so strange and so good to hear her voice again inside the castle.

He opened the door and stood in the door frame, content to take in the domestic scene: his father seated on a stool, his hair tied back from his face, dressed in older, rougher clothes as he worked a file over an arrowhead, dozens more on either side of him; his mother resting on the divan with her feet tucked up, needle flashing in the rosy glow of the setting sun as she hemmed a skirt, the remains of fabric scattered on the ground nearby.

Nahor looked up, and Ephraim stared in amazement as the male's eyes sparkled, happiness and contentment written both on his face and in the emotional pattern that he sensed.

He hasn't been this happy in years, Ephraim couldn't help but note. *I'd almost forgotten what it was like.*

You weren't the only one, my son, came the reply.

"Surely you knocked for a reason," Ling murmured. He turned his eyes to her to see that her needle had stilled as she gazed at him expectantly. Her face, her eyes … they had lost the fearful, haunted expression he had nearly grown used to seeing.

Dear Lord in Valour, it does wonders for her to be here.

"There has to be a reason, an explanation."

Nahor was silent, mulling over things. "Let me ask you a difficult question. And keep your emotions from tangling with your logic." When Ephraim nodded warily, he continued. "Have you considered the possibility that you may have already recovered the princess?"

Ephraim shot him a confused look.

"Elfan— No, be silent and hear me out. She's drawn to you. She can't remember her family. Her age is a rough guess. She's old enough to be Terah. What's to say that she's not my daughter?"

"So now every woman that is drawn to me must be related to me?" Ephraim snarled.

"Shut up, and think clearly. Draw yourself out of the picture."

Ephraim breathed deep, turning back to the serenity of the gardens below, and forced himself to think it through. It was a horrible idea.

He shook his head slowly. "I wouldn't feel this way for a sister."

"You couldn't love a sister? What of Kirin?"

"That's exactly it. I do love Kirin. But not… It's not the same. With Elfan… what I feel… isn't chaste, to say the least."

Nahor heard what he couldn't bring himself to put into words, could hear the nervousness and fear behind his thoughts.

What if I ask her if I could court her, and she refuses me?

Based solely on the small bit of time that I watched the two of you interact, I would hazard a guess that she would not. My only fear is that she may be your sister.

"I can't bring myself to believe that," Ephraim whispered.

"Because you love her."

Ephraim looked at his father. "How sick and twisted would a man have to be to desire his sister so strongly?"

"For your sake, my son, I hope that she is not my daughter by blood. But give me an hour to talk to one of sages, and then take her out into the gardens and walk with her. And about this girl, Oracle—is there any way of getting her to leave the Resistance, even for a short while?"

Ephraim shook his head. "None that I can see, short of kidnapping her."

"We may need to do that clandestinely. If it comes to that, would you be capable of doing it, or would you rather I charge Aramon with the task?"

"Aramon would be the better choice, given his wanderlust and his ability to disappear at the most inconvenient times, but I would rather not get his hopes up only to have them proved wrong." He paused for a moment. "Assumptshun believes that we would be able to do it, provided Thief does not raise the alarm."

"And who is Thief?"

"A human boy with a skill at staying hidden and with knife-play. He is always with her, guarding her, looking out for her. He's madly in love with her, and she returns it. Likely in a few years they will declare themselves married and move into the same chamber in Dothan. There is no marriage ceremony on Amalay Kahelith anymore, or at least not much of one, to the best of Elfan's knowledge."

"Elfan ..." Nahor mused. "Could *she* talk Oracle into visiting?"

"Not likely. Although, if we do not do a kidnapping, you will likely end up with two children coming to Taure En Alata instead of one. I doubt that Thief will let her go alone to a strange place."

Nahor frowned. "Then an abduction may be our best option. I need her alone to have time to watch her gift in action. I don't want the boy interfering." He was silent, thinking through the details, the ramifications. "The court does not need to know about this. Dolon and Aramon do not need to know about this. I would exclude Elfan, but trust is essential to a relationship. I'm getting quite desperate to marry you off to a good woman, and she seems to be one, providing that she is not my daughter. You may tell Elfan. Ling ... doesn't need to know yet. I won't build up her hope only to destroy it. I don't know how many more blows she can withstand."

Ephraim drew himself up. "Then, once you confirm that she is not my sister, I will leave for a short hunting trip or something of the sort and return with a captive, hopefully leaving behind a very irate human."

"Of course, this is unofficial. We never planned this."

Ephraim grinned. "But of course."

"Be in the gardens with Elfan in an hour."

The grin disappeared. "I will."

"And Ephraim?"

The prince turned and raised his brows.

"I hope that you are correct," Nahor said. "On both accounts."

"As do I, *Abbo*. As do I."

"Come for a walk with me," Ephraim coaxed.

Elfan set her knife aside and rose, wrapping the beautiful cloak around her shoulders. Ephraim offered her his arm, and she blushed faintly as she took it.

"The gardens are beautiful, especially in the twilight," he told her as they walked through the castle.

Everywhere they went, eyes followed, making Elfan nervous. "Would that I had brought that knife after all," she murmured to him.

"No one would harm you. They are only very curious."

"Because I am *farrin*?"

"And because you prefer to speak the Common Tongue."

"Then I should work on speaking in Elvish."

"If you like," he replied. "In truth, it doesn't matter. You've learned Elvish once; you'll pick it up again quickly enough simply hearing it spoken again, and you understood everything at breakfast this morning. Which is typically a calmer affair—my brother and I do not usually threaten our father. That was purely for Ling's sake, and for Kirin's, rather than any political reason."

Elfan smiled. "You love your sister despite her sire."

"Of course. I love both of my sisters."

She stared at him. "There is another? I haven't even heard of her."

"Most don't talk about Terah, especially around Ling."

"If I may ask, a scandal or a tragedy?"

"Tragedy. Terah disappeared when she was only four years old. We haven't seen or heard from her since. But, in the strictest confidence—and you are sworn to secrecy"—he smiled faintly at her, and she returned his smile and nodded—"I have reason to believe that I may have located her at last."

Elfan's eyes grew wide. "She still lives?"

"That is my hope. I have been discussing it with my father, and we've decided that Ling and Aramon are not to know until we have some form of verification."

"Wouldn't a mother prefer to know immediately of any news of her child?"

"Ling has been through too much these past years to have her hopes raised and destroyed again. I'd rather have her angry with me. And Aramon would run off and do something rash."

He opened the doors in front of them, and she gasped.

"Ephraim, it's beautiful!"

He smiled wryly. "I assure you, I had nothing to do with its beauty. I'm hopeless with plants."

Elfan let go of his arm to hurry ahead of him into the garden. Spellbound, she reached out to touch the nearest rose, only to pause and look at him. "May I?"

"Of course. Roses have thorns, though," he warned.

She wandered from plant to plant, marveling at them, at the buds and the blooms. He followed her, naming each one for her, telling her of any medical uses it might have.

She grabbed his wrist. "Ephraim, it's glowing. That one is glowing."

He looked where she pointed and smiled. "That's why I wanted to show this garden to you at night. That is called *galdia*. It's very rare and difficult to grow. Do you see how the blooms grow in that shape, like a trumpet or a hunting horn tipped up? *Galdia* forms a nectar inside those blooms, called Numinor's Nectar. If any creature that does not have elven blood drinks it, they will die within moments. But if an elf consumes it, it will bring them back from the point of death. Still, one must be careful of how much one consumes. Unfortunately, *galdia* is incredibly rare and difficult to grow, or our entire army would go to battle carrying the nectar with them."

He reached out and closed his fingers around one of the blooms, producing a thin vial from his pocket. Single-handedly, he twisted the stopper off and held the vial beneath the bloom, pouring the glowing golden contents into the thin tube. Even though the vial was small, it still took three of the large blooms to fill it. He pushed the stopper back in place and twisted a wire around the neck of the thing, forming a loop that he threaded a leather thong through. He knotted it off and handed it to her.

"Should a need, Adonai forbid, ever arise. That vial will not shatter—the crystal forms in a hidden cave and is amongst the hardest substances ever formed. It will keep the nectar safe."

She dropped it over her neck and tucked the vial under her shirt. "Thank you," she murmured. The immensity of his gift was not lost on her. That little vial could save her life—or enable her to save someone else's.

Ephraim stilled as he heard his father's voice enter his mind.

Lady Aelollora has looked into Elfan for the bonds of blood and family and has found none. You were correct when you claimed she was not your sister. I have told Lady Aelollora of Oracle, and she has agreed to meet with her. The quicker you could bring her to Taure En Alata, the better. Lady Aelollora has already arranged for Lord Eolaphos to open a portal to and from Dothan for you and Assumptshun as soon as you are ready.

Send my thanks to Lady Aelollora and Lord Eolaphos, and tell them I will be ready by midnight. Assumptshun and I will meet Lord Eolaphos by the western-most armory.

Lady Aelollora and Lord Eolaphos were two of the oldest and most powerful of the sages. They were also amongst the sanest— several of the others had been driven to the brink of insanity by their gifts, which only seemed to intensify over time. If Lady Aelollora said Elfan was not related to him, then none in her ancestry were likely related to any of his ancestors for at least five generations.

He watched Elfan drift between a climbing rose and an orchid with blooms the size of his hand, watched her as she smiled breathlessly, enchanted by the garden and the beauty she had never seen, by the sweet perfume of the flowers, and by the warm summer night air. Stepping up behind her, he placed his hand on the small of her back.

"Lady Elfan, may I court you?" he murmured.

She spun to face him, eyes wide. "Me?"

"Yes," he replied, smiling down at her.

"But you're the prince," she pointed out.

"I have been made aware of that fact," he teased.

"And I'm nobody."

"You are a beautiful woman with a good heart and an unmistakable skill with a bow. That's not nobody."

He could feel the yearning rising up in her, but whether it was a yearning to acquiesce or to flee from him he did not know.

"You should be courting a lady of the aristocracy, not some peasant girl from Amalay Kahelith," she whispered.

"I don't want an aristocrat. I want a woman who still admires something as small and as lovely as a flower, who has seen so much evil and yet has not let it jade her, and who can shoot a bow as well as any man. You don't have to give me an answer now, and know that you can always refuse me." He flashed her a quick smile even though it hurt. "I won't turn rabid or anything; never fear."

She smiled back. "No, I ... I would be honored if you would court me. I am simply ... surprised you asked."

Ephraim pulled a thin silver band out of his pocket and took her right hand, sliding it onto her finger. It was a little big, but magic quickly fixed it to fit her.

She tugged a hide strap from around her neck, pulling a similar ring off. "I've always had this and had never really realized what it was for. It's not much, but ... it's mine." Blushing, she slid it onto his hand.

He lifted his fingers to look at the small shape etched on the top of the ring. "It's lovely. That's a barn owl, the symbol of the Iada House in northern Ellasar. You may have kin there."

She grinned up at him, and he drew her into his arms amongst the flowers.

"Then someday you may need to take me to meet them."

"Gladly," he whispered.

Ephraim slipped down the dark tunnel, Assumptshun in front of him, scouting ahead in his human form. The dragon's night vision was better than Ephraim's, and both dragon and rider knew it.

Assumptshun paused and sniffed the air at the intersection.

Get back.

Ephraim flattened himself against the rough wall, watching as a small knot of children came walking by. There was an emaciated boy in the back with a bandage around his brow who stopped and glared into the tunnel, eyes narrowing in suspicious.

"Twenty-four, what is it?" one of the other boys asked, doubling back to stand beside his friend.

"I'm not sure."

Ephraim directed his gaze to the ground in front of him, aware that Assumptshun was doing the same. There were some—even amongst the humans—who could tell when they were being stared at.

"I don't see anything," the second boy said. "Come on. Cook will have already made dinner; let's hurry before it's all gone."

The thought of food distracted the boy in black, and he turned and followed his friend down the adjacent tunnel.

At least we now know which way to the central chamber. That may be the easiest route.

And the most obvious, Ephraim pointed out. *I want to take her from her room or from an empty hallway. I hesitate to knock these children out.*

I don't.

I know that.

They paused again at another crossroads, and Ephraim drew a scrap of parchment out of the pocket of his tunic, sliding a glass tube full of glowworms from a pouch by his waist. Elfan hadn't been happy with the kidnapping, but she had reluctantly drawn him a map that detailed where the portal should lead to and where Oracle's room would be, along with telling him who else shared the room with her.

That was Ephraim's biggest concern: her roommates. He dreaded finding Oracle only to have to knock out three other small girls.

Oracle shared the room with Red, Cook, and a girl they called Flit, whom Elfan said had a habit of leaping nimble-footed from high places without making a sound.

Assumptshun had no such worries.

It took them longer than they would have preferred to traverse the tunnels of Dothan, but they eventually reached the room. Ephraim looked up and noted the symbols painted over the doorway, symbols that he could not read or even identify what language it was in. The first was simply enough in its making: three short, horizontal lines bracketed by two slightly curved vertical lines. The second looked like a forked road, except the whole thing was swept slightly to the left and was guarded by two short, vertical lines with the same sweep. The third was stranger—what looked like a crescent moon that was held aloft by a line with a diamond shape in the middle opened downward and attempted to swallow a small, six-pointed star.

Focus, Ephraim. You can ask Elfan about them when we get back.

Ephraim listened at the ragged curtain that served as a door, hearing the voices inside. One was Oracle. The other he didn't recognize. It could be Cook or this Flit. Red's voice wasn't quite that high.

He hoped that there were only the two girls inside rather than a silent one or two.

Do we charge in and grab her and silence the other, or do we wait until the others return and they all fall asleep?

Neither option was ideal.

What if we could draw one of them out? he asked.

He could feel the dragon warming to the idea. *Be careful of the oracle. If her Sight alerts her of us, we've lost the element of surprise.*

Ephraim sprung at his dragon, grabbing the male and slamming him against the rough wall. He felt the echoing pain shoot down his back.

You'll pay for that, elf, Assumptshun snarled.

Later.

He pressed himself against the wall near the ratty curtain as Assumptshun let himself crumple to the ground, careful to hide his face. Ephraim pulled the scarf up over his nose and mouth, tugging the cowl down to hide his eyes.

The curtain was tugged aside as Oracle and a tiny human, who could only be Flit, peered out into the hallway. They crept to Assumptshun, first Oracle and then Flit.

The dragon lay still, barely breathing, as Oracle stooped to find a pulse. On silent feet, Ephraim crept up behind Flit, ready to grab her.

Oracle touched Assumptshun, and the dragon grabbed her, locking his arms around her and rolling to cover her. Ephraim had Flit in his arms within the same second, one hand covering her mouth. He backed the smaller girl into the room and sent his magic—the magic he had gained from bonding with Assumptshun—spiraling into her, knocking her unconscious. Laying her down, he retrieved the sack Assumptshun and he had brought with them and a short letter and left them in the room with her.

Assumptshun was ready to go, an unconscious elven girl bound, gagged, and slung over his shoulder. Ephraim nodded grimly to the dragon, and the two made their way back through the tunnels to the portal that would take them home.

Oracle opened her eyes and knew she wasn't in Dothan anymore. The question was, where was she?

Although, knowing why she had been captured and who had done the capturing would be useful as well. Along with information on what other damages had been done and whether or not Flit had been taken—

Flit!

She scrambled to her feet only to find herself face-to-face with one of the tallest males she had ever met.

"Your friend is fine. No one was hurt in the raid, on either side, and there were no damages done to Dothan," he told her.

"Who are you?" she demanded.

"King Nahor of Ellasar. You've met my sons and my wife."

So this was Ling's husband. "Were you the one who grabbed me?"

He shook his head.

"That was Assumptshun," another voice answered. "I grabbed Flit, and I assure you I did not harm her."

She spun to find Ephraim sitting on a nearby...something. She didn't know the name for the long, low cushioned piece of furniture. Elfan sat next to him, looking uncomfortable.

Everything slid into place. Furious, she flung herself at Ephraim, a small knife in her hand. He caught her and disarmed her easier than she would have thought likely, then simply sat there and held her arms while she cursed at him.

"How dare you! How *dare* you! We *helped* you, and you snuck into Dothan and *kidnapped* me! And *you*!" she snarled, twisting to see Elfan, who wouldn't meet her eyes. "I trusted you! And you let him do it! Bloody likely showed him the way, too—"

Ephraim clamped a hand over her mouth, effectively cutting off her words.

"You may curse at me, but do not talk to her like that," he said firmly. She bit at him.

Someone snatched her out of his hold, and she found herself being carried like a sack to an open door...and out onto a terrace. She started to struggle again when she saw how high up she was, fighting now to get back inside the room.

"Do you want me to drop you?" Assumptshun snapped.

She fell still, clinging to his arm, her eyes wide with fear.

"Look," he commanded her. "*Look*."

She looked out at the land and felt her breath catch in her throat. It was beautiful. It was green and filled with ice blue lights, and there were people milling about in nice clothing down below. There were animals like the one Aramon had—horses—and birds, and others, too, ones she couldn't name. From somewhere down below, music was being played, and meat was being cooked over flame. Her stomach clenched at the smell, reminding her of her ever-present hunger.

"That's enough, Assumptshun," the king said. His voice was low and authoritative, and the dragon carried her back inside and set her down.

She stood where she had been placed, awkward and unsure. Her eyes darted around the beauty of the place, the cushions, and the gossamer curtains. This was a young girl's room, she noted, seeing the cradle festooned in pink ribbons. She couldn't see inside of it, and suddenly she had to look.

Crossing to it, she was aware of everyone watching her, of the king's close scrutiny. Her hands curled over the top, and she stood on her toes to look in.

Empty. The cradle was empty.

Her power—gift, Ephraim had once called it—flared up, and she saw Elfan place a babe inside, a babe with the king's eyes, with Ephraim's eyes.

There was a soft sound behind her, and she turned to see the king still staring at her. She shivered as she finally remembered what Queen Ling had said about her husband hearing the thoughts of others.

"What?" she finally asked. "Whose room is this?"

"It was once my daughter's." He turned his gaze to his son's to shoot him a look she couldn't interpret. Elfan gripped the prince's hand tightly.

"Why was I brought here?" she asked, wary.

It was Elfan who finally spoke. "Ephraim thinks he's found your parents."

"There is someone who has agreed to meet with you," the king added. "Are you willing to be civil with her?"

"Is she my mother?"

Nahor shook his head. "She is one of the sages—elves who have been around since the beginning of the world. She is very wise and very powerful. Her name is Lady Aelollora. Will you meet with her?"

She looked at Ephraim and Elfan, who both looked hopeful. "Sure," she said slowly, uncomfortable with the idea. She was acutely conscious of her torn, filthy clothing, her unkempt hair, the dirt on her skin.

"Lady Aelollora is blind to the visual world," Nahor said softly. "Her gift allows her to see in ways others cannot."

"What is she going to see if she looks at me?"

"Your lineage," he said simply. "I'll bring her in. Ephraim, Elfan, she'll want to meet Oracle alone."

They rose together, and Ephraim place his hand on her head as he passed her. "It will be all right. You'll see."

"It's good to see you again, Oracle," Elfan murmured.

Nahor watched them leave. "I will have a hot meal and a bath and a set of clean clothing brought up for you as soon as your audience with Lady Aelollora is done."

That was more than enough of a bribe for her to behave and not try to flee the room. She watched him leave only to return in a moment with a lady in a hood. He showed her into the room and left.

The dark opening of the hood turned to face her, and pale hands reached up to draw it back. Lady Aelollora looked normal enough for an elf, her hair so blond that it was nearly white, her build tall and willowy. But it was her eyes that marked her as strange. They glowed—like Oracle's did when she had a vision—glowed a constant, pale blue light.

Lady Aelollora smiled at her. "Come here, child," she said. She had a voice like a bell, the tone pure and clear and ringing.

Oracle stepped forward to stand in front of the robed figure, awed by the power she could feel coming off the woman. One hand reappeared, reaching out to cup Oracle's chin and tilt her face up, turning her slightly this way and that. She fidgeted, self-conscious.

"We could sit if you would rather," Oracle offered.

Those lips curved again. "Would you be so kind as to guide me?"

She took the hand that held her face and walked with the woman to the cushioned furniture that Ephraim and Elfan had been sitting on.

Lady Aelollora looked at her. "You have many questions."

"What is this that we're sitting on?"

She laughed a silvery laugh. "A divan, child."

"What do Flit's symbols mean? The ones that she draws everywhere?"

"I do not know your Flit, child, nor do I know her symbols. I cannot help you there."

"Who are my parents? Why would the king get involved?"

"Because the king is your father, dear princess, and the queen your mother. They had a daughter they called Terah who disappeared as a very young child and was never seen again ... until Prince Ephraim found you."

"You're wrong," she blurted out.

"Not about this, child."

"But Queen Ling saw me. Wouldn't a mother have recognized her own daughter?"

"Your mother has suffered much, too much for such a good and kind-hearted woman, and it helped to blind her to your shared blood. You are older than you think, Princess Terah. You have lived one hundred and four years, seven months, and four days. Your soul and your blood attest to as much. I can see that it is true in the same manner as you can see me sitting before you."

"No," she whispered, shaking her head. "I am Oracle. I'm an orphan, and I live on Amalay Kahelith in Dothan, and I'm *not yet eleven.*"

"Your second brother, Prince Aramon, would be better able to give you the answer to that riddle, princess." She reached out and stroked the girl's hair, feeling her shudder as she cried in confusion. "Be of ease, child. Knowing the truth about yourself only makes you stronger and wiser. You are a princess, and your friend the Adkisha is your sister. Blood does not lie. All shall be well. A kinship to the throne of Ellasar does not mean that you cannot still fight for freedom on Amalay Kahelith. It might enable you to do so better."

Terah rubbed at her eyes. Lady Aelollora gave her a kindly smile. "Your father awaits anxiously at the door, waiting to be called in. He hears my thoughts and yours and longs to comfort the daughter he had long thought was dead. Shall I call him in?"

Terah nodded. "Thank you ... for telling me."

Lady Aelollora bowed her head and rose, bending at the waist to kiss Terah's brow.

"Until we meet again, child. May the stars shine brightly upon you." She lifted her cowl up again. "King Nahor, come welcome your daughter home, and I shall take my leave."

Nahor opened the door and ushered Lady Aelollora out to where a male dressed as she was awaited her, thanking her for her time. Then he hurried in, kneeling in front of his daughter.

"You're crying," she whispered.

"As are you, dearest." He smiled. He reached out and touched her face. "Ephraim had said as much, but I couldn't dare hope...I beg for your forgiveness."

She slid unceremoniously from the divan into his arms and clung to him, to the father she had never known, and wept.

Aramon paced, furious. Dolon stood out of the way, stunned by the news.

"Why wasn't I told?" Aramon demanded.

"Because you would have reacted like this, and there was a possibility I was wrong," Ephraim replied.

"What is all the commotion about?"

Both men spun to find Ling standing in the doorway to the breakfast room. Dolon grinned at the sight of her.

"Welcome home, my queen."

She smiled softly. "Thank you, Dolon. It is good to see you again. Ephraim, Aramon," she said, turning back to her sons, "what are you yelling about?"

"Ephraim found Terah, and he's brought her back to the castle," Aramon told her.

Ling clutched at the doorway, stunned. Elfan stepped up, ready to catch her should she fall.

"My daughter. My Terah," she breathed. "Where is she?"

"With Father, *Mai*," Ephraim said gently. "They'll be here shortly. You've met her before; you called her Oracle."

Ling's eyes widened. "How did I not see?"

"You weren't the only one," Aramon replied dryly.

Ling turned as she heard her husband's voice in the corridor. Walking along beside him was a young girl staring about her in amazement.

"Terah!" she cried, running to meet them.

Terah looked up. "Mother," she breathed and flung herself into the queen's arms.

Nahor smiled at the sight and ignored the murmurs of passing elves who were excited and shocked by the return of the queen and the lost princess.

Aftermath

Kirin woke in the middle of the night, overheated. Rising carefully so as not to wake Callian, she left the room to pace in the great room.

Malakieth found her there a quarter hour later. He stood silently for a moment and watched her wear a track in the floor, hair pulled up to bare the back of her neck, her face flushed.

"Are you feeling ill?"

Kirin shook her head. "Merely hot and rather restless."

He crossed to the counter where Natasha often prepared the food and poured her a glass of water from the pitcher.

"If I may ask a personal question, how ... aware have you been of Callian lately?"

"Too personal."

"It may be a side effect of the conversion."

"What, noticing Callian more?" She laughed.

"Your restlessness and the heat under your skin."

"This conversation is growing rather uncomfortable."

"Have you mated with him?"

Kirin choked on her water. "What sort of woman do you take me for?"

"It was an honest question. Because the souls intertwine during the elven conversion, there is a natural drive to unite the bodies afterward—a drive that you are most likely experiencing now. Which is the reason why most elves wait until their wedding night to perform the conversion."

"I wasn't afforded that luxury, and this is extremely uncomfortable to be discussing."

"I was merely explaining things for you," he said mildly. "It should be over soon."

"Good. Define soon."

"Six to twelve hours?"

She glared at him. "Not soon enough."

He forced back laughter. "Good night, my daughter. May your troubles ease by morning."

But when the sun rose a handful of hours later, Kirin was no better off. Natasha came out of Malakieth's room, bade her good morning as she put the tea on to boil, and slipped into the room Kirin had shared with Callian and the dragons. Beau came out moments later, looking irritated and uncomfortable, with Xzylya yawning and stumbling along beside him. The hatchling immediately went to lie down in the patch of sunlight while Beau went to his rider.

"Did I keep you awake?"

No. But I feel it as well. The mating urge. I've never felt it this strongly, and I'm only feeling it through you. I pity you.

Have you felt it before?

Once, when I was near a female in her mating heat. Her male chased me off quickly enough. Any idea when this will end?

Kirin thought of the conversation with her father, letting Beau hear it. The Twilight Dragon cringed. *Poor girl. I should have been awake to intercede.*

I'm glad that you had some sleep, though. How is Xzylya?

She longs for music and moonlight—she grows more and more tired without the moonlight. But she's happy enough. I think that she is too young to feel the desire that you and I feel. There is a spare room; I suggest that you and I make use of it and keep away from Tiamat and Callian.

Kirin nodded, following her dragon as they made their escape. Kirin shut the door behind them and then plucked at her dress and eyed her dragon.

Would you mind terribly if I took this off? I want to wear myself into the ground, and it would seem a shame to get this dress disgusting.

The dragon shrugged. *While you are beautiful, I prefer Tiamat. As your bonded dragon, I will never feel a physical desire for you. And these are extenuating circumstances. Do as you like.*

He moved to lie in front of the door as she twisted out of her dress. Dropping to the ground, she began to exercise.

The knock at the door made Kirin pause. She was covered in sweat, and the cool stone floor felt nice under her stomach.

"Who is it?" she asked.

"Natasha. Sent by Malakieth with a change of clothing."

Beau moved out of the way and opened the door, forcing Natasha to duck under his neck so that Callian, who was pouring over a map, couldn't see in.

"Natasha, you are a miracle-worker," Kirin exclaimed.

"I used to practice in them when I was smaller. I've nearly destroyed them—I've been using them to patch other pieces of clothing. So the sleeves are gone and some of the pant legs. Here is a sash to hold the pants up should they need it; you're rather thin. And I took the liberty of cutting a slit down the back for your wings; we can tie it closed across your shoulders."

Kirin pulled the clothes on, and Natasha tied it closed. The pants ended at her knees, similar to where she used to roll her pants for sparring. It sent a pang of homesickness rushing through her; she forced it away. She had more important things to dwell on at the moment.

Callian caught the door as it closed behind Natasha. "Are you all right?"

"Antsy," she replied, rolling her shoulders.

He offered her her sword. "Care to spar?"

It sounded like as good a plan as any. "Only if you agree to hold nothing back. I'm trying for total exhaustion."

He frowned. "Fair enough."

Callian was momentarily distracted. It was likely the worst moment to lose focus.

The flat of Kirin's blade caught his shoulder soundly, knocking him down, and pain shot through him, effectively dowsing the sudden flash of Tiamat's desire.

In retrospect, he should have stopped sparring when he realized Tiamat had wanted to let Beau touch her wings. *Dear Lord in Valour, no wonder Kirin went crazy when I touched hers. If it felt like that, anyone would.*

Kirin dropped her sword and fell to the ground next to him. "I'm so sorry." Her thin fingers felt his shoulder. "Why didn't you block that?"

"Tiamat distracted me."

She laughed at him. "By?"

"Beau touched her wings. I'm beginning to appreciate yours more."

He ran his palm down one, and her spine arched, lips parting.

She opened her eyes to see him grinning rakishly up at her, fully aware of how that made her feel. She punched him, one quick blow to his chest.

"Rogue. I've been trying for hours to subdue myself, and you've just set me off again."

"Oh?" He laughed.

Kirin grinned back at him, unable to help it.

Heaven and hell, he's a gorgeous creature. She looked down at him, her eyes hooded, feeling the warmth of his hands on her waist. Never had she thought that she would find him more attractive, but immortality had managed to perfect upon his features.

She lowered herself onto her elbows, combing her fingers through his hair, her nails scraping his scalp and sending chills down his spine.

"Remind me to aggravate you more often," he murmured to her.

"That could be dangerous to your health," she whispered against his throat.

"I like danger," he replied, his breathing growing ragged.

Her lips trailed up his throat to his jaw, and she kissed him with a long, drugging pull on his lower lip. He clutched her to him and returned her kiss, tongues dueling in earnest as he gripped the back of her neck. He released her waist to run his hand up and down her wings. Callian could feel the reaction. She gasped against his mouth, and her smooth lips—merely excited before—moved in wild ecstasy with his.

"Easy, love," he mumbled when she drew back for breath.

"No," she cried stubbornly.

He opened his eyes, and they were hungry. Kirin gazed breathlessly back, her intentions written plainly across her beautiful face.

"Careful," he whispered, weakly attempting to fight his own sudden rush of desire.

It was nothing compared to hers. Her thin hands kneaded into his chest and shoulders. It was both strikingly attractive and frightening beyond all means to see her so caught up, so lost in her own desires, her own cravings.

"Careful," he repeated hoarsely, shocked to find his usually strong will crumbling.

"No. I can't be," she breathed, her voice breathless with passion, her eyes wild. She stared at him longingly. "I can't be." She shook her blond head. "I'm out of control."

She lay against him, her flawless lips pressed against his throat again, feeling his racing pulse under her mouth, as her hands frantically untied the back of her shirt. She twisted out of it and reached for the sash around her waist.

Callian focused on remembering to breathe, on not reacting to her touch, on stopping her before she went too far. It was like trying to stop a wildfire with a wet rag. He knew he needed to stop, but he didn't want to. He wanted *her*, and she was more than willing.

"Magic?" he choked out, beginning to lose this fight with himself. How could one girl seduce him so quickly? He turned his head, roughly pulling her face to his and kissing her ardently, holding her recklessly close to him. Could he convince himself that she was close enough? He needed to stop *now* while he still had a bit of coherent thought left in him. No, what he needed was *her*. But he should stop, and he knew it. For her sake. To preserve her honor.

"It's a side effect of the conversion. I don't think I can stop. I don't want to," she said frantically when he let her speak. She managed to kick off the loose pants, pressing her barely-clothed body against him.

Callian hardly remembered to breathe while the room spun dizzily around him. *By Adonai, she's alluring.*

"Are you afraid? Are you certain?" he gasped, holding her to him, pinning her wings to her back, kissing her wildly. He would not be able to fight this for much longer.

She moved uncontrollably in her confusion, her need, hands sliding under his shirt to rub against his bare chest. He burned with want, and in seconds his shirt lay forgotten beside them. "I don't know. There is no fear now, but I don't know about later. I can't see my future," she spoke frenziedly as soon as her mouth was freed.

"Stop," he ordered suddenly, his eyes blazing.

She froze, her muscles shaking. For one second, she hesitated. One second was all he needed.

He grabbed her bare shoulders, wrapping his arms around her back and locking her to him. Carefully, always so carefully, he rolled so that she was under him, and his body pinned down her slim, hot, tempting form. His blood felt as if it had been replaced with lightning. This is where he wanted her—but for reasons other than stopping her. Less noble reasons.

Kirin smiled up at him, alluring and enticing. Her hands rubbed his shoulders, sliding up to the back of his neck. She was breathing rapidly, her eyes wide and glowing, her pupils dilated to an almost human form, which was exactly what he needed. Drawing in the deepest breath he could manage, he kissed her passionately. He held her face with his free hand, keeping her from moving her head, even to breathe. It didn't take long. Frenetically, she tried to break out of his iron grip, craving air as much as she was craving him. He held onto her, refusing to break the kiss.

She collapsed limply under him. Fighting down the panic, the fear for her safety, he didn't let her breathe for a few more seconds. Her body finally grew still against his.

When he was completely sure she was unconscious, he released her, allowing her breath. She didn't reawaken, and he checked to make sure she was breathing normally and that her heartbeat was steady. Satisfied that she would be all right, he rolled off her, kissing her cheek softly one last time.

He slipped out of the room and into the one where his dragon was, snatching the blankets that he and Kirin had used last night and trying to ignore the way Tiamat nosed along her unconscious mate.

I'm sorry, Tiamat. That was my fault.

Our fault, the dragoness corrected. *I likely started it, asking Beau to touch my wings.*

No harm done, correct?

Yes.

He shut the door behind him, closing Kirin in with him. Tenderly, he pulled the one blanket over her, covering her mostly bare body, and folded the other to slip under her head as a makeshift pillow. She was smiling slightly in her sleep. He folded her clothing up, placing it on top of her red dress and her blade, and pulled his own shirt back on. Glancing back at her, even though the blanket hid her body, the temptation hit him nearly as strong as before, tightening the muscles in the pit of his stomach. There was nothing childish about that form, and she had a personality to match. She was a complete wildcat. He wished desperately for water to dunk his head in, for a cool pool or a stream or a lake. Sighing, he forced his eyes off her and sat with his back to her while she slept.

Kirin awoke abruptly several hours later, feeling much more like herself—normal and in control rather than feverish and needy. A deep, deep shame washed over her, and she hid her face under the blanket that Callian must have either carried her to or brought for her. She had been wild before, half-crazed, to the point of undressing herself in front of Callian, to the point of him having to knock her out to stop her. How could she face him after that? How could she have lost control of herself so badly? She had even had fair warning of what was happening, and still...

The tears started to flow, hot and ashamed.

She pulled the blanket over her head to hide, noting in relief that she still wore her underclothes. Callian had managed to knock her unconscious before she succeeded in her frenzied attempt to couple with him.

A hand landed softly on her arm, rubbing her through the blanket in a slow, soothing motion. It took a few minutes, but she eventually stopped crying, feeling her breathing slow to the rhythm of his caress.

When she settled, he drew her up into his arms and kissed her hair. "Hush. It's all right, love. I promise," he murmured. His voice was soothing and perfect, soft and tender and warm. "Hush. Please, Kirin, talk to me. Are you upset that I knocked you out? I'm still not sure I did the right thing. If this is the aftermath of refusing you, then I wish I hadn't. I never wanted to hurt you."

"Stop apologizing," she told him, beginning to cry again. Kirin fought against the tears and lost. She seemed to do nothing more than cry as of late. Defeated, she curled up against him, tucking her head against his shoulder so he couldn't see her tears. "You're only making it worse. I can't believe I did this to you, that I couldn't control myself and you had to make me faint to keep me pure."

He kissed her head again. "I love you. Did you know that?" he teased lightly.

"I know," she whispered. "I'm very lucky." Shame crept back into her voice. "Callian, I am so sorry about that. I can't believe I got so far out of control; it won't happen ever again," she promised rashly.

Callian was silent for a few minutes. "Oh," he finally said, his voice flat.

Her heart skipped a beat. She pulled back and looked up, trying to look into his eyes to read his expression, but his head was tilted back, resting against the wall with his eyes closed. She stared at him, but he didn't move. She ducked her gaze, pressing her lips to the hollow at the base of his throat. His arms tightened fondly around her. Almost rhythmically, his hand ran up and down her bare arm. Her heart thrilled each time his hand touched her skin, making her nerves tingle with each pass of his gentle palm.

"Say something," she pleaded against the smooth skin of his throat.

"Never?" he whispered.

She raised her gaze again to find him staring back at her, his eyes soft and tender and loving, but with a hint of sadness.

"I thought you would be upset over what happened," she admitted, her heart flying.

He shook his head slowly. "But nothing happened, love."

"Nothing?" the inhuman girl argued skeptically. "I went insane. I thought I was going to explode if I didn't... if we didn't... You had to knock me out to stop me from..." she whispered, ducking her head back down to hide against his chest again.

His hand moved to caress her face with the utmost care and affection. "If you are upset because I knocked you out, I'm very sorry. If you are upset because we nearly *did* couple, don't be. We didn't, and what is done is done." He tilted her face up, compassionately pulling her toward him. "If it is because you have some convoluted thought I somehow didn't enjoy that, you're absolutely wrong," he breathed, kissing her lightly, repeatedly. "And if it is because you feel guilty because I seemed upset," he panted softly between kisses, "I merely meant to say I certainly wouldn't mind if you tempted me again, as long as I was strong enough to keep you from jeopardizing your integrity."

He kissed her in earnest. Her heart, which had been racing already, spluttered hyperactively.

His lips were not gentle. There was a new, sweet edge to the way they moved with hers, and it was instantly addictive. She couldn't think. She ran her tongue over his lower lip. It was smooth, warm, soft, and the *taste*. She could barely breathe; the room spun around her. His tongue slid into her mouth, and she thought she would spontaneously combust.

He broke the kiss long before she wanted him to. His hands slid down from her neck and face to rest against her lower ribs, his eyes closing and his mouth twisting into a crooked smile at the feel of her as she gasped for breath. His breathing was just as erratic. She nuzzled against his strong chest, her guilt assuaged.

When her pulse had settled, he asked, "Would you care for something to eat? Natasha came by an hour or so ago, but I thought it would be best to let you sleep. You didn't sleep much last night."

"Food would be wonderful." She pushed the blanket off and rose, heading for the door. Callian caught her around her thin waist, spinning her so she faced the small pile of her clothing. "Oh," she whispered, blushing at his subtle reminder that she was barely dressed.

He playfully mussed her hair. "Why don't you get dressed, vixen," he teased. "You are much too tempting."

She twisted gently out of his arms and slid her legs into the loose pants, tying them around her waist with the sash, and then grabbed her shirt, yanking it on over her head. It stuck irritatingly on her wings. She reached back to work it over, but Callian beat her to it. His patient hands coaxed the soft, worn material over her wings, guiding them through the slit Natasha had cut, tying it together across the shoulders. He moved with the utmost care, allowing his fingertips to caress her as he slowly dressed her.

She was blushing by the time he was finished, but she turned and, finding his gaze already upon her, touched his face and smiled with tender affection. His expression softened, and he kissed her palm and then turned her hand over to kiss her knuckles; his other hand moved in small circles between her wings. It felt divine.

He stepped back and took her hand.

Opening the door, he barely had time to knock her aside. His hand flashed out, acting on instinct, and he caught the blade before it sank into the door. He passed it to her and managed to catch a second one.

Kirin stared at them, shocked that anyone was throwing knives in her father's rooms. They were beautiful in the deadly way that knives often are, a matched set with narrow, straight blades that bore a shallower center groove than most, with wood handles wrapped tightly in black leather.

Malakieth stood across the room, his expression grim. He pointed imperiously to the room with the dragons in it.

Natasha came flying into the great room, face pale, dark eyes wide with fear. She grabbed Kirin by her shirt and half-drug them into the room her master had pointed to. A second later, she threw the blankets and Kirin's dress in with them. Malakieth stood at the doorway.

"Morgan's here. No magic. Stay absolutely quiet." He closed the door, and Kirin heard the sound of something being put in front of it. It would not surprise her if this room was designed to be unnoticeable.

Her hand tightened on the knife. Callian wrapped one arm around her and the other around Tiamat's neck. Beau was crouched over Xzylya protectively. They huddled together, frightened, and listened to the voices in the great room.

Escape from the Sorceress

The knock on the door surprised Malakieth. He had been expecting Morgan to simply barge in and had been prepared for her to do so from the moment he felt her trigger his careful wards.

He took a moment to make sure Natasha was standing in the far corner, head bowed so her hair hid her face, looking inconsequential and unassuming. He checked the door that hid Kirin, looking at the subtle magic coating it that made it look like a part of the stone wall, at the small loom with the half-finished tapestry that was never more than half-finished and the crude basket of thread and carded wool—a prop to make the area seem like a place a *rakasheti* would work.

The knock sounded again. Impatient.

"What the *hell*," he snarled, loud enough that Morgan would hear him. He stormed to the door and flung it open, making sure to look taken aback.

"Morgan?" he whispered. "How— Come in, come in. You look … very much alive."

Morgan flashed him a fanged smirk and sauntered past him, heading to a low couch against a wall. Unlike a vampire, who would only have a single fang in place of a human's canine tooth, she had a double set, the longer ones towards the back. She dropped down and leaned back, the picture of ease, her tight skirt slit up the side to show her thighs.

"Sit. You look tense," she purred seductively. "I could fix that."

Malakieth sat beside her, though not touching her, and kicked his feet out, crossing his ankles. "The dead stands living before me after four thousand years. How would any male not be tense?"

Morgan extended one arm, splaying her fingers, admiring the smooth, pale skin and the sharp, curved claws. "The ceremony worked well. And you, my dearest apprentice, always doubted it would."

"I did not see the logic behind the concept that the death of many would return life to one who is deceased."

"You doubt my master's power?"

"I am fully aware that he is frighteningly powerful."

"Then you are wise."

"I endeavor to be."

Morgan tossed her curls. "I neglect the purpose of my visit."

"To attempt to seduce me?"

She laughed. "Always."

"Sadly, my answer remains no. My heart belongs to another."

"Braw male." She reached out and ran the tips of her claws down his arm. "I'm not after your heart."

He broke out in chills even as his skin crawled. He shifted away from her. "Care for something to drink?"

"Changing the subject?"

"Always. My offer remains."

"As does mine," she purred.

"Right. Girl," he snapped at Natasha, his voice cool. He hated bringing her under Morgan's gaze, but it would change the subject to more important matters. Such as why Morgan was here. "Bring drinks."

Natasha jumped into action. She knew her part well. She could feel both Morgan and Malakieth watching her as she walked with a rolling, long-legged stride to pour two glasses of wine. She brought them to her master without spilling a drop and without raising her gaze from the floor and knelt by his legs, reaching out to touch him. Malakieth gave one to Morgan, ignoring Natasha's touch. He usually didn't let her touch him, but this was under her own volition, and to stop her in front of Morgan would raise suspicions.

"You keep a *rakasheti*? You?"

"I find it helpful. She's fair company, and she can cook."

"And her other services?" Morgan asked, her voice growing a rough edge to it.

Malakieth permitted himself a small smile, though it was more at Morgan's petty jealousy than at any remembrance of passion. "She's good. Very good. Strong and yet submissive."

Natasha's nails bit into his calf in punishment for that comment. He didn't react.

"What species is it even?"

"A Rashek halfling. They tend to be more useful. Stronger, less prone to illnesses." He shrugged.

Morgan turned to Natasha, her fire-red eyes narrowing. "You, slave. Has he sired a mutant off you?"

"No, my queen," Natasha murmured, pitching her voice higher and softer than usual.

"Out of curiosity," Malakieth drawled, "how long have you been back?"

Morgan waved her hand airily. "Oh, a day or two. You might have seen me earlier if you didn't nest up here all alone like a bloody eagle."

"I'm not alone. I'm surprised I didn't hear rumors of your return. Usually all the important things are reported to me immediately. I intend on finding out who neglected to tell me and rectifying the situation."

Morgan gave a low, throaty laugh. "I kept it secret. I wanted to surprise you, but I found myself ... tangled up ... for the first day or so."

He had to work to keep the disgust out of his voice. That hadn't taken her long. "And who is your current consort?"

"General Sisera. Are you jealous, dragon?"

"Hardly. I can imagine what those claws and teeth of yours have done to his skin. If anything, his pain amuses me."

She laughed again. "It seems to amuse him, too. Such a strange creature, but then, his father was hardly sane."

"Speaking of hardly sane, have you seen that wretched Spiriter about? He disappeared a few months ago, and I haven't heard from him."

"I'll pass your regard along if I run across him."

"No, better—rip the skin from his back for me in punishment for desertion, and if it was because of a female, remove a few body parts."

She laughed, her sadistic side delighted. "Malakieth, you have truly done well in my absence. And now that I've returned, I will reclaim my castle."

"I will, of course, have to refuse you in that, dear Morgan. I find I have become quite comfortable with dominance."

Morgan grew still, no longer amused. Natasha gripped his leg, although he was unsure whether she was annoyed at him or frightened of what Morgan would do.

"Are you prepared to fight me then, apprentice?" she asked softly. Her eyes were dangerous.

He kept himself relaxed against the couch, dropping one hand to fiddle with Natasha's hair as if he truly didn't care what she did. "Hardly, fearsome lady. I merely request a compromise."

"Oh? What do you suggest?"

"I give you back the castle, the armies, everything. You rule. But I'm your second-in-command, not that idiot Nephilim—"

"You are welcome to be my consort. You needn't barter for it."

"I don't want to be your consort. Keep the Nephilim. I only want the power and the dominance. As your second-in-command, I would still retain the respect and obedience I've grown used to. I want free rein of the fortress, and I want to retain my privacy up here. Are we in accord?"

"Retention of power, freedom to wander the fortress, and privacy? Of course. I will happily give you those."

"Then I give you the fortress and your bloodthirsty armies."

"Wonderful," she purred, grinning darkly.

Beau rose, the jealousy and protectiveness of a male with his true mate coursing through him and, courtesy of the bond, through Kirin.

Darkin, perhaps it would be best to let her find her own feet, prefer-ably before Beau gets too territorial.

Malakieth released her and stepped back. Kirin walked up to Tiamat, admiring the female's wild, crimson hair.

You make a beautiful human woman, she told Tiamat.

Tiamat's mulberry eyes flashed to Kirin's face, and she blushed. *Thank you.*

Kirin pulled the necklace off and jumped back, colliding with Malakieth as Tiamat shifted back into her true form. Nausea curled through her where her wings brushed his skin, and he hastened to free himself from her, apologizing before disappearing.

Beau's eyes flashed to hers. Then, satisfied his rider was unharmed, he nosed along his mate, and she ducked her head and allowed his administrations. Xzylya squirmed in to rub her cheek against the older female's shoulder, happy to see her again.

Kirin was the first to hear the voices at the door.

Get back! Into the cell!

Graceful despite their size, Tiamat and Beau herded Xzylya into the cell they were to occupy. Kirin froze, Malakieth's knife hidden against her side, as two males stopped by the door and listened.

A meaty fist pounded on the door. "Olcor," a deep voice rumbled. It sounded like a Rashek to Kirin—surely no Nephilim's voice would be so rough. "Why so quiet?"

He rattled the door's handle only to curse. "Idiot locked it," she heard him mumble to his companion.

Kirin backed up, trying to move quietly so that she would be out of sight when the Rashek broke down the door. Her heel caught on the uneven ground, and she fell, landing hard and catching the edge of her right wing. Her breath escaped her loudly; she clamped her teeth on her lower lip to keep from crying out.

It didn't silence Xzylya. The dracling gave a soft cry before Tia-mat or Beau could stop her.

"What was that? Olcor?"

Dazed, Kirin didn't move. Beau flung himself on top of her, stretching out to shield her with his body. She vaguely noted that he was in his human form before the door slammed open.

There was a split second where Kirin was sure that they would sound the alarm.

Then they roared with laughter.

"Olcor, you worm. The least you could have done is let us in and share the bloody girl," the first one said. Kirin flushed, mortified at his assumption, her blade in her palm. Under Beau's arm, she watched his steel-tipped boots walk over to them. "Traznic, brother, there should be others in the far cell if you want one."

Xzylya.

Tiamat's with her, Beau reminded her. *But I can't fight like this.*

The first Rashek reached out and shoved Beau off her.

His death was quick and gory. Kirin spun to see the other tangled with Xzylya, and she ran to help. Back in his true form, Beau grabbed her.

Stop. Look.

Kirin looked, truly looked.

Xzylya stepped back from the body and paced a tight circle around it, teeth bared. The Rashek's throat had been ripped open, and deep slices marred his pale-blue chest. Satisfied that he was dead, Xzylya looked up at her rider, black blood splattered on her scales.

Bad male. My dasha, she said.

Kirin looked on in amazement at the Light Dragon's first kill. *Yes, your* dasha. *Thank you.*

Retrieve your knife, Kirin, Beau told her.

That shook Kirin back into action. Kneeling, she jerked her blade free of the Rashek's eye socket. It caught briefly on the lacrimal bone, and when she managed to wiggle it free, it seemed as if there was even more of the black blood.

"That's foul," she breathed. Xzylya sauntered up, proud of herself, and Kirin used the hem of her shirt to clean the blood off the female's scales, aware that she was ruining yet another article of clothing.

"What happened?" her father rumbled behind her. Callian stood beside him, his hands bound behind his back.

"Xzylya made her first kill," she said simply.

Malakieth looked impressed. "Protecting Kirin?" he asked the young dragon in his native tongue.

Xzylya drew herself up and nodded.

"Good." He turned to his daughter as he freed Callian's hands, switching back into the Common Tongue for the prince's sake. "I will see you anon."

"We'll find Trig by then," she vowed.

Callian smiled. "He'll likely find us first."

Malakieth looked at his daughter. "Be careful. Stay safe." His gaze moved to Callian. "Take care of her."

Callian bowed his head. The dragon ushered them toward the jail cell, locking them in.

"The Resistance should be here within a half hour. I need to be with Morgan. Natasha is up in my rooms. You don't know her name; you've never seen her before. I never helped you. Do you think you can use earth magic, Kirin?"

"I've done it before with Beau."

"Knock the door clean off. Avoid Sisera as best you can—but Molyb and Morgan are the worst of the three evils."

She nodded. He hurried through the door and closed it behind him.

Working quickly in the confined space, Kirin and Callian saddled their dragons and tied on the packs. Callian belted his sword to his hip and tucked his hunting knife into his belt, slipping the one Malakieth had given him into his sleeve and wishing that he had thought to take one of the Rashek's boots.

The dragons curled up with Kirin in their midst, and he leaned his shoulder against the stone and looked out into the darkness through the cell's bars.

"Do you think it would ruin the ruse if I took the Rasheks' boots on our way out?"

Kirin wiggled her own bare toes. "Boots would be lovely. *I* don't think so, but all the same, I'd ask the Resistance. It's not like we could get them now anyway. And what if they were too small for you?"

"You'd wear them, of course. Or one of the Resistance boys. They could grow into them."

"True."

They fell silent, and Tiamat looked at Kirin. *Do you remember that trick with the earth magic that Aramon showed you before we were flung onto Amalay Kahelith?*

Kirin's brow creased in confusion. *Which one?*

With the vibrations in the earth. Using them to see, in a manner of speaking.

Yes, now that you mention it. So much has happened that I had nearly forgotten.

Kirin reached out and placed her left palm on the ground. Closing her eyes, she reached for her magic, calling it to her fingertips.

The fortress came to life in the darkness. There were skinny rats scampering about, guards pacing to and fro, and slaves bustling around. There was the strange tread of a dragon walking alongside a woman and a rather *farrin* creature that kept changing its form—Molyb. Another male walked with them, most likely Sisera.

She searched closer to their cell ... and found a little knot of small figures crouched over, slipping closer to them.

She rose, and the dragons rose with her. "The Resistance is here."

Sure enough, within minutes, the door began to slowly open.

"You can come in, you know," Kirin whispered to them. "The guards are dead. We've been waiting for you."

Thief came in, Captain, a tiny girl with big teal eyes, and two others close behind him.

"How did you know we were coming?"

"We had some inside help," Callian answered softly. "We think Kirin can blow the door down, but it will be loud, and we'll need an immediate escape. You know the way around better than we do."

Captain nodded, accepting this. "Black Twelve, Black Thirty-two, cover Flit and take the rear. I'll stay back with you. Thief, lead

TRAVELING

Nahor tossed his daughter up into her brother's saddle. "Hold onto the pommel," he instructed, showing her what he meant. "Here. Elindil won't like it if you rip out his mane, and Aramon won't let you fall."

She swallowed and nodded.

"You're safe with me, little sister." Aramon grinned, swinging up behind her. He slipped her a warm bun.

"You're trying to fatten me up for the slaughter," she accused playfully, but she ate the soft bread when the stable hands and the courtiers in the courtyard weren't looking.

Nahor, mounted now, guided his horse next to Elindil.

"You make that look easy," she told him. "Guiding that thing."

"That 'thing' is commonly called a horse, and I should, seeing as I've been riding since I could walk," her father replied with an easy smile that she knew hid reservations.

"*Abbo*," she said. "Thank you."

He nodded, rising in his stirrups as Assumptshun took off with Ephraim and Elfan. Twisting, he nodded at Dolon, who was ruling in his stead.

Come home, dear king. Come home with your family intact.

He smiled up at him, trying to lift the man's spirits.

Dolon was the only other—besides his family and Elfan—that knew why he was taking his entire family out of the safety of the citadel, with war armor packed in saddlebags and enough rations to last two weeks, more if they hunted along the way.

Terah's prediction had been dire. The words—words that she had had no recollection of speaking, words spoken in a dual-toned voice—haunted him still: *You will go forth with your family and meet the beloved daughter of your enemy—the hero long awaited, the queen who has yet to be crowned—and the fugitive prince who awaits his throne. Fire, Light, and Twilight travel with her and guard her jealously. The witch's return will mark the shifter's demise and the renegade's freedom, and innocent blood will be spilt for the salvation of all. You will return disheartened, your beloved in agony, and you, oh king, will lose the daughter you have just discovered.*

He hadn't told Terah the end of her prophecy. What oracle predicted her own death?

That in and of itself was strange enough, but Terah managed to surprise him yet again. As soon as it was decided that they would go to meet Kirin, she had requested two pairs of boots and had been able to give specific measurements.

Living with an oracle was going to take some adjustment.

He looked beside him at his wife, at her pale, drawn face. "It will be all right," he murmured.

You can't know that.

I will make it so.

You cannot stop death.

There are other ways of losing someone besides death. It could be quite literal. She could get lost on the way home. She could return to Dothan—and you know that she longs to do that. Perhaps that is what it means. We will lose her to Dothan.

He could see that she desperately wanted to believe him. *Perhaps.*

The prophecy, dreadful as it was, had one good point: it predicted Ling's return home.

He nudged his stallion into a canter, hearing Ling and Aramon and the spare horse laden with armor follow him out of the castle proper.

The prophecy ran through his mind again.

The beloved daughter of his enemy—that was likely Kirin, provided Malakieth was fond of the girl. Her love was Prince Callian of Giladeth. Fire, Light, and Twilight were the three dragons Ling had told him of. The witch—the only one that came to mind was Morgan, and she had been dead for thousands of years. He was certain of it. He had been the one to cut off her head.

So then, who else?

The shifter had to be Molyb, and good riddance to him.

Who was the renegade, though, and what did he or she need salvation from? And who was the innocent whose blood would be split? Terah?

Adonai, please let it not be so, he prayed.

Kirin said her thanks and her good-byes to the Resistance and caught up with Callian outside under the night sky. Xzylya was romping around, rejoicing at being outside and chasing nightbugs. The tiny insects buzzed angrily at her when she knocked them out of the air.

Callian took her hand. "Who do you think took Oracle?" he asked as they walked, skirting the village.

"I don't know, but it must be someone from our world. Who else would leave a note in the Common Tongue and a sack of fresh bread?"

"True. Did you recognize the type of bread at all?"

She shrugged. "I would say Ellasarian. But we've been able to get that at the Academy. Will Trig be able to find us?"

"He should. He's no fool."

They walked on for two hours or so until the village was far behind. Callian shook his head.

"I need to find somewhere to scry. We should have either been found or have found him."

"It's dark out," she pointed out. "What you scry will be dark. How will you be able to tell where he is?"

"You could just ask," a voice behind them said.

They spun.

"Trig!" Kirin gasped. She hugged him briefly; then Callian pulled his friend into his arms for a quick embrace, laughing.

"You fool. How long have you been trailing us?"

The dark-haired human laughed with him. "Since you left the village. Your dragons were agreeably quiet."

Beau chuckled, a low, pleased rumble. *Tell him I'll carry his pack for him. It's likely not all his things anyway.*

Kirin relayed the message, and Trig flashed Beau a grateful smile. "My shoulders and back thank you very much. I've been carrying everything around since the lot of you disappeared, ready to move at the first sign of you."

They stopped so Trig could lash his pack to Beau's saddle.

"So what's this about Ellasarian bread? That's about when I caught up to you."

"You should have said something," Callian replied.

"I had three very good reasons. Firstly, I was waiting for one of you to say something private, at which point I would have let you know I was eavesdropping."

I would have let you know he was there if you and Kirin started to talk about personal matters, Tiamat told him.

"Secondly, I was debating the idea of grabbing Kirin and pretending to try to kidnap her or hold her hostage. However, I concluded that would be a rather painful endeavor, seeing as not only is she battle-trained, but she might also hit below the belt and happens to be from a stronger species than I."

Kirin chuckled. "Very wise of you."

"And thirdly, I was waiting to see how long it would take Callian—who supposedly knows all my tricks—to realize I was following you."

Callian grinned at his friend. "I was a bit distracted by the beautiful woman beside me."

Trig laughed while Kirin blushed faintly. Callian raised their joined hands to brush a kiss along her knuckles.

"I feel like I've missed something important," Trig commented.

Kirin looked up at him. "I'll likely have to explain to my brothers, so would you mind terribly waiting until then for the whole story?"

"Not at all. But may I ask one thing?"

"Of course."

"Is he courting you?"

She smiled. "Yes. I don't usually behave like this around men."

"I thought not, though I was prepared to blame Callian and hit him for you."

She laughed again. "I appreciate the gesture, but it is wholly unnecessary."

"So what about elven bread?"

"Someone—well, a pair of someones—snuck into Dothan and kidnapped Oracle," Callian told him. "Another girl was with her when it happened, a tiny girl called Flit, and she was found unharmed but unconscious in her room with a note written in the Common Tongue and a sack of bread. The note didn't say much— Sage could read it—merely that Oracle would not be harmed, she would be returned in 'due time,' whenever that is, and that she was safe. Her captors apologized for taking her but felt that it was neces- sary to do so."

"Odd. How is Flit?"

"Thief has taken to keeping her with either him or Captain at all times. Everyone protects her, and if you see her, you'll understand why. She looks so fragile—at most four feet tall."

Trig shook his head. "So where are we going?"

"Ellasar."

"To find your brothers and your mother?"

"How did you know they were there?"

"I said farewell to them. Oracle had had a vision of you meet- ing with them there and told them to go. I don't particularly trust future-seers, and I don't take orders from a small girl well, so I stayed behind in the Citadel. Besides, I was convinced that sooner or later you would have to come through there, and I was right. And here I am. How are we getting to Ellasar?"

"I have no idea. Malakieth knows of a way."

He gave her a strange look. "The same Malakieth that set thirty Rashek on you and walked away shortly after discovering you were his daughter?"

Kirin nodded. "My father, yes. We've . . . reached an understanding."

"An understanding? I thought you were supposed to kill him."

"I'm supposed to be *stopping* him. But Morgan and the shifter, Molyb, are much bigger threats."

"Than the creature who rules over a place called the 'World of Fear'?"

"Than the male who saved Callian's life. Who saved both of our lives, perhaps twice."

Trig stared at Callian, who nodded slowly. "I was dying, and Kirin panicked. He calmed her down and told her what to do. And it worked."

I'm landing beside you, Malakieth said, entering her thoughts. *I take it you found your human?*

His name is Trig.

Is he afraid of heights?

"Why are you looking at me like that?" Trig asked warily.

"Are you afraid of heights?" she asked.

"Not to the best of my knowledge. Why?"

"My father wanted to know."

"If he grabs me and tries to fly off with me as some bizarre joke, I'll stab him."

Malakieth landed solidly beside them. "I'll keep that in mind, human."

Trig stared at him. "Bloody huge dragon."

"Yet another reason Morgan chose me."

"Speaking of Morgan, how did you get away from the fortress?" Callian interrupted.

Malakieth flashed a fanged grin. "She actually sent me away to hunt Kirin down. If I happen to run across the Adkisha, my orders are 'to bring back her wretched head but return the princeling alive and relatively unharmed.'"

"Isn't that backward?" Trig pointed out.

Revulsion washed through Kirin. "No, it isn't. She'd only kill me anyway. But she'd keep Callian as a pet or something for a while first."

Malakieth snorted. "The first ever male *rakasheti*."

"Should I even ask?"

She ran straight up to his horse, who pranced and tossed his head in annoyance. There was a huge grin on her face, and she reached out to stroke his stallion's neck as she walked backward beside him.

"I've found them, King Nahor. They're in the grassland beyond the edge of the forest, and they're walking this way."

He didn't smile, but he nodded, returning his bow to his back. "Good. Did you see any sign of trouble?"

"None, unless it's short enough to be hidden by the grass."

"What of Malakieth?"

She shook her head. "Not a sight. Even in his human form, he would tower above the others."

He nodded again. She ran back to tell the others.

Beside him, Ling leaned forward in the saddle as if she were about to ask her horse to gallop. He reached out and touched her hand to stop her.

"They've just come from the Black Fortress. Having a small band of beings come racing up to them is the way to invite a skirmish."

She looked down and started absently braiding small pieces of her charger's long mane. "This pace feels too slow. It may be foolish, but... I am anxious to see that they are unharmed."

As she always was when Aramon wandered home or when one of them came back from a scouting trip or a battle. He twisted in the saddle to see Terah and Elfan walking side by side.

"Care to stretch the horses?" he called back to them. "Likely they're getting bored. I can see Aramon is."

Elfan reached up so Ephraim could pull her into the saddle. Terah swung to look for the younger of her brothers.

He wore a sly grin and was cantering up behind her.

"Oh, no," she breathed. "Aramon, I will kill you."

Her threat went unnoticed. Aramon came cantering by and easily yanked her feet off the ground. He set her in front of him and slowed Elindil to a brisk trot to keep up with the king and queen.

Nemah leapt to her feet the second she heard the bolt being drawn back from the door. She cringed when she felt the power of the creature who entered.

It wasn't Natasha, though it was a female.

A female who had red eyes like some of her dead littermates. But that was impossible. She had killed several of them, and Leader had taken out the rest.

She wished that they were still like that, she and Leader. She wished that Leader still tried to kill her every time he could get near her rather than...

Her mind blanked, not knowing the word. Whatever it was called, she felt that she would rather be dead.

The strange female approached boldly, and Nemah bared her teeth and hissed in warning. The newcomer didn't heed it, except to raise one hand with the same mark Natasha had.

Power exploded out of her, throwing Nemah into the nearest wall. She thrashed and snarled, trying to break free. It was a useless endeavor. The sorceress—she must be a sorceress—clenched her hand into a fist, and Nemah felt her throat constrict, her chest tighten, until she couldn't breathe.

Though she had just been wishing for death, she continued to struggle.

"I am your mistress, you stupid animal," the woman snarled. "I made you. I am the reason you live."

The pressure released all at once, and Nemah crumpled to the ground and lay there in a heap, gasping for breath.

"Wouldn't be wise to kill her simply because you're irate at the Adkisha's escape," a deep, rasping voice said. She looked up to see a tall man standing beside the woman. As she watched, he gave her a cruel grin and changed into Leader. She hissed and scrambled back, baring her fangs at the look-alike. "Honestly, though, I think the girl should have been killed the moment she was drug into the castle. Just rip her head off, and be done with it."

It was strange to see Leader talk, given that Leader had the intelligence and instincts of a wild animal. Which was essentially what he was.

"Next time, Molyb, I will. What's infuriating is not the fact that she escaped—I can appreciate a good opponent—but that it was mere *children* who helped her do it. What the hell are children doing rebelling? Where did that backbone come from?"

"Cathas help us if we knew," Molyb replied. He changed shape again to become a hulking beast-like creature with yellow fangs. "General Sisera and I have been hunting out their families and annihilating them, burning villages, and stealing and raping the females of their families, and they still rebel. It's quite irritating."

"What's quite irritating is your constant shifting," she snapped. "Pick a form!"

He glared at her but obeyed, becoming a huge male packed with muscle the way Leader was, with a strange, branching bone growing out of his head and flaming coals where his eyes should have been. The sorceress looked at him in appreciation.

He regarded Nemah. Nemah looked down, refusing to meet his eyes, the way a submissive beast would.

"Use her," he rumbled, his voice deep.

"Pardon?"

"Use your pet. Take an army. Crush her and her little band. Let the creature out, and see how much damage she'll do."

The sorceress smiled slowly, looking at Nemah. Nemah listened carefully. "I like that. We'll set you loose, wretched creature, and see how many you can kill."

They left, and Nemah allowed herself to smile. They were going to set her loose. She could run.

Run far away.

She couldn't wait to tell Natasha.

REUNION

As they walked, Trig and Callian took turns telling Kirin stories of Giladeth and Castle Haven. Tales of battles and border wars, of balls and courtiers, and of hunting parties came to life in the long walk across the grassland.

Callian told her of life spent growing up in the castle, of watching tournaments, of holiday banquets, and of time spent training with the knights. He described to her the stables and his warhorse and of the battle he had led against Giladeth's enemies to the north.

Trig told her of Wastrel Manor, his childhood home, and of the nearby lake in which he and Callian had learned to sail and swim. He told her of the great plains in the middle of the country and the strange animals that inhabited them, animals that Kirin had never heard of before.

Then Callian described to her the trading expedition he had gone on two years ago and of the long voyage overseas in a ship laden with salted fish and fruit preserves, wood and raw ore, and furs and precious metals, to a strange country far to the south that spoke a harsh, guttural language, whose people had dark skin and dark eyes and wore robes, even the women. He told her of the nomadic culture and how groups of families there banded together in tribes, how the women of the tribe he visited had brazenly come up to touch his pale hair and see his blue eyes. He told her of how the tribe's elders had traded them bolts and bolts of bright, rich material and colorful silks for jewel-encrusted daggers and decorations of hard, engraved leather and for beautiful belts made of leather and hammered metal and precious stones. He spoke of how he had brought along gifts of Giladethian dresses for the women and fine bows for the men and how the people of the tribe had, in turn, given him a carved spear and a dagger and a set of robes and a sash and leather sandals like their men had worn.

"Of course, the court was slightly disappointed when he returned home without a bride-to-be," Trig added.

"You were fourteen!" she protested.

Callian shrugged. "It would have thrilled them to no end if I had brought home a girl from a foreign country to strengthen political ties." He smiled at her. "So they'll have to approve of you, no matter what land you claim as your homeland."

Kirin flushed but smiled. "That's good, at least." Something wet nudged her, and she jumped.

Xzylya stood there, water dripping from her scales.

"Where did you find water?" Trig demanded.

Come, she replied and ran off. The others ran with her.

The stream she led them to was wide and slow-moving, the water cool and clean and about knee-high. Trig disarmed himself and pulled off his boots, then waded in and lay down to submerge himself. Callian and Kirin hurriedly pulled the saddles and packs from their dragons and followed the great creatures in.

It was heavenly to get clean again. They scrubbed themselves down, clothes and all, gulped down as much of the cool water as they could hold, and then just lounged in it.

Kirin smiled at the dragons, watching them lay in the water and scrub each other clean. Nearby, Trig walked up to the bank and lay down in the long grass.

"I could stay here all day and let the sun dry me," he murmured.

Callian nodded, rising slowly. Kirin watched him, admiring the way the water made his shirt cling to him.

Trig was watching him as well, head canted to the side, eyes half-closed. "Callian, you look … different," he finally said. "I've been trying to figure out what it was, and I can't think of it. It's not a bad thing, but … you seem different."

Callian frowned. "Do I?"

"Yes. I don't know. I could be going mad. Or perhaps it's the fact that you are truly, genuinely happy with Kirin. But you're walking lighter, more of a hunter's tread, except that it's all the time and you don't seem to be thinking of doing it. But that could be because you've spent the last few weeks on Amalay Kahelith and we've all been prepared to be under attack at all times. And your voice is a bit different and perhaps even your facial structure. Your hair is lighter, but that might be due to the sun. And you've also put on a bit more muscle—I just noticed that."

Callian looked at Kirin in confusion. She looked back.

You're an elf now, she reminded him. *You look more Ellasarian. The conversion... I suppose you could say perfected... upon your physical appearance.*

Why would it do that?

The benevolence and compassion of the elves—as a whole, mind you—tend to be evidenced by physical beauty. Of course, you were always a handsome man, to the point where I had wondered at one point whether or not you somehow had Ellasarian blood in your family. There wasn't much that the conversion's magic tried to improve on.

Callian turned and knelt back down in the water to see his reflection. The face staring up at him was his own... and yet was not his own. It was slightly different, a small enough difference that only someone who was looking for it or who knew Callian as well as Trig did would notice. His father, his mentor... would they see it?

Trig breathed an oath beside him, sitting up. "Callian, your *ears,*" he murmured.

Callian felt his friend's fingers touch the side of his face, feeling the pointed tip to his ear.

Trig cursed again. "Well, that would explain things. How the hell did you become immortal? I didn't even think that was possible."

"Neither did I until it happened," he replied, turning his head to look at his friend. His closest friend. His *mortal* friend. He stared at Trig, memorizing his face, suddenly struck with the knowledge that this man before him was going to age and die, and there was nothing

Callian could do about it. Not even with his new strength. Not even with his magic. Not even with Tiamat. Death and time were two enemies that he couldn't best.

His thoughts must have shown through his expression because Trig gave him an odd look. "Don't look at me like that, Callian. Heaven and hell, I'm not dead yet and won't be for another fifty or more years if I have anything to say about it."

Trig watched Tiamat come up behind his friend to nuzzle his wet hair and saw Kirin take his hand. He could easily read the guilt in the curve of her shoulders, the set of her wings.

So it had been by her doing. He felt a brief, irrational, and completely selfish flash of ire. *Stop being an idiot,* he told himself. *You've always known that you would have to share your friend with someone else; you should be grateful that he's fallen so hard for her.*

He should be, and he was. But it didn't change the fact that he was going to grow old, and that when he was weak and on his deathbed, Callian would still be in his prime.

But Callian would be happy. And that was what mattered.

Trig felt himself shrug. "Save the story for when Kirin's brothers are with us. But are you happy? Is your immortality a good thing?"

"Of course," the prince replied, his voice low. "Kirin wasn't aging."

"Then that's good enough for me."

"Trig," Kirin said, starting to smile with relief. "You are a good man, and someday you will make a good husband for a lucky woman."

Trig flashed her a smile. "I'm not sure I would call her lucky. I've been told I'm more trouble than I'm worth."

Callian laughed and dowsed him with water.

"That magic is irritating," Trig grumbled. "Though likely useful for sailing."

Assumptshun is coming with a group of elves, Tiamat informed him. Callian relayed the information, and Kirin shot to her feet, calling her brother's name.

She bolted for them the moment she saw them, the one Dark Dragon and the mounted elves traveling across the grassland toward her. Xzylya ran beside her, eager and glad to run.

A rider on a white horse broke free of the group and came galloping at her in a full charge.

Spreading her wings, she flew to meet Aramon, landing beside him as he pulled up his horse. He leapt down and hugged her fiercely, mindful of her wings.

Drawing back, he eyed her up and down as if checking to make sure that she was fine.

"You're soaking wet!" he exclaimed.

"I was lying in a stream." She laughed, shoving her hair out of her face.

"On purpose?" a girl's voice asked.

Kirin looked over her brother's shoulder to see Oracle sitting in the front of his saddle and dressed in nice breeches and a clean tunic.

She had no time to ponder this. The others surrounded her and Xzylya, and she was suddenly embraced by Elfan, who passed her to Ephraim. Assumptshun ruffled her hair and bowed his head to greet Xzylya, who looked up at him in awe.

Then she was in Ling's arms, and her mother held her and stroked her hair, whispering, "My daughter, my daughter. I was so worried for you. Are you all right?"

Kirin nodded, overwhelmed by the throng of people who loved her. *This is family*, she realized. *This is home.*

She never wanted to let go.

"Kirin?" Her mother drew back to see her face and brushed her thumbs along Kirin's cheeks. "You're crying. Are you unharmed?"

"I'm sorry. I'm happy, truly. I'm well. I wasn't harmed. Frightened at times but unharmed. It's a long story. So much has happened."

"But you're safe now." Ephraim smiled. "So now we can finally get you to Ellasar and train you properly."

"Is this Xzylya? The little hatchling?" Aramon said. "She's gotten so big."

She snapped at him playfully. *I'm fierce.*

"She says she's fierce," Kirin told him.

He laughed. "Oh, of course."

"She made her first kill," Callian told him as he and Trig and the dragons joined the group.

"A rabbit?"

"A Rashek."

He sounded impressed. "By herself?"

"She beat Tiamat to him."

"Impressive." Oracle grinned. "Callian, Kirin, we brought you boots."

Callian flashed her a broad smile. "Thank you. You're wonderful."

Ephraim reached over and lifted the small elf down from his brother's horse. She ran back to the riderless horse and rifled through one of the packs, producing two pairs of supple boots. She tossed them, and Xzylya snatched them out of the air and brought them to her rider.

Thank you.

Kirin tugged them on, wings flared to keep her balanced. They fit perfectly and had already been broken in.

"They were secondhand," Ephraim explained softly. "As are Callian's. Terah asked for two pairs of boots and gave us measurements—there wasn't time to make them or ask a cobbler to do so."

"I don't mind at all; it saves me the trouble of trying to break them in. Now tell me why you stole Oracle from the Resistance."

"Do you remember Aramon and I telling you of our sister Terah's disappearance as a child?"

"Yes."

"That's her."

Kirin looked at Oracle, at Princess Terah, and then looked at her mother. Yes, she could see the resemblance now that she was looking for it. Grinning, she walked up to her newfound sister.

"So it seems I have a sister," she teased. "Or half-sister."

Terah smiled up at her. "You are my sister. What Malakieth did to Ling... Knowing that she is my mother makes me hate him all the more."

Kirin shrugged one shoulder uneasily. "He saved my life—and Callian's—perhaps even twice."

"That only makes matters more complicated."

Kirin turned to face the speaker, the tall, male elf she had overlooked in the excitement of greeting her family. He hung back a bit from the knot of people, standing next to his grazing horse and stroking the creature's brown neck. A golden crown wrought in a pattern of leaves and vines encircled his brow.

King Nahor. Ling's husband.

She bowed to him.

Curtsying would have been better, Beau informed her with a sigh. She blushed and straightened.

Amusement pulled at the corners of the king's mouth, making him look uncannily like his second son.

"With all respect, lord king, I do not see the complication."

"You can understand why I seek to kill him."

"I can understand your anger and your hatred, and I agree that Malakieth made many poor choices. But he and Callian saved me from General Sisera, and he helped us escape the fortress."

"How?" Terah demanded.

Kirin said nothing.

But Nahor looked at Callian. "Interesting."

Tiamat hissed at him.

"Unfortunately, I can't help it, Lady Tiamat. Adkisha Kirin, we would accompany you to the castle at Taure En Alata. It is a seven days' journey from here."

Kirin inclined her head. "I would be honored." She glanced back at Trig and Callian, at Beau and Tiamat and Xzylya, who was nose to nose with Elindil and trying to understand what was so interesting about the grass. "We would be honored. If I may make introductions, these are my bonded dragons, Beau and Xzylya. My friend, Lord Trig of Giladeth. And my beloved, Prince Callian of Giladeth, and his bonded dragon, Tiamat."

Trig and Callian bowed while the dragons dipped their heads to the Ellasarian king. "Well met. Prince Callian, Lord Trig, dragons, I would like to extend my gratitude on behalf of my family for protecting Lady Kirin on her journey. From what my sons have told me, it wasn't the easiest task."

"The good ones never are, lord king." Trig grinned.

Callian stepped up to Kirin and wrapped his arm around her waist. "It was my honor, sir, and my pleasure. And it will be my honor to continue to do so."

Subtle, Kirin teased.

No, diplomatic. It's an art you might want to learn someday.

"Lord Trig," Nahor said. "We have a spare horse should you care to ride."

"That would be wonderful."

Kirin, tell him privately I will continue to carry his pack, Beau told her. She whispered the message to Trig as he passed.

Beau looked at his mate. *Tiamat, I will carry your rider if you would like to have an easier trip.*

She looked at him. *Then I will carry—*

"Beau, if you don't mind terribly, I would like to fly now that it's safer."

Beau paused and then nodded his head.

I will carry Callian until she tires of flying, Tiamat decided.

Beau stretched his neck out to nuzzle her cheek. *As you wish.*

They turned and headed toward the tree line. Kirin smiled when she saw Ephraim toss Elfan into his saddle. They were a good match. And seeing them together on a dragon made her think of the Academy.

She flew for several hours, daydreaming about what it would be like to return and settle back into her old life.

Nahor watched Kirin fly, watched her swoop low and rub the top of the dracling's head before pulling up sharply. The Light Dragon leapt up after her, trying to catch her, then tore off after her rider, wings extended, leaping in an attempt to fly. Kirin landed smoothly, tucking her wings against her back, and the dracling leapt on her, knocking her over. The two wrestled, mindful of the other's wings, until Xzylya pinned the halfling and let her up again.

Xzylya loped next to her rider as the Adkisha ran, her pale hair—now dry—streaming behind her.

Watching the two of them play was like watching a celebration of life. He could see his wife smiling, remembering the times when they had been carefree, all the times during their courtship and marriage when they had gone swimming and had ended up wrestling in the water only to climb out to lay on the banks in each other's arms and let the sun dry them.

He promised himself that those days would come again for them.

Xzylya caught Kirin's tunic and tugged on her, and Nahor listened to a one-sided conversation as the dracling begged for Kirin to ride her. It was strange not being able to hear Kirin's thoughts, but he had known that he would be deaf to her. He had never been able to hear halflings. The silence of her mind was both a blessing and an aggravation.

Kirin's wings unfolded, and she beat the air a handful of times, settling on Xzylya's back. The dracling looked back at her with a toothy grin and then arched her neck proudly and cantered to Beau to show him.

You'll make that dragon overly proud, Kirin, he heard Beau say. But even Nahor could hear the fondness in his voice.

What are you thinking of? Ling's thought flowed through his mind, directed to him.

Kirin, he mindspoke to her.

What do you think of her?

That she's beautiful. And, at the moment, that she seems to be celebrating life. And that it will take a bit of adjustment for me to be used to her.

Because she's Malakieth's child?

And because she seems to want to defend him. And because she's fierce for a woman. And a very powerful warrior, and in a matter of days, she will be my student. Not to mention … there is something about her eyes that unnerves me.

They are shaped like a dragon's, and you were always comfortable around Kanna and Kali.

Not their shape, my love. The way they flash. She knows dark magic. There is always the possibility that her dragon, Beau, taught her that. But more than the knowledge of dark magic—which she would have to learn eventually regardless—she smiles and laughs, and I can only see raw fear in her eyes. Something has unnerved her greatly, and I can't figure out what it is that bothers her. I can't hear her mind to discover it, and the dragons are silent on the matter without even seeming to be. It's unnerving that, though the three minds are like one, only one is terrified of something that she won't speak of.

He glanced at Callian and away and then stared hard at the young prince, his eyes narrowed. The wind teased his hair away from pointed ears.

He had been human when he had been captured.

Kirin's voice floated through his thoughts, a memory of her earlier words she had spoken to Terah about her father. *He saved my life—and Callian's—perhaps even twice.*

Had Malakieth told her of the conversion? Had she performed it on the Giladethian prince?

Unfortunately, it seemed the most likely, and he knew from personal experience how potent the aftereffects of that spell were. But for it to terrify her so badly?

He might have to arrange an accident for the prince.

Nemah killed her first warrior when they made the mistake of sending a stranger into her pen—and a male at that. He had been an odd color—blue, Natasha had once called it—and had bled a foul-smelling substance unlike the sharp-tasting red that she and Leader bled.

His death had been a pleasure.

After that, they found a slave woman—not Natasha, but an older one with graying hair and curious lines in her skin. She had been thin and bony and had had cold, shaking hands that had bothered Nemah as they put the thick metal collar around her neck and bound her hands together in front of her with coarse rope.

Morgan herself held the ropes and chain that bound her, and she stumbled alongside a strange, two-wheeled cart that was pulled by a single were-beast. There were ten of the creatures, not including the one that pulled Morgan's wheeled cart, as well as twelve squadrons of twenty Rashek apiece, twenty Nephilim led by someone Morgan called Sisera, Molyb the Shifter, a dragon that could only be Malakieth who looked at her sympathetically, and Morgan herself. And Nemah.

Nemah stared in shock as the sorcerers finally succeeded in getting something called a portal opened.

This was where they were taking her? This lovely place with the bright, blue sky and greenness everywhere? It was wonderful!

Not thinking, she sprung forward only to be yanked back, choking as the collar bit into her throat. She cried out in frustration.

"Idiot," Morgan muttered.

The sorceress cracked her whip over the back of the were-beast, and the army moved forward into the green world.

Nemah looked back through the portal into the world she had known, the world where Leader had been left, the world she would never return to, and bid it farewell. She could only hope that Natasha could somehow escape it soon. They could hide together.

Nemah eyed Malakieth. No, Natasha would never leave her master.

Perhaps Malakieth would come with them.

Nemah sat far away from the fire, not trusting it not to harm her. She watched Morgan just as carefully, listening to her conversation with Malakieth and waiting for her to relax a bit more.

There. Morgan's hand drifted closer, and Nemah shot off the ground, snapping at her.

Morgan jumped and jerked her hand out of the way, backhanding the creature and sending it sprawling. The wretched thing simply shook off the pain and sat up again, watching and waiting in an almost feline way.

"If you fed it a bit more, it wouldn't be trying to eat you," Malakieth pointed out, and she could hear the humor in his voice.

She glared at him, returning to the previous conversation. "I can't believe you."

"She's a child. It's not hard to believe."

"She's an infuriating little mutant! And even if I did want to 'give her time to grow up so that she could be a more interesting opponent,' which I *absolutely do not*, my master gave his orders. Kill her."

Malakieth shrugged at her in his true form. "As you wish."

"You act like you *care* about her. What is it with you and blond females? Do *not* tell me that this is the one you now want since Ling wouldn't have you."

Nemah stiffened, distracted momentarily from the conversation and from aggravating Morgan. She had the strangest feeling that she was being watched. She looked around, suspicious and wary, but saw nothing. She listened but heard nothing unusual. The air carried no new scents.

Apprehensive, she returned her focus to Morgan and Malakieth.

"Women in general are the bane of my existence, regardless of their hair color, and no, I'm not in love with this one. I merely thought that she would make an interesting ally. Who could stand against you and her combined?"

That made Morgan pause. "Still, orders from the master are orders. And when the time comes, can I trust you?"

"I am a very predictable male, Morgan. Of course you can trust me."

Morgan's pet lunged at her again. Morgan swore and drew back to hit her again.

"Stop, stop, before you kill it prematurely and it's no use to you in battle. Give me the thing. I'll go feed it and make sure none of the Nephilim or were-beasts try to kill it in its sleep."

Morgan gladly threw him the ropes and the chain. "Don't give it too much, or it will be no use."

He nodded. "As you wish, fearsome lady."

He nearly had to drag Nemah after him. The girl was stronger than she looked.

I'm not going to harm you, he mindspoke to her. *I'm going to give you food and protect you so you can sleep. I know you understand me—Natasha's said as much.*

She paused and then followed him obediently. Natasha had always praised this male for his goodness.

He led her to a different fire on the very edge of the camp. Freedom called, and she tried to edge away.

Not yet, you don't. Wait until the battle. In the chaos of the fighting you can flee Morgan.

She stared at him, and he picked a whole bird off a branch that had been set over the fire. It burned her hands, her lips, her tongue, but the delicious taste of the hot meat more than made up for it.

That's a pheasant, he told her. *They're common in grassy areas like this. You're in the world of Kyria, in the country by the same name. The world was named after this, the largest country, which is inhabited by humans, along with werewolves and vampires.*

She picked the carcass clean while he talked to her, explaining what was going on, telling her that Natasha was hidden far enough away to be safe but close enough to be able to get to Malakieth in a matter of an hour or so. She didn't understand why he had brought her, and he didn't offer a reason, but it was enough to know her friend was near.

"Lady Kirin, come for a walk with me?"

Kirin looked up at Nahor and then glanced at Ling and at Callian. Ling looked at her expectantly, hopefully. Callian gave her a wry smile that told her that he, at least, understood how uncomfortable a private discussion with her mother's husband was going to be.

"Of course." She rose and left the comfort of the campfire with the king of the elves.

He didn't fool around with small talk but cut straight to the point of the discussion, which she appreciated.

"You are worried. Terrified."

It was a statement, but she still replied to it.

"I thought you couldn't read my mind."

"I'm reading your eyes. You hide your emotions well, but there are ways of telling."

"Like Ephraim and his gift," she pointed out.

"Ephraim is preoccupied with Elfan, and a good thing, too. It's high time that man married."

"Are they engaged, then?"

"No, merely courting, but I have hopes. And it was a good try at changing the topic."

"It was worth a shot."

He smirked briefly at the ground as they walked. "Ling had said Callian was human. However, he now seems to be an elf. I take it you performed the conversion spell?"

"Yes. And if there was some law I broke by doing so, I had no knowledge of it."

"There's no law in Ellasar—or anywhere to the best of my knowledge—against the *animai conveinos*. It's more of a moral law."

"Are you saying it's immoral of me to save a man from dying when I have been given the power to aid him?" she asked hotly, her green eyes flashing fire at him.

"No," he snapped. "But it is immoral to bed a man before you are married to him. I know the spell, Kirin. I performed it on your mother millennia ago."

She blinked. "But I didn't."

"Pardon?"

"I didn't bed Callian. I'm still a virgin," she whispered, blushing.

He seemed taken aback. "*Ehin*," he finally breathed. "I owe you an apology then. I jumped to conclusions."

She smiled at him for the first time. "A problem that has gotten me in trouble with Headmaster Melchizedek many times. May I bargain for a set of answers rather than an apology?"

He returned her smile somewhat ruefully. "If you like."

"Did you wait until your wedding night to perform the conversion?"

He shook his head with a guilty smile. "About a month before. And it was hellacious trying not to dishonor your mother. And what is your second question?"

"Why did you assume I was terrified because of performing the conversion on Callian?"

He looked ahead of them into the darkness of the night forest, his brow pulling down over his eyes. Kirin could begin to see the man her mother had fallen so madly in love with. Nahor had a strong, proud, noble face and a regal bearing, and yet was willing to admit his mistakes to a girl who had not yet come of age.

"I noted that Callian was no longer human, and as the conversion spell is the only known way to become an elf—"

"Unless you're a changeling," she interrupted.

He nodded in acknowledgment but didn't pause. "It was the obvious conclusion that someone performed the conversion on him. Since you were the only elf near him, you were the only one who could. I had assumed that you either didn't or were not able to resist the—shall we call it aftereffects?—of the magic. Since you were the only one of your companions who was frightened, I assumed the others were either hiding something or hadn't realized something was wrong—which would be strange for a bonded dragon. I was worried Callian had harmed you or forced you or that you felt threatened by him now. In truth, I was working on devising an unfortunate accident, but since he has not harmed you, it will no longer be necessary."

She looked at him sideways. "You would protect me?"

He gazed down at her. "You are my wife's daughter, the beloved of my family. If you would permit it, I would claim you publicly to all of Ellasar."

She stared at him, stupidly blurting out, "But I'm a halfling! I don't resemble you."

He smiled gently. "Neither does Elfan, or the woman Aramon loves but will not seek to court because he's a fool. But should my sons ever wake up and marry, I will claim their wives as my daughters. There is an expression in Elvish—*eruanna mir amo menel*. Have you heard it?"

"'Daughter of my heart,'" she translated softly. "I am fluent."

"The offer stands."

They walked in silence for a dozen yards or so.

"Not to be rude or insulting, but seeing as you barely know me and you hate my father, I can't help but wonder if are you offering either because I am the Adkisha and, therefore, a powerful ally, or to spite my father."

"Your title and position as the Adkisha will give you respect in Ellasar regardless of your family—after all, you are a part of King Ishmael's legacy—and you clearly love your brothers, so even as king, I do not offer for political gain. And I offer not to spite your father, but despite him."

"Then why do you offer to call a stranger daughter?" she whispered.

"For Ling. I love your mother deeply, and nothing anyone does to her will ever change that. And for you. I do not want to be the reason you do not visit or stay with your mother and your siblings, whichever is your wish in the future years."

"May I think on it?"

"Of course."

They walked on.

Eventually, Nahor looked at her again. "May I ask what has you so worried? You don't strike me as the nervous sort."

"It's ... I fear an attack."

"An ambush?"

She shook her head. "A full attack. And honestly, I've never been in a full battle yet. Only skirmishes. The biggest was against thirty Rashek."

"Aramon told me of that. He said you fought well for such scant training in magic."

Kirin blushed under the praise.

"Who do you fear will lead the attack?"

"The sorceress Morgan."

"You are aware that I killed her myself in the Battle of Candescere?"

"Her followers remained loyal to her and performed with success a resurrection while I was in the Black Fortress, and she is likely furious we escaped her from under her nose, so to speak."

Nahor was silent for a moment. Then Kirin heard him sigh deeply. "I was afraid she had returned," he said. Quietly, he told her of Terah's prophecy.

Kirin's eyes hardened as she squared her shoulders. "I will make sure nothing happens to Terah. She deserves to have time to be raised in the love of her family."

"You will look after yourself and your dragons as well." It wasn't a question.

"Yes," she said. Then she paused. Morgan would aim for her specifically. "But ... should anything happen to me ... Would you make sure Callian doesn't do anything rash? And see Trig safely home to Giladeth?"

He inclined his head. "But don't think that way, Kirin. It only causes distraction during battle."

She nodded. "Do you think Morgan is coming?"

He didn't answer immediately. "It is a strong possibility. There is the camp just ahead. I will scry and answer your question."

Callian and Trig looked up as they reentered the camp, and Callian smiled at her, patting the space beside him. She sat and rested her head on his shoulder.

"It went better than I thought it would. He's ... honest with me."

"About?"

"He was worried you had compromised my honor after the conversion. I told him he was mistaken, and he seemed pleased. He said that meant he no longer had to arrange an accident for you."

Callian laughed softly. "I'm not sure whether to be more pleased that he cares about your well-being or worried that the king will arrange accidents for foreign princes."

Kirin smiled briefly.

Across the camp, Xzylya started to hum softly one of the tunes Natasha had sung to her. Terah smiled, running a soft cloth against the young dragon's incandescent scales. Like all Light Dragons, her scales reflected the pale light of the moon like diamonds.

Callian stroked her cheek. "You are worried. About Morgan?"

She nodded. "Nahor is going to scry her. I fear she is coming after us."

Across the fire, Aramon frowned, sat up, and then edged closer. Ephraim, Terah, and Elfan came around to sit or stand near Kirin as Ling and Nahor knelt beside her with a bowl of water. The dragons closed their eyes and lay back down, content to view the scrying through their riders' minds.

With a wave from Callian, the water stilled. Nahor nodded to the prince.

He didn't speak to the water, didn't ask to view Morgan as Callian or Aramon would. He merely looked at it, and the water shimmered and brought forth an image.

Kirin didn't have time to admire the sorcerer king's skill, too horrified by the image.

Morgan sat perched on the rail of a chariot, eyes narrowed as she spoke to Malakieth. Nothing was audible, but Kirin doubted from their expressions that it was pleasant news. Around them, warriors huddled in camps, eating, moving to and fro, and sleeping. The tall, trampled grass around them confirmed their location.

But what was more disconcerting was the creature Morgan had bound, who crouched beside the chariot and glared at Morgan with a calculating interest.

She looked human, but the way she crouched was feline. In fact, without the claws and the slim fangs she displayed whenever Morgan glanced her way, she would be darkly beautiful ... almost like a Dark Dragon would be in human form.

"Look at her ears," Trig murmured, leaning closer.

Kirin looked and saw what he meant. They were pointed, but not like an elf's. Instead, there was a double tip, one after the other.

"What is she?" Callian wondered, and Kirin agreed. This creature could not be natural.

As they looked, she suddenly swung around and stared at them, eyes narrowed, darting around as she sniffed the air.

"Impossible," Aramon whispered. "She can't sense us."

But the creature seemed to. Wary, she went back to watching Morgan. And then sprung at Morgan's hand, nearly biting the sorceress.

Morgan leapt, inciting a few snickers, and drew back to hit the girl, who flinched back and steeled herself. But Malakieth intervened, talking quickly and tersely. Morgan threw the girl's bonds to him and swung herself inside the chariot as the dragon walked off.

A new image surfaced in the water, following Malakieth as he half-led, half-drug the girl along. Then she suddenly ceased struggling and followed him tamely to his own fire, where she sat down like a human might. He gave her an entire roast bird, lay down with one forefoot on her bonds, and proceeded to ignore her while she practically inhaled the meat. She watched him and then curled up in a tight ball and fell asleep.

Nahor let the image die.

At first, no one spoke.

"We will make all haste to Taure En Alata," Nahor said finally. "Ellasar's borders are protected, but not against the likes of Morgan and certainly not against Nishron's Three."

"Is Molyb there, then?" Ephraim asked. He wrapped an arm around Elfan's shoulders and tucked her into his side.

"I don't doubt it."

"What is that girl?" Trig asked.

Kirin looked around uneasily as no one answered. "The way she sprung at Morgan reminds me of the were-beasts that attacked us."

"Her facial structure is similar to my people," Assumptshun rumbled.

But not quite, Beau added.

"Those ears are a were-beast's," Aramon added.

"You have time to admire their ears when they attack?" Trig's voice was skeptical, with a slight mocking edge to it that earned him a glare from the wanderer.

"No, but I was in a tavern with a were-beast's head mounted on the wall as a trophy."

"Whatever she is," Nahor said firmly, "and whether she is sentient or not, do not hesitate in battle against her. You've all seen now how quickly she jumps. Be prepared."

All around the tight knot of travelers' heads nodded in accent.

"And I am getting up in the dawn to get a view of their camp and the numbers they bring against us," Kirin said, her voice soft but firm.

Protests went up immediately. Callian's arms tightened around her. *Absolutely not,* he mindspoke to her.

"I have to," she said out loud, looking at Nahor. "We need to know their numbers and how far away they are. I can fly. You *must* let me do this."

"No," Aramon insisted. "*Abbo,* tell her it's stupidity to even try."

The king remained silent.

"Nahor?" Ling whispered.

"As Terah's gift is currently silent, there is no way of telling in advance what the outcome will be either way. It would be better if we knew the numbers Nishron's Three bring against us; *however,* it would be foolishness to risk Kirin. I can argue both sides, and therefore, I will bow out of this argument. But I will say I believe the debate lies mainly between Kirin and Callian, and they should decide together what the best course of action is. In the meantime, I would suggest setting up a guard rotation of which I will keep the first watch."

"I will stay with you," Ling volunteered immediately.

"I'll take second," Aramon added.

Nahor nodded. "First, though, Aramon, I have need of your skill with dreamwalking. Go to Dolon and tell him of our plight; we will not make it back to the citadel without a battle. Ask him to send a full division of archers as quickly as possible to us."

"The Academy will likely be able to help if they can get here in time," Kirin added. "One of my friends is a Time Mage. As of the time that I left, he had very little training, but surely that's changed in a half-year."

Nahor nodded. "You and your love go fight nicely."

Kirin rose, forcing Callian to let go of her, and walked off. He followed, his face set in stone.

"Callian—"

"No."

"Callian, please."

"No."

She threw her hands up and spun away, intent on storming off. "You're being impossible!"

He caught her arm and spun her to face him, backing her carefully into the nearest tree. His eyes burned into hers. Kirin looked away, knowing the moment she met his eyes was the moment he won the argument.

Callian didn't make it easy for her. His hands crept to her throat, his fingertips lightly brushing aside her hair. He pressed his lips to the hollow under her ear and then to the corner of her jawbone. His mouth trailed down her cheek, and he slid his lips across hers, lighter than a butterfly's wing.

His sweet seduction was so much more effective than any force and stubbornness he could put into an argument, and they both knew it. She shoved him away and distanced herself. Undeterred, he wrapped his arms around her from behind and turned her face to the side to torment her with soft kisses.

"Do you think I could live if I let you take yourself away from me?" he breathed against her lips before kissing her in earnest.

She could barely breathe, which kept her from responding too wildly, from conceding right then and there. She let him play with her lips, her left hand hanging lifelessly against his thigh, her right reaching over to cradle his face. Her body lay in a swoon against his.

Callian trailed the fingers of his left hand across her stomach, his lips twitching up into a wicked half-smile as her body arched against his hand. He raised the same hand to trace her face. His right arm supported her limp body, keeping her knees from buckling.

Slowly, he pulled back before she fainted.

She still lay against him flaccidly, her head on his shoulder, her eyes closed, and her full lips parted slightly.

"Are you awake?" he whispered to her.

"No. I'm dreaming."

"Then don't wake up," he teased. Turning serious again, he continued. "Stay here with me," he pleaded.

She shook her head. "I have to go. I need to see her face-to-face before I fight her. Please, Callian. I need to do this. I will be careful; on my honor."

She opened her eyes and turned to see his pained expression. She knew he had been hoping kissing her would have distracted her.

Finally, after several moments of maddening silence, he nodded once and moved to kiss her good-bye.

He was not gentle. He was bent almost in half, cradling her in his arms against his chest, his mouth nearly crushing hers, as if desperately afraid that as soon as he let her go, she would never return.

She felt her knees buckle, and he went with the motion, lowering them both to the ground until he was kneeling in the grass as she lay across his lap. Her fingers were tangled in the neckline of his tunic, holding him to her, suddenly fearing what she had been begging him to let her do.

She could feel his fear and apprehension leaking through his lips as he kissed her. It felt as if her heart was being rent, knowing she was responsible for this pain.

Reluctantly, she broke the kiss.

"I want to sleep with you in my arms," he said.

"Of course," she replied, smiling softly.

"And you will wake me before you go so that I may see you off."

"Of course," she repeated.

He jerked a nod and lifted her, rising easily. Callian carried her in his arms back to the edge of the camp, then set her down.

She placed her palm on his cheek. "Thank you," she whispered.

Wordlessly, he took her hand and led her to where his cloak lay on the ground. She caught Nahor's eye and nodded once.

Then she lay pressed up against her love, her head pillowed on his arm, her cloak over them both. She burrowed into his warmth, and his arm tightened around her. She slept soundly, deep in a dreamless sleep.

Callian opened his eyes to the forest watched by unseen eyes. Tiamat was nowhere in sight, but then, she never was in this wood.

He knelt, waiting for Adonai to speak. His knee barely touched the ground before His gentle voice whispered around him.

"You have done well, but your task is not yet finished."

Callian swallowed. "Am I wrong to let her go in the morning, my lord?"

"Dear prince," the voice murmured kindly. "You have faced so much pain and fear these last months, and you have not allowed the evil around you to touch your own heart. Why do you doubt your actions now?"

"I was given a second chance at life and gifted with immortality," he replied. "My task is to guard and assist Kirin, and yet, I am allowing her to fly straight into the danger from which we flee. That seems a poor choice."

"Prince Callian, Kirin must do what she needs to do. She must face Morgan in battle soon, and I caution you not to try to intercede with the sorceress. If you engage Morgan while Kirin is dueling her, you risk not only your own life but risk distracting Kirin, which would cost her her life."

He took a breath, striving to make his voice polite. "Am I to sit idly by and watch the woman I love fight for her life?"

"Morgan is not the only being who wishes the Adkisha harm. You must guard her back and protect her from the others. Keep her from distraction."

A straight-forward task. Callian felt some of the tension ease from his shoulders. Guarding Kirin was something he could do.

"Do you accept this task, dear prince? Will you see it through to the end?"

"I swear upon the joint life I share with my dragon to protect Kirin, no matter the cost."

Adonai's voice was somber. "You will be held to that oath. This battle will cost you much."

Callian's mind flashed to Trig. Trig had always had his back. How could he live with himself if Trig was wounded—or even killed—because he hadn't been there to save him?

But how could he live with himself if Kirin was hurt because he was too distracted to protect her?

He closed his eyes. Though it hurt him, he banished all worries of his closest friend's well-being out of his thoughts. He would protect Kirin.

"Thank you for her," he murmured to Adonai. "Thank you for giving me this path, this chance."

"My dear son," came the reply, the breeze swirling around him before disappearing.

Callian rose…

He opened his eyes. Kirin still lay curled in his arms, her head against his chest, one wing draped over his side. She looked so relaxed in her sleep. She looked so … young.

Turning his head, careful not to wake her, Callian saw the king of the elves staring at him with wide eyes.

Then the king bowed his head to the prince as if in reverence, and Callian was filled with a sense of honor.

FIRST SIGHT

Ling reached over and touched his hand. "Thank you for accepting her," she whispered.

Nahor looked at his wife. "No daughter can choose her father, and I will not drive her away from her family."

Ling smiled briefly. "All the same... thank you."

He inclined his head, accepting her thanks, unnecessary as it was. With his free hand, he added another small, dry log to the fire. He and his queen had sat at guard for two hours now; Aramon and Terah would be waking up to relieve them soon.

He looked at Ling, at the dark circles under her eyes testifying to her exhaustion.

"Go sleep. I'll wake Aramon up soon."

Ling hesitated and then shook her head. "It will sound foolish, but I don't want to sleep. I... I think that sleep would make me distracted for this battle." *Will it occur tomorrow?* she wondered.

"Likely before evening," he said in answer to her thoughts. She nodded. He hesitated and then said, "You've been having nightmares."

Ling bit her lip and ducked her head.

"It's absolutely nothing to be ashamed of."

"Could you hear them?" she whispered.

He nodded slowly. "And see them." They were silent for a while, and then the king of the elves raised his distraught eyes to Ling's face. "I saw you dreaming last night. It woke me up. I'm sorry, but I couldn't help but listen to and watch your dream. I'm so attuned to hearing your mind in my head. But the things that you were seeing, that you were hearing as you dreamed ..." He trailed off, shuddering and dropping his gaze back to the grass by his booted feet. "It horrified me that I was unable to protect you from those terrors." His voice was almost inaudible. "And all I can do is sit here and move slowly, and hope with all my heart that you will heal from this."

"I am trying," she whispered.

"I know. It will come in time. Relax, and let it happen, my love."

Across the camp, Aramon awoke and stretched, then settled by the fire and nodded at them, relieving them from their post. Terah was supposed to keep watch with him, but Nahor knew his son would never wake his sister.

"Well?" Nahor asked softly.

Aramon yawned so wide his jaw cracked. "Dolon's already actively preparing the archers. He's sending the Third Division. I told him to warn them of that one female."

It was a good choice. The Third Division was comprised mainly of males, and the women that were amongst them were tough and battle-seasoned. Half of the division—and all of the women in it— were mounted; the other half were foot soldiers trained to run for hours. They would travel fast, but to come from Taure En Alata ...

"Dolon made his choice mainly due to the fact that the Third Division was already out on battle maneuvers in practice and is only six hours of hard travel from us. I told Dolon to tell Captain Thavron to rendezvous with us at Amarth Dur."

Amarth Dur. In his mind, Nahor envisioned the lay of the land there, the way the trees suddenly stopped for a mile in a perfect circle, how the ground was perfectly smooth. He saw again the blackened earth at the center of the meadow, the place where so much magic had been released in battle that the grass still did not grow. Amarth Dur. Cursed land.

Strategically, though, it was a good place to battle. The woods ceased for a bit, enabling the archers' arrows to fly farther, giving the dragons the power of flight and room to maneuver. And it was close; they would be able to reach it shortly after noon, if they pushed hard, and would have time to rally the Dragon Knights and his elven archers and prepare for battle.

"Good. And the Academy?"

"Lord Melchizedek believes they will be able to open a gateway safely and bring their knights through. They will prepare at dawn and should arrive at midday."

Nahor smiled. "And?"

Aramon flushed, too faint for human eyes to see in the dim light, though his father noticed. "Niamh is traveling to Taure En Alata. She will be there to greet us when we return. I told her of Terah—and of Elfan—and she has asked me to ask you if she could have the position of Terah's handmaiden."

"I thought she wanted to join the army as an archer."

"Her brother refuses her still, saying that it is not a woman's place. He would rather have her at home but has agreed she may live at court should she be of service in a more ... feminine position."

"Then I shall gladly accept her." Nahor smiled. "She's steady-minded enough to handle Terah's visions. You can tell her when we return."

Aramon nodded. "Fair dreams," he murmured.

Kirin kissed Callian softly. He stretched around her, waking up from a deep sleep slowly.

He sighed against her mouth. "I love you," he whispered, cradling her face to kiss her. She smiled.

"You know I love you dearly," she replied. Her palm ran up and down his side and then gently pressed him back so she could rise. He let her up, and she knelt by her saddlebag, searching through it for a fighting outfit and what armor she had brought with her.

And there they were, folded neatly at the bottom of her bag, the fighting clothes she had brought with her from the Academy but had never thought to have much use for.

She pulled them out and ducked behind Beau, pulling them on, grateful that she had taken the time to cut slits into the back for her wings.

Callian's eyes widened when he saw her step out from behind Beau. He had nearly forgotten how wonderful she looked in fine clothing. The outfit was emerald green, which would blend in beautifully with the deep green of the leaves, and made of a fine, strong weave. The shirt's neck came up high, and she had dropped the crystal pendent over the top. Both the pants and the shirt were cut narrow, made to fit her perfectly without too much extra material. There was a small, simple pattern stitched into the cuffs with silver thread.

She sat down and pulled on the boots Terah had brought for her, lacing them tightly up her calves. Out from her pack came silvery greaves to be fastened over her boots.

"Kirin," he said, stopping her. "The metal will reflect and make you easy to see. Put it on when you come back."

She nodded and repacked her greaves. Leather vambraces went on her forearms, and a leather glove with only three fingers, leaving her thumb and smallest finger free, to protect her fingers from her bowstring. She combed through her hair and then plaited it tightly and wound it up into the warrior's knot he had seen her wear at the Academy. One knife disappeared down her boot, another was tied to her thigh, and the one her father had given her she belted to her hip opposite of where she would later belt her sword. She checked over her arrows and secured them tightly inside her quiver so they wouldn't rattle and then slid her bow in and strapped them carefully on her back between her wings.

Ephraim, who had had the final guard shift, walked over with a skin of water and a plate of fried potatoes and venison.

"Eat while you can," he said grimly, handing her the plate. "And here is water to keep you going should you need it. Aramon says we're meeting up with a division of archers who were out on battle maneuvers and were close enough to come to our aid at Amarth Dur. Are you familiar with the place?"

"I've heard the stories," she said between mouthfuls. "And I could likely show you on a map, but I don't know the land itself."

"We'll be traveling fast and hard. Track Beau and Xzylya in, but give us a warning when you come so we don't shoot you out of the sky."

She jerked a nod, quickly devouring the rest of the food. He took the plate from her.

"Good luck, little sister."

"Thank you. I'll see you before the battle."

Callian captured her face in his hands as Ephraim walked away. "Be careful. Promise me."

"I will be. On my honor."

He leaned forward and kissed her forehead, a silent send-off, and let her go.

She turned and ran, snapping out her wings and taking to the skies, soaring up and around tree trunks until she was in the canopy.

It didn't take her long to find the approaching army. She alighted on a branch and crept along it, shifting her weight carefully to keep from disturbing the branches.

It wasn't hard to find Morgan; she was right next to Malakieth in her chariot, and with his size, he was hard to miss. Kirin stared at her in shock.

She didn't quite know what to expect from Morgan, but this wasn't it. Morgan was her height, with wildly curling black hair that was actually quite beautiful. Morgan herself was one to turn a male's head. She had a figure like an hourglass; her physique was almost impossible. Long, slender limbs and a thin neck, a narrow waist that flared at her hips, and a well-endowed chest that made Kirin amazed she had fit into the sorceress's dresses.

And impressed that Malakieth had the strength to turn her down when she tried to seduce him.

Morgan wore a dress of chainmail with a loose swinging skirt that Kirin had no doubt the sorceress was used to fighting in. A circlet of iron rested in her hair.

As she watched the sorceress and her procession near her hiding spot, a male—with a start, she recognized the Nephilim general and Morgan's consort, Sisera—slipped past Malakieth to walk along her chariot on the side opposite the strange girl, who walked along with her head down, tied to the chariot's frame.

Morgan spoke with him then, keeping one hand on the reins to the were-beast that pulled the chariot, bent and kissed Sisera for a moment, biting his lower lip as she drew back, fangs easily rending his flesh. He smirked and wiped the blood away, pausing to allow the army to swallow him up again.

Disgusted, Kirin looked away, her eyes snagging on the shifter. Molyb flowed from one shape to the next, eventually making his way toward the girl and shifting into what looked like a male version of her, which sent her skittering as far away as she could get, hissing.

Kirin started to count. Molyb, Morgan, Sisera, Malakieth, and the strange girl, plus the were-beast that pulled Morgan's chariot and ten of its kind, what looked like twenty other Nephilim marching under Sisera, and perhaps twelve squadrons of Rashek. Which made for an army of two hundred and seventy-six very strong and very dangerous creatures.

She held absolutely still as the army marched near her tree.

But she evidently wasn't still enough.

The girl looked up and frowned at her. Frantic, forcing herself to be silent and keep hidden, Kirin raised one finger to her lips, hoping the girl would understand what that meant and would stay silent.

Malakieth nudged the girl, and she darted forward. The dragon glanced up but overlooked her.

As carefully as she could, Kirin eased through the trees, slipping ahead of the army. The wildlife was silent with the army's passing.

She strived to be as silent.

She saw them before they saw her.

Beau! Beau, I'm coming. I'm right behind you.

She could hear him sigh in relief and could see him spin to look at her. She dove wildly, flying over his head, and then letting him catch up and run beside her as they hurried to catch up to their companions.

I am glad you are safe.

She frightens me.

And you've now proved your common sense.

They ran up behind the others, and Kirin landed in their midst as they halted.

"There are two hundred and seventy-six, if I counted correctly," she told him. Beau knelt beside her, and she sprang into the saddle. The horses were nudged into a quick canter. "Nishron's Three—and yes, I saw Molyb—the girl, General Sisera, and twenty Nephilim under him, eleven were-beasts, and twelve squadrons of Rashek."

"We should be at Amarth Dur in an hour or so," was all the king replied.

GUILT

"Kirin, can we talk?" Ling asked.

Kirin looked at the queen. "Of course."

"Are you all right?" her mother asked.

The halfling glanced at Nahor riding beside his wife on his stallion and talking in an undertone to Ephraim, who was running with ease beside the bay warhorse; at Callian, talking with Trig; at Elfan and Terah and Aramon teasing each other; at Assumptshun, who was as withdrawn as ever; at Tiamat and Xzylya, walking beside her, one on either side of Beau.

"A little nervous," Kirin answered.

"What's on your mind?"

"Morgan. My father. This war." She sighed. "I'm not ready for this," she said suddenly, ceasing with the short answers, looking down at Beau's beautiful scales, her voice frightened and disturbed and angry. She ran her finger along a vein of gold over his shoulder. "I can't lead an army! I can't go to war! I'm not even sixteen! So the laws will let me battle some of the most evil, foul beings to ever walk the world, and gladly, but I'm not allowed to get *married*?" she cried out in frustration, working hard to keep her voice down. "I can't handle that! What if Morgan's too strong for me? What if I fail? And everyone thinks that I'll be fine with killing Malakieth." She squeezed her eyes shut in an effort to hold back the tears that smarted her vision. "He's my *father*. I... I don't want to fight him. All my life I've wanted a family, a father. But why must it be *him*? Why not a normal being, one that I wasn't expected to battle?"

Ling looked at her husband, who turned his head to meet her eyes. Kirin watched as they had a quick, silent conversation. Then the queen dismounted, saying, "Come with me, daughter." She took Kirin's hand, and the halfling obediently dismounted.

Ling led Kirin into the woods. She sat down, motioning for Kirin to sit beside her.

The Adkisha obeyed, and Ling carefully wrapped her arm around the halfling's shoulders, mindful not to touch her wings.

"Why him?" Kirin asked, sounding broken. "Why me?"

"I've been asking myself that for many years. Why Malakieth? Why wasn't I strong enough to protect myself? Why did he hurt me? Why did Morgan have to twist and poison his mind? Why is this happening? I've always felt... responsible for this war. As if I caused it."

"But that's ridiculous. Morgan started it," Kirin objected.

"No, she didn't. Not truly. Kirin, I... I want you to hear this from me. I want you to hear the truth before Morgan distorts it for you. I don't know what Malakieth told you, and I'm not sure that I want to know, but the guilt that I have been carrying around within me for four thousand years has never been so strong as it is now, watching you, my daughter, whom I love dearly, risk your life and more to stop what was started because of me.

"Long ago, back when I was human and only fifteen years old, I had two men in love with me: Malakieth and Nahor. The general dislike between dragons and elves was amplified between the two of them. Both of them were the crown princes for their respective countries. Both of them were only a little over three hundred years old, both able to appear human, and both in love with the same girl.

"I was young. I was in love. And I had a choice to make. Malakieth or Nahor? Either way, I was prepared to leave mortality behind me.

"Obviously, I chose Nahor. I suppose they both knew my choice beforehand. But Malakieth left, and I saw him less and less. Eventually he left for Gilagaithia. I received word of that from his parents, who were friends of mine, even though I had rejected their son.

"Later, it became obvious what had happened. I had left him, heartbroken and alone, and Morgan had found him. She began to speak her poisoned words, and Malakieth didn't bother to fight her. I guess he had wanted so badly to believe whatever she had promised him that he was blind to the truth.

"And so Malakieth left with Morgan. Morgan took over Gilagaithia, renamed it Amalay Kahelith, and led the attack on Allerion.

"Many elves had been at Candescere in a war council between the two nations—we had expected a war was brewing. Nahor and I were there, as were his parents. It was his gift, the same gift all the dragons often complained about, that saved everyone. In the middle of the counsel, he suddenly leapt to his feet and drew his sword. Obviously, everyone else took offense to this, and one dragon even charged at him. I stood in the way, knowing the dragons' honor would not allow them to attack me.

"Nahor finally spoke. 'War. Candescere's outer wall is under attack. There are hordes of Rashek and Shadow Dragons alongside Morgan. Malakieth stands in their mists. His scales are black. This is treason.'"

She laughed once, without humor, and shook her head.

"You can imagine the reaction that brought about. Nahor shoved me at Queen Kali, your grandmother, telling her to protect me. Kanna, her mate, ordered her to flee, saying that both Allerion and Ellasar would need leaders after this fight. He never returned from that battle, but Kali is adamant he still lives. Nahor hadn't become king yet; his father still reigned—until that day, when both of his parents were killed.

"War broke out and spread. A war that has lasted for four thousand years started because I rejected Malakieth. And I feel even more guilty because I know that deep inside myself, if I was given the chance to choose between them again, knowing what would happen, I would still choose Nahor."

Mother and daughter were silent for a long time, ignoring the danger of the approaching army.

"Do you still have nightmares about him?" Kirin asked.

Ling nodded slowly. "It was traumatic. I was so drugged I couldn't stand, couldn't even speak. What little and selective magic I possess was gone. I could barely raise my head. At first, it was the normal response a friend has when they see someone they never expected to see again. He was worried I was ill, asking me how I had gotten there, if I had left Nahor, if I would stay. Then … it was as if something had changed. As he had been speaking, something had been changing in his voice. Almost as if he were losing his mind."

She paused, drawing in a shaky breath. "He simply started attacking me, and I couldn't fight him off. It was as if he was deranged, as if he, too, had been drugged."

"He was," Kirin murmured.

Ling stared at her daughter in surprise.

"It was one of the things we talked about, what happened that night. It was the *matiasma* in you that made him go mad. He didn't quite know what he was doing. He didn't know you were drugged, that you were scared, that you didn't want him. It wasn't as if you were fighting him." She paused. "He seemed so upset about what happened that night. He said it was his biggest mistake and that listening to Morgan was the second biggest. He said he wished there was some way he could tell you that."

Ling was staring at the ground. Gently, she squeezed Kirin's shoulders.

"Thank you, Kirin. Believe it or not, it helps to know that. And we should likely go back. We've been here too long, and as you said, Morgan is closing in."

They stood.

Kirin took a deep breath. "Do you think I can defeat her?"

Ling looked at her daughter and then reached out and cradled her face in one hand. Kirin could feel Ling's healing magic seeping into her skin. "I think it will be difficult, but I believe you will come out victorious. You have been well trained at the Academy and by your dragons and your brothers and your travels. And I wouldn't worry too much about Malakieth."

She frowned at the queen. "Why not?"

Ling gave her a wry smile. "Because I know him well enough to know that no matter what Morgan tells him to do, he will go after

Nahor. And I know Nahor well enough to know that he will gladly fight your father. They despise each other." Ling gave her a sideways glance. "How fast can you run?" she asked, her voice sly. A smile spread across her face.

Kirin grinned dangerously. "Keep up," she challenged.

Morgan watched the queen and the halfling race back to their pathetic little band. Her lips curled up over her fangs in a snarl.

"Have you forgotten that Nahor defeated you before?" Malakieth stated, his great, dark head looking over her shoulder at the water he was using to scry them.

"Lucky shot," Morgan hissed.

"Not the way I remember it." The dragon chuckled.

Morgan snarled at him, displaying fangs.

He leaned closer to her and sniffed. His expression twisted in revulsion, his lips distorted over his pointed teeth and fangs and his eyes narrowed in slits.

"You smell awful, like Sisera again. At the rate you're going, you'll catch some hideous disease and die before you can claim victory in your war," he commented through his teeth.

She stared at him.

"I was starting to think you wouldn't care whether I lived or died."

He pushed his nose close to her face, that horribly beautiful face.

"I've always cared," he told her. There was no trace of humor in his deep voice.

A slow smile spread across her face. Without the fiery eyes, she almost looked ... innocent.

Malakieth forced himself to return her smile, making his expression gentle.

Behind her, a lone half-Rashek, half-human girl crept up and touched the surface of the water. The image of Kirin evaporated. She grinned at Malakieth, who made no noticeable acknowledgment.

But in the privacy of her mind, he told her, *Well done, Natasha. Be ready and stay hidden. I may need your help.*

FINAL PREPARATIONS

Ling urged her mount faster, moving slightly to the side so that their conversation would be private. Nahor moved with her, perfectly in sync.

"Is something wrong?" he asked quietly.

In a muted voice, she told him of Kirin's worries about facing Morgan and how she feared that she hadn't been taught enough magic for the battle.

A frown flashed across Nahor's face. "I know," he replied, discreetly touching his forehead. "Beau fears the same thing—that Kirin hasn't had enough experience. What would you like me to do?"

"Teach her," Ling said simply. Her thoughts expounded on it. *Teach her everything you know, all of your magic. Show it to her.*

The king's frown deepened, his brows furrowing. "We don't have that time. Even to teach her a rudimentary knowledge of fighting with light magic would take days, if not weeks."

Ling looked down at her charger's mane, twisting it around her fingertips. "There is another way."

Through her mind, he saw what it was that she was thinking of.

"That would be feasible, but it takes time to settle in."

"She's quick and has been trained to think on her feet. You know how the Academy molds its knights to do so. Even if it doesn't settle in, it may create the illusion of preparedness that she needs."

Nahor smiled faintly. "Scheming woman," he teased. Growing serious again, he said, "We should be there in a few minutes. Once she's in her armor and armed, I will draw her aside and offer the spell to her."

"Thank you." *Why must all this evil take place?* he heard her whisper. Nahor kept silent, wishing he had an answer for her.

Squeezing her shoulder with one hand, he vowed, "No one will ever hurt you again, love. I won't let him near you." Nahor looked at his son. *Aramon, look behind us. How close is Morgan?* he mindspoke.

They're moving faster than I would have thought through the trees. Perhaps an hour? At most, two. But there's something else, Abbo, *something darker. I can't see it clearly, as if it's not entirely there. Like a shadow or a nightmare trying to form, if you believe it.* Ehin, *I wonder what it is? It can't be pleasant,* the wanderer answered.

Likely it isn't. Thank you for looking.

They broke through the trees and urged their horses into a gallop across Amarth Dur, the dragons taking off and flying the short distance. Xzylya crowed with success as she followed her brethren into the air, Kirin twisting in Beau's saddle and calling instructions and encouragement.

The mounted warriors dismounted, Trig stretching until his spine cracked from being in the saddle for so long. The horses dropped their heads and grazed, as if relieved to finally have a chance to hold still.

Two elves materialized from the woods, mounted on horseback. One held a banner with an insignia on it.

Nahor stepped forward to greet his captain, pointing out Princess Terah, Lady Elfan, Lord Trig, Prince Callian, and the four dragons before gesturing for Kirin.

Kirin came over with one greave on and the other in her hand. The two elven bowmen stared at her in her man's attire.

"This is the Adkisha Kirin," Nahor said simply. "Lady Kirin, this is Captain Thavron and his standard-bearer."

The young man holding the standard flashed her a charming grin, bowing his head. "Petros, my lady. My name is Petros. Pleased to make your acquaintance."

Kirin nodded regally but couldn't hide her smile when Thavron told him off for flirting.

"Prince Callian of Giladeth is courting her," Nahor said quietly.

Petros looked crestfallen. "My apologizes, then."

Thavron looked at Kirin. "Lady Adkisha, it is an honor to fight with you, as it is with you, my king. My division stands at the ready."

Nahor nodded. "Have them approach and set up ranks with a concentration in the center."

"No," Kirin murmured.

All three of them stared at her. She met the captain's eyes and then turned to the king, acutely aware that he had seen many more battles and was used to commanding these troops.

"Morgan's forces are spread out evenly with the were-beasts and the Nephilim on the front line. The Rashek follow. Molyb is on the left wing, Malakieth on the right, and Morgan in the center with that girl. I don't know what will happen when she's unbound, but I do know that Molyb will hold his spot and that Malakieth will leave his to come for you, King Nahor. Yes, the strength of your archers needs to be in the center, but it also needs to be on the left to hold Molyb. If he breaks through, he'll lead his troops around and attack us from behind. If we are to have any weak spot, it should be on the right wing, rather than both."

Nahor held her gaze, then began to smile. "Captain Thavron, I believe you have your orders. The lady's strategy is good."

Captain Thavron bowed and turned his horse, cantering back into the woods with Petros eagerly following him.

Nahor turned back to Kirin. "I have another proposition for you."

"Stay back and let you command the army?"

He smiled again. "No. Come walk with me."

They headed off away from the group, pausing briefly so that Kirin could strap her other greave on.

"Ling was expressing your concerns regarding the amount of training you have received."

"Yes."

"There is a way to quickly teach you all that I know of light magic. But you would have to allow me in your mind, allow more than simply my voice in your mind. It is a breech of privacy. But it could be done if so you desired."

Kirin nodded quickly. "Thank you," she breathed. "Where would you prefer to . . . ?"

"Out of sight of the others. No need to unnerve Callian."

He led her through the trees until they were out of sight, hidden by the thick trunks. Ling stepped around one of the trees.

"She's going to try to keep you calm," Nahor murmured. "Are you sure you want to do this? I cannot stop in the middle."

"I'm sure."

"Then lie down."

She obeyed, curling on her side to keep from laying on her wings, and Ling knelt beside her, taking her hand. Nahor knelt beside her, placing Kirin's head on his lap and brushing his hands over her hair.

His hands stilled, one over her forehead, the other cradling the back of her head.

"Just relax," he intoned, his voice slow and deep. "Feel your mother's magic. Close your eyes, and focus on that."

Minutes passed, and nothing happened. Nahor was perfectly still until she nearly forgot about his hands on her head. Ling's magic seeped into her, soothing her.

There was a gentle pressure in her head; an image rose in her mind of a mage's hand outstretched, palm up, light floating in glowing tendrils around his fingers, illuminating a text.

That image was replaced with another and another, flowing faster and faster. The pressure increased to an uncomfortable level until the images were speeding by, faster than a dragon in flight, and the pressure became pain, and the pain became agony, and she thought that she might go mad from it. Her mouth opened in a silent scream.

And then, impossibly, miraculously, it began to ebb away, replaced by Ling's healing magic. Finally, it was gone, and Kirin could move again. She rolled off Nahor's lap and held herself up by her arms as her stomach heaved, threatening illness.

When her stomach settled, Ling and Nahor helped her back to her feet.

"Thank you," she whispered.

Nahor inclined his head. "Go; finish preparing for the battle. Then settle somewhere and rest."

She nodded, and they walked with her back to the camp. Callian and Trig helped her strap on the rest of her armor—except for her breastplate and helmet. The breastplate would no long fit, due to her wings, and the helmet was cut in the human style, which meant that it would cover her ears. With her sensitive elven hearing, a blow to the head with a metal helmet covering her ears could prove debilitating. Callian, too, would go without a helmet.

The Dragon Knights still hadn't come.

Callian touched her face, his expression grim.

"Be careful," she whispered to him.

"As careful as I can be. Same goes for you." He clasped her to him, catching her face between his gloved hands.

His lips crushed against hers almost roughly, his hand gripping the back of her head, locking her mouth to his with a brute strength that was impossible to resist.

So she kissed him back, her fingers knotting into his soft, tangled hair. Her wings covered him, rubbing up against as much of him as was morally right.

Callian's hand trailed down her ribs, and even with the armor on, she could feel his gentle touch. She wanted to stay like this forever. But destiny was calling, and she couldn't allow Morgan to kill her family.

They drew apart reluctantly.

Callian drew an uneven breath and then jerked his head in a quick nod. "Right. I'll let you rest."

"I love you," she said simply.

He gave her a haunted smile and bowed to her, then turned and walked off, heading toward his friend. Kirin curled up against Tiamat—Beau was busy teaching Xzylya how to fight—and dozed off.

BATTLE

Kirin sat on Beau's back, fighting to keep the fear down. Her brain kept churning awful memories of pain and agony, and she wondered if she was going to die in this fight. She wondered if it would hurt *very* much ... dying.

Dear Lord in Valour, how can anyone stay sane waiting *for battle? It is so much easier on one's nerves to simply be attacked and respond.*

Ephraim could sense her turmoil and smiled at her, trying to reassure her. "It's almost time."

"We can handle Morgan and a few of her brigands," she dimly heard Aramon mutter. She could feel Beau and Xzylya's distress in her mind. They, too, were impatient for the battle to start, impatient for it to be over, one way or another. The howls of the were-beasts tracking their scent into the clearing was worsened only by the high, keening cry of what could only be the female.

She looked at Callian, and he smiled at her. It didn't touch his eyes.

"This is the worse part," he told her, and she was suddenly reminded that not only had he been in battles before but had also commanded armies to victory in war.

Determination was set in his eyes, and she feared that he might do something dangerous in his desire to protect her.

He wasn't allowed to die for her. She couldn't bear it if he was hurt because of her.

Closing her eyes, she sought out the king and mindspoke, *Please, Nahor, protect him.*

He caught her eye and nodded slightly to show that he had heard her.

But for me, child, Ling's safety comes first.

Kirin managed a half smile. She had known that would be the case.

Here they come, Xzylya murmured.

Thank you, sweetheart. Kirin swallowed hard and drew her sword. Callian gave it a panicked glance.

"Rather I didn't use it?" she murmured softly. She didn't have it in her to be sarcastic or snap at people, especially him. Her eyes never left his face, trying to take in every familiar detail. Just in case. If she had to die in this battle, she wanted his sublime angel's face to be the last thing she saw.

"I'd rather not have you in the battle at all," he answered, his vivid blue eyes tortured and anxious. "But I'll tell you one thing. When we get through with this and get to Taure En Alata, I am going to celebrate our survival and the fact that I am now seventeen and steal you from the crowds of admirers you will have. We will fly across Ellasar and sleep under the stars in safety."

She couldn't help but smile. "And I will wear dresses just for you, my love."

"Tiamat and I have got your back."

Beau locked his gaze with his mate's. Tiamat's beautiful, dark eyes were wide, twin windows into her emotions. Beau could see what she wouldn't admit, especially with Morgan and her company nearly in the clearing.

Tiamat was scared. She didn't want Callian to enter the battle. She didn't want him to be hurt.

But at the same time, she wanted his strong reassurance beside her. It steadied her, strengthened her.

Beau's golden eyes burned into hers, calming her, preparing her for the oncoming fight.

Fire simmered in her belly for the first time. Her mouth and throat were baked and desiccated as she prepared to breathe flame.

Despite the situation, excitement danced in her eyes.

It will burn the first time, love, he warned.

She was quiet for a few minutes. *I love you, Beau.*

I will always be yours, sweetheart, he promised solemnly.

Morgan ran her tongue over her lower lip in excitement. She cracked her whip over her pet's back one last time for good measure and then hauled her in closer as her army punched through the last of the wretched trees.

The small army that stood ready to greet her surprised her, but then she smiled. More fun to be had.

"Kill them all," she commanded.

Her army surged forward as a single unit, and the Adkisha's pathetic band prepared to meet them. She released her pet, and the creature took off, racing just behind the Nephilim and the were-beasts and just ahead of the Rashek.

Morgan drew her sword and her magic, swearing viciously as Malakieth roared a battle cry and changed course, racing straight for Nahor.

Predictable dragon.

Still, that left her the Adkisha to kill.

Morgan smiled as the armies collided.

The archers shot with good accuracy, felling many of the Rashek and two of the were-beasts before the armies collided. The archers in the front abandoned their bows and drew their knives and swords while the ones in the back kept shooting.

A were-beast and a Nephilim came racing straight for Tiamat. The Fire Dragon opened her mouth and shot out fire, burning her own throat. The Nephilim screamed as he was engulfed in flame, and Beau surged forward, catching the were-beast as it leapt and rending it in two.

Over his head, Kirin shot arrow after arrow with one goal in mind: take out the were-beast pulling Morgan's chariot.

Tiamat lashed out and snapped around her, and Callian swung his sword, cleaving the head off a Rashek. The madness of battle surrounded him.

Something slammed into Tiamat, and he was thrown off. He rolled with the impact and brought his blade up in time to block the strike of a Rashek. Callian struggled to get off the ground, trying to force the other warrior back but to no avail.

Suddenly, something rammed the Rashek from the side, taking him down and ripping into his throat.

The girl. She sprang up, but before he could thank her, she darted off...and he watched, stunned, as she took down one of the elven archers in her path.

He looked for Tiamat only to see that see she had taken to the air and was picking up her enemies and killing them above the throng below. Xzylya rose up to join Tiamat.

He ran for where Kirin and Morgan were drawing ever closer and closer together.

Morgan saw the dracling flying and looked about. Molyb was closest.

"Molyb!" she screamed. "Kill the little one!"

Molyb launched himself into the air, shifting into a griffin. The dracling took off over the trees, the shifter hot in pursuit.

Flashes of magic and fire lit up the center of the battlefield. Malakieth had assumed his human form and was locked in a mages' battle with Nahor.

Callian was dueling Sisera, his handsome face set in grim determination, blue fire dancing in his eyes. Sisera wasn't grinning, but his eyes were scornful and mocking. The prince was fighting dirty, hitting Sisera with magic whenever he could. Sisera fought worse. They danced about on the battlefield, oblivious to the rest as they crossed blades, both determined to reach Kirin.

The general was skilled, but Callian met him blow for blow.

There was a terrific roar, and fire filled the air, but Callian barely noticed.

"Oh, look," Sisera snarled. "Your precious Dragon Knights are here to help. How sweet of them to come."

"What does Morgan see in you?" he shot back through his teeth. "I'm seventeen, and I'm as good as you are, if not better."

Adrenaline coursed through Kirin, making her aware of everything at once: of Callian dueling Sisera and forcing the Nephilim back; of Nahor and Malakieth dueling with magic nearby; of Morgan's steady approach; of Xzylya darting in and out of the trees, forcing the bigger shifter to work harder; of her wonderful Dragon Knights flying overhead to dive low on the other side of Amarth Dur to surround the enemy.

Morgan must be protecting her beast! Beau roared in her mind. *Off my back. I'm going to take it out.*

Kirin leapt free. *Be safe.*

The Twilight Dragon surged up and circled, landing in a clear space behind Morgan. He fought his way to her, finally leaping and ramming the beast pulling her cart. The sorceress lashed out with her foul magic, missing him by inches as he ripped the creature's throat free. He scrambled back and fought off a Nephilim and a group of Rashek, struggling to get back into the air. Once there, he circled, looking for a place to land near his rider, only to see that he was too late.

Morgan ran for Kirin, who braced herself to duel the witch.

Lightning hissed through the air, filling Kirin's nose with the awful scent of burnt flesh and the metallic smell of blood. As the dust cleared away, she could see Malakieth in his true form slowly circling Nahor, his expression full of dark triumph. Nahor was on his knees on the ground, clutching his charred side, blood pooling on the ground from another large wound in his leg. His young face was twisted in pain from her father's strike.

Malakieth circled for the kill. And froze.

Ling stood crouched in front of her husband, her sword drawn, her face streaked with tears.

"Move," Malakieth snarled, glaring past her at his rival.

Ling refused, merely looking up at him. "If you wish to kill him, you will have to kill me as well. He is my husband, my love, and I will not live without him!" she shouted.

Malakieth's gaze flickered back to Nahor again. His eyes burnt with hatred and resentment.

"I despise you," he muttered at the male elf, loathing filling his voice. Then he turned back Ling. "I never meant to hurt you, love," he whispered.

A furious roar ripped from Nahor. Even in so much pain, that still evoked rage and jealousy. Malakieth had always been a personal threat.

Malakieth gazed at Ling wistfully.

"And I will never hurt you again," he swore.

Nahor wanted badly to respond to that statement, but held his tongue. He would never forgive himself if Malakieth snapped and harmed Ling by accident in an attempt to get to him.

Allerion's one-time prince turned and flew off, casually dispatching a Rashek as he left.

Ling turned to the smaller Dark Dragon fighting from the air a few yards away.

"Assumptshun! Please, help me!" she screamed.

Assumptshun, with Elfan on his back, dove beside her, missing her by inches. As he soared upwards, she could see Nahor safely ensnared in the dragon's claws.

Callian and Sisera continued to duel, dancing around the blood-soaked battlefield.

"You're nearly the only one left here," Callian called out to him. Sisera's magic struck him in the chest. The chest plate of his armor buckled, making breathing harder.

"You know, you have a pretty female," Sisera shot back, his blade whistling over Callian's head. The prince ducked and lashed out at the Nephilim's knees. "I'll enjoy bedding her."

Callian couldn't ignore that comment, and his enraged bellow rent the air. Blinding white-hot magic exploded out of Canath, smashing into Sisera's torso and blasting him twenty feet backward. There was a sickening crunch as his head smashed into a tree.

Tiamat leapt on him, ripping him in half and breathing flames at the same time.

If Callian had bothered to look, all he would find of the great Nephilim general was a blackened hole in the ground by the time Tiamat was finished with him and had taken to the skies once more.

Morgan screamed, and with inhuman speed, she changed course and raced for Callian.

Something hit her from the side, and she and Kirin both fell to the ground. The halfling rolled aside and jumped to her feet.

Morgan bared her fangs as the two squared off, swords knocked aside by the fall. They both held their hands up in a guarding position, as if this was merely a sparring match at the Academy. No one grinned. No one spoke.

The two powers circled each other slowly.

Morgan was the first to attack, breathing a volley of fire at Kirin. Kirin didn't even blink as the fire blew harmlessly past her, slamming into a small knot of Rashek fighting with Callian.

Left, Kirin, Adonai's voice commanded in her head. Kirin obeyed without hesitation, and Morgan's killing spell just barely missed.

Duck. Lightning crackled over her head, striking the ground and blowing earth into the air.

Relax, and let the magic come to you. Respond.

Kirin sucked in a deep breath and opened herself to her instincts, to Nahor's knowledge.

And they were fighting. It was deadly—that was an understatement. Morgan fought with all the black magic she could draw. Kirin was relying solely on instinct, her Academy training, and the knowledge Nahor had given her.

Kirin disappeared into thin air just before another wave of magic passed over her, reappearing on the opposite side of Morgan and actually landing a blow.

Trig struggled to get closer, nearer to the front line. His horse was nowhere in sight; he had been knocked out of the saddle by a Rashek.

He paused when he saw the girl running toward him, covered in red and black blood, her fangs bared, eyes wide and wild, and claws arched. She leapt at him.

He drew back and swung his sword, catching her shoulder with the flat of the blade hard enough to throw her to the ground. Her head cracked on the earth, and she didn't move. But Trig could see the steady rise and fall of her chest, and he stooped and grabbed her under her arms, hauling her up and dragging her out of the thick of battle so that she wouldn't be trampled, his sword held out to defend the two of them.

Flashes of light and fire and dark magic lit the center of the battlefield, easily marking where Kirin and Morgan dueled. The deadly dance was beginning to get out of control. Kirin could only hope the elves and Dragon Knights had scattered to give them room as they fought, rather than trying to get in the thick of things. But Callian was out there, she knew, and Beau with him.

Somewhere above her, she heard a dragon scream in pain, a human cry rising with it. Far to the left, out of the corner of her eye, she saw a Fire Dragon fall from the sky.

Morgan's lips curled back into the parody of a grin. "What if that was your lover?" She sneered.

Kirin jerked, panicked, and only just managed to dodge another killing blast. The black light hurtled past her, toward the elves, only to be blocked by Ephraim's own magic.

What if Morgan is right? What if that was Callian?

What if I end up dead because I actually believed one of Morgan's lies? she snarled at herself.

Kirin feinted left and then let her magic loose. Light crashed into Morgan's waist, sending her flying.

Frantically, she looked around. Beau was grappling with one of the last remaining were-beasts, bleeding from his shoulder. Tiamat was nowhere in sight.

There. Callian was standing shoulder-to-shoulder with Ren— she recognized his red hair—and Trig, Terah standing nearby with her knives drawn. He was still alive.

Relief washed through her, and then she felt Xzylya returning, Tiamat beside her. The dracling looked winded and tired, but she had a triumphant smile on her face, which must mean that—

Lost him, she said proudly. *Doesn't fly well through trees.*

The dragons landed beside Beau, who was now guarding a fallen Water Dragon. Kirin recognized Mist, looking around frantically for Peter.

Peter appeared, stumbling toward his dragon. Trig threw one of his knives, intercepting a Rashek before the monster could harm Peter more. The Dragon Knight collapsed on the ground by his dragon.

An inhuman scream brought Kirin's attention back to Morgan.

The sorceress stood, trembling with fury, staring at something on the other side of the field.

Kirin turned to see a yellow-and-black-spotted feline-type creature racing toward them, a blade clamped in its mouth. Evidentially, Molyb wasn't as lost as the dragons had taken him to be.

But what was more startling was the great dragon who flew behind him, tight to his back, claws out to catch him, and death written across his face. Malakieth. No other dragon was that big.

Kirin was swamped by the immensity of what had occurred. Her father was betraying Morgan, had chosen Kirin over the sorceress.

Malakieth couldn't breathe fire—there were too many of the elves and the Dragon Knights around.

Looking at the cold fury on his face, though, Kirin realized that she had never truly feared the male until now.

She felt the crackle in the air and threw herself to the side. Morgan's magic raced past her. Leaping to her feet, Kirin met the sorceress head on once more.

GOING HOME

With a brief respite from the battle, Callian looked on, watching as the fight between the two women grew faster still. He could no longer tell who was who or which one was throwing what magic. Dust and sparks flew through the air, lit only by the rapid flashes of magic.

Everything happened at once.

Tiamat screamed a warning. Callian twisted to see what could only be the shifter running for Kirin with a knife, Malakieth in close pursuit. Molyb shifted into a human form, knife in hand.

There was no time to think. Callian reacted, racing to guard Kirin from the shifter.

Molyb threw the knife. With a dull thud, it buried itself in Callian's chest, piercing armor and flesh. He reeled backward, his face twisted in pain. Dimly, he saw Kirin's face as she fought Morgan.

Tiamat was screaming out loud and in his mind, leaping to curl around her rider. He felt her nuzzling him, holding him close against her.

He was gasping for air, each breath taking more and more effort. His heart burned as it struggled, as the world began to dim.

Malakieth grabbed Molyb in his claws, rocketing skyward again. There was a high keening sound that ended abruptly as the dragon ripped the shifter apart.

Kirin's fight unexpectedly stopped. The halfling stood triumphantly, Morgan kneeling before her, Kirin's magic wrapped like a python around the sorceress. Both combatants heaved for breath.

Morgan's eyes darted to Callian, and she began to laugh. A black cloud descended nearby.

Kirin froze. Her green eyes darted to follow the sorceress's, and a wordless cry of pain ripped from her. Kirin's hand drew back, her sword striking Morgan, wounding her. She ran to where Trig was kneeling, tears streaking down his shocked, pale face. The halfling dropped by Callian's side, touching his face as he breathed his last. Her hand shook as she gently closed his staring, deep-blue eyes.

"He's dead," she sobbed, hugging his still body against hers, leaning her head against her beloved dragon. "He's gone."

Beau roared in pain, a tear shimmering on his cheek. Xzylya sobbed with her rider, torn between her fear of going near the dead dragon and her desire to be close to Kirin.

Kirin was only faintly aware of the lull in the fighting, of her sister standing near, of her brothers running up.

"It was Molyb's knife," Ephraim murmured. His voice was laced through with sorrow. Trig couldn't speak past the lump in his throat. Instead, he slid the knife out of his closest friend.

Nahor came limping towards them, Ling pressing against his wounded side, healing it. There were some quick, terse words exchanged between father and younger son over the wounded king and his queen's presence on the battlefield, but Kirin couldn't hear it.

"Malakieth killed Molyb," Aramon added shakily.

Kirin stared unseeingly at the black cloud as she felt her world collapsing around her. It didn't seem possible that they could have won this battle when Callian had died.

She clenched her teeth, trying to choke back her sobs as she felt the horrible pull of dark magic gathering. Tears blurred her vision as the black cloud beside Morgan solidified.

He was young, he was handsome, and he was the most frightening thing Kirin had ever laid eyes on.

Several of those around her swore. Kirin ignored them, sliding her hand into the rent in Callian's armor and pushing her healing magic into him. It was a futile attempt, and she knew it, but she felt compelled to try. The skin sluggishly started to heal but then reached the point when it could go no further, when Callian had been dead too long.

"Cathas," Nahor hissed.

Ling's eyes grew huge, and she shot her husband a panicked glance.

Kirin looked at her Light Dragon, at her precious Xzylya. The dracling looked back at her, eyes wide and scared.

Kirin reached out to rub her head. *I love you.*

Through the bond, she felt Xzylya's answering love.

"Arise," the devil commanded the sorceress.

Morgan struggled to her feet and walked slowly to his side, injured and in pain from Kirin's strike.

Malakieth dove again, this time trying to end Morgan. Cathas calmly directed a bolt of lightning skyward, piercing Malakieth's wing. He dropped out of the sky and landed hard but staggered back to his feet, his anger driving him.

Nahor shouted orders to his elves, and all who were able rallied around their king. The Dragon Knights spread out, completing the circle around Cathas and Morgan.

"Morgan, do me a favor," Cathas murmured, gesturing with one long hand to the wounded Nahor and Ling.

The sorceress bared her double fangs.

Kirin stood up slowly, raising Callian's sword. No more would die today.

Dark magic exploded from beside Kirin.

"Go! I've got Morgan!" Malakieth yelled.

Morgan couldn't have looked more surprised to suddenly be fighting Malakieth. Ling raced into the battle, fighting for the first time with the former prince. Ephraim and Aramon fought with her.

Cathas raised both hands, tilting his head back to look at the sky.

Through her tears, Kirin could see everything go dark, as if the sun had given up with her heart.

Cathas laughed quietly. It was the only sound.

Kirin's hand rose to clutch the crystal pendent around her neck. As always, its healing powers soothed her. She glanced up. Ling had an arrow drawn and was standing between her sons, protecting the wounded king and the two girls who stood beside him. Elfan's hands steadied Terah. Malakieth had Morgan pinned under one foot, the sorceress's own sword at her throat.

Cathas stood tall, a confident, cruel smirk on his face, his hands raised as he blocked the life-giving light of the Kyrian sun, a star they called Vullania.

Everything was cast into an eerie blood-red shade.

Xzylya's scales glowed, as did the air surrounding Kirin, shining from all of her magical glory.

She knew what was coming. She had to make him release Vullania.

"All right, now we bargain," she said, her voice soft and, thankfully, steady.

His sneer grew more pronounced.

"You know what I want," Cathas returned, triumphantly.

"State it."

"You. Out of my way. I want you dead."

She dropped her eyes down to Callian's face, handsome even in death. His expression was serene, and that gave her a bit of peace. With his eyes closed, he looked as if he was going to wake up and pull her into his arms and tell her that he was dreaming.

"I love you," she breathed under her breath, softly enough that no one could hear her. "Please forgive me."

"Make him stop," Malakieth snarled at Morgan.

Morgan blasted him off her. "Charmed to have you over me, but sorry, no. I'm a liar, not a betrayer." She raced to stand at Cathas's side, slightly behind him.

"Time is racing, Kirin. Do we have a deal?" Cathas was asking.

"If I let you kill me, you'll release Vullania?" she confirmed, not bothering to raise her gaze off Callian's face.

"Yes."

She stood tall, her back toward Callian's body, facing Cathas's darkly gleeful face. Her gaze moved over all those present: elves, dragons, Trig, the Dragon Knights… She had no way of knowing whether or not he would keep his word, but she also had no way of overpowering him. Her eyes rested on Nahor, hearing again in her memory his offer to call her his daughter, and even without the king's gift, she could tell that his mind was racing, trying to find a different choice. He was leaning on Ling, who was pale, clinging to her husband in an attempt to heal him. Ling, who had just regained her family after spending years suffering at the mercies of Cathas's followers. And Ephraim, shielding Elfan between his body and Assumptshun's ... Terah, who, like Ling, had finally found her family ... Aramon, his bow drawn, ready to shoot the moment the opportunity presented itself ... Trig, who had moved from her side only to close Tiamat's eyes, who stood there even now, one hand on the trembling Xzylya, the other resting on the fallen dragon's shoulder as he breathed a Giladethian prayer. All around her, the Dragon Knights shifted, nervous and impatient and filled with dread. These were her family, her friends. She hadn't been able to save Callian, but if she could save them ...

Her eyes lifted briefly to Vullania. If the sun's light was blocked for too long, her beloved homeland would sicken and die. Her friends would suffer, die ... her family ...

She looked at Callian once more, reaching out to stroke his cheek as Xzylya moved closer, then rose and stood tall, her back toward Callian's body, facing Cathas's darkly gleeful face.

"Deal," she said, her voice little more than a whisper.

"No! *Kirin!*" The cry came from everywhere at once, from her parents, from Nahor, her siblings, Trig and Elfan, and from the Dragon Knights she had been raised with.

Beau lay curled around his dead mate. He raised his head and roared to the sky, a cry of mourning for Tiamat, before dropping his head to rest against hers and closing his eyes. Xzylya lay nearby, curled in a tight ball, as if she were about to go to sleep, her muzzle resting near Callian's head.

Cathas's black blade rose in air as he paced toward her, stepping callously over Tiamat's tail as if it didn't matter that she was dead. Even with death seconds away, Kirin felt no fear. Her green eyes closed, and she fixed Callian's face in her mind's eye.

Please forgive me, she thought, *but I have to save them. I have to try. You won't be alone for long, my love.*

There was a sharp pain and then ... nothing.

"Fool." Cathas sneered at her lifeless body as she dropped with a soft *thud* to the ground. "Did you really think you could bargain with *me?*"

He turned and grabbed Morgan's arm as Malakieth surged forward and as one of the Dragon Knights broke ranks. They vanished with a whip-like crack, leaving the echoing sound of his cruel laughter. Vullania's light remained blocked.

Ling and Malakieth raced for Kirin. They hardly noticed as Ishmael's crystal, which had begun to glow brighter and brighter, broke free of the chain that bound it and shot like a backward meteor toward the sun, no longer bound to Kirin's life force.

Daylight flooded back to the horrific scene.

Ling broke down, crying over the dead body of her daughter, the stress and fear of the long, long day far too much for her.

Nahor had drawn his blade as Cathas had approached her, his mind working frantically in an attempt to find a different solution. Nothing had come, and now he knelt with the tip of his sword in the earth, his hand on the hilt, murmuring an ancient elven prayer for the fallen warriors. All around him, the elves were murmuring the same prayer.

The Dragon Knight who had broken ranks leapt off his Fire Dragon and jerked off his helmet, throwing it aside as he ran to Kirin's side. Ethno reached out and touched her cheek, silently screaming for her to open her eyes, to snap at him so that he could snap back and they could fight.

Nahor rose. He had seen her mind when he had performed the spell on her earlier that afternoon, had seen past the power and the destiny. He had seen the emotional young woman in love with a man who loved her back. He had seen the girl behind the expectations of several worlds. Others felt the loss far worse than he did.

Malakieth wrapped his arm around Ling's shoulders, helping her walk as she grieved the loss of their daughter.

"Where are you taking me?" she whispered. He could have given her any answer, and she wouldn't have cared. Ling didn't care what happened to her right now.

"Where you belong," he murmured softly to her, but she could hear the grief in his voice as well.

He let go of her, gently pushing her forward. She stumbled. Familiar, strong arms caught her, and Nahor held her close to him, her ear over his heart.

"I do not understand," he stated quietly to Malakieth, standing right next to them. Ling raised her head from her husband's chest to look at her old friend.

"He is a better man than I," Malakieth said, looking only at Ling. He looked down at the still body of his daughter, remembering the brief span of time he had had with her. "Until we meet again." And with that, he turned and ran, leaping into the air and exploding into his true form, flying awkwardly out of sight on his wounded wing. The huge black dragon *was* different, though. Between his eyes and over his chest, two patches of shimmering white scales had replaced the jet-black.

Nahor watched, knowing how hurt not only his beloved wife was but his bitter rival as well. He held her closer, his hand moving in comforting small circles on her back.

Lord Trig of Giladeth, the new heir to the throne, stood nearby, eyes dry now, as if he were in shock. "They look as if they're sleeping," he whispered faintly. "They look so *happy*."

And they did. Both Kirin's and Callian's faces were completely at peace. She had fallen in such a way that her body rested against Callian's, her serene face turned toward his.

Ephraim held Elfan close; Aramon, leading the ever-faithful Elindil, moved closer to his family. Terah stood awkwardly alone until Aramon picked her up and hugged her and carried her over to their parents. Jonathan dismounted and walked up to his friend, gripping the young man's shoulder. Melchizedek and Zedek approached.

"Your Majesties, my son is a Time Mage," the headmaster stated in an undertone, placing a hand on Zedek's shoulder.

"I can stop time around them. It is the least I do. For her. For them," he whispered.

"You knew her personally," Elfan murmured.

Zedek nodded and began to cast the spell that would halt time and keep the bodies of the two fallen heroes and their dragons perfectly preserved and perfectly visible. Many would desire to come and pay homage to the great couple.

"We all must continue to fight this war. This madness has gone on long enough," Nahor murmured under his breath to Melchizedek.

The headmaster nodded. "You have our support, Your Majesty."

"And you ours," Nahor replied.

"She was never afraid," Ephraim whispered, his voice breaking. "She was ... completely at peace."

The elves and Dragon Knights stood silently, some praying, some with tears in their eyes. And Kirin lay in the arms of her lover, where she would be for the rest of eternity.

EPILOGUE

Trig stood near the limp form of the strange girl. "I can't accept that," he stated quietly.

Nahor and Melchizedek looked on grimly. All around them those with healing magic worked to save as many as they could while the dead were being gathered.

"Even if she is sentient—which I am not sure she is," Nahor replied. "She's been damaged beyond repair by Morgan. She's ruined, Trig, not broken."

He shook his head. "I want to save her. If anything, what happens to her is my decision, seeing as I was the one to take her out of the battle."

"I believe King Nahor is correct, Lord Trig," Melchizedek said. "Sometimes it is more merciful to end a creature's suffering than prolong it in hopes of saving it. And there are some creatures who do not want to be saved."

Trig's attention drifted back to the girl. She was awake, staring at them from the ground.

"King Nahor, what is she thinking?"

"She's a halfling, Trig. I cannot hear her thoughts, if she has any."

Trig watched her watching them. Her eyes were keen and still so frightened. Yes, she had killed multiple elves, but she had also killed Rashek. She hadn't bothered to discriminate, and there were some who had only been wounded by her. The path of destruction she had wrought had flowed in a straight line, as if she were fleeing from Morgan.

"I can't let you destroy her. There's been enough death today."

"Then what would you propose to do with her?"

Trig looked at the king, at the leader of the Dragon Knights. "I'm going to go back to Giladeth. Someone needs to tell them..." His throat tightened, and he had to swallow before he could continue. "Tell them what happened. I'll take her back with me. If she truly can't be saved, then I'll put her out of her misery. But I want a chance to try to save her."

Nahor looked out over the battlefield, seeing the elves that had perished being wrapped in cloth and tied to horses, seeing the horses that had been killed being buried by those few elves with earth magic, seeing the Dragon Knights gathering the few of their own who had died to be cremated. In his mind's eye, he saw again Kirin clutching Callian's body to her, sobbing as her heart broke. *Eruanna mir amo menel.* The daughter of his heart.

"If that is your wish, Lord Trig, then I will agree to it. The girl is your responsibility."

Trig bowed. "Thank you, sir."

Melchizedek looked at the king. "My lord, what are you going to do with their bodies?"

Nahor sighed. "The Giladethians deserve their prince's body back, and his dragon will go with him. I hesitate to separate them, as foolish as it seems. I thought to have Kirin and her two dragons taken to Giladeth as well, unless you would prefer to have her laid to rest at the Academy."

"No. I think that Giladeth is a fine place for her to be laid to rest. I think that she would have liked that," Melchizedek said softly. "My son can always open a gateway for those who wish to pay their respects to her."

"So be it."

"*Abbo.*"

Nahor turned to see Aramon carrying Terah in his arms.

She's had another vision.

"What did you see, daughter?" he asked, praying it was not more ill news.

Terah looked at him. "A bright flash of light that illuminated a castle of grey stone. It silhouetted a young woman in a dress with a long cloak on. Wind from a storm rushed around her, making her blond hair blow wildly. That is all I saw. But, *Abbo?* In the vision, I could have sworn I heard Kirin's voice."

ABOUT THE AUTHOR

Victoria Weber is studying Occupational Therapy and English at Ithaca College in New York. She started writing when she was fourteen and completed her first novel, Rising Sun, by fifteen. She spends her free time riding her two horses, Theo and Tootsie, reading obsessively, playing her harp, and sitting glued to her computer—writing, of course. You can visit Victoria online at www.victoriaweberbooks.com.